Earth's Mother

Hazel McBride

Copyright © 2021 Hazel McBride
All rights reserved.
ISBN: 9798743009497
ISBN-13:

Paul,

You are my new dream.

1.

"Ah crap." She cursed.

Slowing to a halt outside the newsagents, she sighed in exasperation and removed her feet from the ginormous puddle she had failed to spot. Shaking and stamping her squelching trainers, she grumpily tucked the newspaper into her raincoat and pulled up her hood against the drizzle.

In most places, August brought with it heatwaves and conjured up images of lazy afternoons and late-evening barbecues. Not in Scotland. Unfortunately their good weather had turned up earlier in the year and had failed to return.

Riva hoisted her bag of shopping into the crook of her elbow and set off home, her toes growing colder with each step she took up the high street. Her damp feet not helping her bad mood. Being kicked out of the house because your recently reunited parents wanted some alone time was bad enough, but did they really need to make her walk to the shops in the middle of a rainstorm?

Stomping her way down the main street, she tried to banish the images of her canoodling parents from her mind. She was sick of them acting like lovesick teenagers.

Of course she was happy that they were together again, but she hadn't been expecting how much her father's return would change things.

Granted, as far as excuses for abandonment went, his was pretty good. Eighteen years imprisoned in an underwater kingdom by his late father who just happened to be the King of the Mer was a pretty reasonable excuse to be unable to return to the love of his life and daughter. But she was finding it increasingly difficult to both remember that he hadn't had a choice in the matter and control her temper these days.

Sighing heavily, she wondered vaguely where all this anger was coming from. As she pounded her way up the pavement, she realised that the newspaper under her jacket was probably now illegible thanks to the fact that the rain was coming down in sheets, so she ducked into the doorway of the local café where her mum usually worked for some refuge. Shaking the back of her hood to get rid of the icy droplets, she dumped her shopping bag at her feet and felt the blood return to her fingers.

"Crap!" she cursed under her breath. Several potatoes had escaped and had started rolling back into the street. She quickly ducked down to grab them, stuffing them unceremoniously back into the bag beside the obnoxiously large bar of chocolate she had bought as compensation for her troubles.

The windows of the café were thick with steam and she could only imagine how lovely and warm it would be on the inside. She was just about to push open the door and spend more of her mum's money on a large hot chocolate, trying to prolong the outing so that she wouldn't have to walk in on her parents doing something she would definitely rather not see, when she heard muffled voices coming from the other side of the door.

"Can you believe it Janet? Turned up out of nowhere after almost twenty years and she just takes him back without so much as a question!"

"I know Lorna, I was shocked when I heard."

"Have you seen him then?"

Riva's stomach turned over uncomfortably. This was not a conversation she was supposed to be overhearing, but she quickly decided that she didn't want the village gossips to discover her accidentally eavesdropping either.

Just before the door could open she pulled herself and her shopping bag into the shadowed alcove and called upon her magic.

Accessing that pulsating ball of energy inside of her gave her the usual thrill of exhilaration as she bent both light and rain around her, rendering her practically invisible. A neat little trick that she had learned during her stay in Oceana earlier in the summer, she had found that it worked just as well up here as it did at the bottom of the ocean.

The bell tinkled daintily as the door opened outwards, its cream paint chipped and warped from the elements. Three middle-aged women hesitated on the threshold, eyeing up the severity of the rain.

Deciding it was better to wait it out, they halted, the door swinging shut with a bang behind them. They soon continued their conversation, oblivious to Riva's magically cloaked presence.

"I mean it was bad enough that she got herself pregnant so young, and my heart goes out to her for being left with a bairn, but to just take the man back so easily after he abandoned them?" The woman that spoke was looking for something in the depths of an overstuffed handbag.

The other woman was shaking her head. "Just terrible. You know we all thought that Helen would make something of herself didn't we? Now look at her. No respect for herself or her daughter."

Riva could feel her temper bubbling close to the surface once again. Her magic, so recently summoned to shield her from view seemed to want to make an appearance again. Begrudgingly she noted that her increasingly fragile hold on the well of magic within her was probably behind her flaring anger.

The first woman who had spoken finally managed to locate what she was looking for within her handbag and brandished her umbrella wildly. "That poor girl. Can you imagine how she must be feeling? To have a strange man turn up at your door and turn your life upside down?" she said.

For a brief second Riva had to admit, the woman had a point. It wasn't their fault that they had gotten the wrong end of the stick about her father's mysterious re-appearance. Of course people were going to jump to conclusions in a town as small as Glendale.

She had walked past these women and their gossiping her whole life. They seemed to make a hobby out of it. She would catch snippets of their conversations as they hung about the village hall clutching their yoga mats, or find them staring at her over the lipstick-stained brims of their off-white china cups as she visited her mum in the cafe.

They had no problem sitting at their usual table and ordering slices of her mum's delicious baking, but as soon as her back was turned, they chewed up everything from her appearance to her job as fast as they did her Victoria sponge. All of them jealous of the handsome stranger who had suddenly appeared one day almost eighteen years ago and had fallen madly in love with her.

Things like that just didn't happen on the Isle of Skye. The whole scandalous story had been village gossip for so long that it was almost folklore. Little did they know that the truth was much closer to a fairy-tale than they could ever have imagined. The image of her father swimming around with a blindingly white tail drifted into her mind and she smirked. Until another image replaced it, that same tail criss-crossed with bloody scratches as she hauled him onto the shingle of a secluded bay, his skin grey and pallid as he floated closer to death.

Riva shivered and paid more attention to the conversation to distract herself from the memories of the night she saved her father.

The third woman sniffed loudly and looked between her companions disdainfully. "As far as I'm concerned, Helen showed her true colours years ago. Nothing but a tart who couldn't keep her legs shut long enough to get a ring on her finger."

In a great rush, Riva's temper flooded back to the surface, magic pooling in her veins.

"Lorna, that's a bit harsh." Umbrella lady said, sounding shocked.

The other woman, Lorna, pursed her lips. "I'm sorry but that's how I feel. No moral standards whatsoever. Allowing herself to be taken back in by the very same philanderer who ruined her good name. Her parents must be turning in their graves. God rest their souls."

Riva's magic was begging to be released. She was allowed to irrationally resent her dad for the abandonment that hadn't been his fault, even after everything she had went through to bring him back, but no one was allowed to insult her mum. Ever.

These women had no idea what her mum had been through. The deep depressions that swiftly carried her away for sometimes months at a time. Or the secret that her mum had kept from the whole world, even from Riva, until just a few months ago.

"No, I agree with you." Janet said. "I think it's just outrageous. She is setting a terrible example for that daughter of hers. Just you watch, I bet she turns out the same way."

The café bell tinkled again and a wiry old man stepped around the three ladies crowding the entrance, clearly unwilling to finish their conversation. Riva, still cloaked in shadow, was attempting to get her powers, and temper, under control before it got too cramped in the doorway and she popped into view like a magical jack-in-the-box.

What was that saying her mum always used to tell her? Eavesdroppers never heard anything good about themselves? Well it was a little late now.

"Mark my words, it's only a matter of time before her daughter ends up pregnant too. Wouldn't surprise me if she's already sleeping around, didn't you hear that she disappeared for more than a month after the kids finished their exams?" Lorna sniffed.

The woman with the umbrella tutted and shook it out into the downpour as if wanting to make a break for it, clearly uncomfortable with the turn in the conversation.

"Don't you look so shocked Pauline! Isn't your son in her class at school? Better keep a close eye on him."

Distracted, Riva looked more closely at the woman's face, as recognition slowly came to her. She had the same red hair and kind eyes as her son. It was Kieran's mum.

Riva hadn't seen him since she had returned from Oceana two weeks ago. He had been calling her a couple of times a week but she had been studiously ignoring his messages. That was until a couple of days ago when she had finally agreed to meet up with him at Alex's insisting. They still needed to come up with a believable lie about where she had been all summer.

"Riva isn't like that. Kieran always speaks very highly of her." Pauline said.

Lorna folded her hands across her ample bosom. "Well I heard that no-one could find head nor tail of the girl for weeks. Even that best friend of hers, what's her name? Alice? Was knocking on doors and dropping in at the police station every other day. If she's anything like her mother I'll bet that she ran off with someone unsuitable and is now back here nursing a broken heart, undoubtedly with a bairn on the way as well."

Pauline was shaking her head. Riva was losing the urge to keep her temper in check.

"Young girls these days have no standards, teasing every young man around them without expecting there to be any consequences." Lorna finished, finally stepping out from under the roof of the café.

Suddenly, a face flashed in Riva's memory, with a voice that chilled her blood as he uttered those very same words; *'You are such a tease, you wanted this."*

She snapped.

At the exact moment Lorna decided to step out from underneath the lip of the café roof, the awning split and a tidal-wave sized deluge of water cascaded down to drench her. Her shocked screams soon had Riva's magic writhing to be let loose. Where the rain had been dropping down steadily in great fat plops, now it more closely resembled the rainforest in monsoon season.

Janet and Pauline almost bumped into her as they scrambled back towards the relative shelter of the café door, narrowly avoiding the frigid water splashing into their boots. Lorna however, was soaked to the skin, her perfectly set hair now plastered flat to her scalp and her thick make-up running in great dirty streaks down her cheeks.

Riva took immense satisfaction at the bedraggled state of the woman as she continued to shriek about the cold as she hurtled herself back into the increasingly cramped doorway to get out of the rain.

Riva took a deep breath to steady herself and tried to coax her magic back into that safe place deep in her chest and simultaneously calm her anxiety about the face that had jumped into her mind. Every night she was still waking up from nightmares. The overwhelming feeling of suffocating under her attacker's weight had become a nightly occurrence for her.

She breathed her way through the panic as her magic calmed, until gradually the rain went back to its steady drizzle, leaving all three women bewildered. She flexed her still-invisible fingers as they tingled with Earth magic and briefly wondered if she should start being more subtle.

"Mary and Bride, you alright Lorna?"

"Aye Janet, I think so." Lorna replied breathlessly, her cheeks flushing scarlet while she tried to dry her face with a single Kleenex.

The other two women leaned out from under the roof gingerly, both looking up at the dull sky. "You think we should risk it or go back inside and wait until it calms down a bit?" Pauline asked.

"I cannae. Rhys has his piano lesson in half an hour, I've got to get back." Lorna sighed, taking out a small compact mirror from her handbag, eyes bugging when she took in the state of herself.

Bracing themselves, the three women dove out into the sheeting rain, leaving Riva alone and invisible in the shadows with her magic, clutching the bag of potatoes to her chest.

Perched on the window-ledge, the dampness seeping through her jeans, she bit her lip. Her powers were now coming through with almost no noticeable effort. Wriggling her numb toes to try and bring some feeling back into them through her wet socks, she had to admit to herself that her magic was growing more powerful and more uncontrollable by the day.

Ever since her elderly neighbour Lillian had passed the power of Mother Nature of all things into her, she had been feeling more and more unstable.

There was no wonder she was still having nightmares of Stuart's attack, she hadn't really been given any time to process what had happened.

Sighing, she pushed herself up off the window ledge and back out into the rain, removing her cloaking as she passed the bus stop. This time, the torrent of sheeting Scottish rain didn't touch her. As she walked past the boundary of the main village and started traipsing up the country lanes towards the cottage, not a single drop fell on her.

The truth was that she could have done this at any moment. The real reason why her mum and dad hadn't felt bad about sending her out into the freezing cold while they stayed warm and dry at home. She had pretty much complete control over the elements thanks to Lillian's little gift. Why then, had she not chosen to use her powers in the first place?

The truth was that they were staring to frighten her. Every time she tapped into them she wanted to use more. The rush of euphoria that came with their use was addictive, but sometimes the magic, especially the Earth magic, seemed to have a mind of its own.

As if that wasn't enough, the daily news reports of accidents at sea, capsized naval vessels and injured scuba divers were causing her anxieties to skyrocket to dangerous levels. Clearly her uncle was busy enacting his human-hating regime of power in Oceana to great effect.

To say that she was massively overwhelmed would be an understatement.

Finally reaching the cottage, she opened the front door with a creak and slipped off her now-dry trainers in the hallway. Her hair was steaming as she heated up the air around her, the ends curling as they dried.

"I'm home!" she called out.

Her only answer was a muffled giggle followed by a thump coming from her mum's bedroom.

"Ew." she whispered to herself as she padded through to the kitchen in her socks, the stone floor frigid under her feet. It took seconds to heat the air around her, but the thick stone of the cottage was another task entirely.

Dumping the shopping bag onto the kitchen worktop, she headed for her attic bedroom but before she could take three steps, her mum's door opened.

"Hi darling, thanks for doing that for us." Her dad said, emerging into the kitchen in that supernatural way that made him look far too big for the space.

"Breakfast in the middle of the day is it?" she said somewhat scathingly. "We've got no honey left." She said as her dad wandered barefoot into the kitchen and started opening cupboards.

"I'm sure you could fix that for us."

Riva bit her lip uncomfortably. Her dad was eager for her to start exploring the extent of her new powers, or 'gifts' as he called them. She didn't really want to think too much about what gaining these powers meant, or of the responsibility this ancient magic brought with it.

"Why don't you go back down to Lillian's garden today and see if you can connect to the bees? You were getting so good at expanding your consciousness back in Oceana." Her dad said while pouring out his cornflakes.

"Yeah but back in Oceana it was just talking to dolphins for fun wasn't it?" Riva said.

Her dad looked up from the kitchen and out to the small hallway that connected to her mum's bedroom. He plucked two thick slices of plain bread out of the bread bin and slid them into the toaster. She had to admit that it was nice to have someone else around to help her take care of her mum.

"Chatting with marine life just because I could was one thing. 'Communing with nature' using the powers of Mother Nature herself is something entirely different dad." Riva said, still attempting to back away to the sanctity of her bedroom and escape this conversation.

"My darling, you know as well as I do that you can't ignore these powers forever. They were given to you for a reason. And I know you don't want to hear it but Duncan will be looking for you. I'm surprised we haven't heard or seen any of his scouts up here already, searching for us. We need to be prepared for any eventuality and your magic gives us the best chance of surviving."

Her dad now poured copious amounts of milk into the bowl so that the stream hit the cornflakes the wrong way and half of it splashed out onto the scrubbed countertop.

"We're going to run out of milk again if you keep using that much." Riva said cuttingly.

Her dad, good-natured as always, simply chucked to himself and licked his fingertips with a faint squeaking sound, "It's alright love, I'm sure you can pick us up some more when you're in the village again this afternoon. Don't think I don't see how good you're getting at changing the subject." He paused, realising that he wasn't going to get an answer. "Is it just Alex you're meeting up with?"

"No, Kieran's coming too."

Now her dad raised his eyebrows, blue eyes sparkling. "A boy?"

Riva rolled her eyes, "Not that kind of boy."

"I wasn't aware there were multiple kinds." Said her dad as he picked up his bowl and hopped down the little step that separated the kitchen from the living room. He sat down at the rickety wooden table and picked up her dog-eared copy of *Harry Potter and The Prisoner of Azkaban* that she had left sitting there the night before.

"He's just a friend dad." Said Riva, unwilling to admit that Kieran would have been more than happy to be more than that.

"Okay, whatever you say." He said, digging in to his cornflakes with a crunch. "I still think that you should go over to Lillian's when you come back from the village. It is good for you to be close to her energy." He opened the book, leaving Riva to stare at the illustration of Buckbeak on the front cover.

She wished that hippogriffs were something that existed in this mad world she had discovered a few months ago. Then she would have been able to fly away from this conversation.

"I've been going there every day and it hasn't helped me so far. What more do you want me to do?" She asked, rubbing the Mark on her palm subconsciously. The Mark that looked like a scar but twirled into a spiral from where Lillian had transferred her magic.

"So I made the garden come back to life the day Lillian died. That doesn't mean that it will give me any answers." She said, temper once again flaring, her magic egging it on.

She backed out of the living room and up the stairs to her bedroom before she could say anything that would cause the faucet to explode or the apple tree branch to fly through the window again.

Closing her bedroom door quietly behind her, she pulled on her fluffy dressing-gown. Taking up her usual position on her window seat, she hugged her knees to her chest and stared out across the crofters fields towards the sliver of blue that she could make out on the horizon. She had no idea where her home was anymore. Her month spent in Oceana with the Mer had taught her that she didn't quite belong there, but now she felt just as out of place in the cottage as she had done under the waves.

She had tried to ignore the headlines that had been on her dad's newspaper. Humans were dying at sea at an unprecedented rate with little to no explanation. But she knew the reason why.

Her uncle Duncan, her father's younger brother who had succeeded her grandfather as King of the Mer had made it his mission to restore power to the Mer by destroying human presence in the oceans. They hadn't exactly parted on good terms given that he had ordered her execution and tried to incapacitate her father.

She fiddled with the raggedy hole in her dressing gown. Two weeks later and she was still no closer to figuring out how she was going to save the Mer and their dying world or what she was supposed to do with her Earth magic either. She wasn't sure that Lillian had been thinking straight when she had chosen her.

Riva smirked at the memory of her mum rushing down to their elderly neighbour's cottage in her slippers after Riva had appeared in their bedroom, palm glowing gold from her Mark and completely overwhelmed with magic. She would never forget her mum storming back in, just as the Mark had finally stopped tingling, hair a birds-nest on the top of her head, screaming for them to call the police as Lillian had been abducted.

It had taken several whiskies before she had calmed down enough to listen to Riva's insane-sounding explanation. That her daughter now possessed the magic of Mother Nature and that the woman with the green thumb from down the road had too.

But now she was gone, once again leaving Riva to figure everything out alone. Weren't magical beings always supposed to have some sort of spirit-guide or fairy godmother to help guide them?

She really wished that were true. Then they could help get her out of this terrible mess that her life was becoming.

2.

"I can tell something's on your mind. Spill." Alex said as they walked from the cottage into the village together.

Riva's eyes darted across to her best friend, wondering why she seemed extra-perceptive today. "Nothing. Just wondering why you came all the way up here instead of getting off on the main street."

"The twins have the chicken pox and I so do not want to be in that house right now, so I got an earlier bus. Didn't feel like standing outside the café all on my tod. Technically you're doing me a favour." Alex replied.

"Are they really that bad? Surely your mum would appreciate your help."

Alex linked her arm through hers. "When I left, my mum was practically duct taping woollen mittens onto their hands to stop them from scratching. Even though you kick in your sleep I've been getting more kip sleeping here for the last week than I did back home this weekend." Alex nudged her playfully with an elbow. "Why? Are you sick of me already?" she laughed, the sound like bells. And foreign to Riva's ears. She couldn't remember the last time she had laughed, so instead of replying, she just looked down at her feet, concentrating on avoiding the muddy puddles.

"Okay, I was joking but now I'm offended." Alex continued, her tone still light but with an edge of concern.

She was quiet for a minute, the only sound the squelch of two pairs of wellington boots down the field path. Their usual short-cut.

"Riva. Don't cut me out again. I know these last few months haven't been easy for you but I don't want to go back to what happened at the beginning of the summer. You swore there would be no more secrets remember?" Alex said quietly.

Riva stuffed her frozen fingers deeper into her pockets, stubbornly ignoring the pull of her magic that was urging her to warm the air around them.

After she had emerged from the sea two weeks ago with her merman father bleeding to death in her arms, there had been a lot of things Riva had needed to talk about. Most things she hadn't even understood herself, but Alex had been there for her. They had spent almost every night curled up in Riva's small bed with Alex hogging her favourite pillow and playing the part of therapist like she already owned her PhD.

Describing Oceana to her best friend had been exciting. The luminescent palace that rose from the sea floor like a mighty seashell, the vibrant reef that bordered it, full of fish every colour imaginable. And the Mer themselves, terrifying, beautiful and just a little bit creepy. Explaining the horrible mistake she had made in trusting Em, who had betrayed both her and her father, had been difficult. She was still torn between wishing she could have her witty, sarcastic Mer friend back and wanting to throttle her with her bare hands.

She sniffed loudly, the bite of the wind across the open fields making her nose run.

"Here." Alex said, fishing around in her lilac and cream handbag – only Alex would choose to wear such a clean looking accessory in the middle of a muddy field – and handed her a packet of Kleenex.

"Thanks." Riva replied, blowing her nose loudly.

Alex was fidgeting with the strap of her bag and Riva prayed that she would have the good sense to keep her mouth shut. There was only one thing that she was still keeping a secret from everyone, and it was for a good reason.

Unfortunately, Alex opened her perfectly lip-glossed mouth. "So about that voicemail…"

Riva sighed loudly, already shaking her head. "Not this again."

Alex grabbed her arm and forced her to stop. "Yes. This again. Every time I bring it up you refuse to explain or you change the subject. Don't think I haven't noticed." She crossed her arms across her chest.

Riva had to stifle a smirk. She looked like an angry teddy bear.

"All you said was that it was about feeling like your powers were overwhelming you, but you sounded scared Riva. Really scared, not just overwhelmed." Alex said, "I'm not stupid you know. I can read between the lines."

Riva resisted the urge to roll her eyes. "Believe me no-one could be forgiven for thinking you stupid."

In actual fact Alex had spent the last four weeks of their summer holidays enrolled in summer school. Not because she needed to make up the extra grades, but because she wanted to get a head start in learning course material for when she went off to university next month to become a hot-shot doctor.

Alex ignored her look and simply narrowed her eyes. "I mean, you told me that you got your powers the day you fell out of the boat, which now makes total sense to me. Remember how I found you paddling by yourself after I went to get us ice creams? I thought that was really weird because for like, the whole time I've known you, you've been terrified to even dip a freaking toe in the sea. And then how your voice healed in like, an hour? I mean that's just medically impossible."

She stayed silent, hoping that Alex would manage to talk herself off the subject.

"Sure, you seemed weird after the accident, well, weirder than usual at least, but you never seemed scared about the fact that you had just been flung out into the open water. Which again was totally weird because you had been terrified to get in that boat the whole week we had been planning the trip."

Riva wiggled her frozen fingers in her pockets and gave in to the magic, the small space warming deliciously until her fingers tingled. Was it really possible that the accident that had awoken her Mer blood and sparked her powers had only been three months ago? Her powers had changed so much since then, grown into something she was struggling to understand.

Alex was still yammering away. "So no, I don't buy it. I don't know what scared you so much that you - literally the only person more stubborn than I am - would have called me to ask for help in the middle of the biggest fight of our entire friendship."

Mouth dry, she didn't know what to say. She hadn't wanted to tell Alex about the assault. She hadn't wanted to tell anyone. She had been hoping for months that his image would fade from her mind or that his voice would stop taunting her every time she lay down to go to sleep. Looking out over the fields, she might as well have been back on that storm-tossed beach. Stuart's vicious face shouting at her as the rain battered both of them on the inky dark beach.

"You and your lies, your attention-seeking stories, getting me into trouble and then walking around the school pretending like you are a victim. Look at you right now! Waist-deep in the water, taking off your clothes in public like a whore!"

Then he had come at her. Forced her down into the sand. He battered her body until she couldn't fight him anymore, screaming obscenities.

Embarrassingly, tears were swimming in her eyes and she quickly turned from her friend, brushing them away angrily. "God this wind is a pain. When is the summer weather coming back?"

Alex ignored her question but followed her quietly, just a couple of steps behind, as if realising that Riva needed a bit of space. That door she had fought to keep closed for months had just swung wide open thanks to Alex's insisting. Well, she had been able to keep it closed in her waking hours at least. There had been no escaping him in her dreams.

Riva squeezed her eyes shut, as if to try and block out the images of that night on the beach.

"You asked for this" he had growled *"You deserve this."*

His hands crawled all over her, such pain in her body from where he had beaten her. Terror at the thought of what was about to happen.

She had been trapped, powerless. Until the ocean had saved her.

Tapping into the full extent of her magic for the first time, she had managed to fight him off. But she couldn't forget the dark edge her magic had taken on as she held him captive under the waves, watching him struggle. She had wanted to drown him. She would have enjoyed it. Sometimes she was still unsure as to why she let him go. Perhaps she would have felt less afraid now if he was dead.

"Riva what's the matter? Whatever this secret is, you can tell me." Alex's voice pulled her back to the windswept field.

His face kept swimming into her mind's eye, bringing with it a wave of nausea as she recalled the choking sand.

"Look. You need to tell me what happened. I'm not going to get scared and run away. Whatever you tell me I will believe you." She paused and made to reach for Riva, but let her hand fall back to her side at the last minute. "I'm on your team remember."

She felt panic creep up her throat. Her heart had given an almighty lurch and was now galloping away inside her chest like an outsider overtaking to win the Grand National as she thought back to that voicemail that she now wished she had never sent.

"Hey Alex, listen, I need to talk to you. Something crazy has been going on with me lately and I was wrong to keep you out of it."

The first part of the message had been ok, in fact it had already been explained. But she wasn't sure if she could get away with blaming the second part of the message on her powers for much longer.

"But something awful happened last night and I really need you ok? Just call me back please."

She shook her head to try and banish the memories. She had coped so well down in Oceana. Granted, there had been a million other more pressing issues for her to deal with during her time at the bottom of the ocean – like survival.

"What happened to you the night before you disappeared?" Alex asked again, her voice soothing, like she was trying to coax a scared animal towards her.

Riva realised that her best friend was never going to drop it. The wind was lifting all of Alex's baby hairs out of her ponytail so that they whipped around her head, creating some sort of mad halo. If there was anyone she could tell, it was Alex.

She stuffed her hands deeper into the pockets of her rain jacket, their warmth soothing, but also so that Alex wouldn't see that they were shaking.

Then she looked away from the path they were standing on, across the rolling hills that surrounded them. The smell of wild grass and sheep was strong in her nostrils, as the sun flitted weakly in and out behind heavy grey clouds. It was a safe smell. It smelled like home. A far cry from a storm-tossed beach in the middle of the night, but she still had no trouble imagining it.

As soon as she let the memories come back in full force, the flood gates opened and her windpipe tightened. Her breathing started coming in short gasps as the rolling hills disappeared from her view, replaced suddenly with darkness and the angry smell of salt water. Her mouth gaped open, her lips pursed like a fish as she tried to drag some air down into her lungs.

Alex quickly closed what little gap remained between them and clasped Riva's shoulders tightly, steadying her, "Hey, it's just an anxiety attack, you're going to be okay. Try to breathe deeply, I'm here, I'm not going to leave you."

Repressing the memories and focusing her anger and hatred on Duncan instead of Stuart had allowed her to survive in Oceana, but that had only left her feeling more broken now, months later, when she knew that she should be getting over it. She hated acting like the victim Stuart had told her she was.

She leaned heavily on Alex as her legs turned to jelly and her friend, unable to support her weight, let her go. Landing heavily on her knees, palms down in the damp grass, she tried to remember how to breathe.

His shadow looming out of the darkness behind her.

Breathe.

His hot breath on her cheek.

Breathe.

The white-hot pain of her nose breaking when he punched her.

Breathe.

His crushing weight on top of her.

Breathe.

His fingernails scraping her skin as he tried to undress her.

"ENOUGH!" she finally screamed.

The primal cry had come from the very depths of her soul, as the flashbacks wracked her mind and body. She gripped the long grass as if it was the only thing holding her onto the earth as she forced air down into her lungs and rode the wave of panic.

"Riva, it's okay." Alex started sobbing, down on her knees beside her, clearly now very aware that this was not some trivial secret between friends.

"It's not okay." Riva choked out, realising that she was also crying. "It will never be okay."

She screwed her eyes shut tightly until the stars swimming in front of her eyelids replaced her vision of Stuart. It really didn't feel like this misery was ever going to end.

One night, just one night of her life was going to ruin all the others.

I can't let that happen. If I let that happen then he wins.

So she looked up into Alex's face, brown eyes heavy with concern, and finally spoke the words aloud.

"Stuart." Her voice cracked. "S-Stuart, tried to rape me."

She had thought that the words would have come out angry, or afraid, but instead they sounded flat and hollow. Like they held no meaning anymore.

The shock in Alex's red-rimmed eyes was swiftly followed by disgust, then anger and eventually pity. The exact reaction that had stopped Riva from telling anyone anything in the first place. So she averted her eyes and focused on the damp grass stalks beneath her instead.

"We have to go to the police." Alex breathed, sounding like she'd been knocked over the head.

Riva laughed, verging on hysteria. "I think it's a little late for that don't you think?"

She spotted a ladybird climbing over a strand of grass that was so long it almost tickled her chin as she knelt there on all fours, her breath still coming in great gasps. She was almost able to hear the gears turning in Alex's mind as she searched for a solution.

"Even if a lot of time has passed, you need to report him to the police. A statement can still start to build a case against him even if you don't have any b-biological evidence anymore." she said, stuttering over the word.

Riva screwed her eyes shut as a wave of nausea washed over her at the thought of anything of Stuart being left on her skin. The thought made her want to douse herself in bleach.

"What if he does it again to someone else?" Alex hissed.

"Don't you think I've thought of that?" Riva growled, resisting the urge to turn towards her, temper flaring in sheer frustration. Taking deep breaths to calm her now-roiling magic, she reached out a finger towards the ladybird. As its tiny feet scuttled, she felt herself calm down a fraction as it manoeuvred its stout little body onto the tip of her finger.

"If I report him then I will have to see him again if he gets charged, and I worry about what will happen if I do." She said quietly.

The ladybird scuttled around her finger, realising it wasn't in its proper place.

"What do you mean?" Alex asked. "No one will let him hurt you."

The ladybird then opened its bright shell and spread its wings, flying away with the help of the breeze to find a more suitable perch.

Riva sighed, finally getting control of her breathing and straightened slightly, resting back on her heels. "I almost killed him." she admitted, still staring down at the grass.

Alex snorted sceptically, "I highly doubt that."

She finally turned to look at her friend. She was sitting sprawled out in the dirt, completely muddying the seat of her jeans. Her best Levi's.

"No Alex, I did." She sighed, her chest still uncomfortably tight, "These powers that I have, they are capable of great things, but not all of them are good." She had finally spoken aloud the words that had been worrying her. "I wanted to kill him. I wanted to see him suffer. So I summoned a wave to drag him into the water and I made the tide hold him under and I watched him choke. I watched him fight to get to the surface. The moment I saw true fear cross his face for the first time under those waves felt, good. I wanted to finish it. I wanted justice. To make him pay."

The sound of sheep rustling in the distance was the only thing to fill the silence, before Alex asked quietly, "Why didn't you?"

She seemed to be looking for an easy answer, but Riva had been searching for one for weeks and remained unable to find it. "I don't know. Sometimes I find myself wishing that I had killed him. Then maybe I could stop worrying about seeing him again. And like you said, other girls would be safe from him. But who am I to deliver justice like that? What gives me the right to take a life? I'm not a God. I'm just, me."

Alex seemed to consider this seriously, wringing that obscenely clean handbag strap in her grip. "You may not be a God Riva, but these powers have raised you to a level above human standards. I know you don't want to hear it but Mother Nature isn't far off God-like you know."

Riva gritted her teeth, "And how do you think that makes me feel? Because it sure as hell is a lot of pressure to put on a teenager."

"Look, all I'm saying is that we need to research these powers a little more before you're too hard on yourself about how they are manifesting." Alex had ploughed on.

"How the hell are we supposed to research any of this? There are some things that you just can't find in books or on the internet you know." she ran her fingers through her hair, stifling a curse when her fingers got stuck in the tangled curls thanks to the wind that was still swirling around them. "You can justify killing all you want Alex, at the end of the day it's still murder." Riva said, her temper quelling the majority of her earlier panic.

Her tone put an end to Alex's commentary. They knelt in the path for so long that the sheep trotted over the hill and the sun was higher in the sky, bright but not exactly warm as it peeked out from heavy grey clouds. Riva realised that they would have to get a move on otherwise they would be late to meet Kieran.

"I'm so sorry that I wasn't there for you. I should have sensed it." Alex finally breathed. "All of those lunches when you would go out of your way to sit on the opposite end of the bench from him. The way you would go quiet around him. How you looked at Kirsty every time she flirted with him. It all makes sense now."

Riva felt the tears leak out from beneath her eyelids again, temper fading. "It's not your fault, it's mine."

Alex knelt up and gripped her firmly by the shoulders, forcing Riva to look at her. "Don't you dare think that for a second. This was in no way your fault." She said, brown eyes fierce.

"He threatened me before though, at school. He bullied me frequently, cornering me when I was alone and I didn't report him when I could have." Riva angrily wiped away her tears, leaving a long streak of dirt on her cheek. "I went down to that beach in the dark. Alone. I should have known better."

Alex was livid. "No. You were *not asking for it*. No one is ever asking to be raped. He should have known better than to sexually assault women."

Riva grimaced at the words as well as at the venom in her friend's voice and looked across the hills towards the direction of the ocean. "I don't know how to get past this. It was so easy to ignore when I was away, but here… I know it's only a matter of time before I run into him again."

Her voice had tailed off feebly, not knowing what to say.

"You are the strongest person I know Riva, you will find the strength to face whatever this is too."

"I don't feel very strong right now." her voice came out even quieter than she had been expecting and it almost scared her. She focused again on the bright grass beneath her, hoping that the swaying stalks below her hands would replace the image of Stuart's hulking figure. Waiting to grab her. To finish what he started. The grass tickled her palms pleasantly.

"Then find some strength from somewhere and let it help you." Alex said.

Something about her words hit home.

Find some strength.

She focused on the blades of grass again and curled her fingers into the dirt.

Of course... Earth, I need your strength.

She closed her eyes and felt the dirt under her fingers soften, loosen and grow warm as the Earth magic rushed up to meet her. The spiralling Mark on her palm began to glow like a beacon and the two girls were suddenly surrounded by the scent of wisteria and lilies. The wind lost all of its chill and instead it warmed their cheeks and lifted their hair playfully.

Riva didn't loosen her hold on the Earth or its magic, but she felt the power surge inside of her as it rushed through her body, warming her very soul until she finally smiled.

She felt Alex exhale in incredulity as she experienced Earth magic for the second time.

"Are you doing this?" she breathed, sounding as exhilarated as Riva felt.

Not bothering to answer, and at the Earth's urging she opened up her emotions and finally, truly let herself feel.

She felt her power pour through her veins, vibrating through her body. The magic changed as soon as she let go.

As her emotions became more unstable so did her powers. The temperature dropped significantly as the breeze became a crisp autumn wind, and as Riva poured out all of the emotion she was too fragile to keep locked up inside of herself anymore, the temperature plunged further until it was practically an arctic chill.

"Alright Elsa, calm down now. When I said let it go I didn't mean this." Alex said through chattering teeth.

Both girls were shivering, but Riva barely heard Alex, instead she thought that she had never felt more broken. She felt as barren and dead as the trees in winter. As the harsh wind whipped around them, her tears froze on her cheeks and she welcomed the burning pain caused by the ice.

She allowed herself to feel it, to feel everything that she had kept buried inside for weeks as her magic burned her soul and froze her heart.

"Riva, please stop this" Alex cried above the howling wind, her words frosty.

But she was too far gone to stop now and she finally, truly allowed herself to feel her pain, her sorrow and her anger. At Stuart but also at herself for being so stupid in letting him get away with so much for so long. She felt the shame and disgust at her own body after being touched by him, violated. She wallowed in the agony of not knowing who she was anymore. Of losing the old Riva and having no idea how to find her way back to the girl she had once been. Perhaps she never would.

As the icy wind buffeted the girls on the hilltop, the cold air scared away the sheep and they ran across the hill in search of a warmer corner of their field, baaing indignantly. Alex was huddled in a shivering ball, arms crossed tightly across her chest to stave out the cold, button nose angrily pink. Riva saw none of it.

Each ferocious gust felt like a slap in the face. She thought that she could hear the cracking of ice and briefly wondered if it was her heart. But with each unwelcome sensation came another realisation. That she may have been a victim, but she didn't have to let that define her.

The ice raced through her, coating her skin in a shimmering, crystalline net, as well as freezing her very bones. As she exhaled, a long stream of steam came out of her mouth.

The old Riva was changed. Irreversibly, inexplicably changed. But that didn't have to be a bad thing.

"Riva, seriously, please stop this." Alex said, barely able to get the words out as her lips were so numb, looking like all she wanted to do was curl up and go to sleep.

Where there was ice, there was fire.

She would fight to get past this. Her magic would help her find a way. She would give her pain to the Earth as many times as it took until she could finally bear it herself.

Riva looked over at her friend and before Alex could get frostbite, the air warmed significantly. The ice crystals that had formed on the mud thawed and some of the pain dulled. Feeling came back into her own fingers and toes and she felt Alex sag against her in relief.

The air was suddenly filled with birdsong and the strong scent of new grass, and just like a heat pack easing joint pain, she felt some of the hurt she had been carrying inside of her heal too.

Alex was on her feet, arms still folded tightly across her chest, still shivering even though the air was warm once again. "The next time you decide to magic us into a snow globe please warn me in advance so I can bring thermals." She said grumpily, rubbing her nose.

Riva lifted her palms from the dirt, releasing the Earth magic as she did so, feeling it pour out of her hands and back into the ground. She felt it go with a brief sadness. That was the most Earth magic she had ever used, and although it did her bidding gladly, she didn't feel as comfortable with it as she did her ocean magic. Perhaps it was just because it was still so new.

Alex looked like she was going to take a step closer as Riva stood up but stopped herself at the last moment.

"Please don't be afraid of me. I need you." Riva said, wiping her dirt-streaked hands on her jeans, seeing the last of her magic fade from the shining Mark on her palm and hoped that her gold, glowing eyes were fading fast. Thankfully, after a moment of hesitation, her best friend closed the gap between them and pulled Riva into her arms.

"I'm so sorry these things are all happening to you. I wish I could have helped you sooner." Said Alex.

Riva, drained from the magic use, sagged against her. "You're helping me now." was all she said.

With a squeeze and a sniff, Alex released her and tightened her ponytail. "Alright. Any chance you can do that hairdryer trick again until we get to the café? I feel like you froze my bones a second ago."

The corners of Riva's lips lifted in a smile and she summoned her magic again, letting a current of warm air run across the surface of their skin.

"Much better." Alex sighed, pouting. "Now come on or Kieran's going to think you've ran away and abandoned him again and there's only so many times you can let a boy like that down."

3.

"Riva?" Alex's voice jerked her out of her thoughts as she stared into the depths of her mug.

"Sorry, what?" she asked.

Alex rolled her eyes and threw her curtain of golden hair back over her shoulder. The action seemed to dazzle every boy sitting at the tables nearest to theirs.

They had managed to snag their favourite table by the window. Not only did it have an excellent view of the main road and make for great people watching, but it was also the main thoroughfare for service within the café, meaning that they always got frequent refills on their hot drinks. Granted the café was stiflingly warm and the street outside bitter cold with the wind so they couldn't see much thanks to the steam on the glass.

"You weren't listening to a word I said were you?" Alex sighed.

Taking a great gulp of the thick hot chocolate, Riva shook her head, "Sorry I was miles away."

"You're still thinking about it?"

She looked up at her best friend warningly. The sugary drink hitting her bloodstream was making her feel jittery, "I wasn't actually. I was thinking about the fact that I almost drowned Hannah's mum outside that door yesterday."

Tucking a loose strand of hair behind her ear daintily, Alex glanced around to make sure no-one was listening and leaned closer, "I think it would do you good to talk about it."

Riva kept staring down into her steaming mug, stubbornly silent.

"You know most victims say that they feel like a weight has been lifted once they give voice to their experiences." Said Alex.

Riva snorted, "Did you quote that from WedMD?"

Wounded, Alex straightened up. "No. It was Psychology Today actually, but what matters is getting you the help you need. It's been two months and you still won't talk about it to anyone. You only just told me for goodness sake." She hissed.

Hands clenched tightly around her mug, Riva replied, "Yeah well, the way you keep going on about it I'm starting to regret telling you anything at all."

Alex had the good grace to look ashamed for being so pushy.

"It's fine." Said Alex in a tone that indicated it wasn't actually entirely fine. "This is a difficult situation for you, I can't even begin to understand how you must be feeling. But please remember that I'm here to help you."

Riva rolled her eyes, "Are you training to be a doctor or a counsellor?"

"Very funny."

"Speaking of, are you going to be heading off to Dundee in a few weeks or are you going to make your parents mad as hell and postpone for a year?" asked Riva.

Alex fiddled with the salt shaker, unscrewing and tightening the lid. Even though it was Alex's lifelong dream to cure cancer, or Alzheimers, or some other horrific disease that Riva would struggle to pronounce, she had been considering delaying her degree in order to help Riva figure out how to overthrow her uncle and restore peace between humans and the Mer.

Besides, she wasn't sure how much help Alex could actually be, lacking magical powers and all that. She could just imagine her swimming a dainty breast-stroke in her hot pink bikini giving King Duncan a firm talking to. But she also knew that no-one should underestimate he best friend once she got an idea in her head.

"You've been working towards this next step for years. Dreaming about it." Riva said. "You should go."

Alex started tapping sprinkles of salt out onto the table top, "I know, but what kind of person would I be if I left you alone to deal with all of this…" she waved her hands around vaguely, searching for the right word. "Ridiculousness."

"I love your enthusiasm but if I can't see how to get out of this mess then I don't know how you can." Riva laughed bitterly while Alex pouted. "Don't be like that, you know what I mean."

"Just because you have special powers and I don't." Alex continued to pout and started drawing swirls in the carpet of salt she had poured out.

"I mean if you want the responsibility of saving an entire race of beings from a tyrant king who is hell-bent on destroying everyone you love, as well as having to find a way to heal the Mer-human relationship, then by all means I'll find a way to transfer them to you just like Lillian did to me." She said, raising her palm and summoning a gust of wind to blow the salt off the table top and into Alex's lap.

Before Alex could throw the salt-shaker back at her, the busty waitress wormed her way to their table through the crowd of villagers seeking a warm drink and refuge from the rain.

"One chocolate fudge cake and one strawberry tart." The waitress said sliding in between them awkwardly.

"Chocolate fudge is for me." Riva said eagerly. It was one of her mum's best recipes and she never left it in the house for them to eat as it was such a favourite in the café.

Alex, finished brushing the salt off of her tights, drank from her mug and grimaced. "Eugh, it's stone cold." She muttered, wiping her hand across her lips.

Looking down at the pink smear on the back of her hand horrified, she quickly rummaged around in her handbag for her lip gloss.

Quietly, Riva reached forward and clasped Alex's almost-full mug of coffee in her hands. Almost subconsciously she raised the temperature of the liquid until soft tendrils of steam were once again coiling out of the top.

Snapping her make up bag shut briskly, Alex fussed the corners of her mouth with one perfectly manicured fingernail.

"Still freaky that you can do that, but bloody useful." She said, picking up the mug and taking a gentile sip. "Delicious."

Riva leaned back in her chair while holding her own reheated hot chocolate and wondered briefly about exactly how much power could come from her two hands. As always, she dreaded the answer.

Alex drummed her nails on the table. "You have to admit you're getting the hang of them now. You'll figure out what you need to use them for when the time is right."

Riva looked over at her, sceptical. "Oh yeah, how do you know that?" she asked.

Alex rolled her eyes. "Because that's what always happens in the movies." Drawing her gaze towards the window, her eyes bugged. "Shit, he's not as late as he said he would be. We totally forgot to get our story straight and he's right there." Alex swore loudly, earning some scandalised looks from the pensioners at the next table over.

Riva whipped around and could just make out Kieran's red hair crossing the street through the misted window. She suddenly lost her appetite.

"Crap. What am I supposed to say?!" She asked Alex.

She could almost hear her best friend's brain whirring under that mane of blonde hair as she scooted over to make room for Kieran at the table.

"Just let me do most of the talking. I know enough of the real story to make something up that's believable." She replied.

"Alex, you know I don't want to lie…"

Alex's face went deadpan. "Oh alright then, you want me to sit here and watch as he calls up the local psych ward once you tell him that you spent the last four weeks underwater and that you're actually a mermaid possessing the reincarnated spirit of Mother Nature and some seriously freaky magical powers? Be my guest." Alex sat back in her chair, arms crossed and eyebrows raised.

Knowing that she was right, Riva replied snarkily, "Half mermaid actually." Grumbling into her mug by way of reply.

The bell above the door chimed brightly as Kieran pushed it open. Riva sunk down in her chair further, with no idea what she was going to say.

"Riva, Alex!"

He covered the distance to their table in just a few strides. Setting her mug down on the table, she nervously sat up higher in her chair and turned to face him, brushing her hair behind her ear as she did.

His exclamation of joy at seeing her again was brought to an abrupt and awkward halt when he saw her face. It had been clear that he had been planning on scooping her up into one of his massive bear hugs, but the sight of her had rendered him momentarily speechless, so his arms stuck out stiffly from his sides, awkwardly frozen mid-gesture.

"Hi Kieran." She said quietly.

The confusion on his face was hard to stomach. Sometimes she could barely remember what she had looked like before all this had happened. The physical changes that had come along with the manifestation of her powers and the awakening of her Mer blood had been gradual but drastic. Even more so ever since Lillian had dropped her little 'gift' off without so much as an instruction manual.

The last time she had seen Kieran had been the day of their final exam. Not one of Riva's finest days. He had grown up used to her being a frizzy-haired, blotchy, stunningly average-looking human being. Even though he had been there the day of the accident and had seen some of the early changes, now he was being greeted by someone who looked closer to Goddess than mortal.

In the weeks following the accident her friends had put the changes in her appearance down to coloured contact lenses and good hair extensions. But as much as Riva didn't want to admit it, technically she wasn't fully human anymore. She was something... else. And that something else looked nothing like the Riva from a few months ago.

Her hair now fell in luscious dark waves past her mid back, without a flyaway in sight. Her once plain blue eyes now iridescent even inside the dull café. Her skin glowing like pearl, illuminated from within. Her whole life she had been used to heads turning whenever Alex entered a room, she still wasn't used to it happening to her.

Alex cleared her throat loudly, "Sit down Kieran."

Evidently still dumbstruck, he dropped his arms to his sides and did as he was told. The waitress came over and took his order while Alex nibbled away at her glazed strawberries and Riva tried to look anywhere but at Kieran's face, her fudge cake forgotten on the plate in front of her.

The silence between them was almost unbearable until finally the arrival of his carrot cake and coffee seemed to steady his nerves and he found his voice again.

"I'm so happy to see you Riva, you have no idea. We couldn't believe it when you just left without saying where you were going. We thought all kinds of crazy things, didn't we Alex?"

Kieran looked across at Alex but she stayed silent, licking the whipped cream off her index finger.

"We did go up to your house to try and talk to your mum but she didn't seem to want to say anything which made it even stranger, you know? People were spreading all kinds of rumours around the village about where you had gone. That maybe you had done something bad. Then when you didn't return any of my messages I started wondering if you were ever going to come back, with school being finished and you not going to university…"

Riva narrowed her eyes. She had a good idea where Kieran had heard those rumours, judging by what she had overheard his mothers' friends saying the day before.

"But when Alex finally called to say that you were back in town, God, it was such a relief."

His brown eyes were warm and crinkled at the corners as he smiled at her. Her stomach twisted with guilt as she realised how worried he must have been about her. And she had made him wait two whole weeks after her return to get back in touch. She really was a piece of work.

She had hoped that he would have forgotten about his little crush on her, after all there were plenty of girls in the village desperate to snap him up. In fact, as she looked at him she could see that he had changed over the summer too, in those subtle, swift ways adolescence rushed into adulthood.

"So…" Kieran picked up his coffee and sipped it slowly, "Where exactly did you disappear to?"

Still having failed to come up with a cover story, Riva took an enormous bite of her chocolate fudge cake which effectively welded her jaws shut, rendering her unable to answer.

She looked pleadingly at Alex, who narrowed her eyes, but sighed theatrically, "Really Kieran, how tactless are you?"

Kieran looked like a puppy who had just been hit over the head. "What?" he asked.

"That's really the first thing you are going to ask her?" Alex said.

"But, did you not-, I mean, I have a right to know, I mean, don't I?" he babbled.

Swallowing her cake, Riva softened. "It's okay Kieran. You do have a right to know." She said.

Besides, if getting a version closer to the truth out there might help to squash the rumours that she had ran off to have an unsuitable affair and had come back bearing a love child then she was all for it.

Scrambling for some sort of reasonable explanation, she said, "Do you remember how weird I was acting during exam week? And how Alex and I had a massive argument and fell out?"

Kieran looked uncomfortably between both girls and nodded, "Yeah, probably the most awkward week of my life, why?"

"Well I had been doing some research, with Alex's help, into my dad's disappearance at sea before I was born." Riva replied, fiddling with her fork.

Alex raised her eyebrows and sat back in her chair, clearly very interested to see how far Riva could run successfully with this story.

"Alex helped me look into old shipping records of accidents and we managed to find an incident where a man had washed ashore in-" she hesitated as her panic made her forget her own birthday"-August just a few weeks before my birthday on Lewis. They took him to Stornoway apparently because we found a record of a John Doe there-." Riva had to look down at her plate because she didn't think Alex's eyebrows could go up any higher, "so we thought that man could have been my father."

I mean, she did think it sounded a little like an episode of *Grey's Anatomy* but it was Alex's favourite show for a reason. Maybe people would eat this story up as fast as they did one of Meredith's never-ending plot lines.

Kieran had been listening wide-eyed, genuinely invested in her tall tale. "Jesus Riva, why didn't you tell us any of this? We would have helped you find more information. Laura's mum works at city hall you know, maybe she could have found something out." he rubbed the back of his head, making his hair stick up on end and he looked to Alex at his side, "Well, with this one I'm sure you did alright."

Startled to realise that she hadn't so much as thought about the others in their friend group since she returned home, that guilty feeling intensified. "How is Laura?" she asked.

"Yeah, fine. She's already down at Strathy, their start date is a bit earlier and she wanted to get a head start enrolling for some clubs and stuff." Kieran replied through a giant mouthful of carrot cake.

All of her friends off to university. She wondered how she would have felt if this past summer hadn't changed everything for her. Would she have just been left to wander the island alone, looking after her mum? Maybe she would have needed to start working in the café too.

"Anyway... Riva, you were saying?" Alex aimed a swift kick to her shin under the table.

"Ow, right. Well, we struggled to find any more information for a while. Besides we figured if he had survived the accident and washed ashore so close to Skye then he would just have gotten onto a ferry and come home to us, you know? But, uh, apparently the John Doe had... amnesia."

Alex snorted so loudly that she had to turn it into a fake cough to get away with it.

"Amnesia, really? Like in the films?" Kieran asked, incredulous.

Through gritted teeth, Riva replied "Apparently."

"So what happened?" Kieran asked, looking between the two of them, clearly on the edge of his seat. Maybe she should submit this story to the writers of *Grey's Anatomy*, apparently it was riveting.

"Well, they took him to the mainland to try and figure out who he was, thinking that he had set out sailing from Ullapool. But obviously they didn't find much and the next record we had of him was in America."

"America?!" Alex and Kieran exclaimed simultaneously.

Riva aimed another kick at Alex under the table but missed and smacked the table leg instead.

Ouch! Crap!

"Yes. America." She replied, eyes watering.

"Wow, that's unbelievable." Kieran whispered. "What happened next?"

Smiling sweetly at her friend, fork hovering above her plate of cake she asked, "Why don't you fill him in on what *we* found out next will you?"

Alex pursed her lips together so tightly she looked like she had just eaten a bag of *Haribo* Tangfastics.

"What's wrong? Was that strawberry a little too tart?" Riva smiled sweetly at her.

Narrowing her eyes, Alex continued the ridiculous tale that was about to become even more far-fetched.

"Yes. Well, we couldn't quite believe it either. In fact, I told Riva on several occasions that I wasn't actually convinced this man was her father at all. Although of course I understood completely her desire for it to be so, being such a good friend and all that." Alex smiled just as sweetly back at Riva, but thankfully Kieran failed to detect the heavy sarcasm lacing her words,

"So apparently the John Doe arrived in America and set to making a new life for himself since his memories had yet to come back. Retrograde amnesia you see usually wears off after a short period of time. It can be seen when people get concussion or other minor head injuries and it affects the short term memory, however it is much more unusual for it to affect the long term memory for a period of so many years. I mean it would actually indicate some severe brain damage…"

Riva sent another kick Alex's way and this time made contact.

"Ouch what the he—"

"Get to the point, Doctor." Said Riva.

"Fine." Alex folded her arms, "So, apparently her dad made a life for himself working over in America but fell in with the wrong crowd and ended up involved in a criminal circle."

What the-

"Seriously?"

This time Riva joined Kieran in voicing his utter disbelief.

"Yes, he got into some real trouble and ended up in prison for a very long time. Didn't he Riva?" said Alex, her eyes flashing.

It took her a second to realise that Alex was completely out of ideas and only just managed to wipe the look of utter confusion off her face before Kieran turned to her, eager to hear the rest.

"Y-yes, that's right. Um, by the time his, uh, memories came back he was unable to even get back to us, you see, because he was in prison."

Kieran looked confused, "Couldn't he have at least called you guys or something?"

Crap.

"Um, well you know. A long time had passed by then and he still had a lot of time to serve in prison, you know the American system's really hard to get out of I hear. So he felt, you know, ashamed of what he had become and, uh, thought that we would be better off without him. He thought that we would forget about him and move on." Riva said, her tone becoming convincingly sad by the end since that part at least wasn't all that far from the truth. Her father had effectively been a prisoner for almost twenty years within the borders of Oceana with no way of contacting either of them and no hope of ever returning.

"So when we found out that he was a criminal with possible brain damage, of course I didn't want Riva to go and find him." Alex interrupted.

"My dad is not a criminal with brain damage!" Riva spluttered.

This time the two pensioners at the table beside them did get up and leave, clutching their carpetbags close to their chests.

"I mean, his amnesia is gone now so you know, no lasting damage anyway." Riva lowered her voice and glared at Alex. She was starting to sweat slightly and hoped that Kieran wasn't going to ask any more questions. "Things are complicated. But basically Alex and I fell out because she didn't want me to go to America and find him once exams were over and I did. I didn't tell my mum why I was going away in case he turned out to be a horrible person, so that's why she couldn't tell you where I had gone. But thankfully he turned out to be great and he came home with me. Ta da, the end." Riva finished by shovelling the rest of her cake into her mouth because she wasn't sure she could keep expanding this ridiculous story.

"That's unbelievable." Kieran said.

A damn sight more believable than the truth that's for sure.

"So you actually went to America and brought your dad home. Your mum must be so happy." He said.

Riva struggled to speak, her teeth were stuck together with cake. "She's thrilled. I've never seen her happier." She said genuinely.

Kieran smiled, looking so utterly delighted for her that Riva feel terrible for lying.

"And how are you? You look… different." he continued, gesturing across the table towards her.

"Oh you, know. American air, a change of scenery, and a good curling iron can work wonders." She laughed awkwardly, combing her hair across her face a little as if she could hide the new angled cheekbones and sapphire eyes.

"I'm just so glad you're back safely." After a moment of hesitation, he reached forward and covered the hand that wasn't holding her fork. "I've been really worried." he said.

The kindness in his eyes and the warmth in his words was the only thing that stopped Riva from wrenching her hand away. She knew that he had meant well but she still wasn't ready to be touched. The minute his fingers had made contact with her skin all she had felt was disgust.

Not at him, in fact she had to admit that he was looking really good, better than good actually. But it was the memories of the last time a man had touched her that made her feel dirty. Used. So she moved her hand away slowly and didn't miss Alex's look of concern as she did so.

Kieran cleared his throat and chuckled to break the awkward silence. "Look at both of you eh? It's like I'm sitting at a table with Athena and Aphrodite. Aren't I the lucky one?"

Riva rolled her eyes but Alex looked quite pleased and shook out her curtain of gold hair, the spitting image of the goddess of love.

"Well you're wrong there, I'm certainly no Athena. Goddess of wisdom my backside, I barely scraped a pass in any exam." Riva said, thinking back to the morning two weeks ago when she had opened her exam results and had to resist the urge to throw the envelope straight in the fire. Her mum had done her best to cheerfully celebrate the two Bs and three Cs that she had managed to somehow scrape by with.

But Kieran was staring at her with something burning in his eyes. "I didn't say that you were Athena."

Her heart skipped a beat. Right then, with his eyes the colour of her favourite chocolate and his fringe flopping across his forehead, she wondered if she might have felt differently about him if her own circumstances hadn't been so complicated. It was suddenly very warm in the café.

Alex was smirking, eyes darting between Kieran's shy grin and Riva's flushing cheeks.

She decided that a swift change of subject was needed.

"So how were your exam results anyway?"

"Good enough thankfully." said Alex with the audacity to sound like she had been worried.

"Come on, you couldn't actually have been worried about them. You had already been accepted onto your course." Kieran laughed, digging into the last of his cake enthusiastically.

"What about you?" Riva asked him.

"I got what I needed to get my conditional offer turned into an acceptance. Mum's thrilled." He said.

"Congratulations." Riva replied, genuinely meaning it. "I'm just glad I passed any considering my mind was half underwater during exam week."

Crap!

Both girls glanced quickly at Kieran, wondering if he had noticed Riva's slip-up.

"I know what you mean, my head felt foggy for weeks! Man, I don't know how I'll make it through uni. I don't want to have to sit another exam in my life." Kieran said, stretching his arms behind his head.

Relived that he hadn't understood what she meant, she silently kicked herself. She was being sloppy. Not having a cover story prepared, using her powers in public with only the barest hint of control, and no real plan of attack in place weeks after escaping Oceana? She needed to do better than this. As soon as Kieran went home and told his mum about where Riva had disappeared to (no doubt she would be waiting by the front door for news), she needed to get her backside in gear.

Whereabouts in America did she say she had tracked down her dad again? Had she said? This was about to get way too complicated. Stomach churning with anxiety, she pushed her half-finished chocolate fudge cake away from her and slouched down, earning herself a glare from Alex, who looked pointedly at Kieran.

Sighing, she sat up slowly.

"So since you're back, I was wondering, uh." Kieran fidgeted with his collar, it was only then that Riva realised he had dressed rather smartly for coffee with two of his school friends. She looked down at her own bobbly jumper, suddenly feeling like she should have made more of an effort.

"I um, wondered if maybe you would like to hang out sometime? Before I head off to uni that is." He asked, blushing slightly.

Confused, she replied. "We are hanging out. Right now."

Kieran looked at Alex sitting beside him out of the corner of his eye. "Well yeah, I mean, technically. But I wondered if you might want to do it again? Maybe, just the two of us?"

Feeling like a rabbit caught in the headlights she looked towards Alex for help, but she was just grinning and giving not-so-subtle nods with her head behind Kieran's back.

She groaned inwardly while trying to keep the expression off her face. Why on earth had he asked her this now? Things were difficult enough as it was without adding this into the mix. But as she looked at his honest eyes and the face that pretty much every girl in the café was eyeing up, she thought that maybe it wouldn't be such a hard thing really, to go on a date with him. Maybe Alex was right and she needed to start taking some steps to get past the assault.

"Um, uh." She felt flustered and didn't know where to look. It certainly didn't help that Alex was eyeballing her.

Kieran's expression changed, he was already preparing for disappointment as he drew in a long breath. But before he could say anything, Riva jumped in. "Sure, why not?"

Surprise was clear on all three of their faces, none more so than Riva's. But as she looked across at him, now grinning shyly, she felt at the very least glad to make him happy. Granted, it wasn't exactly a butterflies in the stomach, first love kind of deal, but she wondered why she had been so hesitant for so long. Putting the Stuart stuff to one side, he had been interested long before anything had ever happened.

Alex cleared her throat loudly and Riva realised that they had been staring at each other for far too long.

"So, enough about my summer, how's yours been?" she asked Kieran in an attempt to get the conversation going again.

Looking delighted that she had asked, he launched into a long story about his apprenticeship with his dad and how much he was enjoying work.

"It's been a good laugh. I've saved up a decent amount of money and he even told me that he would take me on once I finish uni, if I want." He ran his fingers through his hair, Riva briefly wondered if it felt as soft as it looked and then blushed immediately for thinking it.

"Spent more time with my dad than I have since I was about four!" He looked adorably embarrassed about how much he was enjoying this newfound father-son time.

"Stuart's dropped by quite a bit too. Have you seen much of him?" he asked.

Riva's mug slipped out of her hands to clatter onto the table loudly, splattering her with the last dregs of hot chocolate.

"Wow, careful!" He chuckled, reaching across Alex to grab some napkins, completely oblivious to the fact that both girls had just frozen.

He's seen Stuart. He's here.

Fighting the urge to look over her shoulder at the door, her chest tight, she took the napkin that Kieran handed her robotically to wipe off the brown chocolate spots now decorating her jumper.

"No, we haven't seen him." Alex said somewhat breathlessly.

Wiping the stains ferociously, all Riva could hear was his name echoing madly against her skull. Stuart, Stuart, Stuart. It had been stupid of her to think that he had gone away. But the more time that she had spent at home and in the village without seeing him, she had started to think that maybe he had. At least she had hoped so. She tried to remind her lungs that she could breathe, that there was no sand blocking her airway and she clutched the table trying to stop the panic from taking over.

"That's a shame, he's really struggling at the moment. You know his dad isn't easy and his mum doesn't keep well so he's been trying to pick up work here and there." Kieran continued obliviously.

There was a high, cold, voice that joined the conversation and it took Riva a second to realise that it was coming from her.

"*Stuart* is struggling?"

Kieran looked up, confused by the look on her face. "Yeah, I mean you know he's had it tough growing up. I thought things were getting better for a while there, when he started boxing I mean, but he's been really down these last few weeks. I think there's some trouble at home again."

A half-hysterical laugh burst from her lips and surprisingly, instead of panic, came anger. The sheer injustice of someone thinking that her attacker was the one who deserved sympathy, that he was the one struggling, made her blood boil. Regardless of whether or not Kieran knew all the facts, she didn't ever want anyone to see Stuart in a favourable light again.

"Stuart's been feeling *down* Alex, did you hear that?" She said still choking on that maniacal laughter.

She felt her magic push itself towards her, nudging insistently. Use me, it was saying. I'll help. She should have finished it that night on the beach. If he had been dead then she wouldn't have to spend her life looking over her shoulder, worried that he was about to come back and finish what he had started. Or worse, wondering if he was out there doing it to another girl instead. More than once in the last two weeks she had found herself lying in bed at night wanting to go out and find him, wanting to finish the job.

"Riva, are you ok?" Kieran asked, looking worried.

"She's fine." Alex said firmly, but Riva could hear the slight edge of panic in her voice.

Magic was flooding her system, muffling every sound and making her feel like she was floating somewhere far away. The window beside them grew darker and the clouds grew heavy with rain that soon started pelting the window. Thunder rumbled directly overhead, loud enough that it rattled teacups and the windowpane shook. Several other customers jumped or cried aloud at the unexpected crash.

"Holy shit!" Kieran swore, laughing uncomfortably. "I was not expecting that!"

Why had she been so weak as to let Stuart go free? She had had him completely at her mercy ready to pay for what he had done to her and she had chickened out, too scared to use her powers for what they were clearly meant to do.

Her magic nudged her again and she let some of it go in a glorious rush. The thunder grew louder and, with a great gust, the door to the café blew open, drenching the customers sitting nearest. As they leapt up shrieking in the cold spray, the power went out plunging them all into near darkness. More than a few people screamed before the manager could be heard shouting for calm and grumbling about the fuse box.

"What the actual hell is going on with this weather? Some summer this has been eh?" Kieran laughed nervously. "At least we got a couple of good weeks at the beginning."

By this point Riva was shaking with the effort of holding her magic in while fighting with her rage. She wanted to leave right now and hunt him down, to be free of him. She needed him to suffer like she was suffering.

She looked up at Alex pleadingly. She needed to get out of here, now.

Alex's mouth plopped open like a dead fish as Riva looked up. Her glowing golden eyes were like two great beacons in the dark café.

Thankfully, Kieran was looking over at where the manager was attempting to locate the blown fuse. Alex mimed at Riva to keep her head down and eyes closed.

"You know I think I'll go and help him. My dad taught me a thing or two about faulty wiring a few weeks ago" Kieran said.

"Good idea." Replied Alex decisively.

He got up and made his way behind the counter with his phone torch held aloft to try and help, when Alex scraped her chair back and grabbed Riva by the shoulders.

"It's time to go." she said firmly.

Alex half pushed, half shoved her out into the street where she finally opened her eyes again, the driving rain good cover for the glow. Alex frog-marched her up the street until they came to a deserted alleyway that smelled strongly of rotten lettuce.

"For God's sake!" Alex shouted furiously, "you need to get control over yourself somehow. I know that can't have been easy for you but if you want to keep this a secret at all then you can't have your magic bursting out of you like this all the time!" Both girls were drenched. The rain was still coming down in sheets around them. Alex looked like a fluffy pampered cat that had just fallen into a bath – sopping wet and very annoyed.

"Oh for God's sake Riva, can't you make this stop already!?" Alex finally shouted, waving her arms around madly.

It took her a second to realise what she meant. Stop the flashbacks of the attack? Stop letting her powers get the better of her? A very exasperated Alex gestured upwards at the heavy clouds and it clicked.

"Oh crap, I'm sorry." Riva said.

It barely took any effort. In fact, no sooner had she thought it, the rain stopped and the clouds lightened to their usual wispy grey.

"Subtlety has never been your strong suit. But thank you." said Alex, wringing out her hair gingerly. "Great, now I'm going to need an appointment at the salon tomorrow." She fished around in her handbag for a hair-tie.

Riva sighed. "There's no need." She reached out, Mark still glowing from all the magic use and touched her friend's arm. Summoning her powers, it felt like they were standing in one of those full-body blow driers that you found at theme parks by the side of the log-flume ride. Steam curled off their clothes and hair as they dried.

"Don't think that gets you off the hook." Alex grumbled, inspecting her dry-clean-only clothes for damage. "Can we talk about what happened in there?"

Riva pulled her cardigan tighter around her. "It's just a lot to deal with Alex. And I will, I'm getting there, I just wasn't expecting it to come up that's all."

Alex stopped, hair-tie clutched between her teeth, expression unreadable. "You can't just keep running away every time things get difficult anymore."

Riva pulled her hood up and shivered as several fresh droplets of rain found their way under the collar of her jumper.

"I know, I know. You're right. I'll get it together I promise."

Alex smiled, shaking out her now dry hair. "Good. Because I need you to learn how to do this on the regular, it will cut my styling time in half."

Riva gave her a shove and then linked arms, leading her back up the main street and away from the village. It took her until they were within sight of the cottage to realize that they had once again abandoned Kieran with no explanation.

4.

The rain had finally stopped, but there were still some steady drips plopping off the leaves and petals around her. She was once again sitting in Lillian's garden, although for the first time not due to her father's insistence.

After Alex had unceremoniously shoved her onto her bus home, she realised that she had better figure out why she had these powers and what she was supposed to do with them before she blew up. Or blew someone else up.

She was sitting at the white garden table and the metal of the ornate chairs was digging uncomfortably into her back. If only Lillian hadn't disappeared as soon as she had transferred her powers, maybe she could have explained what she was supposed to do now. What had the old woman done with her powers anyway? All Riva could remember of her was a quiet woman who enjoyed gardening.

But we never saw her very often did we? She thought. *Maybe she had been disappearing in secret without us knowing...*

The thought of the wizened old woman controlling the elements clad in her tatty old rain mac and bright yellow welly boots brought a smile to Riva's face and she stood up from the uncomfortable chair, stretching.

Her phone pinged and she unlocked it to see a message from Kieran waiting for her.

You left without saying anything, are you ok?

She sat down on the chair again, the cold, damp metal soaking through the seat of her jeans. She replied;

Sorry, family emergency, didn't want to distract you from helping the manager but everything's fine now.

His reply took a couple of minutes this time and she watched a great, fat bee buzz importantly through the bushes. She wouldn't blame him for being mad at her. All she ever did was mess him around.

She thought about that look in his eyes back at the café and the way his jumper had showed off his broad shoulders. When her phone finally pinged again she surprised herself by hoping that he wasn't going to be mad at her.

No problem, it was just a blown fuse. Do you still want to go out tomorrow night?

She stared at the blank message box for a few minutes, not knowing what to say. Well, that wasn't quite true. She wanted to go out with him. In fact, she was craving something normal in her life, but could she do it? Forgetting everything that had happened with Stuart, was it fair of her to bring Kieran into this crazy world she now lived in? Potentially put him in danger at worst or vanish every time something went wrong at best?

She clicked a button and her phone screen went dark. She would think about it later.

Remember what Alex said about running away from your problems? The little voice in her head said.

She stuffed her phone angrily into her pocket.

This isn't running away. Just postponing.

Remembering what she had come to Lillian's garden for in the first place, she lay down flat on her back on the grass, almost instantly regretting her decision as the damp soaked through her clothes. She had come here for some answers and she wasn't going to leave until she found some. Crossing her hands over her stomach she closed her eyes and waited, praying that the rain wouldn't start suddenly pouring down.

As the cold seeped into her bones and she started to long for a hot bath, she continually reminded herself to bring her mind back to her magic and her connection to the Earth. Alex had been harping on about 'mindfulness practice' as a way to control her flashbacks. She hoped that she was doing it right.

Every time thoughts of Stuart flitted into her mind she concentrated on the feel of each damp grass stalk that tickled her fingers. As anxiety welled in her stomach at the thought of having to save the Mer, she concentrated on the birdsong in the trees surrounding her. She let the heady scent of lavender and roses help her drift off until she felt almost detached from her body. It wasn't until she had been doing this for some time that she realised she had been subconsciously summoning her magic. It seemed as if the Earth itself had come up around her like a cocoon, protecting her from the outside world and all of the worries it held for her.

She opened her eyes.

Crap.

Sitting slowly upright, it was immediately obvious that she was no longer in Lillian's garden. In fact, she was nowhere she had ever been before.

The grass under her jeans was pleasantly cool but no longer damp, and the air around her was warm like an early summer's day. A far cry from the dreary Scottish August she had been present in moments before. She seemed to be sitting in some sort of meadow. Raising one hand up to her forehead to block out the faint sunbeams, she glanced around.

Wildflowers were dotted all over the place and friendly-looking oak trees guarded the perimeter, making her feel safe. A lively spring was babbling away in the far corner and just over the tops of the trees she could make out glorious mountains that soared into the sky.

"I've stepped right into a freaking Enid Blyton novel." She muttered.

"You have finally found your way my daughter."

Jumping at the strange voice that had sounded behind her, she whirled to her feet. Only to find herself looking up into the dazzling face of a woman standing several metres away from her. She was tall, with skin like burnished copper and eyes that swirled like limitless pools of liquid amber. It took her a minute to realise why she looked so familiar.

"You're the woman from my dream…" she whispered.

The dream she had had the night that Lillian had disappeared. The dream that had been both a vision and reality. The dream that had changed everything.

It had woken her up in the early hours of the morning and she had sprinted down to her neighbour's house in a panic. Unfortunately, when she got there she had realized that the dream had been all too real. The garden which only hours before had been alive with colour was at that moment blackened, dead under her feet.

In that moment she discovered that her ocean magic had evolved into something much greater as she had brought the garden back to life. The swirling Mark that now sat on her palm was proof of it.

The Goddess who had appeared in that dream, and who now stood before her, had given her more responsibility than she thought was entirely fair. So as she gazed upon her in the meadow, she found it difficult to tell if she was friend or foe. Perhaps she was neither.

As Riva stared now, it was difficult to truly see what she looked like. Flowers were blooming in bright splashes of colour in her hair, only to fall to the ground at her feet to be replaced by new pink buds. The folds of her dress rippled in the light breeze, like gold and brass waves whipped up into a froth, making it hard to see her outline. She looked like she was made from everything and nothing, all at the same time.

"Am I dreaming?" she finally asked.

The woman smiled, and Riva thought that she would cry with the beauty of it.

"Yes… and no."

"Who are you?" she whispered.

"I have many names. But you may call me Gaia." The Goddess said. Her melodic speech seemed to echo with a thousand voices, it managed to be both soothing and harsh all at the same time. Girlish and husky. A perfect contradiction.

She tore her gaze from her and looked around the picturesque meadow. "Is this…heaven?"

The Goddess laughed, the sound as pleasing as church bells and as cruel as a raven's cry. It sent shivers up Riva's spine. "No my daughter."

Riva felt somewhat unsteady as she brushed the grass off her jeans and looked up at Gaia, unsure of whether or not she should curtsy or something. What was the protocol when you met a Goddess? She had never been particularly religious or interested in mythology, but there was a small part of her that couldn't help but be glad that the first Deity she met was a woman.

"Welcome to Eden." Gaia said, opening her arms in welcome.

She looked around again at the serene meadow which positively glittered with radiance and she couldn't think of a better name for it. She had never seen anything so perfect in her life.

"Wait, isn't the Garden of Eden a Christian thing?" Riva scrunched up her nose, her head was starting to hurt.

Gaia smiled. "Like the roots of a tree almost all things come from one. It matters not what a place is called, but rather what it symbolises." She said.

Riva nodded heavily, trying to pretend that any of this made any sense. "Not that I'm complaining, because this place is pretty incredible, but how did I get here?"

Gaia gestured towards the woods. "Shall we walk?"

The two of them set off through the soft grass and into the shade of the oak trees. The sounds of birdsong and small animals scurrying about were muffled inside the shelter of the large boughs, but pleasantly so. She had never heard so many creatures before. More than once a fox or a badger scurried across the path in front of them.

"That's amazing!" Riva exclaimed as the furry black and white animal disappeared between the roots of yet another towering oak. "I've never seen a badger in real life before. They're like, really endangered and I'm pretty sure they're nocturnal. I've seen a couple of foxes before but they were always a bit mangy looking. Mr MacGregor, our neighbour down the road, shot one for eating his chickens once."

At the condescending smile on the Goddess's face, Riva blushed and immediately ceased her nervous ramblings.

"What makes you think that this is not real life Riva?" Gaia asked.

She looked up into the Goddess's face and she felt stupid. Of course there would be badgers frolicking about in Eden. For heaven's sake a unicorn was probably about to prance out from behind that tree.

"I dunno. It's all just a bit surreal." She breathed.

"You have journeyed to an underwater kingdom have you not? Discovered your abilities to control the ocean and its inhabitants, and yet now you question your reality?" Gaia asked in that same contrary tone, flowers of all colours still streaming from her like a flourishing waterfall.

Riva had to admit that she had a point. Was this really any crazier than mermaids and Oceana?

"You're right. It's just a lot to take in. I need a sec." She sat down heavily on a tree stump and closed her eyes. "Are you here to tell me what am I supposed to do? Why I have these powers?" she asked, not daring to open her eyes. "I went to Lillian's garden for answers. I need help with all of this, with these new powers. I don't know what to do or how to control them."

She jumped when she felt a warm hand brush against her face, soft as the touch of a feather. Looking up she could see sadness etched onto that beautiful face, and a glimpse of a withered woman behind the façade.

"My ancient magic is almost gone." The Goddess said. "As humans grow more powerful, the Earth suffers. Many of the old God's have passed into memory and continue to exist only in stories. We are all that remains."

"Why do you keep saying we?" Riva asked, looking around uncertainly.

As much as she felt safe in Gaia's company, there was still something about her that put her on edge. She wasn't sure she liked the sound of being surrounded by other ancient beings like her. If this was Gaia without the majority of her powers then she decided that she did not want to meet her when she had them all. Magic was practically seeping out of her pores.

"Do not worry my child. The others will not bother you here while you are under my protection." She said. "But I am no longer strong enough to sustain the Earth alone." She gestured to where Riva was still sitting on the tree stump. "So I choose a mortal host every few centuries who can do what I cannot. We are no longer free to leave Eden, our powers are limited to its boundaries. But sending my magic down to a mortal who can wield them with strength, yes. That I can still do."

"Hold up. Wait. Every few centuries?" Riva stuttered, "Does that mean-."

Gaia smiled. "That you will be blessed with long life? Yes."

If she hadn't already been sitting, Riva was sure that she would have keeled over.

"Lillian had lived for hundreds of years." It came out not quite as a question.

Huh, no wonder she was so wrinkly.

"She was the right host until someone stronger came along."

Riva gulped. "You mean me?"

There was a look of pride, but Riva couldn't mistake the hint of greed on the Goddess's face. "The strongest host in a millennia. Blessed with your own powers over the elements and the ability to wield them. The blood of your father gives you a connection to the ocean, and with the addition of my own magic..." The Goddess smiled, and she could see both the joy of birth and the fear of death in it. "You could be the one to finally restore balance to the world."

As Riva watched her, she was no longer sure that her dress looked like waves, now she thought they more closely resembled a raging fire, or writhing snakes.

She swallowed uncomfortably. "That's an awful lot of responsibility for someone who doesn't even have their drivers' license yet."

The writhing snakes calmed to a flicker of candlelight as the Goddess once again grew peaceful. "My daughter. You were destined for this."

Closing her eyes so that she wouldn't roll them, Riva groaned. This Deity was sounding annoying like her father. The only thing she wanted to be destined for was a Nandos. She was seriously regretting not finishing her fudge cake as her stomach grumbled.

"What happened to Lillian?" she asked.

"When her duty was over and she found you, she moved on. However she remains a part of me, of us, and of this place." Gaia said.

As Riva looked around, she realized that there were signs of her old neighbour all around her. The roses that were blossoming all over the base of a tree in a way that definitely didn't look natural. And the watercolour wildflowers back in the meadow had looked just like those in Lillian's garden.

"You see? We are all connected." Gaia said, stretching out her hand.

"I swear if you say anything about a circle of life I'm ending this dream right now." Riva said holding up a finger warningly.

Ignoring her quip, the Goddess continued. "We have faith in you."

Then she reached out her hand, long delicate fingers adorned with green vines and clasped her upper arm just as Lillian had when she had passed the spirit of Mother Nature into her. What felt like an electric shock ran through her again and she gasped at the contact. Hundreds of faces flashed in her mind's eye. Hundreds of women. All women like her who had been chosen to try to save a dying world.

Riva pulled away and broke the contact. "It's too much. I don't even know where to start!" she cried.

The Goddess backed away slowly, face shadowed. "Begin with the destiny of your blood and the rest will fall into place."

She began to fade.

"No, wait! I have more questions!" Riva cried, jumping up from the log, attempting to follow, crashing through the trees back into the meadow.

The Goddess backed into a shaft of sunlight, flowers blossoming at her feet as she went, and then, in the blink of an eye, was gone. Nothing but a beam of light remained.

What the- Seriously? Thought Riva, sweeping her hand through the sunbeam and finding nothing but air. *Double crap.*

Sitting down with a thump on the lush grass she hugged her knees, feeling seriously overwhelmed. Why did no-one ever give her a straight answer? Picking at the grass stains on her knees, she looked around the meadow again until her eyes fell on the stream to her right. Wondering if she was even allowed to explore Eden alone, she wandered over, wanting to quench her thirst.

As she knelt down beside the small stream, she looked down at her reflection. While on Earth she might look like a Goddess, she was dull in comparison to Gaia's otherworldly radiance. Gaia was as terrifying as she was beautiful but at least her cryptic message had given her some direction.

The destiny of her blood, that had to mean the Mer.

Riva cupped some water in her palm and lifted it to her mouth, and as she did so she looked up into the tree line.

There was someone looking back.

Crap!

Heart pounding, the water fell from her palm with a splash and she scrambled to her feet.

"Who are you? What do you want?" she asked, voice shaking, immediately wondering what kind of God or Goddess was lurking in those shadows.

The figure in the trees didn't reply, all she could make out in the darkness was a tall shape and the flash of amber eyes.

"Gaia?" She called out nervously, keeping her magic close.

The figure did not reply, instead they kept to the tree line, cloaked in shadow.

She remembered what Gaia had said about being safe in Eden while she was under her protection. Well the Goddess had left her alone and she wasn't entirely sure that her magic would have any effect on the other *beings* that she had mentioned lived here with her. Certainly not if they were as powerful as Gaia herself was.

She backed away slowly. Prey retreating from a predator.

Hoping that she would be allowed to come back, she closed her eyes and desperately thought of home.

When she opened them she was once again lying in Lillian's garden, her jeans soaked through to the skin. Heart still pounding.

"And I didn't even need a pair of ruby slippers…" Riva muttered out loud, shaking out her still-wet palm.

It wasn't until she was almost back at the cottage that she realised that perhaps it was a good thing that she hadn't drank from the stream. Who knows what kind of magic it held.

Whoever had been lurking in the tree line, had possibly saved her from making a huge mistake.

Summoning her magic to her, she walked home with renewed vigour.

There was no more time for avoiding things. King Duncan was going to wage his war on humans and half-breeds whether she did something about it or not. She shuddered at the image conjured in her head of him sitting on the throne that had belonged to her grandfather and should now rightfully go to her father, with Em by his side, amassing his Guards.

Em.

She needed to stop avoiding everything. Goodness only knows how much damage had been done in the two weeks since she had returned.

Well, there was one thing that would be easy to stop running away from. She pulled out her phone and replied to Kieran's message.

I can't do tomorrow, but it's my birthday on Thursday. Want to join the party?

Taking a deep breath, she pressed send. She didn't feel ready to go out on a date with him alone, but thinking of him being there with her parents and Alex to celebrate her turning eighteen? That didn't sound half bad at all. Baby steps.

It was time for her to stop being afraid of these powers and embrace her destiny. After all, it wasn't like she was expecting to receive an acceptance letter from a university this year.

Stopping at the gate, she clutched the wet wood and closed her eyes, summoning the Earth. It came to her in a joyful rush, warming the air around her and lifting the dampness from her clothes. A steady confidence began to ebb through her, as if the warmth of Gaia and the Earth had passed through from Eden with her.

It was time to start planning. She had an underwater world to save.

5.

"I don't need any fuss mum, honestly." Riva protested

Her mum, painstakingly applying lipstick in the hall mirror, rolled her eyes. "Don't be daft love, you only get to turn eighteen once. Of course we're going out!"

Riva squirmed in her new dress. Her mum had looked so happy giving it to her that morning so she had felt obliged to wear it out to her birthday dinner, but it itched something terrible under her arms. Plus the biting wind outside meant that she had to wear it with tights that she had borrowed from her mum and they kept rolling down her hips.

At least the deep purple colour was lovely.

"Are my girls ready yet?" her dad called out as he strode out of the bedroom, looking more dashing than ever in a pale blue shirt with his dark curls in their usual disarray. No wonder the ladies of the village liked to gossip about him, no human could ever look that good.

"Almost, we're just waiting for mum to put on her face." Riva said, sticking her tongue out in her mum's direction.

Her dad glanced over to where her mum was now fiddling with a mascara wand. "Ah, you don't need to be bothered with all of that my darling, you are beautiful just as you are." He made his way over and looped his arms around her mum's waist, making her squeal delightedly.

"Dylan, you'll make me smudge it!"

Riva rolled her eyes, trying her best not to scratch at her armpits. "Do you guys really have to be so PDA all the time? Can you maybe act your age until my birthday is over?"

Her dad released her mum, not looking even the slightest bit embarrassed. "Sorry love, this is your night." He put his hands on her shoulders and looked her over. "That colour really suits you, I can't believe how grown up you are."

"Well maybe that's because you missed the nappy stage and the crawling stage, and the…"

"And the stroppy teenager stage?" Her mum said warningly. "Birthday or not, watch your attitude."

Riva felt guilty at the look on her dad's face and reached out to him. "I know it's not your fault you missed all that." Seeing him smile she felt glad that he shared her dry sense of humour. "Don't worry, I resent you much less now than I did two months ago."

"Riva!"

Her mum was giving her 'the look' from behind her dad's shoulder but he laughed, affectionately, mussing up her curls.

"Stop squinting your eyes mum, I thought you didn't want to smudge your mascara?" Riva said drolly, pulling her coat off the overflowing rack beside the door. "We're going to be late for our reservation, Alex already messaged to say she's almost there. And Kieran's been there for ten minutes already."

"Hmm. Punctual. I like him already." Her dad said, reaching across to grab his coat.

"Eye-witness reports are saying that it was one of the most devastating things to happen in European waters. The Star of the Sea sunk so rapidly that the majority of the passengers were unable to make it to the safety of the lifeboats. As of the current moment, the exact number of lives lost is still unknown."

The three of them turned to the TV that had been left on in the background and froze to watch the news report. The images of a large cruise liner in the Mediterranean was followed by images of the stricken faces of the people who had managed to escape. It was then followed by drone footage of the extensive damage to the hull of the ship as it sank.

Throat dry, she picked up the remote with a shaking hand and turned it off.

"We're running out of time." She whispered.

Her dad buttoned up his coat purposefully. "Riva. You are only one person. You need time to figure out a plan of action. Don't blame yourself for the things my brother is doing."

She shrugged on her own coat. "I know. But I feel guilty every time something like this happens. We know why and we know who's behind it, and I need to stop him sooner rather than later."

"Darling, you are only just eighteen and you didn't ask for any of this. None of it is your fault." Her mum said, smoothing her hair.

Riva fidgeted with her dress, no longer quite as hungry as she had been five minutes before.

Her dad reached across to fix the collar of her good coat. "Come on. Put it out of your mind for now and enjoy your birthday dinner." He said, forcing a smile. "You need to think about which wine to pick with dinner now that you are legally allowed." He winked.

Appreciating his attempt to lighten the mood, she followed them out of the house, but it took most of the drive to town before she was able to get the images of the overcrowded lifeboats and floating bodies out of her mind.

By the time they had finally found a place to park in the teeny car park beside the beach, Riva's stomach was once again growling. She was kicking herself for saying no to that roll and Lorne sausage at lunch. Her dad was looking wary, having borne the brunt of her snappiness when she went hungry in Oceana thanks to her aversion to seafood.

Thankfully seafood was not on the menu for her birthday dinner.

"Finally! What took you so long?" Alex groaned, shifting from one foot to the other outside the door of the Indian restaurant.

"Sorry, the kids took too long getting dressed." She replied, nodding her head back in the direction of her parents where they followed a good six metres behind. She had sprinted off in Alex's direction once free of their simpering conversation in the car. The sight of her dad's hand sliding up her mum's thigh as she drove had almost been enough to make her lose her appetite again.

"Aw, I think they're cute together." Alex smiled over at them, where her dad was now protectively wrapping her mum's shawl more firmly around her shoulders to stave off the biting wind flying in from the ocean.

"Yeah, you don't have to live with them." Riva said.

Alex's gaze travelled back to her best friend. "Why have you dressed like the purple sweet from the Quality Street tin?"

Thankfully Kieran appeared at that moment and spared Alex the bite of Riva's hangry tongue.

"Hey sorry, I forgot your present in the car." He said, jogging up to them, looking seriously good in a tight-fitting long sleeved navy jumper. He'd even worn dress shoes with his dark jeans. Alex wiggled her eyebrows as if to say 'someone made an effort.'

"You didn't need to get me a present." Riva said shyly, spying the gift bag he was trying to hide behind his back.

Kieran bent over and leaned in, and for one terrifying second she was worried he was going to try and kiss her, but he just barely grazed her cheek with a peck instead. Heart racing, she wasn't entirely sure if it was nerves or excitement so figured it was best to simply usher everyone inside the cosy restaurant.

"Come on let's find our table before we lose the reservation or before you lose a toe to frostbite." She looked down at the glittery black monstrosities attached to Alex's feet. "What possessed you to wear those down here?" The entire street was cobbled.

Alex sighed at Riva's lack of appreciation for fashion. "I wouldn't expect you to understand." She glanced down at Riva's simple black pumps and pushed the heavy door open so that they were both engulfed in a warm cocoon of aromatic spice, Alex almost losing her balance as she did so. "Besides they're too high for me to walk in properly and at least wearing them to a restaurant I can sit down for most of the evening."

Giggling their way to the cosy corner table, Riva started enjoying herself more and more as the evening went on, sunken cruise ship forgotten. Her parents were just as loved up as they always were, and Kieran had seemed too intimidated by her father's arresting force of personality that he thankfully hadn't brought up anything to do with him being an ex-criminal. Good thing too, as Riva had completely forgotten to fill her parents in on her impromptu cover story.

Happily eating her way through her own chicken madras and an entire well-fired naan bread, she was even willing to forgive her mum and dad their embarrassing PDA.

Although there had been some looks exchanged when Kieran produced a gorgeous silver charm bracelet as a birthday gift. Riva had been completely speechless at both his thoughtfulness and also at the gentle touch of his fingers on the sensitive skin of her wrist as he attached it. Feeling rather brave, she leaned over and returned his peck on the cheek in way of thanks, his freshly-shaven cheek smooth and smelling of something decidedly masculine.

She had also been doubly thankful that she had invited Alex along when she had failed to finish her own massive portion of korma, meaning that she happily took seconds. Nursing a rather prominent food baby, the cool evening air was welcoming on her face as they left the restaurant a couple of hours later, well stuffed but with just enough room for birthday cake back at the cottage.

"Are you sure you don't want to join us for some cake?" her mum asked Kieran as they stood outside the restaurant.

"Sorry Ms McLaren, I promised my dad I'd help him late tonight at the shop. He's got a rush order to finish by tomorrow." He replied. Lowering his voice slightly, he whispered to Riva. "Walk me back to the car?"

Blushing, she looked embarrassedly at her parents and Alex who had all heard him but were too polite to say anything. Her mum was making shooing gestures with her clutch bag.

"You know, I quite fancy a walk on the beach now." Her mum said a little too forcefully.

Alex, cottoning on, grinned and happily stepped out of her heels. "Great idea, I need some relief from these blisters."

Before they could say anything else, Kieran had put one hand on her lower back and started guiding her towards the smaller car park on the other side of the village, closer to where he lived. His hand was pleasantly warm, and the arm around her back felt protective, not threatening. Yet being so close to the beach where the attack had happened, combined with the feeling of walking away from the safety of her parents and off alone with a man was just enough to make her feel uneasy.

Don't be ridiculous, this is Kieran. She said to herself.

You said that about Stuart in the beginning too. The voice in her head replied.

Screwing up her eyes, she tried not to think about it.

"You okay?" Kieran asked gently.

"Oh, yeah. I think I just ate too much that's all." She replied.

They reached the small car park and Kieran stopped beside the stone-dyke wall, leaning casually against it.

"Thanks for inviting me tonight. I honestly thought that I would never get you to say yes to going out with me. But I had a great time." He said.

Riva softened. "I'm really glad you came." She lifted up her wrist so the tiny charms began tinkling, "And thank you so much for this, it really was too much."

Kieran smiled. "Only the best for you." he paused, and then he leaned towards her. He was close to her now, so close that she could smell the bite of his aftershave again. "Happy birthday." He whispered. She could count all of the freckles smattered across the bridge of his nose, her heart pounding in her chest. She didn't even have time to ask herself if she was ready for this before his lips were on hers.

They were soft, but urging, and as she automatically tried to kiss him back, he pressed his body closer to hers.

"Stop!" she cried out, wrenching herself away, the roaring of the ocean loud in her ears. She took a large step away from him and tried to calm her racing heart. He made to come closer to her and she held out her hand to stop him.

"What's the matter?" he asked, utterly confused, holding up his hands like he was surrendering.

Trying to gather herself, she shook the memories of what Stuart had said to her out of her mind. 'Frigid bitch' is what he had called her. Well Kieran was definitely going to think that now. She had ruined everything.

"Hey, Riva, talk to me. I'm sorry if I moved too fast, I just. It seemed like you wanted to." He said, backing away a few steps in response to her obvious need for space.

His attitude took her completely by surprise. He had stopped. He hadn't tried to push her.

"I'm sorry." She gasped, getting her breath back.

"Don't apologise." He said understandingly, running a hand through his mop of red hair, making it stand up again at the back. "But can you just tell me what I did wrong? I thought you liked me back."

She looked at the hurt clearly etched in the tense lines around his mouth. The same mouth that had just been on hers. That had been so gentle.

"Nothing." She said, stepping towards him. "You've done nothing wrong. It's me."

She sat down next to him on the wall, ignoring the friction that told her that when she stood up she would have a ladder in the back of her tights.

"I just. I need to go slowly ok?" she said.

Kieran rubbed his palms across his thighs. "Alright. I kinda already thought that we were but, if that's what you need. I respect it."

She let out a steadying breath and only realised that her hands were shaking when Kieran took them in his own.

"Riva. I would never hurt you." he said sincerely.

She turned her head to look at him, those chocolate eyes were concerned.

"Why did you say that?" she asked, her heart fluttering like a caged bird.

Kieran smiled sadly. "Because when you pulled away just now, you looked. Scared. Really scared. And I've only ever seen you that way once before."

Riva swallowed. "The day of the boating accident."

He nodded. "I'm not blind you know. I know something happened that day and for whatever reason you won't tell me or anyone else what it was but after that you changed."

She tried to swoosh her hair back over her shoulder casually and fluttered her eyelashes to get him to laugh. "You mean this?"

Kieran just stared seriously into her cerulean eyes. "No. I don't mean that." His eyes roved across her face, far too perceptive for her liking. "I watched you during exam week, I know you put it all down to nerves but there was something wrong. You were a wreck. Constantly looking over your shoulder, fighting with Alex, and I barely got two words out of you before you disappeared."

Riva was shocked at exactly how perceptive he had been.

"Look, if something bad happened, or if something is going on I can help you." he squeezed her hands tightly but somehow they didn't feel restricting, instead those strong hands made her feel safe. "I can protect you."

She didn't know whether to cry or laugh as the guilt ate her up inside again. This magic had turned her into a liar. So many secrets that she was forced to keep. She didn't think she would ever tell her parents about Stuart and she was certain that Kieran would run a mile if she showed him her powers.

She raised her hand and cupped his face. Realising as she did so that it was the first time that she had initiated contact between them, that she wanted contact between them. The fact that he thought he could protect her from what she was facing was laughable. And commendable. Anyone that was connected to her was in danger from the Mer as long as the King wanted her dead.

She took a steadying breath and dropped her hand from his face, clutching the uneven wall for support. "Look, Kieran. You're right, something happened at the beginning of the summer and, I'm not ready to talk about it. I might never be. But just know that I do, l-like you." she blushed at his smile. "But I need to take it slow, okay?"

He reached up to tuck one flyaway strand of hair behind her ear and where his fingertips grazed the soft skin, suddenly her body was telling her she didn't want to take it slow. Was she actually starting to have feelings for him?

"I get it." he said, pulling away before Riva could change her mind. "I heard some – rumours and, you don't need to explain anything, just if-."

Feelings gone.

"Wait. No. Hold up a second." She sat up straight, temper flaring. "Whatever *rumours* you've heard. They aren't true." She spat, reassessing her opinion of his mother if she was repeating what those hags at the café had been gossiping about.

Kieran blushed to the very roots of his red hair, not wanting to even repeat what those rumours were about. She steeled herself for what she was about to say.

"Kieran I'm, a- I'm a v-virgin okay?" she stuttered, having to look down at the cobblestones to avoid whatever look was on his face. "I didn't run away with someone, I wasn't sleeping around. Something bad happened before exams started and then I went away to get my father back. That's all."

Kieran just took her hands back in her own. That stoic calm enveloping her and dissolving her temper.

"I already said that you don't need to explain yourself to me. It's completely up to you if you do want to sleep with people and I certainly wouldn't have cared if you were a virgin or not. It's your body." He said.

Taken aback, she relaxed. "Kieran, I had no idea you were such a feminist."

He chuckled, the tension finally broken. "My big sister. She dragged me along to the women's march last year. I learned a lot." He looked beyond her, down towards the beach. "I'm nervous too you know. I've wanted this for so long, well you know that." His cheeks flushed as red as his hair. "I don't want to mess it up."

They shared a smile and Riva felt like they had passed some kind of test. Whatever had been intangible between them earlier had somehow solidified.

"You should get back before they wonder where you are." He said, standing up, pulling Riva to her feet and she felt her tights rip. "You've got a birthday cake waiting for you at home."

"I suppose. Thanks again for the present." She said, trying to pull the dress down to cover the back of her laddered tights.

He plucked her hand up and bowed exuberantly, making a show. "Mi lady." He said pompously and kissed the back of her hand with a wet smack that had her squealing. He flashed another grin at her before opening his car door.

"See you soon yeah?" he asked, a hopeful note in his voice.

Riva nodded. "Soon."

She watched his car drive away, not quite able to place the feeling swirling around inside of her. It was similar to the rush of her magic, but she definitely hadn't summoned any.

A horn blared behind her and she quickly jumped out of the way as the driver shouted out of his window for her to get off the road. She quickly darted across the street and around the corner back onto the promenade to catch up with her parents.

She found Alex sitting on the railing, swinging her bare feet to and fro as her mum and dad sat happily on the bench behind her, people-watching.

She skipped her way over to her best friend and looped her arm around her waist, dragging her backwards off the railing with a squeal.

"Ooooh, tell me how it went!" Alex asked excitedly, "Did you kiss?" Riva's blush was telling enough. "Eek, you did! How was it? Did he use too much tongue?"

"Alex, stop." Riva whispered, looking over her shoulder.

"Oh, shit right. The 'rents. I'll save it for when we're home." Then she saw Riva's face and her expression became serious. "What is it?"

Riva had the uncomfortable sensation that someone was watching her. Turning around to look down the street, she could just about make out the greengrocers and the small flat that sat above. Her heart jolted painfully in her chest. Even though she could barely make out the front door, she stared at it as if she expected Stuart to walk out and come get her.

"Riva what is it?" Alex asked, following her gaze. "Oh."

She had been avoiding this beach for months. But unfortunately her favourite restaurant was located in the middle of the promenade, and her mum had booked it for her birthday without asking. She wasn't exactly mad about it, but she definitely felt strange being this close to Stuart's house.

"Hey, it's okay, the lights are off and the blinds are shut. There's no-one there." Alex said "He's not coming after you, I promise."

She smiled weakly, "I know, I just got a weird feeling that someone was watching me." She shivered despite the fact that the wind had died down, "I wish I'd brought a jacket."

"And cover up that gorgeous new dress? I should think not!" Alex laughed and traced the outline of her hips with her hands, "You look fabulous! No wonder Kieran kissed you."

"Leave off Alex people are staring." Riva smiled self-consciously and tapped into a little of her magic to warm the air around them. As her goosebumps disappeared she smiled. "You know, getting to use my magic without feeling the crushing weight of responsibility feels much nicer."

"Tell me about it." Alex sighed, shaking out her impossibly smooth hair and enjoying the relief from the chill, "I don't know what finally convinced you to embrace it but I'm all for it."

"It's a long story." Riva breathed.

Alex turned to look at her, curiosity written all over her face.

"Happen to know anything about a Goddess named Gaia?" Riva asked.

"You mean the mother of the titans?" Alex replied, baffled. "Why do you want to know about her?"

Riva sighed heavily. She was much too full to be having such a serious conversation. "Let's just say we need to do some digging on her and her offspring."

She called the strength of the Earth around her like a bubble, safe in the knowledge that if Stuart ever did try anything, at least she would have the upper hand this time.

Without a backward glance, the girls hurried to catch up to where her parents were now walking along the promenade towards the car park, the gentle breeze playing with the bottom of her mum's dress as she strolled hand-in-hand with her dad.

"You know I would give anything for my mum and dad to look that in love." Alex said wistfully.

"Yeah well, I'm not sure that two four-year old girls are exactly conducive to marital bliss." Riva snorted, "I think it's kind of hard to get in any canoodling when you are dealing with tantrums and toddler TV."

Alex rolled her eyes, "Yeah, I guess you're right. It's probably better if they don't have sex again, you know, just in case there are any more surprises. The twins were bad enough."

Riva giggled. "I have to sleep with my headphones in every night. It's delightful."

Covering her mouth to stifle her own giggles, Alex replied. "Do they at least put a sock on the door knob?"

Riva grabbed one of those lethal-looking stilettos out of Alex's hand and pretended to thump her over the head with it.

After Alex had finished wrestling it back from her and shoving her feet back into them delicately, wincing at her blisters, she looked out at the calm surface of the ocean. With the sun just sinking below the horizon, casting shadows of pink, orange and yellow across the clouds, Riva really could believe that things would work out.

Her gaze drifted across the sand where some families just like theirs were enjoying an evening stroll in the brief respite from the month-long rainstorm they had been having. A small girl was barely visible within the folds of her puffer jacket, only a small angry fist that battered on the top of her plastic pot with a red spade. She breathed in the salty smell of the ocean deeply, filling her lungs. The tang of it making her want to plunge beneath the waves once again.

Opening her eyes she gazed out at that overwhelming expanse of water and wondered when it would be safe for her to return. If it ever would be.

Then, almost as if she had summoned her by thinking about her, she spied a dark figure silhouetted against the setting sun, lounging on the rocks at the far end of the beach.

Someone had been watching her after all. But it hadn't been Stuart.

She froze.

"Dad!" She called out in warning, her voice coming out half-strangled.

Her father turned around slowly, his smile slipping from his face as he saw the expression on her face and he hurried back to her side, dragging her mum with him.

"Who is it?" He knew immediately. Someone had found them.

She inclined her head towards the figure on the rocks and felt an intense hatred build up inside of her as she stared.

It was Em.

6.

Em was sitting atop the rock wall that separated the long stretch of beach from a smaller alcove down on the other side. A hundred yards away from them, she sat wearing black boots, ripped jeans and a leather jacket of all things. Her tattoos and severe haircut making her look like a badass. With legs. A badass that looked completely at home on those legs.

She was also attracting a fair amount of attention from the people walking at the seafront who quickly began muttering about tourists from the big city. Everything about her appearance screamed 'dangerous'.

"Who is that girl?" Her mum sounded scared, pulling her shawl tighter across her shoulders searching hers and her father's face for an answer, "Riva, darling, who is she?"

Her mum was right to be scared. Em had betrayed both of them by secretly working for Duncan and hadn't hesitated to try to kill her father on Duncan's orders.

"That's Em."

Helen and Alex's eyes widened as they turned to stare. Both had listened to her account of her and her father's dramatic escape and were rightly terrified of the girl who had once been an Elite Mer soldier before she had become a double-agent.

Riva's mum clutched her dad's arm tightly, as if Em could magically teleport her father back into the depths of the ocean with one glance.

"What is she doing here? How did she get rid of her tail?" Alex blurted out.

Riva was past caring about her lack of fins. Just the fact that she was here was enough to make fury flood her system and her magic sprang to the surface, ready for anything. Staring up at the girl she had once thought of as a friend had her feeling like she could spit fire. That girl was the reason she was now an outcast. The reason there was a price on both of their heads. She had been making so much progress with the Mer, to the point where her grandfather had been willing to publically accept her before he had tragically been killed in an accident at the border of Oceana. Then thanks to the information Em had been drip-feeding into Duncan's ear, he had been able to twist everything to his advantage and turn the entire Mer community against her.

"There could be others here too." She said in a low voice, looking suspiciously around the promenade. "You all need to get out of here."

Struggling to control her anger, she advanced up the beach towards where Em was still lounging nonchalantly against the rocks. That chilled-out attitude made Riva want to punch her. Hard. Preferably in those perfect teeth.

She had barely taken two steps when she realised that the other three made to follow. She turned to them.

"Where do you think you are all going? Seriously, get out of here." When none of them moved, she raised her voice. "I mean it! I don't know if she's alone." She said.

Her father stepped forward, already rolling up his shirt sleeves. For what, she didn't know. "Not me, I can help you."

Riva rounded on him. "Are you serious? Especially not you. *You* have to be the reason she is back here. Duncan wants me dead but he wants you returned to Oceana alive. You need to get as far away from her as possible do you hear me?"

He paused, halfway between Riva and her mum, his dark curls dancing in the sea breeze. He looked over his shoulder to where her mum stood, clearly on the verge of tears and reluctantly nodded.

Riva steeled herself. "Take him back home." She said to her mum.

"No darling, we'll stay with you. We won't let you face this alone." Her mum said, trembling.

Riva rounded on her. "I didn't fight my way out of Oceana, making myself number one on the Mer-Most-Wanted list for me to allow Em to march up here onto *my* island and take dad from us again. You take him home. Now."

Her mum actually backed away from her. "Riva, your eyes…"

Aware that her magic was surfacing and her eyes were probably two golden orbs in her face, she continued. "Do you want to lose him again?"

Harsh, cold words. But true. Her mum's bottom lip started wobbling and she shook her head.

"Then run. If I'm not back in an hour you pack your bags and get to the mainland." She said threateningly. "The further he is from the sea the better."

This time her mum nodded, setting her jaw. Pinching the bridge of her nose to stop her tears, she swiftly took her partner's hand and dragged him away to the car. He kept casting glances back to where Riva and Alex stood until her mum had practically folded him into the passenger seat and shut the door forcefully.

Her magic was pooling in her veins now and she tried not to shiver at its delicious power. She locked eyes with Em, but for some reason, instead of advancing, she turned around and jumped casually off the rocks towards the other side of the beach, effectively hiding herself from the view of passers-by. An invitation.

All the better for Riva. She didn't want witnesses for this. Her magic was crackling in her palms and she had to clench her right hand into a fist to mute that beacon of light pouring from her Goddess Mark.

"What about me?" Standing, now shivering in her little black dress, Alex was trying valiantly not to look scared but wasn't doing a very good job of it.

Riva turned her glowing eyes on her friend. "You wanted to be involved remember?"

Alex reached down and slid off her high heels once more, suddenly four inches shorter, the top of her head just reaching Riva's chin. She hooked them both under her index finger. "Reporting for duty, captain."

Despite the tension, Riva stifled a smirk. "Alright, you stay up here and make sure no one makes their way down onto that side of the beach. I don't want anyone to see this."

Shaking her shining blonde hair out down her back, Alex set her shoulders, looking like a Chihuahua trying to be a guard dog.

Riva turned and made her way down the path to the other side of the beach, the wall behind her obscuring her from view as she descended the ramp. As she turned the corner, Em was waiting for her beside the rocks.

She rolled up the sleeves of her dress and channelled all of that power that had flooded her system moments earlier down into her hands, her Mark blazing. This close to the water, Em was no match for her. She had to have known that. Riva cast another glance around her towards that rock wall now towering at her back and the other man-made one to her right.

Is this a trap?

She couldn't see any other Mer, but they could be biding their time. Perhaps they lurked, unseen under the waves, waiting to drag her back to Oceana with brute force. Or maybe they thought that Em could finish the job alone.

As she drew closer, Em's cocky grin faltered slightly, nervous hands betraying her true feelings as she fidgeted with the corner of her jacket. She didn't know why, but that made her angrier.

Riva advanced, her magic threatening to overwhelm her, setting her eyes and Mark aglow and she finally spoke.

"Why are you here?" Her voice reverberated as she channelled her power. Em visibly paled. Good, she wanted her scared.

"I need to talk to you." Em replied, daring a few steps towards her.

Riva's hands crackled as she ran an electrical current over her palms. She knew that it wouldn't do much damage up here without the water as a conductor but it looked mighty threatening.

"I think you've done enough talking these last few weeks Em. Or is that even your real name?" Riva needed to raise her voice as a fierce wind whipped up from the ocean, a by-product of her temper. She could hear the beach-goers begin squealing and shouting as they were caught up in the resulting sandstorm.

Em took a few more steps towards her, looking far too steady on her new feet, her smile gone. "Please, Riva, you have to understand, I would never have passed information to Duncan if I hadn't had any another choice."

Riva laughed, a sound so cold she almost didn't even recognise it as her own. "There's always a choice. And why the hell should I believe anything you say anyway? You've done nothing but lie to me."

The wind whipped up across the beach, the waves now crashing their way onto shore just a few feet in front of them. She heard car doors slam behind her as the locals abandoned the beach for the safety of their homes. Riva felt her temper stretch to its limit and she squashed down that thread of hurt that rose to the surface when she looked into Em's jade green eyes.

"I thought you were the only friend I had down there. Do you have any idea how scared I was? How lonely? I had lost everything in those first few days, trapped in that room, never knowing if or when I would see my family again. So I confided in you. When you started opening up to me about your family and your own problems I began to trust you. And how did you repay that trust? You tried to kill my father!"

Her emotions so unstable, her power shot out from the golden spiral on her palm before she could stop it. Shooting two crackling fingers of lightning in a low arc that landed directly in front of where Em stood.

Both girls jumped back a foot from each other, shocked by the power of it. She could taste metal on her tongue as Em stared at the blackened sand in front of her.

Well that's new.

Staring down at her Mark, she felt another charge welling up, like a faint pressure that built and built until she could no longer contain it. Her magic was practically singing to her. She released another bolt.

Em dove out of the way just in time.

"Riva what the hell are you doing?" Em yelled at her over the howling of the wind, stumbling across the sand, dodging another lightning strike.

She released another, then another, until Em was practically dancing as she scrambled to avoid them. The biggest bolt yet crackled out of her fingertips and split the rock directly behind Em in two.

Those jade eyes were filled with fear and Riva basked in it. This is what owning her power felt like.

A flick of Em's eyes and Riva saw what she was about to do before she did it. Em bolted for the waves, clearly hoping to seek sanctuary under the surface. Or lure her into a trap.

As her foot made contact with the surf, Riva shot both of her palms out towards her, lightning forking from each of her fingers to form a net of electricity that sparked across the waterline. Em, caught like a fish in a net, started to shake violently as Riva shocked her.

Standing there, her hair whipped up into a frenzy around her head by the violent wind, she watched as she electrocuted the girl who had once been her friend.

Just like with Stuart before, the two warring voices in her head were screaming at one another. The first, urged on by her magic and her anger, was telling her to finish it while she still had a chance, while her family was still safe. But the second reminded her of the Mer girl who had made her laugh during state functions, the girl who had kindly made her clothes to protect her modesty, the girl who had saved her sanity with her dry, sarcastic humour.

Not entirely sure she was making the right choice, she released her magic in a great rush and felt it drain some of her energy just as Em slumped to the wet sand.

Coughing and slightly charred, but conscious.

Riva advanced towards her. The dainty black pumps she wore a perfect contradiction to the justice she would unleash with her steps. Em was shaking her head, clearly trying to get her vision straight. She should strike now before she got too close. Magic or not, she knew that Em could definitely take her in a fist-fight.

But for some reason she hesitated.

"Looks like I wasn't the only one keeping secrets Riva. I thought you said you only had control over the ocean, not the skies too." Em said with a cough, clutching her side.

Furious that she still hadn't apologised, or at the very least thanked her for sparing her life, she fought to control her temper, even as the waves behind them roiled in anticipation, as if waiting for Riva's order.

"This magic is new to me, it came to help me save my father's life after you tried to kill him."

She had Em backed right up to the rocks, crawling away from her on the damp sand so she had no way of escaping.

"I didn't try to-."

"Stop lying!" Riva yelled, abandoning her magic completely, forgetting everything she had just told herself about the idiocy of getting too close, and instead drew back her fist and punched Em square on the nose. Pain shot up her wrist and forearm making her eyes sting with tears.

"Oh crap, ow, freaking hell…" she exclaimed cradling her right fist in her left hand, knuckles already bruised from the impact.

Annoyingly Em's face looked untouched. In fact, she had actually started laughing as she cupped her nose, apparently forgetting her fear in the face of Riva's pathetic attempt at a right hook.

"Maybe you should just stick to fighting with your magic from now on and leave the hand-to-hand combat to the experts alright?" she drawled.

Riva cradled her sore hand, funnelling her magic into it to heal herself. "Not all of us trained since birth to become killing machines alright?" She flexed her right hand and grimaced as a couple of the knuckles popped audibly but hissed in relief as the pain began to fade. As much as she didn't want to admit it, Em was right. Without her magic she was pathetic.

"I am not a killing machine Riva, I still have feelings." Said Em, brushing her fringe back from her face and righting herself.

Riva scoffed. "Oh just a Mer with no morals then? No sense of loyalty or compassion? Or generally any concept of what the word *friend* might mean?"

She watched as Em ground her teeth behind her smirk. "Is that all you think of me now? Everything we built between us back in Oceana is now gone because of one mistake?"

Riva could barely believe her ears. "One mistake?" Her lightning was no longer crackling in her hands but the windstorm was still whirling around the beach in its place.

"You knowingly fed information to Duncan the *entire time*. Personal things that I revealed to you in confidence! You knew that Duncan hated my being in the palace. You know how much he hates half-humans and how he campaigned for my execution even while the king was still alive. Then even after you got to know me and *by your own admission* accepted me, you still remained loyal to him. Why?" Her voice cracked on the last word, the hurt she had felt and had tried to keep buried deep down underneath her anger was now surfacing.

Em looked just as hurt as she was. "Please, just hear me out. It is hard to put aside a lifetime of prejudices in the course of a few weeks Riva. When I was summoned to Oceana, before you arrived, Duncan approached me and gave me purpose again after being cast out from the Elite."

"Oh yeah? What purpose might that have been?"

Em let her hands drop to her sides and sagged against the rock, defeated. Hair flopping into her tired-looking eyes. "To eradicate humans from the ocean for the greater good of the Mer."

Riva struggled to keep the shock off her face. Staring at the girl in front of her, she barely recognized her, and it was nothing to do with the fact that she no longer had a tail. Images of capsized cruise ships, dead scuba divers, and missing mariners flooded her mind. Had Em been behind some of those news reports? Had she enjoyed it? Her fury built to a point where she didn't know what to do with it anymore.

"And what – exactly – did that involve?" she asked through gritted teeth.

Speaking over the roaring of the wind Em replied. "Whatever needed to be done. We would reactivate mines, exterminate dive teams sent on 'research' expeditions in places they had no business being, or we would destroy and sink submarines and other metal machines."

Riva could barely grasp what Em was telling her.

"You didn't even care that you were killing innocent people? How can you stand there in front of me and say that like it's no big deal?"

"No big deal? Riva my people are dying. *Dying,* because of humans. Every single day we suffer a little more because of what they are doing to us, so no. None of them are innocent. If they aren't doing anything directly to hurt us then they are complicit in the acts of others, so I'm sorry if you have the luxury of being able to sit on your high horse and judge me, but I did what I thought was best for my people." She paused for breath and looked up at her, jade eyes meeting sapphire. "Until I met… you."

They both looked away from each other, Em gazing at the sand, Riva towards the churning waves, uncomfortable with the turn in the argument.

"You appeared at the palace and all of a sudden things changed. I saw that you weren't that different from any of us. That you wanted the same things. That you were willing to help. I saw you master your powers and for the first time in a long time I felt hope for our future. That was when I stopped reporting to Duncan, I refused and tried to break our deal but he wouldn't let me."

Riva interrupted, looking back to where she still lay against the rock, "What deal?"

Those jade eyes welled with tears as Em gripped the rocks behind her for support.

"He promised me that in exchange for my *services,* he would find Flora." Em said, voice cracking.

Flora. Em's girlfriend. The one she had been caught with and the reason for her exile to Oceana in the first place. Unfortunately the Mer had some seriously archaic ideas about breeding and they wouldn't tolerate two reproductive systems going to waste, so they had separated them.

The wind calmed slightly so the girls no longer had to scream at each other to be heard.

"So Flora wasn't made up?" Riva asked, the bite of her temper still evident in her words, but calm enough for her to listen.

"No she wasn't." Em practically hissed back at her. "That's why I agreed to pass information to Duncan about you. He promised me that if I did what he asked then he would tell me where she was. That if I handed him the information he needed to take you down, then he would pardon us both and allow us to live in peace, together." Em's voice was quiet, but lethal.

Clearly Riva wasn't the only one with strong feelings about the new king.

"So you thought that it was okay to betray people who loved you and work for a man with some seriously questionable ethics just as long as he gave you the information you wanted? For goodness sake Em I could have helped you! My grandfather was days away from accepting me and granting me an ambassador role within the palace, I could have pleaded your case! Hell, I could have used magic to find her!"

Unbridled tears were now running down Em's cheeks. "She was the love of my life Riva. You don't understand what it is like being institutionalized your entire life, especially in a society where being your true self for someone like me means a lifetime of oppression. Ever since I can remember I have been part of the Elite, we know our duty and we obey orders. I thought I was doing the right thing." She paused and her voice dropped to a whisper, full bottom lip wobbling. "But it doesn't matter anymore."

"Why? Because I escaped and Duncan won't tell you anything until you bring me back? Well I'm sorry to tell you this but I won't come quietly" Riva interrupted, crossing her arms.

Em was shaking her head. "No. It doesn't matter because she's dead."

All of the fight seemed to go out of her with those last words and she sagged onto the rocks. Riva was left standing on the beach a few feet in front of her, growing cold in the now-calm breeze, unsure of what to do or say.

Surprising herself, she felt sorry for her.

"I didn't ever mean for things to go so far. I certainly never expected us to become friends. I wanted you to be just another mission, a means to an end-." Em tailed off, face tired and drawn. "I didn't hit your father hard enough to kill him, I made sure of that." She whispered.

It wasn't enough.

"But if I hadn't managed to escape with my father then you would have happily handed him over to Duncan to be executed in exchange for the information you wanted." Riva said, arms crossed.

Em leaned her head back against the rocks but didn't deny it. "Riva, I didn't come here to fight. I just lost the last shred of hope that I have been clinging to for months. There is nothing left for me back there besides misery and regret. I came to apologise."

Riva stared down at her. She couldn't just welcome her back after a simple 'sorry'. Her temper was screaming at her to never forgive her. But that little emptiness that had been lurking within her for the last two weeks was saying otherwise.

"How do I even know you are telling the truth? Do you seriously expect me to believe that you aren't working for him anymore? How did you even get here if it wasn't with an Elder's magic and with Duncan's permission?" she asked.

Em sighed and stood up slowly, sandy hands rasping on the rock. She pulled back the collar of her leather jacket. "This is how I got here."

The blood drained from Riva's face and even the faint breeze vanished. The sudden stillness made it sound like they had been sucked into a vacuum.

The necklace…

It sat daintily on her collarbone, interlocking pieces of white lichen working their way halfway up her neck, as if she was wearing a very distasteful choker.

It took Riva a few minutes before she was able to find words again. Her stunned silence quickly giving way to suspicion. "So you're telling me that you managed to escape Oceana, break into the Vault, steal a highly coveted ancient magical relic, and find me here despite the cloaking magic I've put around pretty much the entire side of this island?"

Her signature smirk flitted briefly across Em's face. "Yes."

"Impossible. Duncan sealed all of the currents in and out of Oceana before I left. He must have opened one up especially for you to follow us."

"Wrong." Em countered. "He opened all of them immediately after you escaped, sending every Guard out across the oceans to bring you both back. It was easy for me to slip out unnoticed."

Riva crossed her arms. "How did you break into the Vault without being caught?"

Em raised one eyebrow cockily. "I'm just that good."

She rolled her eyes. "A little heavy on the arrogance there Em, I thought you were here to humbly apologise?"

"Apologise yes. Humbly? Never." she drawled.

Ignoring her quip before the corners of her mouth could turn upwards in a smile, something else occurred to Riva. "Hang on. You need royal blood to be able to enter the Vault. How did you get in if Duncan didn't go with you to spill his own blood at the entrance?"

Em shifted guiltily and stared at the wet sand.

"I still had some of your father's blood on my hands from where I hit him, it was enough to grant me entry to the Vault once I smeared it across the rock."

Her temper soared again at the thought of her father's blood on her hands, and she heard the ghost echo of the sharp *crack* as that rock had found its mark across the back of her dad's skull. Taking a deep, steadying breath, she calmed her magic.

"Well at least you have the grace to look ashamed of yourself. But that still doesn't explain how you found me."

Now it was Em's turn to roll her eyes. "You literally told me where you lived Riva. I may not know Glendale off the back of my hand, but I sure know how to find the Isle of Skye and from there it wasn't that hard to track you. Especially once I realized that someone had heavily cloaked the area around those creepy-looking rocks on the other side of the headland. Figured you couldn't be too far away."

Riva could have kicked herself for thinking that her cloaking would have been enough to stop someone from tracking them. "So I assume that the Guards are on their way soon?" She asked, already planning an escape route for her mum and dad. Maybe she could get them to Inverness by the morning.

Em crossed her arms, the leather of her jacket creaking. "Why would you think that?"

"Well, didn't you whisper that juicy piece of information into Duncan's ear the first chance you got? Eager to help him find my family, to provide you with some leverage?"

Em actually looked offended. "I never revealed your location to him."

Riva narrowed her eyes. "I don't believe you. After everything you've done you're lucky that I'm even standing here listening to you at all. I should have blasted you backwards into the waves ten minutes ago."

"But you didn't." countered Em.

There was an awkward silence and Riva looked up to check on Alex who was still standing at the entrance to this part of the beach.

She had abandoned her guard dog position now that it was no longer looking like it was going to turn into a fight and was instead sitting on the wall, swinging her feet, looking at both of them with deep interest, clearly straining to hear their conversation. Thanks to the wind Riva had been creating, her hair was a bird's nest on the top of her head.

"When you told me that your mum was living there alone, I chose not to tell Duncan about your home. I didn't like to think what he might do with that information. You seem to love her very much and-." She paused, pain displayed across her face. "-and I didn't want to be the reason she was taken away from you."

Caught off guard, Riva was finding it more and more difficult to see an enemy where her friend stood. "Well, thank you." She replied stiffly.

"But even though I never disclosed your location to Duncan personally, I would expect him to send Guards here as soon as he can get his hands on enough magic to make it possible. It was where they found your father eighteen years ago after all."

Riva felt anxiety well up in the pit of her stomach as she stared out at the flat grey expanse of water in front of them. Maybe her parents should go to the mainland after all. They had tried to convince her mum a few days after Riva had returned but she had refused to leave the cottage with more gumption than either Riva or her father had thought she possessed.

"So. What's the plan?" Em asked.

"What do you mean plan?" replied Riva scathingly, dragging her eyes away from the waves. "Even if I had one, I wouldn't be telling you what it is."

"Please." Em scoffed. "I escaped because I want to help you."

"Help me? I think you've *helped* enough in managing to destroy my reputation among the Mer, turn my own family against me and chase me out of Oceana with a price on my head." Anger swiftly returning, "Don't think that your apology changes any of that."

She cast one last scathing look at Em and then turned on her heel to march back to where Alex, her true friend, was waiting for her.

"Oh I think you'll want my help Riva." Em called out after her, voice amplified by the wind rushing in with the tide.

Riva gritted her teeth and kept walking, refusing to turn around and look at her. "Oh yeah? What makes you so sure?" she called out behind her.

"Because I know where to find Duncan's half-human son."

The words hit Riva like a punch in the gut and she whirled around to find Em, standing with her arms crossed and that signature lopsided grin across her face as she willingly handed over what could be the key to overthrowing the King.

Riva didn't know whether to kiss her or kill her for being so cocky.

"Well happy birthday to me." She said with a reluctant smile.

7.

When she finally traipsed up to the cottage with Alex in tow, her mum burst from the front door in a panic.

"Riva! Oh I'm so glad you're alright. Your father is packing our bags now, hopefully we can be on the mainland within a couple of hours." She garbled, rushing down the drive to sweep Riva up into a hug. "I was so worried that she might have taken you away."

Pulling away from her mum, feeling tired from the magic use, she replied, "Apparently that wasn't what she was here for."

Her mum frowned.

"Come on, I'll tell you both inside." She said reaching for her mum's thin hand.

Having called her father out of the bedroom where he was wrestling with the zip on their oldest suitcase, she had them both assembled in the living room while she started a fire.

Fumbling with the lighter as it sputtered, she cursed, "Screw this crap." And pointed her index finger at the logs. Figuring that if she was able to summon lightning then a few flames shouldn't be an issue. She smelled the burning of tree sap and felt the heat of summer's day surround her as her magic soared through her and moments later a fire was flickering merrily in the grate as if it had been burning for hours. She smiled at the rush of exhilaration that always came with her magic, cold legs warming through her thin tights.

"You might want to sit down." She said to her family.

Both her parents and Alex squeezed themselves onto the sagging sofa and Alex busied herself scrolling through Instagram while she caught her parent's up on the story, having heard it all from Riva in hushed whispers on the bus ride up from the beach.

When she had finished, her dad spoke first. "I cannot believe it. I can't believe that my brother was going behind father's back for months, authorising strikes against humans." He had his head in his hands and Riva was more than slightly worried that he was going to pull his curls out. "I just cannot believe it." He got up and had started pacing the living room, wearing the already tattered rug even thinner.

"Well I can." Riva scoffed.

Her dad gave her a look.

"What? Come on, we both know that Duncan's an arse. He's never made any secret about how much he hates humans."

"Language Riva!" her mum admonished

She crossed her arms and started back at her. "I think we have more pressing things to worry about than swear words mum."

The look on her mum's face told her otherwise, so Riva thought it best to change the subject.

"Well there's one in every family, and good ol' Uncle Duncan is clearly ours."

Her dad stopped his pacing. Much to Riva's relief. She was rather attached to their antique Persian rug – ugly as it was.

"I just don't know how he got away with it for so long." her father continued, "Surely at least the Captain of the Guard had to know. Unless there were more people in on it? Surely not, but then there's no way any missions would have been successful had Emerald been acting alone."

It hurt Riva to see how upset this news was making her father. But an even worse thought flitted through her mind. "What if Duncan wasn't going behind the King's back at all? What if he knew about it?"

She wasn't prepared for her dad's face to turn to stone.

"No."

Riva stepped away from the fire. "But maybe he-"

"I said no, Riva!"

For the first time, her dad had raised his voice to her, and she wasn't entirely sure how she felt about it. Alex's eyes widened but she remained resolutely staring at her screen, keeping out of it. Riva's mum closed her eyes as if trying to block out the noise.

His nostrils flared but he quickly reigned in his temper. "My father would never have approved of such a scheme. He was a good man and a good King who wanted peace. You saw how willing he was to accept you."

Riva sat down in her chair by the fire. "I also saw how willing he was to execute me when I first arrived." She fiddled with the lumpy cushion. "You know as well as I do that if I hadn't had my powers I would never have made it out of that audience chamber. I wouldn't even have met you."

Her mum made a strangled noise as she said the word 'execute' and her dad again ran a hand through his curls and sat down heavily beside her, taking her hand.

"My father was a fair man and a good King. When he delivered the order to execute you he was simply following the law."

He realised his poor choice of words when everyone else in the room stared daggers at him.

He held up his hands, his face showing his exhaustion. "Hatred for humans and humankind runs deep in the minds of the Mer. We are raised to loathe their very existence, taught that they are the reason why we are suffering. But when he really got to know you Riva, when he saw that you were not a thre-."

"He only agreed to let me live after I had used my powers against the Mer. After he had realised I could be useful." Riva interrupted.

Her dad nodded tiredly, "I know that my darling. What I am trying to say is that my father believed in justice. You also saw how his mind changed after he was in possession of all the facts. Even Kings make mistakes sometimes."

Her dad was now staring into the fireplace, a look of extreme sadness on his face. She sometimes forgot that he had watched his father die only two weeks ago. She clutched the cushion tighter.

"I'm sorry, Dad. I'm just trying to figure everything out. You're probably right. I only knew my grandfather for a month and he only knew me as his granddaughter for a day. Who am I to judge?" she said quietly. Tilting her head, she could hear footsteps crunching up the gravel drive. "But I think you should start unpacking that suitcase. You aren't going anywhere."

"What do you mean?" her mum asked.

As if on cue, there was a knock at the door.

The four of them were silent, the only noise the frequent crackles and pops as the logs burning in the fire released their sap. Her mum and dad exchanged a nervous glance as Riva stood up, feeling like this was the worst birthday present in the world.

"It's open!" she called out.

All four heads turned in anticipation as Em strode into the living room, shaking her head like a dog, casting droplets all over the carpet. Apparently it had started raining again.

"Good evening." She said stiffly.

Her mum let out a small scream and Alex had to bury her face in her cardigan to stifle her laugh.

"It's fine mum. I asked her to come." She said frostily. While she had invited her here, that didn't mean that she had forgiven her.

Riva had asked Em to wait a full hour before knocking on the door. Either the Mer were unable to tell time or she had gotten bored of standing in the rain.

Her dad was sitting up, stiff as a poker and her mum was clutching her heart, the expression on both of their faces was a mixture of fear and fury.

"Whiskey's all around then I think." Alex said, extracting herself from the couch and flitting off to the kitchen in search of the biggest bottle of scotch she could find before Riva's dad could hit something or her mum fainted.

"After everything she has done, how can you allow her into this home?" Her dad said, his hand clenched so tightly on her mum's knee she was worried he would shatter her kneecap.

Riva walked into the middle of the room and stood there, in between Em and her dad, not entirely sure which one would need protecting. "I told you what she said to me down at the beach. We don't have to trust her completely, but if what she said is true, if Duncan really does have a son, then she can help us. And we are in no position to refuse help right now." Said Riva as her father continued to stare straight through Em.

Her father nodded stiffly and got up off the couch, back straight and shoulders tense. He made his way into the kitchen to help Alex in her search, conveniently putting himself as far away as he could physically get from Em.

Em walked awkwardly towards the only remaining armchair and sat down. Her mum eyed the large biker boots apprehensively, obviously fearing for the state of her pristine wooden floors. Still shaking her dripping fringe, she extended her long tattooed fingers towards the fire, sighing in appreciation when she felt its warmth. "This is still new to me but now I know why you were always complaining of the cold in Oceana." Em smirked at Riva, curling her hands in and out of fists.

No-one replied.

Alex crossed the room and handed a large glass of whiskey to Riva's mum. "I'd drink up if I were you Helen." She said.

Riva's mum raised the glass and tipped the entire contents down her throat.

Alex's eyes widened and she glanced at Riva nervously. "Or down it in one. Sure, why not." She said taking the now-empty glass out of Riva's mum's hands and returning to the kitchen.

As the minutes passed and Em visibly thawed out, she tried again.

"Sir, I owe you an apology." She called out towards the kitchen, rubbing her now-pink hands together.

Her dad's eyebrows almost disappeared under his curls as he set whiskey glasses down onto the counter methodically. "That. Would be the understatement of the century." He said drolly.

Riva bit her lip. Apparently her sarcasm was rubbing off on him. Alex, Riva and Helen looked between the two Mer-turned-human's in the room with interest.

Her father didn't speak again.

Em swallowed nervously, she was after all having to apologise to a member of her royal family. Riva had never seen her look more uncomfortable.

"I acted out of poor judgement. My motives for betraying your daughter as well as for working for your brother were out of love. I am sure Riva has already explained, but please let me tell you how sorry I am for my part that hurt both of you. I never meant for any of this to happen. I just wanted my Flora back."

Em's eyes remained dry and her face was set as she stared at her father across the tiny living room. He stared coldly back at her.

Alex, Riva and Helen's eyes were flicking between the two of them like they were following an invisible ping pong ball.

"I was wrong to do what I did. I not only lost the love of my life forever, but what few friends I had left." Em's eyes darted towards where Riva stood. She was wringing her hands so hard that it looked like she was trying to take her skin off like a pair of gloves. "Please accept my humblest apology. If you will allow me back into your confidence, I will never betray your trust again."

Her dad looked over to Riva and, despite her own misgivings, she nodded ever so slightly in encouragement. Whether she wanted her father to accept her just for the information she could give them or because she still saw a faint glimmer of hope for their friendship she didn't know.

Her father unscrewed the top of the bottle. "I accept your apology" He said stonily.

Em visibly relaxed.

Seemingly restored by Alex's generous measure of whiskey, Riva's mum got up from the sofa and appearing to want something to do with her hands, she started clattering some pots and pans.

"Well, dinner was some time ago now and we can't let Riva's birthday cake go to waste can we?" She announced.

The whiskey had returned some colour to her cheeks and now she seemed to want to calm her nerves doing what she did best.

Em breathed a sigh of relief, and deciding that she was safest with the only person in the room who was eyeing her up with a scholar's curiosity and biting her lip with the effort of keeping all of her questions in, Em settled herself down at the table with Alex.

Riva quietly moved over to join her mum in the kitchen where she was fiddling with a piping bag, and she watched Em like a hawk from across the breakfast bar.

Em and Alex leaped into conversation, seemingly determined to learn as much about each other as possible in the next five minutes. Alex's need to understand how the Mer world operated clearly won out against any reservations she had about Em's loyalty, while Em seemed determined to learn the proper use of a can-opener.

"So you keep food in these metal tins and then eat it years later?"

"Is your society not matriarchal then? Riva explained to me how your physiology is very similar to that of cetaceans so it's a little surprising to me that you would be governed by men."

After getting bashed several times by her mum's clattering, her dad huffed and made his way out of the kitchen, and moved stiffly to the far end of the couch, pointedly not looking in Em's direction.

Her mum handed her a bowl of icing sugar. It seemed as if Em was going to be staying for their midnight cake-feast.

As she watched those jade eyes sparkle in the firelight, something knotted in her stomach and she felt silly for wanting birthday cake when both of her worlds were going to hell.

"Alright. Enough with the cryptic clues. Time is running out. There's a new maritime accident every time I turn on the news these days." Riva said to the room as she threw the empty bowls into the sink. "What did you mean when you said you knew where to find Duncan's son?"

Her mum's hands tightened over the piping bag and icing shot out of the nozzle all over the countertop.

"For goodness sake Riva, look what you made me do." She groaned.

"Can't it wait? We just got over the last awkward conversation." Alex sighed, clearly annoyed that she had interrupted Em's breakdown of the Mer hierarchical social structure.

Riva met her eyes with a serious stare. "No it can't. You've all been telling me that I have a destiny to fulfil and apparently it turns out you were right. So I need to actually start doing something about it." She grabbed a sponge and helped her mum wipe up the mess. "I can't afford to waste any more time."

Em sat back in the rickety chair and nodded. "Of course. I'll tell you everything I know." she said sincerely.

"Well, let's wait until the cake is ready at least" her mum laughed nervously, "I don't think this is the kind of conversation you should have on an empty stomach."

Riva turned on the faucet and the water shot out of the tap forcefully thanks to her rising temper. "I don't think this is the kind of conversation that can be made better with cake mum." She grunted as she wrapped her hands around the faucet to stem the violent flow of water.

"Well, it won't be made any worse by it either…" her mum finished, swatting her out of the way as she started twisting the piping bag again. "And you watch your attitude missy. I don't care if you are some all-powerful being nowadays, you're still my daughter and I'll still ground you."

Temper simmering, Riva started herding everyone towards the dining table. Only Em and Alex looked comfortable to be there. She wrapped her hands around the back of Alex's chair, fingers gripping the worn wood so hard she thought she might snap it.

"Better watch out Riva, you don't want to get grounded, then you won't be able to go out on your next date with Kieran." Alex said, wiggling her eyebrows.

Riva's mum sighed. "Such a lovely young man."

"Who's Kieran?" Em asked.

"None of your business." Riva replied, relaxing her grip on the chair. "I think I have more important things to worry about than a date."

Alex pouted. "Don't say that, you'll break his heart for one, and all work and no play makes Riva a dull girl."

Riva threatened to pick up the wet tea towel and Alex squealed, throwing her hands up in front of her face.

She thought back to when he had kissed her, and the panic that had swiftly followed. Too many warring emotions that she couldn't make sense of. Not to mention the fact that she definitely wasn't in a position to commit to anything or anyone right now when she was very likely about to disappear into the ocean for an indeterminate amount of time. Again.

She sighed. "I don't know Alex. I just don't think it's a good idea to jump into a relationship when you think that either one of you might get themselves killed in the near future."

Both Em and Alex looked up, shocked at her blunt words.

"What do you me-." Alex began, but stopped as a screeching chorus of 'happy birthday to you' made its way out of Riva's mum's mouth. Her mum came around the corner of the kitchen brandishing the world's largest birthday cake, clearly oblivious to what Riva had just said. Leaving the two of them to awkwardly join the chorus, Em joining in confidently with each line and then accidently singing over everyone when the lyrics changed.

Riva just stood there and slowly realised that this was definitely the strangest birthday she had ever had.

8.

Fifteen minutes later, they were all crowded around the wonky dining room table. Each of them shoulder to shoulder, like the most awkward gathering of the Knights of the Round Table ever.

Her dad finally cleared his throat. "Excellent cake Helen, as always."

Alex nodded vigorously as she poked at the frosting while massaging her stomach, clearly a thick slice of birthday cake after a curry was too much for her.

"Ouch!" Em cried out, her spoon dripping with the thick, delicious custard that her mum had just whipped up. "It's hot!"

Riva rolled her eyes. "Of course it's hot. We actually cook food up here? I thought you would have remembered me telling you that at least." She said scathingly.

Gratefully accepting a glass of water from Riva's mum, looking slightly embarrassed Em replied, "Yes, sorry. But it's quite different experiencing it for yourself for the first time. It does give rather a pleasant sensation in the stomach. No wonder you were always complaining about the raw fish."

Narrowing her eyes, Riva bit back another snappy retort. The warning look from her mum also told her that being a bitch to Em wouldn't help anyone at this point. If her father was able to sit across the table from her and eat calmly, then she could too.

"Yeah well, you still haven't tasted a Nando's." Riva said.

Em looked up at her hopefully, another spoonful of custard halfway to her mouth.

"We can go get you some Peri-Peri chicken and then you will really have something to talk about." She offered Em something that was halfway to a smile. The beginnings of a truce. Not trust, but not quite suspicion either.

"Glad to see you think so highly of my baking." Her mum said, looking more than a little put out.

"You know what I mean mum." She sighed, feeling some of her hatred melt away as Em slowly chewed her mouthful. The warm food had brought colour to her marble cheeks and Riva found herself thinking that there may be hope for their friendship after all. If Em was telling the truth.

"This really was delicious Helen, but I can't eat another bite after that enormous curry tonight." Alex said, massaging her belly.

Riva gave her a very confused frown as she practically hoovered her cake up from her plate. After all of the magic use down at the beach she was starving again. Like she hadn't even eaten a curry in the first place.

"Are you seriously going to make me eat your leftovers again? You didn't even finish your korma." Riva scoffed, reaching over with her fork and slicing off a thick piece of frosting.

Alex grimaced. "We don't all have the appetite of a horse you know. I stopped swimming for the summer and don't even think I'll try out for the Dundee University team. Medicine is such a taxing degree choice, I think I'll need every spare moment to dedicate to my studies."

Riva stopped chewing. "So you've decided? You're going then?"

Alex was quiet for a moment as four pairs of eyes stared at her. "Well I mean, I know I said I would help but you know, you have Em now. And clearly she can help you much more than I can." She gestured at Riva who had put down her fork. "Besides you kept telling me that you wouldn't let me come to Oceana with you so. Yeah, I think I'm going. Classes start on the twenty fifth." She finished.

Riva's stomach dropped. Even though she would only be going to the mainland and technically Riva would be much further away in Oceana, she had been dreading the moment Alex went off to university for the best part of a year.

"That's in three weeks." Riva said.

Alex nodded.

"Well that's wonderful news Alex dear. I'm sure your parents are thrilled. You've always wanted to be a doctor and now you're on your way." Riva's mum said brightly.

"Thanks Helen." Alex replied shyly, and Riva could hear the guilt in her voice.

She reached over and took her friends hand. Pushing her own negative thoughts out of her head. "Hey, don't worry about it. If I need your help from afar there's always Skype or FaceTime."

"Not at the bottom of the ocean." Alex rolled her eyes.

"Yeah well, hopefully by the time we're down there we will have figured out a plan." Riva said dryly. "Besides, it might be useful to have access to a university library. I bet there are all sorts of old, dusty books about mermaids tucked away in some moth-eaten corner somewhere."

"Or about titans." Alex said knowingly. The look in her eyes told her that she hadn't forgotten their conversation just before Em had appeared. That had made one of them, she had forgotten all about Eden and Gaia and the mysterious shadow in the wake of Em's appearance. All thoughts of titans and Goddesses pushed to the back of her mind as she dealt with a more pressing issue.

Riva's mum was looking at their three plates, cutlery sat down, cake mostly untouched. "You girls are going to give me a complex between you, you know that?" her mum scoffed, clearly wounded at the lack of appreciation for her hard labours.

"Sorry mum, it's just been a bit of a night you know?" Riva apologised.

Her father tried to come to the rescue. "Don't worry my darling, you know how fantastic your baking is." He said, gesturing to his empty plate and towards Em who was in the process of drinking custard straight from the bowl.

"Thank you dear, but I would feel a little more confident about that if the two people who had cleared their plates hadn't been raised on a diet of seaweed and tentacles." She said, glaring pointedly at Alex and Riva's mostly untouched plates of food.

"Honestly I'm stuffed, I couldn't eat another bite." Alex said despairingly.

"Mum, it's fine. It was delicious." Said Riva. Remembering the advice that Gaia had given her, she made up her mind. "But we should probably get down to business. We all know that I need to find a way to overthrow Duncan, Not only because he is quite probably still trying to find a way to kill us both." She shared a pointed look with her father. "But the Mer deserve their lives back. Humans have taken so much from them, what I saw down there… that's not how I ever imagined them to be living. I want to fix that." She said.

With that announcement, everyone sat their cutlery down on top of their plates, and all eyes turned to Em as she chewed her last mouthful of custard-soaked cake.

"Okay." Em said, swallowing, a slightly embarrassed blush creeping up her neck. "Where do you want me to start?"

Riva's questions were practically fighting each other to get out first. "How do you know Duncan has a son? Where did you get the information? How do you even know it's true?"

Em looked a little startled and picked up her glass of water again.

"Just start at the beginning." Her father said, eyes narrowed across the table.

Em sat her glass down on the table with a soft thump. "So after you both fled Oceana-." Em started.

"You mean after I escaped Oceana, dragging my unconscious father away from persecution." Said Riva, arms crossed.

Em sighed and rubbed a hand across her face tiredly. "If you want to hear what I've got to say then you are going to have to listen. Preferably without judgement."

Riva bit back another nasty retort and sat back in her chair, the wooden back digging in to her spine. "Fine. Continue."

Em ran her fingers through her lopsided fringe and settled back in her own chair. Well, as settled as she could get since Riva had given her the one with the wonky leg on purpose.

"Alright. After I heard Prince, I mean, King Duncan's declaration in the infirmary, I knew I was on the wrong side. Looking around that cave, seeing the looks exchanged between you and your uncles, I knew I had made a mistake. Betraying you was more painful than I could have imagined Riva. The way you looked at me before you blasted the wall open made me feel unimaginably guilty."

Riva stayed silent.

"So I left. While Duncan was summoning every Guard in sight and ordering them after you, I slipped away. I watched as the Guards formed ranks and the Elders opened up current after current in an attempt to find out where you had gone. Ten or more Guards disappeared into each exit current and there was panic among the people. The city was chaos. Rumours spreading like wildfire that the King was dead, sightings of you fleeing with Prince Dylan in your arms, Guards bolting across the open ocean in pursuit. It was easy enough to fade into the background myself. Especially with our new King shouting orders and causing even more alarm."

Riva smiled in spite of herself. She hadn't been able to do much, but at least she hadn't made his first day as King easy. It was a minute before she realised that Em was smiling with her.

"I have known since that day you cracked the pillar outside of the palace that you are the one who can save us. When you healed that little boy I allowed myself to hope, to think that maybe there was a better way than the one Duncan was offering me. I want my people to be the way they once were. You can help us be that again."

"Yes, Em, it's all part of my great destiny, get on with the story." Riva said sarcastically.

Pretty words, but she was waiting for the girl's actions to change before believing her. Her mum looked furious at her attitude but both Alex and her dad were hiding smiles behind their hands.

Em gave her a look that said she knew exactly why she was still being so cold, and continued, "I found out that Duncan had a son thanks to Flora. As part of our work as Elite, we are stationed all across the wider ocean. You hear and see things that most other Mer don't. We are also trained to notice what others miss. She was covering a coastline in California about a decade ago, keeping an eye on humans that had started using dolphins to carry out their work beneath the surface. Bizarrely the dolphins remained fiercely loyal to their human keepers and returned to them again and again even when we freed them from their harnesses. I mean you would think that they would have thanked us but Flora told me that they had looked at her like she was the enemy."

Riva cleared her throat.

Pausing mid-breath, Em realized that she had been getting off topic. "Right. Anyway, she saw a young boy get into a surfing accident near where she was stationed. Apparently he had come too close to the rocks and bumped his head as he fell. Of course Flora hadn't been going to interfere and had watched as he was taken further under the surface by the waves crashing above him-."

"Oh, of course she left the little boy to drown. Whatever else could she have done?" Alex scoffed indignantly. "You're right, Riva, the Mer seem just charming."

Em smiled lopsidedly, looking almost pleased with herself. "Can you blame us?"

"Well… I know we aren't doing the ocean any favours…" Alex stammered, colour flushing her cheeks.

Em flicked her fringe out of her eyes and ignored Alex's huffing. "No. You aren't. Anyway. Flora didn't want to get involved until she saw something glinting on his wrist. Intrigued, she swam over to see what it was."

"I thought mermaids weren't interested in shiny treasure like they are in the stories?" Alex asked, pretending to be all innocent.

This time Em replied through gritted teeth, "Do you want me to tell *this* story or not?"

Riva snorted.

"Anyway..." Em started, looking between everyone sat around the table as if making sure there would be no more interruptions, "The boy was unconscious but attached to his wrist was a woven bracelet with a small medallion attached. Now, it hadn't meant anything to Flora at the time and when she recounted the story to me, she hadn't focused particularly on the bracelet at all – simply describing how the medallion had been engraved with the figure of an ugly looking man. We laughed about the strangeness of humans together." The collective looks from the three other women at the table told her that they thought otherwise.

"Don't look at me like that, you are all strange to us. You should have seen some of the things Riva did when she first arrived in Oceana. There were rumours going around the palace that she wasn't right in the head."

"Hilarious." Riva said drolly.

With a lopsided grin that showed how much she was gaining in confidence, Em continued. "So after we had laughed about the ugly bracelet, she told me that the little boy had started shaking and appeared to have a fit under the water. So she swam away to leave him to his watery grave."

"Well she sounds like a delight." Alex said with a pout. Riva readied herself to jump across the table to protect her friend as Em gave her a look as cold as ice.

"I was a different person back then." She said instead of lunging towards Alex, jade eyes ablaze, but seeming to think better of it.

"I don't even know what kind of person you are now." Riva said. "Just because you're giving us information doesn't mean that we trust you. You're still skating on thin ice remember."

Em looked confused. "Who said anything about ice? It's still the beginning of September. I knew Scotland was cold but I didn't expect summer frosts."

Resisting the urge to roll her eyes she replied, "It's just an expression. Keep going. I'm guessing the underwater seizure Flora saw this boy have was his Mer blood awakening."

"What do you mean?" Asked both her mum and Alex at the same time.

Looking between them, she remembered why she had never told them what it had felt like.

"The day I fell out of the boat I was unconscious for a while."

Alex interrupted with a snort. "A while? More like an hour. We were worried sick. I remember all I kept thinking was that I would have to tell your mum that you had drowned."

Riva's mum closed her eyes as if Alex's words had conjured up an unwelcome image in her mind.

"Thanks Alex." Riva fixed her friend with a warning glance. "At least we all know that I didn't drown. But I wasn't unconscious the whole time. From the moment that I touched the water I felt pain. The worst pain imaginable. Like my blood was burning in my veins, and my skin was melting. The pressure that built up inside of me was unbearable. Like I was going to explode from the inside."

Her mum shuddered and Alex had turned white.

"Do you feel that way every time you go into the water?" her mum asked, looking so small and fragile sitting next to her dad's broad figure.

"No. No of course not. Otherwise I don't think I would ever have gone back in. No, I think the pain was just part of my transformation from human into something... else. My Mer side awakening or something."

"I can't believe that I was stupid enough to believe that bullshit you told me after the Coastguard had pulled you out." Alex breathed.

Riva smiled. "Well, I seem to remember you being a little distracted by said Coastguard...."

Alex shimmied her shoulders and sighed at the memory of him. "Oh my gosh yes, he was *gorgeous*. I wonder if he got stationed elsewhere because I haven't seen him all summer."

"So what happened to this boy?" Riva's dad butted in and put a stop to the reminiscing, his face serious.

Em held up her hands. "I don't know. Flora left him and when she passed the same place later in the day to get back to her transport current he was gone. She assumed that his body had been recovered or carried away. However knowing what I know now, I agree that he probably awoke under the water with the same abilities as Riva."

At Em's comparison, she was surprised that she felt almost threatened and even a little jealous at the thought that someone else may have the same powers as her. May have had them for longer.

Well, not all the same powers. Even if he has ocean magic, he certainly doesn't have the magic of Gaia.

"How did you figure out that he was Duncan's son? He could have been the child of any Mer who had gotten close enough to the coast to reproduce. We don't need to have legs to procreate with humans after all." Her father said.

"Dad, ew." Riva said, scrunching up her eyes as she flung the dishtowel at him. Now there was a visual she hadn't asked for.

Clearly feeling the stress of the conversation, her mum got up from the table and started clattering around in the kitchen again, pulling chipped mugs out of the cupboards to make them all hot chocolate. She could practically feel Alex groaning beside her as she readjusted the skin-tight LBD she was still wearing from the birthday dinner.

"The bracelet." Em said. "Duncan wears one just like the description Flora gave me."

Riva bolted upright in her chair, almost knocking the plates flying as one of the table slats came loose. "Crap, you're right. I remember it. He was wearing it at the banquet." Into her minds-eye swam the image of a bracelet exactly as Em described. A thick, ugly woven rope that looped around a ghostly pale wrist with a dull, metal medallion attached. Riva had thought that it was a coin.

"Oh he never takes it off." Em continued, "Every time I saw him it would catch my eye and I would think of Flora. That's probably why I paid so much attention to it. Because it reminded me of the story she told me."

Granted, it wasn't much to go on, but it was something. A human boy who wore the exact same bracelet as the new King of the Mer.

"He could have picked it up at any tourist shop or boutique when he spent time on land. This doesn't prove anything." her father said sceptically.

"Dad, come on. This is the only lead we have!" Riva swung around to look at him, arms folded so tightly she could be forgiven for thinking he was wearing an invisible straightjacket.

"I wouldn't-." Em started before Riva cut her off.

"If you were about to say that you wouldn't lie to us I would rethink that statement before you end up wearing your hot chocolate."

Em wisely shut up and Riva turned to her dad again.

"You should want to believe her story more than anyone." She said.

Clearly puzzled, her dad stared at her with his periwinkle blue eyes, "What do you mean?"

Riva sighed. "If Duncan really did this. If he really does have a half-human son, it means that he had been able to put aside his prejudices for long enough years ago to be able to, you know-." she faltered here for a second, blushing. "-do it, with a human. Perhaps we actually stand a chance of changing his mind."

Her dad didn't answer, but the steely glint in his eyes faded and he uncrossed his arms. "How old was this boy when Flora encountered him? And what year was it?"

Em looked a little taken aback and exhaled, trying to remember. "I know that she had said that he was small, but I suppose that if he was old enough to be surfing there alone then he must have been at least nine or ten I think."

"Yes, and the year?" her dad pressed.

She threw her hands up in despair. "How am I supposed to remember that?"

"Try." Her dad said stiffly.

A couple of awkward moments passed as Em wracked her brains. She stood up and walked behind her chair, leaning forwards on the frame, tattoos contracting as she interlaced her fingers. "Flora and I met four years ago and she had worked off the coast of California for seven years prior to her posting with our group. If I remember rightly, I think this had happened pretty early on in her stationing."

"Why do you need to know that?" Riva asked her dad as her mum sat down an enormous mug of hot chocolate in front of her. Alex stared at the mountain of whipped cream like it had personally offended her.

Her dad held up a finger to shush her as he calculated in his head. "If the boy was nine or ten at the time of the accident and said accident happened eleven years ago then it could be possible." he finally said.

"How can you be sure?" Riva said thickly, through a gulp of whipped cream. "Didn't you say that he hadn't been ashore for long? Something about rushing back early to try and save your mother?"

"Queen Noelani, May she rest in peace."

They all looked at Em who had surprisingly bowed her head in memory of the late Queen. Even more surprisingly was that her father was now looking at the Mer girl like she had earned back a grain of respect.

"You're right." He told Riva. "Duncan had used the necklace to come ashore before me. Like I told you, I had been putting it off initially and he had jumped at the chance. After the, um, the accident, he returned to Oceana in the January of 1991, the month my mother died." He looked around the table at his riveted audience. "So if my brother has a son and he is still alive then he would be twenty-one years old. If this boy was the age you estimate, then the timing is right."

Everyone around the table let out a breath. With this confirmation from her father, Em's revelation was quite probably true.

A horrible image popped into her head, "Wow. Duncan got someone pregnant." She started giggling with Alex, "That poor woman."

"Riva!" her mum admonished.

Em looked unsure as to whether or not she could join in with the laughter and settled for a shaky smile instead.

"Come on mum. The man swims around like he's got a fish bone up his backside and he has absolutely zero sense of humour." She replied. "He clearly has no clue that he has a half-human son. He was only too eager to have me executed when I showed up in Oceana. I mean, with the Mer being so worried about dying out and their own failing reproductive systems, they should welcome us instead of trying to exterminate us."

"Riva." Her dad said in a warning tone.

"What? You know it's true." She replied.

Her dad sighed heavily. "Please remember that despite what he has done he is still my brother. You knew him for only a handful of weeks, I have known him my whole life."

Taken aback by the fact that her father was attempting to defend the person trying to kill them, her temper spiked. "Yeah, and for the majority of your life he has persecuted you for loving a human. They shackled you for it. Stripped you of your crown for it. And now we find out that he is just as bad! What a filthy hypocrite. Ordering executions and secret strikes against innocent scuba divers and holiday makers when it suits him but he doesn't think twice about going to bed with one as long as he gets his rocks off…"

The comparison hit her like a knife between the ribs. The king who was trying to kill her and the boy who had tried to violate her. Both with so much hatred in their hearts, both not caring who they hurt or used as long as they got what they wanted.

Riva had a momentary, terrible thought. What if the mother of Duncan's son hadn't been willing? What if he had forced himself on her? She knew her uncle could be vindictive and ruthless, but would he have stooped so low? She shuddered and pushed the thought from her mind.

She remembered the promise she had made to herself after she had survived Stuart's attack, that she would never again let a man put her in that position. That she would never again feel so weak and helpless. Duncan didn't deserve her compassion any more than Stuart did.

"Riva!"

She vaguely noticed the cottage beginning to shake but her vision blurred and the face of the Goddess sprung into her mind. Like she was standing with one foot in reality and one foot in Eden. Birdsong trilled in her ears and the thick scent of roses flooded her nostrils. Gaia didn't need to speak for her message to be clear. She was the powerful one now. And Mother Nature was as ruthless as she was nurturing.

"Riva! Stop this!"

Popping sounds brought her back to reality, both feet on the cold stone floor of the cottage as she realised she had made the lightbulbs explode. Behind her the fire was roaring dangerously high and leaving dirty black streaks of soot up the mantelpiece.

She quickly reigned in her magic "Crap, sorry." She apologized, taking in the four nervous faces sitting in front of her. Her mum was hovering beside her, as if she had wanted to reach out and touch her but had been afraid of what she would do. Alex was looking nervous but was trying to hide it. But both Em and her father, both slightly more used to the supernatural, seemed less fazed. Em was sat with one eyebrow raised and her signature boyish grin plastered across her face.

"You're getting dangerous." She said, sounding positively delighted.

"I'm sorry. I don't know what came over me." Riva apologized. "I'll go buy some more bulbs tomorrow mum."

"It's fine pet, don't worry about it. You can't control it yet." Her mum replied breathlessly, padding off in search of the brush and shovel.

"Well she needs to learn. Quickly." Her father said stiffly, and as everyone made to finally rise from the table, he cut in. "I have a few more questions for you." Her dad said to Em, sounding suspicious once again.

Riva took the opportunity to drain her mug of hot chocolate and sat back down heavily in her chair before she managed to smash the mugs too. Now that she had information, she was itching to track down her supposed cousin.

"How did you get your hands on the necklace if you aren't working for my brother?" her dad asked quietly.

"Oh, she already explained that to me at the beach dad. She still had some of your blood on her hands. Literally and figuratively speaking that is." She said, raising a sarcastic toast towards her with her now-empty mug.

Her father said nothing.

"It is as Riva said. I smeared some of it onto the entrance to the Vault for it to open."

A quick flash of anger rose up at the mention of how Em had practically split her father's skull open, but she pushed it down.

"But you never explained how you got out of the Vault without being caught." Her father continued, his tone insinuating more than he was letting on. Alex quickly dropped the phone she had been scrolling through back onto the table.

Em smirked, "I was trained as an Elite, I know how to get around." She ruffled her hair and stretched.

"I don't buy that." Her dad said, his tone dangerous. "No-one attempting to raid the Vault escapes. You can't honestly think you are the first person to have done it?"

"The first to do it successfully maybe." She drawled.

Now Riva was wondering if she needed to jump in front of Em to save her from her dad.

"Tell me how it is that you sit with us now. If you remove an artefact from the Vault there are wards in place to ensure that the thief is apprehended. If you were caught stealing anything from the Vault you would have been locked up in the bowels of the palace by now."

So they do have dungeons. Riva thought, quietly thinking that they couldn't have been much worse than the stark, empty shell of a room they had given her. She had never been more grateful for Netflix, or a simple book, in her life after spending three weeks literally staring at the walls.

Em was quiet, until she finally looked up from the table. "Fine. Elder Iolana found me within the chamber. I was just about to remove the necklace from its plinth when I heard her voice behind me. I had thought that she was going to arrest me but her voice had gone all gravely like it does when she awakens the enchantments around the city and her eyes were cloudy. Like a frothy tide."

Riva shivered. If Iolana was the same Elder who had cornered her during the summer solstice then she was very glad Em had been caught in the Vault and not her. While the ancient Mer had seemed to support her efforts to integrate herself with the people of Oceana, she definitely gave off a creepy vibe.

"I had frozen with the necklace in my hand but she made no move to restrain me. But as I was about to swim through the doorway, she started chanting."

"Chanting?" Riva's dad asked, sounding sceptical.

"Yes, Your Highness, chanting." Em bit back.

"What did she say? Was it like a prophecy?" Alex asked, hanging on Em's every word.

"It was a little cryptic now you mention it." Em cleared her throat and then started rhyming.

'On the sand in Venice she will find, the man who can help her unwind, the problem that they together will face, shall see the Mer in their rightful place. Where one brother went, the other did first. Look to the seed that was further dispersed.'

"Well it all sounds like gibberish to me." Riva said, more impressed with Em's memorization skills than anything else.

"Come on Riva, it wasn't really that difficult." Em said, "Well, at least the last two lines weren't. Not for me anyway. That's how I figured it out. *Where one brother went, the other did first*...We all know the royal's 'tradition' of coming ashore when they come of age."

Alex giggled. "It's like spring break for Mer-people."

"It's supposed to be a secret." Her dad said.

Em sighed dramatically. "Yeah, well. Fish talk."

"So the last two lines of her vision helped you make the connection between the story Flora told you and Duncan's bracelet." Riva clarified.

"Exactly." Said Em. "With that figured out, I knew that this prophecy was to do with you. That helped me to figure out some of the beginning. The bit about *shall see the Mer in their rightful place*." Em glanced over at Riva shyly. "Like I said, I knew you would save us. As soon as I heard those words I knew I was making the right choice."

Riva swallowed uncomfortably. As much as she wanted to hold on to her anger over what Em had done, she was proving mightily useful right now.

"Was this Elder by any chance wearing a stingray-bone cape?" Riva asked.

"Um, yeah it marks Iolana's rank, why?" said Em

So it was the same Mer woman then.

Alex butted in with, "I told you two weeks ago Riva, it's fibrous cartilage. Stingray's don't have bones."

"Whatever." She muttered resisting the urge to stick her tongue out at her know-it-all friend. Whether it was bone or cartilage, the image still creeped her out. But she wasn't at all surprised that Iolana had been the one to make this prophecy. If anyone was to be believed down there, it was the Mer woman who held the entirety of the remaining magic that had been siphoned from the bottom of the ocean.

"Putting aside her questionable fashion choices, I think we need to listen to her." Riva said. "So apparently this cousin of mine will help me overthrow his dead-beat dad and somehow save the Mer. I mean, still no idea how we *do* that exactly but first things first. Where do we find him?" Riva asked.

For the first time in a while, her mum piped up, "That's the easiest part sweetie, it was in the poem. Venice."

By this point, Alex was practically bopping up and down in her chair like an imitation Hermione Granger. Riva was surprised that her hand wasn't in the air and was fervently glad that she wasn't sitting in the wonky chair.

"Yes, Alex?" she drawled.

"Not Venice, Italy." She said, grinning.

"What?"

"The poem. It's not talking about Venice, Italy." Alex stated, apparently still waiting for the rest of them to put together what her genius brain had already grasped.

"Well how many other Venice's are there?" Riva asked, impatient.

"Just one that I know of." Said Alex, smugly, "Venice, California to be precise. I mean, if California is where Flora saw Duncan's son surfing all those years ago then it makes sense right?"

Riva bit her lip, "I mean, maybe. But how do we know he hasn't moved since then? I mean, that was more than ten years ago now."

"True, but I think she has a point. It's better to start where the clues are leading us right?" Em asked.

Alex was shaking her head, eyes gleaming. "There are no beaches in Venice Italy. And the poem said specifically 'on the sand'."

Riva looked at the five of them gathered in the cottage and sighed.

"Well we'd better buy some sunscreen. We're heading to California."

9.

"At least we have somewhere to start now." Riva said as she sat on a cool, flat stone by the stream in Eden, delicately dipping her toes into the crisp water.

Whoever had appeared in the tree line hadn't been trying to stop her drinking from it. Gaia had assured her it was quite safe. Although she had refrained from mentioning the shadowy figure for some reason.

"I have faith in you my daughter." The Goddess replied softly, "You are on the right path."

Riva stretched luxuriously as the dappled sunlight warmed her face. "I mean once we find my cousin I still have no idea what we're going to do but yeah, one step at a time right?"

Gaia just smiled knowingly, as always. Riva secretly found it a little infuriating. "You will know what to do."

Then, just like she always did, she faded mysteriously away into the sunbeams leaving a pile of lilies behind. Their scent was strong amongst the subtler fragrances that drifted across the meadow and she wrinkled her nose.

"Everyone sure seems to have a lot of confidence in me." She said to no-one in particular.

She was getting better at manifesting whatever dream-state was required for her to drift off and find herself in Eden. The past couple of days had been frantic with packing cases and organizing flights. Having an escape from reality had certainly come in handy when Em had started panicking when the plane had taken off. She had jumped at every sound or announcement and Em's anxieties certainly weren't helping her own as a first-time flier either.

Alex's smug smile as she strolled calmly through duty free had been enough to make Riva want to throttle her. A seasoned flier thanks to her dad's air miles, Alex had simply popped in her Air Pods, slid on an eye-mask and went promptly to sleep without so much as glancing at the safety card.

Despite Em's exclamations over the clouds, Riva had found herself preferring not to look and had instead retreated inwards, seeking the sanctuary of the meadow to soothe her anxieties.

The excitement that was shared by everyone else about the trip was overshadowed by her trepidation of the task that awaited them. Finding her cousin, convincing him that he was half Mer, and figuring out a plan to overthrow his father as king. She had decided to conveniently leave out the part where she wasn't entirely sure about how exactly she was going to make that happen. She had the vague idea that Duncan was never going to rescind his throne willingly. She was prepared for that, in fact there was a dark part of her that was secretly hoping for it, but were the rest of them?

Standing up slowly from her perch on the rock, she gleefully rubbed her toes into the long grass. Breathing in the fresh scent of gardenias and dewy leaves, she stretched her shoulders. The long plane ride had made her stiff. She knew she wasn't technically here physically, but it still felt like she was.

There was a slight breeze in the meadow today, stirring the buttercups and lifting the ends of her hair.

A twig snapped to her right and she whirled towards it. There it was again, that shadowy figure creeping in the tree line.

Instead of running away this time, she walked towards it. "Hey! Who are you?" she called out across the stream but the figure didn't move. It didn't retreat either.

She dipped her toes back into the stream and made to cross it. "What do you want?"

Giving her just a flash of those amber eyes, the person disappeared into the shadows again.

"Hey! Earth to Riva!"

Her vision of Eden swam in front of her as the voice started to pull her out of her dream state.

"Ugh. What?" she asked, annoyed at the interruption.

The ugly motel room came back into view with abhorrent clarity. The threadbare carpet, dirty lampshades and buzzing of the insect catcher made her want to smack Alex for bringing her back to such a dismal reality.

"We're going down to the beach, you need to get ready." Alex was clutching an oversized beach bag and wearing equally oversized sunglasses as she brandished a bottle of sun cream in her direction.

She thought again about the mysterious stranger who kept appearing in Eden. Why were they only ever there once Gaia left? Why didn't they reveal themselves? She had asked Alex about titans during the never-ending long-haul flight here but had quickly grown bored with her long explanation which sounded confusingly political. All she retained was that they pre-dated the Greek Gods. Apparently.

"Seriously, you need to slather this factor fifty all over your pale arse." She continued.

Em snorted.

"I don't know what you're laughing at. You're next." Alex flung the bottle onto the bed in front of her. Riva was surprised that a cloud of dust didn't bounce up around it.

Standing up from where she had been sitting against the front door as it was the only patch of carpet that didn't look like someone had been sick on it, she uncapped the bottle and smeared some of the heavily coconut-scented cream on her face.

"We're not here to have a holiday Alex, you know that." She said, "Besides we're all still jet-lagged." She sniffed the cream again. "God this stuff is strong."

Sitting down on the questionable duvet cover, Alex grimaced. "The best thing for jet lag is a strong coffee and adapting as quickly as possible to the time zone you're in." she pulled out a small compact mirror from her bag and adjusted her lip gloss, "It's almost lunchtime, so we'll get you an iced latte on the way to the beach."

"I don't like coffee." Riva grumbled.

"What's a latte?" Em asked.

There was a knock at the door and the three of them jumped. The motel looked just like the ones she had seen in American films. She was expecting an axe murderer to storm his way in any second.

"Girls, it's me. We'd better get going." Her dad called through to them.

Em walked over to open it, but not realizing that Alex had slid the chain on the night before, she ended up wrenching the chain and lock away from the wall entirely.

"Sorry, damn thing was stuck." She said, looking at the dangling chain, perplexed.

"Em you practically broke the bloody door frame." Alex complained, strutting over to inspect the damage in her wedges. "We need to sleep here tonight you know, and I for one would rather have a functioning lock when we do."

With the door open, the arid, midday heat was wafting in and she was already starting to sweat uncomfortably. Em started fanning herself with the romance novel Alex had been absorbed in. "Don't worry princess, I'll protect you." she waggled her eyebrows suggestively.

Alex narrowed her eyes, "Ha-ha very funny. You're scrawnier than I am."

"You're clearly forgetting that I'm an Elite." Em smirked.

The two girls had gabbled incessantly for the past two days, trying to absorb as much information from each other about their different worlds as possible. It had been annoying enough that Riva had spent thirty minutes searching for a decent pair of ear plugs in the airport.

"Maybe with fins you are, but I'm still pretty sure I could beat you in a race up here. You've only had those legs for a few days now. I've got eighteen years on you with feet." Alex said, making a grab for her paperback.

Quick as a flash, Em was out of the faded red chair and hopping across the double bed, Alex squealing indignantly after her.

Ignoring them, Riva turned back to her dad, "Where's mum?"

"She went to go and get us all some breakfast." He said.

"Oh no! I wanted to try iHop." Riva pouted, forgetting that she had just told the girls that this wasn't supposed to be a vacation.

Her dad looked over his shoulder and down towards the car park of the motel, beyond which lay the freeway and some dodgy-looking construction work. "I don't think you're missing much."

A crash followed by a thud sounded from inside the room and they both turned to look. Em was sitting on Alex's back and the latter was face down on the ground, red in the face and furious that her pristine make-up was touching the grimy floor.

"And then Stephan approached her. He had never felt an attraction like this in his life. His member was bursting forth, ready for her…" Em read aloud from Alex's novel in a theatrical voice, causing Alex to squeal and thrash underneath her.

Biting her lip to stop from laughing, Riva went to rescue her friend.

"He removed his shirt, the beads of sweat glistening in the candlelight…"

"Alright that's enough you two, come on." She gave Em a shove and she fell backwards good-naturedly, still thumbing through the pages of the romance. "We've got work to do."

Alex swiped her book out of Em's hands as she creased with laughter from some no-doubt thoroughly inappropriate paragraph. Shoving it back into her beach bag, cheeks ablaze, she strutted out of the room, clacking all the way down the hallway in her wedges.

"Is she really going to the beach dressed like that?" Riva's dad asked, casting a worried glance over the rickety-looking metal staircase that Alex was now navigating.

"When it comes to Alex's fashion choices, I've learned to stop asking questions." Was all Riva said as Em attempted to get the door shut.

Ten minutes later they were all squeezed into the rental car with Riva and Em devouring the enormous blueberry muffins her mum had brought back from the bakery around the corner. Alex was busy checking Google maps for potential locations where Riva's cousin would likely be.

"I still think we should check in the obvious place first. Just like was said in the prophecy, we head to Venice beach. I say we try to blend in with the rest of the tourists and beach-goers while we look for a twenty-one year old wearing a rope bracelet." Alex said confidently.

"Yeah, sounds super easy." Riva said thickly through a mouthful of muffin. "Not at all like looking for the proverbial needle in a haystack."

"Do you have a better idea?" she asked huffily.

Riva shook her head.

"I didn't think so."

"I might have an idea." piped up Em, who was crushed between the window and Alex's ginormous beach bag.

Riva looked across Alex's lap at her. Still a little unsure as to whether or not to completely trust her. Granted, she hadn't tried to throw anyone out of the plane so there was that. "What do you have in mind?"

Em looked nervously out of the window, a cornflower blue sky was brushed by the tall palm trees that lined the side of the road. In the bright sun it almost made her eyes water looking at it. "Assuming that Duncan's son is still surfing, which I think he must be if the Elder's prophecy is to make sense. Why else would it be leading us to one of the most popular surfing spots in California?"

"Since when do you know so much about surfing spots in California?" asked Riva.

Em jerked a thumb in Alex's direction. "Her friend Google told her."

Alex started giggling.

"Stop winding her up. It's just going to end up with you on the floor again." Said Riva, warningly. "None of us need a repeat of what happened on the plane."

Both girls had the good grace to look embarrassed. None of them wanted to see that air steward again. Or his pretzels.

"Explain." Riva asked.

Em leaned forward, to peer over the wide brim of Alex's sunhat.

"The Mer have an ability to sense one another. It's the reason why you and your father can't go into the ocean right now, and it's also-do you really have to wear that in the car?" she swatted at the sun hat.

Alex peered out from underneath her obnoxiously large hat like a 1930s movie star. "Yes, I do. The sun's rays are crazily strong in this part of the world and I want to avoid any premature wrinkles."

"Keep going." Riva reminded Em as she looked like she was about to make another catty retort.

Still frowning at Alex, she continued, "It's also how the Guards found you when you first stepped into the ocean." She said, peering at the brim of the hat as if she was hatching a plan.

The memory of six dark figures swimming towards her drifted across Riva's memory. She remembered the Mer Guards' eerie song as they had honed in on her. She had been under the water for less than fifteen minutes.

"But how does that help us find Duncan's son if we can't go in the water? Or do you think we could sense him on land?" Riva asked, intrigued by the idea.

Em was shaking her head. "I don't think so. That's why they had so much trouble tracking down your father when he was living with your mum. We can't sense each other up here. I certainly couldn't when I came ashore. I had to wait at the beach and hope you would come down one day. I mean I could have started knocking on doors until I found your house but I wanted to respect your privacy."

Riva snorted. "You mean you were afraid I would attack first and ask questions later?"

Em grinned, flashing her white teeth. "I needed a public place to be sure you would actually listen to me."

"Well, I still got in a few good shots at first." She said, wiggling her fingers threateningly, allowing a few sparks to shoot between them. Her dad cleared his throat from the front seat and she dropped her hand. "Okay, so what is your plan?"

Em smiled cockily, "I go in to look for him."

Alex's giant hat swivelled so quickly that Riva was worried her head had been knocked out of joint. Her mouth dropped open and she looked down at Em's pasty white legs where they stuck out skinnly from ripped denim shorts.

Riva was already shaking her head. "No. You've been away from Oceana for too long. Even if Duncan hasn't figured out that you're helping us yet, you'll be wanted for treason for escaping and breaking your exile. You were as much a prisoner there as I was."

Em reached across Alex, who was still staring dumbly at her flip flops as if fins were about to spring from them any minute, and grabbed Riva's hand. "Let me do this for you. If this is what it is going to take to get you to trust me again then I'll do it. I won't get caught."

Riva stared into those almond-shaped eyes and for the first time realised that she wasn't angry at her anymore. There was still a little resentment lingering deep down, but if Em really was willing to do this for them, if she would really risk being caught just to give them a better chance of finding Duncna's son? She had to trust her. The thought both comforted and terrified her.

"You know that we might need to come back here every day for the rest of the week to find him. Are you really prepared to take such a huge risk for us?" she asked.

Em brushed her fringe out of her face, indigo tattoos a dark contrast to her pale skin. "Subterfuge and evasion. This is what I excelled at in my training." She replied.

Riva groaned. "Yeah, that's a great way to regain my trust. Remind me how good you are at lying."

Even though Alex sucked in a breath, Riva shared the first genuine smile with Em since she had turned up on her birthday.

Riva squeezed her hand. "Alright. If we need you to go in then fine."

"If you don't go too far out then they won't be able to sense you." Riva's mum piped up from the driver seat.

"What?" all three girls asked.

"There's a boundary of course. Where the land meets the sea. If you pass that boundary then you belong to the sea and if you don't then you stay under the protection of the land."

Everyone else in the car eyed each other awkwardly. Riva's dad reached out to place a hand on her mum's knee.

"Did your mum bring her meds with her?" Alex whispered in her ear.

Riva smacked her.

Her mum just smiled pityingly on the rest of them in the rear-view mirror, as if they were all extremely slow to figure it out. "It's quite obvious really."

Thankfully her phone pinged, distracting her from her mum's ramblings. It was a text from Kieran.

Good morning gorgeous, how is your first day in The Golden State?

Looking at her messages, she realized that he had sent her three texts already. The first wishing her a safe flight and the second checking to see if she had landed safely. She groaned inwardly. She was a terrible person.

Hey! Sorry I didn't reply, jet lag is a killer! It's really sunny, we are all just heading down to the beach now.

At least she was keeping the lying to a minimum. When she had called him to explain that she was leaving again, he had sounded worried. She had spent a good five minutes promising that it was going to be a short trip and that she would definitely be coming back. Blocking out Em and Alex's playful banter, she opened her phone as another message came in.

Wish I was there to rub some sunscreen into your back for you.

Her stomach clenched as she imagined those strong hands on her back and she quickly hid the screen from Alex. Unfortunately the movement was way too suspicious and her best friend made a grab for it.

"Whose message don't you want me to see then?" she asked, her acrylic nails acting as claws as she scrambled for the phone.

"Girl's be careful back there, your mum needs to concentrate on the road." Her dad said over his shoulder.

By this point Alex was practically on Riva's lap as she held the phone aloft. Then her phone was plucked nimbly out of her fingers and both girls turned to stare as Em casually unlocked it and swiped for her messages.

"Hey not fair, I was distracted!" Alex whined, readjusting her sundress.

"How the hell do you know my password?" Riva asked indignantly.

"More to the point, how do you know how to work a smartphone?"

Em gave both of them a condescending look and pointed first at Alex "You need to learn to focus on more than one thing at a time." Then Riva. "And you need to be a little more observant." She peered down at the text messages and frowned in disgust. "Ew. I wish I hadn't bothered now."

Riva blushed but intrigued, Alex grabbed the phone.

"Ooh let me see…" Peering at the messages, she pouted in disappointment. "That's it? Wow boy needs to work on his lines." She said sarcastically, dropping the phone back into Riva's lap.

Blushing furiously and trying not to glance at her parents in the front seat, Riva opened her phone in trepidation as it pinged again. She could practically feel Alex craning her neck to get a good look.

Sorry, I'm not very good at this. Have fun at the beach, I wish I was there xx

Riva couldn't help a smile lifting at the corners of her mouth. She vowed to be nicer, all she ever did was run away and ignore him but he still remained just as patient and kind as he had from the beginning. She shot back a quick "me too." Text and promised to call him later on to talk to him properly. She wasn't entirely sure if this was what a normal relationship was like at the beginning, but she was willing to see where it went.

None of them spoke again until her mum had parked the car in one of the few vacant spots still left on the street near the beach. She could already see a lot of wetsuit-clad figures floating in the swell and her heart clenched at the sheer number of people lounging on towels in the sand.

"What was that you said about a needle in a haystack?" Alex breathed.

The three girls exchanged glances full of trepidation as they made their way across the street until they stood at the entrance to the Santa Monica pier. Side-stepping people taking photos and tour groups waving their fluorescent flags, they took shelter in the shade.

The September sun was stifling. Riva soon wished that she was in possession of Alex's broad-brimmed hat and wondered how she could swipe it off her at the earliest opportunity. Em was eyeing up the waves with longing on her face.

"Alright. I say we split up. Your mum and I will take that side of the beach if you girls take the other. We'll meet back here for dinner if we haven't found him yet." Her dad said decisively.

"I love your optimism." Riva laughed. "You really think we're going to find him in one afternoon when we have no idea what he looks like or what his name is?"

"You're underestimating how much I don't want to sleep in that motel again." Alex said, dragging her down to the right. "We are finding this boy as soon as humanly possible."

They walked down the beach, the white sand scorching hot underneath their sandals and they were soon skipping across it, panting like lunatics.

Alex was keen to lead them nearer to the shirtless guys in the acrobatics park closer to the road, where they were busy showing off swinging on rings and bouncing on ropes, but Riva grabbed her arm and marched her off down the beach, closer to the waves.

"Come on Riva. They were gorgeous…" Alex pouted as she dragged her away from the muscle-men showing off by the jungle-gym.

"Motel, remember?"

They stopped short of the wet sand and plonked themselves down in a heap on top of their towels, already exhausted by the sun. Looking out at the sparkling surface just a few metres away from them, her breath caught. She had been close to the ocean since her return from Oceana, living on an island there wasn't really any getting away from it. But here she could feel the tide pulling at her again. Not as strongly as it had back when she had first awakened her Mer blood, but strong enough that she wanted nothing more than to plunge down into those waves.

"So what now?" Em asked impatiently

"Now we wait. And watch." Riva replied.

Alex soon took advantage of the situation and stripped down to her hot pink bikini, placed another blob of sunscreen on the bridge of her nose, stretched out on her towel and closed her eyes.

"Wow. You're super concerned about premature ageing. So much help, thank you." Riva said sarcastically, reaching over her friend's body to grab her sunhat.

"Well we did tell my parents that this was a last-minute getaway before I started uni didn't we?" she replied, pulling out her phone for a selfie.

The guys who were walking up and down the beach with their surfboards were casting appreciative glances in Alex's direction as she snapped away. Their eyes soon drifted to Em, where she sat in a floaty black shirt, dark tattoos a stark contrast in the bright sun. Thankfully Venice beach attracted a more eclectic sort of crowd than the Isle of Skye and most people seemed interested rather than threatened.

"This seems to be a main throughway for the surfers. Good location." Em nodded happily, looking all around them, surveying the surroundings.

Well at least someone is focused on the goal.

Riva eyed Alex, who was now trying to select the appropriate filter to upload her selfie to Instagram.

From underneath the offensively large hat that was now protecting her from the worst of the sun, Riva was free to check out the majority of the male surfers in their radius. Unfortunately she couldn't spot any glinting of metal on wrists or rope bracelets. Em didn't need a hat to hide behind. She was clearly a master at observing without making it obvious that that's what she was doing.

An hour passed and Riva had drained her water bottle and sweated her way through her t-shirt. The waves had never looked more inviting. She could feel Em straining to hold herself back from them beside her. For a brief moment she worried that this trip would end up driving all of them crazy as the intoxicating salt spray coated them both.

"This is getting us nowhere." She complained, wiping sweat off her nose for the zillionth time.

"My offer still stands." Em said.

Riva looked at her, knees drawn up to her chest, lichen necklace that definitely didn't scream 'beach-chic' still clawing at her neck.

"I don't want to have to ask you to do this." She said quietly, despite everything that had happened, she would never forgive herself if Em got caught because of her.

Em raised one eyebrow, "You aren't asking. I'm offering."

Glancing at the waves one more time and then the hundreds of people on the beach, Riva made her decision.

She poked Alex in the ribs.

"Ow, what was that for?!" she squealed.

"Hi sleepyhead, snore much?" Riva replied.

"I don't snore!"

"Well I guess you'll never know. Can you go get us some water from the truck up there? We're out."

Alex groaned. "Ugh, fine."

She slowly stood up, adjusting her bikini straps. Rooting around in her bag, she grabbed her purse.

"And I'll take that back thank you very much." She said grumpily, swiping the hat back off Riva's head as she shoved her feet into her sandals.

Em turned to her once Alex had gone. "Why did you send her away?"

Riva sighed, peeling off her pale blue cotton shorts and flung them on top of her sweat-soaked t-shirt.

"I know Alex. If I let her watch you get your fins back we would never hear the end of her questioning. That girl makes it her mission to understand anything and everything."

Em looked inclined to agree. "Fair enough. The other night she asked if she could examine my nipples." Em said nonchalantly.

"I'm sorry, she did what?!" Riva spluttered.

"Yeah, she thought that I must have two sets since when I'm in my Mer form I have mammary glands on my tail too." Em said casually.

Despite herself, Riva found herself wondering.

Em caught her looking at her shorts. "I don't have two sets of nipples Riva."

"No. of course you don't." she replied, blushing. "Come on, let's go."

In only a few short steps they were at the water's edge. As the first trickles of salt water made contact with the bottom of her feet, she felt like she was connecting with herself again.

"Ahh, I missed this." She sighed in contentment as they walked in, the water cooling her overheated skin refreshingly. The ocean rushing to her like an old friend.

"We still need to be careful." The Mer girl said glancing around them, anxiously fingering the necklace, "I'll try not to be under for too long. There are a lot of people in the water today so hopefully even if there are Guards in the area and they do sense me, it won't be easy for them to find me."

"Yeah maybe." Riva said faintly. "Maybe my mum was right too though."

Em looked sceptical.

"No, really." She said, "The first time I was in the ocean, after the accident, I was out past the headland for more than an hour and none of the Mer found me."

"Flora hadn't sensed any Mer blood in the boy while he was under the waves either." Em pointed out.

Slightly disappointed she replied, "Fair enough. Maybe our Mer side doesn't fully awaken the first time or something."

They continued on into the waves until they were waist deep. Being back in the embrace of the ocean had Riva's magic going crazy. It was practically roaring at her to let go. Her hands were shaking with the effort of keeping it contained.

"Good luck." She said to Em, squeezing her hand.

She nodded by way of reply and bent her knees so that she was now submerged up to her neck. She went to unlatch the necklace.

"Wait! Maybe give me your shorts in case they rip. Otherwise what are you going to wear to come back out again?" Riva said.

Em laughed nervously, "Good thinking." She wriggled out of them.

Holding the sodden denim shorts in both hands, she watched as Em removed the necklace, and passed it to Riva. At first nothing happened, but then almost in the blink of an eye, her tail appeared with a sleek flash of light.

Em smiled in relief.

"What does it feel like?" Riva asked, looking at her grey fins curiously.

Em grinned, "Like I've been curled into a ball for days and now I get to stretch."

Riva found herself smiling with her, despite the potential danger, when suddenly an idea occurred to her. "Wait! How have I never thought of this before?"

She grabbed Em's hands in her own and tapped into her magic, drawing from both the Ocean and Earth.

"What are you doing?" Em asked, sounding uncomfortable.

"Ssh, let me concentrate." Riva whispered, "I'm trying to cloak you."

Em's tail twitched in excitement, "Seriously? Can you do that to someone besides yourself?"

"You knew about my cloaking?" Riva asked.

Em rolled her eyes. "You still underestimate my abilities as a spy after everything we've been through together?"

Riva smirked slightly, summoning the magic. "Yes sorry, I guess I was too focussed on your ability to be a two-faced liar."

Despite the words, they both knew that Riva no longer meant them. Closing her eyes, she imagined the sun's rays shaping themselves to Em's body, making her both see-through and reflective at the same time. When she opened them again, she could feel Em's hands but she couldn't see them. All that was left of her was her head above the water.

"Okay it's done. Now go."

With a wink, Em let go of her hands and submerged herself carefully under the waves. She shot off so quickly that Riva couldn't even make out where she had gone. She only hoped that her cloaking magic would work the further away Em swam from her.

Sighing, she realised that she didn't want to leave the water. She tucked the necklace carefully into the body of her swimsuit. It was swelteringly hot up on the beach, she would just take five minutes to cool down. She spread her palms flat on the surface of the water and connected with the waves.

Smiling, she felt the tiny little eddies and currents swirl around her calves, like they were happy she was home. Silently, she hoped that her mum was right, and that she was too close to the beach for any Mer to sense her. With her toes buried in the soft sand she knew that she should be getting out of the water now but found that she really didn't want to. That familiar tug behind her belly button where the ocean always hooked her was coming back.

She started manipulating the tide, enjoying the repetitive feeling, like pulling an elastic band taut and then releasing it with a snap as the wave rolled out, white and frothy towards the sand. She could hear the surfers whooping and cheering as the swell grew and their boards darted across the surface. Her hands flitting to and fro, she rolled the waves higher and higher, like a baker kneading bread.

"Yes man! Get under it!" one surfer shouted out in the distance.

Riva kept her eyes closed, fighting against that voice in her head that told her to go back to the beach. She wanted to listen to her heart that was telling her to dive forwards and submerge herself.

"Dude there's a dolphin here!" another called to his friend.

"Awesome!"

The sun was hot on her face, but in the cool water it was no longer uncomfortable. A far cry from the picturesque meadow of Eden and nothing at all like her rainy island home. But what she was coming to realise was that on this earth, there wasn't just one type of perfection.

"Hey watch out!" someone cried directly in front of her.

Opening her eyes she saw a surfer careening towards her on the crest of a wave of her own creation before his board cracked her on the head and everything went black.

10.

The tide had calmed and as she regained consciousness resting on the sand in the shallows, she felt very confused.

Wait, how did I get here?

Her head was throbbing and she felt sure she would have a giant lump on it tomorrow. She rubbed it and winced. Panicking, she grabbed the front of her swimsuit and the pounding of her heart eased when she felt the necklace still securely in place. Taking a breath, she felt the ocean pass through her and smiled ironically.

Well I guess it was inevitable that I'd end up down here. Did Em pull me out of the way?

Looking around she tried to spot the Mer girl or the surfer who had hit her but found nothing. It was very light under the waves, and visibility was excellent. Nothing like the dark, murky waters of the North Sea around the Scottish Highlands. She could make out some surf boards bobbing around at the surface and wondered which one of them had smacked her.

From the underside, the soft swell of the waves and the muffled whoops and cheers of the surfers gliding across them was immensely soothing. Her ocean magic was practically purring in contentment at being back in its element. She kicked out with her feet, and ran her hands through the fine sand, it was warm between her fingers as she floated in place.

She knew that she had to get out. Despite the fact that her mum seemed convinced that as long as she remained close to land then the Mer wouldn't sense her, she wasn't so sure.

Either way, it wasn't worth the risk and she needed to give Em the best chance possible. She was already swimming around in full mermaid-mode and Riva didn't want to add to their scent or sound or whatever it was that the Mer used to track them.

Before she could push off the bottom and surface, a strong pair of arms were slicing through the water above her. She got an eye-full of some serious abs and beautiful dark skin, before the boy plunged, aiming right for her.

Crap.

She frantically scooted over, hoping that he would think she was a snorkeler or something but before she could even react, he was in front of her. Clearly surprised to find her floating nonchalantly at the bottom, he froze.

Then she noticed that he was breathing.

Holy crap.

There was nothing of Duncan in his face but he was definitely breathing the same way she did, letting the ocean pass right through him. His onyx eyes widened and his handsome face was a picture of shock. Automatically glancing down, she checked for a bracelet but came up empty.

Another one?

"Impossible." The mystery boy breathed.

Despite feeling like she should try to pretend that she wasn't half-Mer and protect her secret, there was something honest about his face that made her drop all pretenses.

Unable to think of anything else to say, she replied. "Well hitting me over the head with your surfboard is one way to get an introduction I suppose."

His jaw dropped. Underwater conversations weren't exactly alien to her after her time in Oceana, but this boy was looking at her like she was from another planet.

"Sorry the Scottish accent can be a little hard for most American's to understand." She said, attempting to lighten the moment with humour. He didn't reply.

"Okay, I see we're going to have to take this more slowly. Maybe a more normal setting will help." She grabbed his wrist and pushed off the bottom.

As their heads cleared the surface, droplets flew from his hair as he shook his head. He looked at her wide-eyed and exclaimed, "Who the hell are you?"

She glanced wildly around, making sure there were no floating surfers nearby. "Ssh, keep your voice down idiot, don't attract so much attention." She hissed as they treaded water.

He was still looking freaked out, "How can-, I mean can you-, um, you-."

She rolled her eyes, "If you are trying to ask how I can breathe underwater then I think you already know the answer to that considering you were doing it too."

He was shaking his head dumbfounded. "I've never met anyone like me before. This is wild. Who-who are you?"

"I'm Riva." She said, and bizarrely, found herself holding out her hand for him to shake it.

He didn't.

"Yeah sorry, I'm a little awkward sometimes." She said, crossing her arms over her chest. Scanning his face for any sign of her family she again came up empty. His smooth dark skin, tight black curls and obsidian eyes were completely unfamiliar to her. Although her grandmother had been Hawaiian, perhaps there was some resemblance there. "What's your name?" she asked.

"D-Douglas." He stammered, looking like he had been the one to take a surfboard to the head.

Well what would you know? Another D name. He might be our ticket after all.

"Strong Scottish name." she said, hesitating. "A family name?"

He shook his head. "Uh, no. At least I don't think so. I don't have much family. It was always just me and my mum."

Bingo.

"Interesting." She mused. "It's nice to meet you Douglas, but should we maybe make our way back to dry land or do you want to keep treading water all day?"

He looked behind them towards the beach, "Oh, sure. Uh. Fine."

They both turned and swam in, awkwardly slowly, both of them knowing they could go much faster but neither of them willing to show it.

As they scrambled back onto the damp sand, Riva became painfully aware that she was standing in her faded swimsuit, incidentally the last one she had raced in. Even if this guy was her cousin, it was still totally embarrassing. Giving him the once over she grimaced. Especially when he had the body of a Marvel's Avenger.

"If you've never met anyone else like us then suppose you have a lot of questions." She said quietly, the water already drying from her body in the hot sun.

He still seemed a little at a loss for words. "Yeah, you could say that I guess."

Riva searched for the right thing to say. She needed a way to talk to him, privately, without freaking him out. She had a feeling that if she told him that her whole family was currently combing the beach for him and that she also had a mermaid out in the water searching for him then he would bolt. But despite the obvious shock on his face, at least he was still standing in front of her.

"Do you want to meet me back here later tonight when it's a little quieter? We can talk more then?" she suggested, suddenly worried that Em was about to pop her head out of the waves behind her or that Alex would come barrelling in with her usual lack of tact.

He ruffled his tight curls in thought and looked behind Riva towards the pier. "Uh, sure, if you want. Meet me at eight by the entrance to the pier?" he said.

"Okay." She replied, her heart racing. "Sorry, I would talk now but I'm here with family and I'm pretty sure you don't want to meet them yet." She finished with a weak laugh.

He raised his eyebrows in surprise. "Your family know your secret?"

She grimaced. "It's a long story."

"I've got some time."

"Yeah, not for this story you don't."

He stepped back and observed her, those black eyes narrowing. "You're new here aren't you?" he said.

Riva fiddled uncomfortably with her swimsuit strap. Thanks to her lack of chest to hold it up, it had an annoying habit of wandering. "What gave you that impression?"

"That accent for one." he seemed to be relaxing, "and that pasty complexion for another."

"What's wrong with my accent?" Riva asked indignantly.

He chuckled, "Nothing, it's just. Different."

She chuckled, noticing his visible relaxation.

"Oh you want different?" Harnessing her magic, she pulled another huge wave in to the shore, surfers going crazy in the shallows. Just as it crested she pulled its edges together around where they stood. Rising up beside them it came crashing down on top of Douglas's head, completely drenching him while Riva stood bone-dry beside him.

"What the hell?!" he exclaimed, coughing and spluttering as he wiped his eyes.

"Different doesn't even begin to cover it." She smiled warmly as he shook his head like a dog, "I'll see you at eight."

She turned to make her way back up the beach when he called out to her, "You'll definitely be there won't you?"

His tone of voice was different this time and she looked back over her shoulder to where he stood, eyes full of hope. She realised that he was just as alone with this secret as she had been before she had discovered Oceana. Painfully lonely and feeling like an outcast.

She smiled sadly. "I promise."

Turning her back on him, stomach churning with excitement, she practically ran to their towels. She couldn't believe that she had actually found him.

Well, she hoped it was him. But how many other half-Mer could there be swimming around Venice beach? Especially half-Mer with a very Scottish name beginning with the same letter as his suspected father and uncles. Granted, her twin uncles Murray and Murphy didn't have names beginning with D but they always seemed to be a rule unto themselves.

Reaching the towels, she grabbed hers and started furiously rubbing the itchy dried salt off her skin. Now she had to figure out a way to meet him alone. No doubt the entire clan would want to tag along.

Alex would insist, Em would want to play security guard, her father would see it as his business and her mum would go wherever her father did.

A slight prickle of anxiety told her that she was stupid for not getting his phone number, but that look in his eyes made her certain that he would want to meet her again.

Grumbling in annoyance already, she looked around for Alex. Surely the queue for water hadn't been that long? Eyes roving across the beach, she finally spotted a pink bikini in amongst five or six hulking men over by the volleyball nets. She pulled her t shirt on over her now-dry swimsuit and marched up the beach to where Alex was shamelessly flirting with men twice her age.

"Wow that's totally impressive." One of the men was saying.

"Yeah, we should give you a tour, you'd love Mel's drive in." said another.

She marched up to where the group was playing the most stationary game of volleyball she had ever seen.

"Hey Alex! Having fun?" she called over.

The whole group turned to see who had called out and it was suddenly like Alex didn't exist. The men who had been falling over themselves to take Alex out on a tour of Santa Monica five seconds ago suddenly found themselves speechless as Riva approached. Her endless waves a deep chestnut as they dried in the sun, sapphire eyes ablaze with irritation at her best friend, and pale skin practically luminescent in the reflection off the sand.

"She your friend Blondie?" One of them managed to ask.

Alex, realising what was happening managed to look both ashamed of herself and put out at Riva stealing her thunder. "Yeah, she's got a bit of a temper."

"And you haven't seen the half of it yet." Riva practically growled as she grabbed Alex's arm.

"Ooh, fiery! I like it." one of the men whooped idiotically.

Rounding on him, she lit up her thousand-watt smile. "You like fire?"

Before she could summon her magic, realising what Riva was insinuating, Alex practically started running. "Sorry guys, we've got to go now. Thanks for the game!"

As they dragged each other back down the beach to the moans of disappointment from the volleyball players.

"Come on Barbie, don't go!"

"I thought you wanted to try a basket catch?"

"Your friend can join in!"

Alex tried to get her arm free and slippery as it was with sunscreen, it was a struggle for Riva to keep a hold of. "Were you seriously going to use your magic in front of them?" Alex hissed once they were out of earshot.

Throwing her down on their towels just a little too hard, Riva replied. "Of course not. But I needed to say something to get you away from them."

Alex pouted. "It was just a bit of fun."

"Are you kidding me?! Get your head in the game would you?" she practically growled at her, still on her feet, now scanning the shallows for any sign of Em.

"Hey, stop freaking out." Alex cried, "I got you your water."

Riva grabbed the now lukewarm bottle. "Fantastic. Really great work Alex. Meanwhile, I just found Duncan's son."

Alex's eyes went wide as she gasped. "Shit, seriously?!"

"Yeah, no thanks to you." She spat back, grimacing as she swallowed the tepid water.

Alex had the good grace to look ashamed. "Where's Em?"

Riva gestured back down the huge stretch of beach towards the waves dramatically by way of an answer.

"No!" Alex covered her mouth with her hands and jumped to her feet. "She's a *mermaid* right now?"

"Keep your voice down." Riva said, eyeing the people sun-bathing closest to them. Luckily they all either seemed to be asleep or have headphones in. "Where are you going?" She groaned as Alex started walking towards the surf.

Alex was shaking her head. "Can you please stop moaning at me all the time? I was just trying to have a little fun with those guys. I got your water and then one of them called over to me. I didn't see any harm in talking to them. It's not like there's anything I can help with anyway."

Riva fell into step with her. "What's that supposed to mean?"

"It means I feel useless. And I'm not used to feeling that way. Especially-." Alex stopped herself, biting her lip.

The words hit her like a knife wound. "Especially around me you mean?"

The guilty look on Alex's face told her that it was true. Riva shouldn't have been surprised. All their lives, Riva had been the plain one, the one who failed tests and never excelled at anything besides swimming.

"Look, I don't mean that I'm not happy that you've turned into this amazing, beautiful, powerful person." Alex sped up as Riva started walking again. "Because I knew that's who you were all along! There's just a lot of big things happening and I don't know where I fit in to all of it."

The girls stopped as they reached the waves again. The swell had calmed without Riva's magic and the lapping around their toes was soothing.

"You fit in as my best friend." Riva said quietly, staring down at the small grooves of sand under the glassy surface. "I can't do this without your support."

Alex took her hand. "You know I'll always support you. I'm sorry for not acting like finding Duncan's son was a priority."

Riva turned to look at her best friend, the bridge of her nose freckling in the sun already and she looped her arm around her waist, almost instantly regretting it as the slimy sunscreen smeared all over her.

"It's ok. I forgive you. And I get how hard this must be for you. But you are the only one without any true ties to Oceana. Wait, hear me out." She quickly said as the hurt crossed Alex's face.

"You are the only one with the ability to walk away from this, and you can do it at any time. I wouldn't judge you for it."

"Not a chance." Alex said, staring stonily out at the waves.

Riva smiled. "Good. Because even though I just said that, I don't know how much of it I really meant." She started walking towards the quieter stretch of beach, scanning the waves for that familiar dolphin-like tail.

"So when did she say she would come back?" Alex asked.

Starting to get worried, Riva kept scanning the waves. "She didn't."

"How did you find your mystery cousin then?" she pressed.

"I'll tell you both together, but it was either fate or a very lucky coincidence." She said, squinting at a shadowy figure closer to the pier. "I think she's there. Either that or it's a small shark."

Pointing to the figure, Alex raised a hand to her forehead to block out the sun, even though she was still wearing the sunglasses that made her look like a bug.

"She's there!" Alex squealed as Em's head popped up at the surface, dark hair plastered to her head and a frustrated look on her face.

Riva dug her elbow in to her ribs. "Ssh. Don't draw attention to her." but looking around she saw that everyone was either too busy surfing or sun-bathing to care about two teenage girls. "Why isn't she coming out?"

Em was gesturing for Riva to come towards her.

"Come on." She said, grabbing Alex hand and marching into the waves. Alex followed excitedly behind, clearly desperate to get a glimpse of the tail.

When the girls both reached Em, the Mer girl looked furious.

"Where the hell are my shorts?" she asked, eyeing Riva's empty hands. "I've been scanning this part of the beach for fifteen minutes already!"

"Oh crap!" she said "I must have dropped them when Douglas knocked me out with his surfboard."

"Who's Douglas?" Asked Alex.

"Who knocked you out?" Asked Em.

Riva sighed, the waves lapping at waist height. "Long story, I'll fill you all in back at the motel when we track down my parents." Em was crouched uncomfortably, trying to hide her tail. "Alex, do you have anything spare that she can borrow?"

"I always bring something spare. You never know when you might need it." Alex said as she not-so-subtly squinted under the waves at Em's tail.

Em had noticed and winked at her. "You can touch it if you like."

Alex hesitated and then blushed as she saw the suggestive look on the Mer girl's face. "I'm going to go, uh, get you something to, um, wear." She stuttered, swimming lithely away to shore. Em grinned like the Cheshire cat.

"You shouldn't tease her like that." Riva said, smiling despite herself.

Em pretended to look innocent. "What? I thought you said that humans were more tolerant than the Mer?"

Riva rolled her eyes, "I mean you're in California right now so pretty much anything goes, but not with a straight girl."

"Shame she's so annoying. She's just as beautiful as you said she was." Em sighed dramatically.

Riva dunked her.

Em surfaced chuckling and launched herself at Riva, lithe tail making easy work of the take-down. Until she grabbed exactly the tender spot that had become target practice for a very solid surfboard.

"Ouch, watch it!" she hissed through gritted teeth, "That's where I got hit."

"Hit by what?" Em asked.

"A surfboard."

Em was quiet for a moment before she fell about laughing.

"Yeah, yeah. It's hilarious." Said Riva sarcastically.

"Wow you actually have a lump. It's like there's an egg growing out the side of your head." Em exclaimed.

"Mmhm. I'm sure." She said, unamused as the lump smarted. She reached down the front of her swimsuit and pulled out the necklace. "Right, Alex is coming back, put that around your neck and let's find my parents. I think we found our ticket to freedom."

11.

The sun was setting in the most glorious splash of fire that Riva had ever seen. As she walked down the broad, palm-tree lined boulevard with her best friend, she wondered what it might have been like if they really had been able to come to California for a holiday.

No stressing about the fate of an entire race of beings on her shoulders, just sightseeing and eating good food. Maybe after this was all over she might be able to do just that. Although she would have to wait for the summer holidays if Alex was to join her, Riva knew she would never skip classes.

After they had finally extracted Em from the water and practically forced her into the baby-pink kaftan that Alex had held out for her, they had caught up with her parents back at the motel. Over a lunch of some seriously questionable take-out, she recounted the story of how she had, quite literally, bumped into her cousin.

Em had been all for high-tailing it back to the beach, knocking him out and stuffing him in the car, but one deadly stare from Riva's father had her quickly forgetting that idea. Deciding that the whole group turning up would feel too much like an ambush, they had agreed that Riva and Alex would meet him at the pier together.

The clattering of the rollercoaster and the excited chatter of both locals and tourists made for a jittery atmosphere that reflected her own nerves. How was she going to start this conversation? How did you explain this to someone you had never met before? How much did he already know?

"Stop fidgeting, you're making *me* nervous." Alex hissed as they crossed the road and walked under the bright blue archway of Santa Monica Pier.

She had to admit, it was a good place to have a secret conversation. Between the crashes and bangs of the ancient rollercoaster to the pings and whoops from the arcade, there wasn't much chance of them being overheard.

"Where do you think he'll be waiting?" asked Riva.

Alex looked around. "I dunno. Maybe we should just wait in an obvious spot?"

"If you say so." She replied, spying a bench a rambunctious family had just vacated near the entrance to the pier. "Let's sit here. If he walks further down the pier we'll see him pass by, besides it's too crowded down there, I think he'd struggle to spot us."

The girls sat down, both of them looking extremely stiff, heads on a swivel. Alex had her arms and legs crossed so tightly it was hard to see where her limbs ended and began.

As the sun finally set, the sky went from a watery orange to a blush pink and then finally a deep red as eight o'clock came and went. Then eight fifteen. Then eight twenty.

Riva was seriously regretting not asking him for his phone number.

With the sky dark above them and the glaring lights from the arcades illuminating their faces, at eight thirty Alex announced that she was going to go try to find a bathroom. Finally unravelling herself, she walked away into the crowds of people that had been growing thicker ever since the sun set. Riva briefly wondered how she didn't have a dead leg.

She kept looking around even though her neck was getting sore from how much it had been craning around. He had seemed so eager to talk that she had been convinced he would have been there before them. Why hadn't she found out more about him earlier? At the very least a second name, that way Alex could have Facebook stalked him.

"Thank God, I thought she'd never leave."

Jumping almost completely out of her skin, she whirled around to see Douglas leaning over the back of the bench.

"How long have you been here?!" she exclaimed, clutching her chest.

151

"About twenty minutes." He grinned, his long-sleeved t-shirt rolled up to the elbows. "You aren't the most observant person in the world are you?"

Riva frowned. "What if we had given up on you and left?"

He looked confused. "Well, I figured that you couldn't shake your friend. I thought I would wait until you got rid of her for a bit so we could talk."

Also confused, Riva replied. "She knows everything."

"Wait. You've told more people?" he asked, surprised. "I thought you said it was just your parents?"

Riva shrugged. "Some people. The ones that I trust."

Douglas seemed taken aback by this and sat down heavily beside her. He was wearing stylishly ripped jeans and flip flops of all things. The excited chatter coming from tourists all around them filled the awkward silence between them.

"Your family and friends? Boyfriend?" He asked, somewhat judgementally.

Riva crossed her arms. "My parents and exactly one friend." She figured that Em didn't count since she was technically guarding more of a secret than Riva was. "And I don't have a boyfriend."

She squirmed slightly on the bench, thinking of Kieran and his tentative kisses. Was she ready for that?

"So how did it happen for you?" he asked, jerking her out of her thoughts about running her hands through auburn hair. "I mean, the first time?"

Riva swallowed, her throat dry. Why did this have to be so painfully awkward? "Uh, boating accident. Three months ago."

His eyes widened in disbelief, the dark irises reflecting the flashing red and blue strip lights. "You've only had your powers for three months?"

She nodded.

"Wow. That's impressive. It took me years to figure mine out but you're out here creating waves already." He rubbed his hand across his mouth, making a rasping noise against his stubble. "I definitely don't have as much control as you do." He looked almost disappointed in himself.

Internally she was both a little disappointed and secretly pleased that he didn't seem to have as good a handle on his powers as she did. "Look, my story's a little complicated." Riva said, searching for the right words, "It's going to take some time to explain."

"Well, you best get a move on then before your friend gets back." He said, scanning the crowd.

"I told you, I trust her."

Douglas raised an eyebrow, "Yeah well, I don't know her at all. I haven't kept my secret for more than ten years only to have every blonde in Santa Monica knowing about it by the end of the week."

"She isn't Californian. She's Scottish too."

Another raised eyebrow, "Hmm. She doesn't look it. Nowhere near as pasty." He once again ran an eye over her bare legs. Thanks to the neon lights they looked almost fluorescently white.

Riva wondered if he was this cheeky to everyone he just met. "Yeah, well. She was in Dubai last month." Crossing her arms, she took a good look at him, elbows balanced on both knees, chin in his hands. "You found out about all this ten years ago?"

He nodded slowly. "Yeah, I got into a surfing accident in my first lesson. Thankfully I've improved." He laughed in an endearingly self-deprecating way.

"Are you sure?" Riva asked, rubbing the bump on her head.

Douglas grinned, shrugging. "Yeah well, I'm not used to people floating in the middle of my waves. I did try to avoid you but Tommy was on my right and I just didn't check my balance on time, I came right off you know. It took me ages to find you, I thought you would have floated back up."

But Riva had stopped listening. As he had put his hand to his head she had spied what he was wearing around his wrist. A rope bracelet with a medallion attached. Her breath caught.

"Nice bracelet." She said, slightly breathlessly, trying to keep the excitement out of her eyes. She had been right. It was him.

Douglas looked taken aback at her interruption and fiddled with it, resting his wrist on his knee. "Oh this? Yeah my mum made it for me. It's a St Christopher medallion, she used to make them for sailors and fishermen. You know, for safe travels."

He sat up, putting one arm across the back of the bench, the tarnished silver medallion glinting in the light.

"You weren't wearing it earlier today."

"Nah. It might not look like much but it's- important to me. I don't want to risk losing it when I'm out surfing you know?" he said, Riva could tell that her questioning was making him uncomfortable.

"Look, I know you came here for answers, and I promise I will give as many to you as I can but, I need your help in return." She said, gripping the wooden bench, wondering how much crazy he could take in this initial meeting.

Douglas nodded seriously. "What kind of help?"

Oh not much, just disrupting your life with a trip down to the bottom of the ocean, a meeting with your long-lost father who may or may not try to kill you on sight and restoring peace to the entire ocean.

"Um, why don't we start with the questions first and then you can decide if you want to help us or not?" she asked, hoping that his curiosity would win out.

His gaze levelled with hers for a moment, onyx eyes meeting sapphire before he nodded once.

"Alright. Well, uh, how much do you know about where your powers come from?" she asked.

He shook his head slightly, but seemed a little more relaxed as he leaned back against the bench again, hands clasped behind his head. "Honestly? I have no idea. I was hoping you could tell me."

Oh my god I have to explain everything. Crap.

Trying to find a linear way to break it all down for him she wished that Alex had had time to make a spreadsheet or portfolio about it or something that she could give to him. "Okay, so how much can you do with your powers?" she asked.

Douglas exhaled and looked skywards. "I mean, I can breathe underwater which is pretty cool. Definitely helps whenever I wipe out. I can control the waves a bit too, but nothing like what you did down on the beach this afternoon - that was freaky. But using my powers like that in surfing competitions made me feel like a cheat so I gave it up about five years ago. I just do it recreationally on the weekends now."

Riva felt sympathy with him there. "Yeah I gave up swimming too." She sighed and he looked at her with interest in his eyes. "I competed for Scotland until the summer." She explained.

He whistled appreciatively.

Embarrassed, Riva looked at her hands, pale and ghostly under the harsh pier lights. "Yeah well, gold medals don't really feel like gold medals when you've got a seriously unfair advantage over the rest of the competition." As she said it, she realized that she actually didn't miss it. Not the early morning training and definitely not the tang of chlorine that used to cling to her like a second skin. She did miss the rush of competition, but she had something else now that gave her a bigger thrill.

She felt a quick tug from her magic from that space in her chest behind her heart where it seemed to live and she smiled.

"So are we like demi-gods or something? Because I watched a movie once about the son of Poseidon who could do some of the same stuff. That would be pretty epic." He said, clearly only half-joking. "I've had a lot of theories over the years."

His mention of demi-gods had her thoughts turning to Gaia and that shadowy figure who she had decided to try and unmask the next chance she got to visit Eden. She tried to wrack her brains for some of the information on titans that Alex had given her, but then realised it was better to stick to the basics for Douglas's sake.

Riva grinned and shook her head. "Sorry no. I used to wonder if I was a superhero who was about to be recruited into the Avengers or something."

Douglas grinned again, his full lips parting over pearly white teeth and Riva had to suppress an involuntary shudder. Yupe, he was Duncan's son alright. If those lips could curl to the side in a sneer then they would be two peas in a pod.

"I can imagine you giving the Black Widow a run for her money, but don't you think our powers would be more suited to X-men or something? I mean that stunt you pulled with the wave is definitely more Storm than Spiderman." He said, still grinning.

Riva rolled her eyes but grinned back. "Haven't you heard of Thor?"

Ignoring the small voice that told her not to be so obvious, she channelled her powers and released her magic in a joyous rush as a peal of thunder sounded directly overhead, shaking the very foundations of the pier. Douglas's eyes widened as he looked skyward to see thin strips of lightning zig zagging across the cloud she had conjured.

"Is that you doing that?" he breathed, still looking at the heavens.

Riva scrunched up her eyes and sat on her right hand to hide her glowing eyes and Mark from view.

"Hey, you ok? Does it hurt or something?" he asked, putting a hand on her shoulder.

Feeling the magic drain away and hoping that her eyes had gone back to their normal blue she turned to look at him. From his double take it was obvious that not all of the gold had faded.

"No it doesn't hurt. But you're right. The truth is probably even crazier than you've imagined so I hope you're ready for it." she replied.

He looked at her earnestly. "I've been waiting for answers for a decade."

She took a breath and decided to go for it. "How much do you know about your father?" she asked.

Clearly her line of questioning surprised her but he answered willingly. "Not much. I know he left my mum before I was born but she died just after I turned eighteen so I never got the chance to ask her. Wasn't really interested in knowing some deadbeat who ran scared after getting a girl pregnant though. Why?"

Riva gritted her teeth and summoned the courage to blurt it out.

"Well, for both of us it seems, our powers came from our dads. I grew up just with my mum as well. I'm so sorry that you lost her. I don't know what I would do if I ever lost mine."

He cleared his throat loudly and rubbed his chin with a loud rasp. "Thank you."

"You're welcome." She took his other hand, hoping that it would give them more of a connection, or at the very least stop him from running away. "Both of our dad's left our mum's when they were pregnant. Both of us have a connection to the ocean." He was staring into her eyes and she hoped he would take this well. She took a deep breath and blurted it out.

"Both of us were raised by human single mothers, because our fathers have fins."

He looked a little like she had done earlier after he had hit her with his surfboard. Panicking, she decided it was probably best to just finish this as quickly as possible. So much was riding on him believing her.

"Our dads are Mer. They exist. There's this whole underwater kingdom called Oceana. I've been there, well actually I was, you know technically, held prisoner there."

"W-what?!" Douglas choked out, eyebrows slowly climbing his forehead.

Desperately backtracking and cursing her poor choice of words she continued. "No! I mean, I wasn't locked in a dungeon or anything, like I had my own room and stuff and I was only there for about three weeks-ish. And technically I was a guest in the palace because the King of the Mer is my- sorry *was*- my grandfather. I'm his eldest son's daughter. So you know, even though he originally wanted to kill me, he kind of had to change his mind in the end. Thankfully." Realising she was rambling, she paused to draw breath.

"Your father is my father's brother, the new king of the Mer. My uncle. We're cousins."

Douglas looked like he was going to pass out as he stared off into the middle distance. She had no idea what he was thinking.

"I mean it's a lot more complicated than that and I'm trying to make it simpler for you but I know this is a lot of information so please don't freak out. I want to help you with this and I'll take more time to answer all of your questions, just please, please let me explain."

Before she could say anything else he completely surprised her by throwing his arms around her. The large muscles squeezed her, although not uncomfortably, as he held her.

"Thank you." he choked out gruffly.

"Um, sure." She said, patting him awkwardly on the back, "For what?"

His arms still around her, he was clearly fighting with his emotions. Riva noticed that he smelled pleasantly of salt water, something spicy and the unmistakeable scent of fresh air. He pulled back slowly, obviously trying to get a grip on himself.

"You have no idea how long I've been waiting for the truth." He finally said, eyes brimming with tears. "And yes, it is crazy. But no crazier than anything I've been thinking for years already." He sniffed, "and to find out that I still have family?" He shook his head and blinked forcefully to stem the flow of tears. "You have no idea how much that means to me. I want you to tell me everything. Cousin."

Tears threatening in her own eyes, so relieved that he hadn't run a mile, she went to give him another hug when a voice sounded beside them.

"Oh my god the queue for the bathroom was a mile long, so I grabbed us these on the way ba-." They were interrupted by a very indignant sounding Alex, clutching two repulsively large burgers wrapped in white paper.

Douglas cleared his throat and pinched the bridge of his nose, Riva quickly brushed her own tears off her cheeks.

"Um, I'm clearly interrupting something." Alex said, not knowing what do to, until she spied the bracelet. "Oh my God, Riva is this *him?!*"

Riva dropped Douglas's hands and grabbed the burgers before Alex flung them on the floor in her excitement.

"Clearly." She said, pulling Alex down to her level by her wrists. "Calm down please." She growled in her ear.

"Sorry." Alex replied breathlessly, her now-empty hands flitting around her body adjusting her skinny jeans, crop top and hair simultaneously. "I um, didn't think you were going to turn up so attractively."

Riva aimed a kick at her shin.

"I mean, turn up so late. Really late. Why were you late?" she continued.

Douglas turned up his movie-star smile full blast, "I was waiting for you to leave." His tone warm but his words more than a little cutting.

Alex looked like a spanked puppy. "Oh, I mean, of course. You needed to talk to Riva." She looked between both of them, "Did you guys talk?"

Riva nodded. "We had a very interesting conversation."

"But it's not finished yet." Douglas said, his tone very clearly suggesting that he wanted Alex to leave.

Alex, not used to such treatment from any straight member of the opposite sex, pouted.

"Well, you guys enjoy the burgers then. I guess I'll just head back to the motel."

Riva rolled her eyes. "Don't be daft, it's dark. I don't want you walking around alone, we don't know the area." Riva stared daggers at Douglas for even making Alex think this was an option. "We can all hang out together. We'll get another burger for Douglas and have a good long talk about all of this crazy stuff together." Riva looked between them both. "Alex can help me explain some of it. She was there when it all happened, even if she didn't know what was going on at the time."

Douglas was lounging against the back of the bench arms crossed, Alex was clutching her handbag and studiously avoiding his gaze while trying her best to stick out her butt and suck in her stomach.

Before Alex could make more of a fool of herself Riva stood up and shoved the burger into Alex's pouty mouth, the cheese dripping down her chin. She wiped it off indignantly but the delicious greasy food clearly wiped all other thoughts from her mind as she chewed.

"Right, show us where you got them and we'll pick one up for Douglas." Riva asked, taking a bite out of her own burger. Cheese, bacon, plus a beef patty with crispy onions and some kind of spice relish. Only American's could make something so bad for you so delicious.

"No thanks, I don't eat meat." Douglas said loudly "That stuff will give you cancer."

Riva rolled her eyes as Alex went from foodgasm to looking like she wanted to spit her mouthful out on the street.

"Well, life's too short to deprive my taste buds of a real American burger on my first trip to the States so I'll take my chances." Riva said, pointedly taking another enormous bite, her taste buds thanking her. She turned on her heel and watched as the two of them followed her, both haughtily avoiding getting too close to the other.

They weaved in and out of people loudly chattering as the flashing lights from the arcades cast manic shadows across their faces. When they reached the end of the pier it felt like breaking out of a bubble. It was still noisy but much less crowded. Riva made her way to an empty corner and stared out at the horizon while taking another massive bite of her burger.

"How can you not eat meat when you have access to food like this? I've never tasted bacon like this before." Riva said with her mouth full.

Douglas looked amused but also faintly repulsed. "I mean, you know exactly how much water and land it takes to farm beef? Not to mention the CO2 emissions from cattle farms and then how inhumanely they are slaughtered and..."

Out of the corner of her eye she saw Alex chuck what was left of her burger into the nearest bin.

Riva took another huge bite. "I get that, and I have huge respect for you being able to do it, but it's not a choice everyone can make. Try telling my mum to give up her famous cottage pie, she'd have a heart attack. At least I don't eat seafood, although that has a lot more to do with the fact that I don't like the taste of it than ethics."

Douglas smiled. "Me neither. After knowing what we can do how could you right?"

"I suppose. Although it's all the Mer ever eat. It was a nightmare down there at dinner, I really struggled. After almost a month I was practically starving. If you had went through that then you would have been kissing anyone who handed you a burger like this."

Douglas looked sceptical, but intrigued. "What is it like down there?"

"Impressive, intimidating, magical, a little creepy." Riva said, chewing thoughtfully, wiping grease off her chin with the back of her hand. "Oceana I mean. That's all I've ever really seen of the ocean, aside from the Scottish coast and this beach. I haven't really had a chance to go further since the Mer are technically hunting me down right now."

Douglas's eyes bugged. "Hunting you down?"

"Yeah, I escaped from the palace and took my father with me. He's human now by the way." Riva finished her burger and immediately wished that Alex hadn't thrown hers in the bin. She would have finished it too.

"Wait, how is that even possible? Human?" Douglas was looking more overwhelmed by the minute.

Riva shrugged, licking her lips. "Don't worry I don't think you have the power to turn anyone human. That's all Earth magic." She shook her head at his quizzical glance, Alex was despairing at her blunt delivery of all of this information. "Another long story. Hey, I have a question for you - how have you never been found? If you've known about your powers for ten years, and been using them, then surely you've went out far enough for them to track you."

Douglas looked confused. "What do you mean?"

Alex piped up, "Riva's mum thinks that as long as half-breeds stay close enough to land then the Mer can't detect you. Basically meaning that as long as you don't go too far out, you're protected."

"Half-breeds?" Douglas asked, clearly offended.

Alex blushed and looked deeply embarrassed at her choice of words. "I didn't mean it like that."

"Alex it's fine." Riva said dismissively. She'd never seen her friend look so flustered before. "We don't know how true that actually is. It's just a hunch that she has, and my mum doesn't always have the most reliable ideas. It's all contradicted anyway because when I had my accident and fell in to the water for the first time I was out past the headland and no-one found me."

"What do you mean found you?"

Riva leaned against the railing, the waves whooshing underneath them and looked at Douglas's face. "I'm sorry, I'm not doing a very good job of explaining."

"I can help fill in the gaps." Alex said, pushing in between Riva and Douglas.

Douglas pushed himself off the railings and stood in front of the two girls with his hands in his pockets. "Tell me everything." He said, looking between them both.

Riva and Alex shared a glance, both remembering the last time they tag-teamed a story like this. Hopefully Douglas would get a more coherent version than Kieran did. At least Douglas had the benefit of hearing the truth.

"Ok. Let me start from the beginning."

The three of them stood there as the crowds on the pier thinned out and the rollercoaster eventually ceased its clattering around as they gave Douglas the whole story. Everything that had happened to her since May. Leaving out only the details of Stuart's assault. She definitely didn't know him well enough to tell him about that. By the time she had finished, they were all sitting cross-legged on the wooden slats, the waves lapping calmly below them.

"You know, I've been waiting my whole life to hear something like this." Douglas said wistfully. "I can't believe that you only found out about your powers a few months ago and have learned more than I have in a decade."

Riva laughed, "Yeah but only because you weren't stupid enough to actually go looking for Mer though."

He had started fiddling with his bracelet again. "Well my mum never told me anything about my father before she died so I didn't even know where to start."

"Didn't you ever want to go out and explore though?" Riva asked. "I mean, we both know how amazing it feels to be in the water so why didn't you ever go deeper?"

Douglas shrugged. "I'm a surfer. I like to be on top of the waves not under them. I mean yeah it feels great to be able to breathe underwater and stuff but I always liked to get a good swell going for me and the boys instead you know?"

"Maybe, but it's lucky for you that you did, otherwise you would have ended up just like me and I'm pretty sure your father wouldn't have been as welcoming as mine was." She said, her bum slowly going numb on the stiff wooden planks. "I'm sorry about that by the way."

Douglas waved her off. "Nah, don't worry about it. I gave up hoping that my old man was a decent person a long time ago. When he didn't even turn up to my mum's funeral I knew he was a dead-beat. I just never thought that he could be a dead-beat at the bottom of the ocean." He said with a grim smile.

Riva looked out at the horizon, blanketed in stars. "I just hope we can stop him before he causes any more damage."

"Guys they're closing the pier, I think we should go." Said Alex.

They both looked up at her. Trying to ignore the pins and needles shooting up her calf, Douglas helped her to her feet.

"I know this is going to be hard for you." Riva said quietly.

Douglas across at her and cocked an eyebrow, "You mean following you down to an underwater kingdom to meet the father who doesn't know I exist and will quite probably try to kill me?"

"Yes." Riva said.

Douglas grinned, "Sounds like the most fun I've had all year."

12.

"Mum, Dad?" Riva called out as she knocked on the door of their motel room.

She was standing with both Alex and Douglas on the grimy landing, growing increasingly annoyed by the buzzing from the mosquito lamp.

"God they better not be doing it in the shower or something." She muttered.

"Seriously?" Douglas laughed.

"They were apart for almost twenty years, so they're basically two lovesick teenagers now. It's very romantic." Alex said wistfully.

Riva turned to look at Douglas. "It's nauseating."

Douglas looked inclined to agree. She resumed her hammering on the door.

"Come on guys, let us in!" she yelled.

Finally, the door opened to reveal her dad, bleary-eyed with his curls standing on end. He was pulling on his dressing gown. The woolly tartan dressing gown that he had insisted on packing and bringing to California. Where it was currently almost forty degrees outside.

"Sorry darling, jet leg you know?" he croaked out, blinking in the glow coming from the harsh strip light behind them, he didn't even notice the presence of the tall, handsome stranger standing beside her. "Come in."

"Dad, I think you need to wipe the sleep from your eyes." Riva looked pointedly at Douglas.

Her father blinked slowly a couple of times, rubbing his eyes comically until he finally registered all six feet-something of broad-shouldered Douglas. His mouth plopped open.

Maybe she needed to take her dad for an eye-test, given that the Mer tended to live longer than humans, despite the fact that he looked no older than forty, he could quite well be a couple of centuries old. Now that she thought about it, she was surprised he didn't have cataracts.

Her dad was still gaping open-mouthed at Douglas. "It can't be." He breathed.

Riva nodded excitedly. "Well, short of a DNA test we've got about as much evidence as we can get." She triumphantly grabbed his wrist, holding up the bracelet. "Starting with this."

Her dad leaned forward, eyes narrowed to peer at the medallion, giving Riva even more cause for concern about his eyesight, and then whooped loudly. She heard a small start come from the double bed inside the room as her mum finally woke up. Douglas held his hand out politely for her father to shake it.

"Riva tells me you're my uncle."

Her dad brushed Douglas's hand away, beaming, and instead wrapped his arms firmly around his nephew.

"I certainly am my boy. I certainly am." Her father replied, clapping him firmly on the back. "Let me get a good look at you." he pulled back, clasping either side of Douglas's head, giving him an appraising look. "Well, you wouldn't see the resemblance unless you were looking for it. You must favour your mother quite a bit. But there is something there of my brother, in the chin and the shape of your face."

Douglas didn't seem to know what to say to this as he shifted uncomfortably from one foot to the other, Riva's dad still grasping his cheeks.

He finally let go. "Lucky for you I say." Her dad continued with a wink, "My brother certainly isn't the best looking in the family."

"Dylan, don't be so rude." Riva's mum piped up from inside the darkened room, manically combing her fingers through her hair. Quite obviously trying to make herself somewhat presentable, she pulled her beach robe on over her pyjamas, creating quite a startling clash of colours.

"Come on mum, the man tried to kill both of us, he deserves a few insults." Riva said, making her way into the room, turning on lights.

"Fine, but I don't have to like it." her mum said, squinting. "I raised you to rise above Riva. Don't forget that." She peered at the harsh light, eyes narrowed.

"Don't tell me I need to take you for an eye test as well?" Riva huffed, sitting down on the mattress beside her, watching her squint at the room.

"What?" her mum asked, with a small huff of drowsiness.

Riva kissed the top of her head, inhaling her sweet-smelling shampoo. "Never mind."

Alex drifted into the room like an afterthought with a sideways glance at Douglas. Only Riva noticed her quick check in the mirror as if to verify her good looks before she settled herself into the chair quietly.

"I figured you were back. I heard Alex's outrageously inappropriate footwear clattering all the way down the hall." Em said drolly, appearing at the still-open door. "Do any of you know what time it is? I could have done without the yelling Riva, some of us are trying to overcome this jet lag." Her boyish grin was plastered on her face.

"Well we were getting eaten alive by mosquitoes outside and dad took his sweet time answering the door so what's a girl to do?" Riva said innocently.

"Go to her own room?" Em suggested, flopping down into the only other vacant chair.

Riva stuck her tongue out at her.

"So I'm guessing this is half-breed boy?" she asked, waving her hand up and down Douglas's body

"Can everyone please stop calling us half-breeds?" Riva piped up, "I know you guys don't mean it to be offensive-."

"Don't we?" Em interrupted with a sly grin and Riva threw the pillow at her.

"There has to be a better name for us."

Everyone in the room was silent, especially Douglas as he tried to keep track of all these new people he was meeting that suddenly seemed to know his secret.

"What about sirens?" her mum suggested quietly.

Alex shook her head. "That's a whole other type of mythical creature Helen. Plus it would send mixed messages about what you're able to do."

"Maybe kelpies?" Alex mused to herself but then shook her head. "No, that's not right either. You're people not horses, although we're getting closer in the folklore. Maybe selkies would work better, those stories did originate from our islands after all…"

"Is she always like this?" Douglas asked over Alex's ramblings.

Everyone in the room nodded.

"But of course selkies wouldn't work either since historically they appeared in seal skins." She looked across the room at Em. "Are there any Mer who have tails like seals, or are you all genetically predisposed to take after cetaceans?"

Douglas's head swivelled to the chair that Em was still lounging on. "Wait, you're one of us too?"

"No!" A look of disgust passed over Em's face which she quickly tried to disguise. A lifetime of being trained to hate humans wasn't erased overnight. She cleared her throat and then said regally, "I'm fully Mer."

Douglas looked down at her pale, obviously human, legs.

"But I don't…"

Em pointed to the garish collar around her neck. "I'm not wearing this as a fashion statement believe me."

"Okay…" he said, looking extremely confused.

Riva's dad clapped him on the shoulder. "In this family, just because you are born with a tail doesn't mean you will keep it."

Douglas looked like he might pass out, Alex was still muttering to herself and Em was looking thoroughly pleased that Riva's dad had inadvertently referred to her as part of the family.

"Welcome to the family Douglas. Another Demi-Mer to tip the scales in our favour."

Alex stopped her muttering and smiled warmly. All her talk of titans and Greek God's had finally given Riva an idea of what to call themselves. Something that would make them sound more acceptable and less like a blight on the Mer populace.

"Demi-Mer." Her father mused. "I like the sound of that."

Her mum started snoring softly on her shoulder and Riva looked around the room at her family, heart swelling with love.

"Alright cousin, let's talk about how we overthrow your daddy."

*

"Why are we hiking to see a sign?" Em asked, "Wouldn't you rather hike to a good viewpoint? I mean there are signs everywhere here…" she gestured to the stop sign at the intersection they had just passed.

Riva laughed. "Aw Em, this is probably lost on you but it's a very iconic sign. You'll see." She pulled at her t-shirt, the sun was so hot it was sticking to her.

When Alex had begged and begged to be able to do at least one touristy thing before they left California, Riva's parents had finally given in since their flight home wasn't until the evening. So that was how they had found themselves on the dustiest, hottest hiking trail in the entire state, on their way to see the Hollywood sign while her dad took her mum to a spa.

"Are you sure this is the right path?" Riva asked for the millionth time. "We haven't seen any other hikers for ages."

"It's fine. Most people don't come this way because there are coyotes or something."

"What?" Em exclaimed, looking at the scrubby brush that surrounded them, clearly feeling underprepared for attack on land.

Douglas raised his eyebrows. "Don't you mean mountain lions?"

Em looked ready to bolt back to the car while Douglas chuckled. Alex frowned at them but remained determined.

"This path is fine. I've seen loads of photos of people coming this way. Just less people know about it that's all. The blog I found it on was written by someone who lives here and she swears that this is the best place to see the sign. It's like one of those 'off-the-beaten-path type thingies."

She grabbed Em's arm and walked off on the decidedly un-beaten path through brambles. Em was reluctantly following, eyes still searching their surroundings as if something was about to pounce on her.

Bringing up the rear with Douglas, Riva couldn't help feeling slightly apprehensive. "Do mountain lions even come this close to the city?" she asked, readying her magic in case they would need it.

"Yeah sure, it's one of the only cities in the world where big cats will come into residential areas. But then I guess that's what we get for building on their land." He said.

Riva swallowed nervously and Douglas elbowed her in the ribs, chuckling. "I thought you said you could communicate with animals?"

Riva pushed him back. "Yeah in the ocean." She glanced behind them as if a pair of great yellow eyes were about to blink out within the bushes. "I haven't had cause to try it on land yet and I don't really want my first try to be when we're an inch from a mountain lion's claws."

"I think you'll be fine. With all the chattering Alex is doing she'll get eaten first." He replied with a cheeky grin.

Punching him again, they soon fell into step with each other and they walked in companionable silence. He had been true to his word in helping them. Calling his work immediately and putting in emergency vacation for a few weeks.

He had surprised them all when he said that he was an accountant, a far cry from the surfer-dude image they had all been forming of him. Alex's ears had certainly pricked up.

All that had been left to do was get him a seat on the plane and bring their own reservations forward by a week and they were Scotland-bound in just a few hours.

Riva couldn't quite believe how easy it had been. Perhaps Elder Iolana had done more than just prophesize their meeting. Although she had a sneaking suspicion that the rest of the challenge wouldn't be quite so simple.

In the quiet, desert heat, she heard the muffled ping from her phone coming from her backpack. As she saw the message she groaned.

"Oh no. I totally forgot." She muttered, coming to a stop.

Douglas stopped with her as Alex and Em meandered up the hill, oblivious.

Riva pulled at her ponytail, the ends already wet from the sweat on her back. "It's Kieran. I told him I would call him last night but then after we met up with you I totally forgot and then Alex was yammering on about this hike and you were calling your boss and my mum was on hold with the airline…"

"Your boyfriend?" Douglas asked.

Riva scrunched up her nose at the word, thinking. "Something like that." Was all she said.

"So you forgot to call one time, it happens." Douglas shrugged.

Riva fixed him with a despairing gaze. "It's not just one time. I do this all the time." She rubbed the toe of her tatty trainer into the dirt. "And he doesn't even get mad, he's just always so understanding it makes me feel even worse about it."

"So you want someone who will yell at you and get mad?" Douglas frowned.

Riva smacked his arm. "No of course not. I just want to deserve him that's all."

Douglas was shaking his head and muttering something about not understanding women at all.

I'm so sorry. Again. Something came up, but we're catching a flight back to Glasgow tonight. I'll be home by tomorrow. Can we talk then?

Heart in her mouth, she waited anxiously for his reply. Then when it came, she wasn't sure that she wanted it after all. It was just one word.

Sure x

"What's the matter?" Douglas asked.

She showed him the message. "Just one word. What is that even supposed to mean? Do you think he is mad at me now? Ugh, I feel like such an idiot."

"Nah, don't worry about it. The dude seems chill. He's probably just busy, and look he sent you a kiss. I don't ever send girls kisses at the end of a text. You're fine." He said brushing it off.

Riva continued to frown at the screen, wondering if she should message him back. Sighing, she shoved the phone into the back pocket of the rucksack and started walking again. She had no precedent for dating but she had a sneaking suspicion that an almost-boyfriend shouldn't be this much of an afterthought.

It was bad enough that she had all of the Stuart drama to deal with in their fledgling relationship, never mind her own scatter-brained-ness.

Thirty minutes later they finally caught up with Alex and Em who were in the middle of an Instagram photoshoot for Alex.

"Well you have to give her credit. This is a pretty spectacular view." Riva said appreciatively as Douglas' long, low whistle confirmed his agreement.

The rolling hills that were strangely bleached by the sun gave way to the sweeping cornflower blue sky and like oddly-shaped teeth, the Hollywood sign loomed in front of them.

"It's further away than I thought it would be though." Douglas whispered and Riva poked him in the ribs.

As they walked closer, Riva had to work to contain her giggles. "Poor Em, she's trying really hard to be enthusiastic, but it's so obvious that she has no idea what we're doing." She whispered to Douglas, making him laugh as Em was now on one knee as instructed by Alex to get the best photo angle.

"Well she's much better at pretending to be interested than I am." He muttered.

Riva smiled and gave him a nudge. "That's a family trait. My mum calls it my glass face. We can't ever hide what we're thinking. It's a real pain."

She made a show of assembling a smile on her face and went to save Em from Alex.

"But it's only showing my face." Em said, blinking at the screen.

"Yes it's on selfie mode, just press the button with the arrows at the bottom and it will flip around." Alex sighed.

Riva scooted in between them just in time as Em was looking more and more inclined to hurl the phone off the cliff.

"Here, let me." She said, Em threw her a grateful glance and walked off to look at the view with Douglas instead.

Five minutes later they were passing around the water bottle and cereal bars that Riva's mum had packed them, all in dire need of a break and some shade.

"These are really great Riva thanks!" Alex said happily, thrusting the screen in Riva's face. Mouth full of cereal bar, she couldn't do anything more than nod and mumble.

Douglas crossed his muscular arms, his workout shirt straining across his chest. "I expect these will be posted all over Instagram in about five minutes?" Douglas asked.

Alex put her phone back in her stylish bum bag. "Considering I don't have any signal out here, no. Not in five minutes they won't." She answered haughtily.

"Just as soon as you get back to the motel then."

Riva glanced at Douglas warningly, but saw what Alex couldn't. That there was no spite behind his words, he was just thoroughly enjoying teasing her. And she was giving him the exact reaction that he was looking for.

This is going to get interesting...

Before Alex could make a bitchy retort, Riva stepped in again. "How about we all take some pictures? Then we can all look back and remember the whirlwind trip we took to California."

"Great idea!" Em said, catching on quickly and went to stand between Douglas and Alex. The two of them stopped glaring at one another long enough for Riva to take some snapshots of the three of them with the sign in the background.

"Alright now you two!" Alex said, shooing Douglas and Riva together.

Trying not to stand like two family members who had been strangers to each other until the day before, they put an arm around each other and smiled for the camera.

Photoshoot done, Alex took one last look at the view. "What do you guys think? Was it a good choice?" clearly proud at having found this secret spot.

"I would have gone to Disneyland myself." Douglas said.

Watching as Alex's face turned puce, Riva saw him stifle a grin. "But we never would have found this spot without you."

Confused at his not-quite compliment, Alex just stood there brows furrowed, looking like a lost puppy.

Enjoying watching her try and fail to figure him out, Douglas just scratched the back of his head and started walking back down the hill with Em.

Alex turned to Riva. "I mean logistically Disneyland would never have worked. I mean when you factor in queuing time and traffic we would have been able to do, like, three rides tops and would have missed the fireworks." She pouted.

"I don't think that's what he meant." Riva soothed. "I'm glad we did this instead."

Secretly she would have much preferred a trip to Disneyland even if it would have been a short one, but there was no way she was about to mention that to her best friend when she was already one hairs-breadth away from a freak-out.

Trying not to show visible relief when they finally turned off of the hiking trail and on to the main road, she drained the last of the water from her bottle, throat itchy from all the dust.

"Where did you park the car again Douglas?" she asked, scanning the trail, wondering how much further they had to go.

He pointed behind a small hill. "It's just round that corner at the back of those houses."

Riva could see the roofs shining in the sun, wavy lines radiating off them in the heat. She was dying for air conditioning, or a dip in the ocean.

Turning another corner, they heard scuffling sounds.

"Stop." Riva breathed, pulling the other two girls to a halt and unlinking their arms.

"What is it?" Em asked, automatically assuming a defensive stance, looking worriedly down at her feet. "A mountain lion? Cayato?"

Alex rolled her eyes and hissed. "It's pronounced coyote."

"I don't know what it is but both of you shut up." Riva barked.

Alex looked around, frightened. "Spidey senses telling you something?"

The group stood frozen to the spot as Riva tried to cast out her consciousness. Then out of nowhere, bursting from the trees on their right…

"Aaaahh what is it?!" Screamed Em, jumping behind Alex to save herself.

Relaxing, letting out a relieved breath, Riva watched as the possum darted into the trees on the other side of the path.

Douglas snorted loudly with laugher and even though Alex looked like she was biting her lip to keep from laughing as well, she shook her head at Douglas for being so insensitive and turned to comfort Em. "It's just a possum, don't worry. They aren't dangerous unless you threaten them. Strange though, aren't they usually nocturnal?"

"How should I know?" Riva shrugged. "Come on daredevils, let's get back to civilization and see if we can't find another burger like the one we had last night shall we?"

At least Douglas's look of disgust at her mention of processed meat stopped his chuckling. Then his face turned pensive.

"I'll take you guys to my favourite restaurant." His voice grew quieter, almost shy. "My mum used to take me there every Sunday night."

Riva smiled at him. "I'd like that."

Em didn't talk much during the car right there, still thoroughly embarrassed at losing her badass credibility over a large rodent. But twenty minutes later, Douglas had parked his car in a seriously questionable-looking part of town and all three girls shared a look as they slammed the doors shut.

"What?" he asked, hands shoved deep into his pockets, flip flops now firmly back on his feet post-hike.

Alex looked around like she wanted to douse herself in a bottle of hand sanitizer.

Douglas pursed his lips and nodded. "Alright. I thought you wanted the best burgers in town but if you're too good for this place…" he went to open the driver's door again but Riva quickly stopped him.

"No, don't be daft. It's fine. We're starving anyway." She pushed him up the street, keeping her feet out of the puddles that lined the pavement, silently praying that the general state of the area was not indicative of the hygiene in the kitchen of wherever they were going to be eating.

Em strolled confidently behind them, trying very hard not to look fazed by anything that was going on around them.

"How much further is it?" Alex asked, tiptoeing between discarded food wrappings and several questionable stains in her Air Jordans.

Douglas pointed. "Just a couple of streets ahead, first right and round the corner. It doesn't look like much but we used to love it here." He grinned, dark eyes sparkling wickedly. "I might even allow myself to have a burger in her honour today."

Riva smiled back at him, she thought it was sweet that he wanted to share such a special part of his history with them.

That was until something stopped her.

"Ouch, Riva. Don't just stop in the middle of the street like that I was right behind you." Alex complained, grabbing Em around the neck to stop herself from falling. The Mer girl made a strangled squawk and shoved her away.

"What is it?" Douglas asked.

She held up a hand to shush them as she listened.

Alex tutted. "Don't tell me it's another possum. Make sure Em has sufficient warning this time so she doesn't wet herself."

Riva blocked out Em's swipe at Alex and listened to whatever it was that was telling her something was wrong. She could hear dragging feet on concrete, the scruff of rubber soles.

Summoning her magic, her eyes and the mark on her palm began to glow.

"No. It's not a possum." She said, her voice taking on that otherworldly quality that it did whenever she summoned her magic.

She turned into the next street, stepping carefully through a child-sized gap in an otherwise locked chain link fence. A pile of disused cars waiting to be crushed stood between her and the noises. The heat of the sun in this concrete jungle was suffocating and her face was stinging with sweat.

Douglas stepped through the fence towards her. "Riva, come back here, Alex was kinda right, it isn't the safest neighbourhood and I don't want-" his words choked off in surprise when she turned and he saw her now-golden eyes. "Holy shit."

But Riva, still focused on whatever was making that space behind her navel tighten in alarm, simply turned back towards the noises.

"Let her go." Alex whispered to Douglas, making her way through the fence just behind her.

Riva heard the hard smack of something on metal, a dry crunch that accelerated the growing panic in her veins. Straining her ears she tried to work out why she felt drawn towards it. Was it just someone working in the junkyard? It definitely wasn't an animal. All she knew was that she had a very bad feeling about whatever was behind that pile of scrapped cars – so why then did it feel almost familiar?

She blocked out the pounding of the three racing hearts behind her and pushed her senses to the limit. Heavy breathing, the acrid stench of sweat, and fear. Followed by… excitement?

Riva's stomach twisted the exact same moment they all heard a muffled voice cry out.

"No!" she growled.

Golden eyes ablaze, she launched herself into a sprint and she was swiftly around the small heap of cars, trainers squeaking on the hot tarmac. A large grey wall met her, along with a very faded sign reading 'Tony and Sons Motors.'

In the shade underneath this sign was a man pressing a woman down behind some tarpaulin. With her consciousness still expanded she could feel the girl's panic even as her muffled shouts grew weaker and the scent of the man's excitement was enough to make her gag.

Without even stopping to think and with one swipe of her hand, her Mark a golden arc in the air, the man went flying. The gust of wind she had summoned throwing him into the chain link fence with a crash. The girl sat up, whimpering as Riva rushed towards her.

"Are you okay?"

The girl let out a choked scream as she beheld Riva's eyes. Already terrified, she scrambled to her feet and pushed past her. Knocked off-balance, Riva's hand hit the hot concrete, little stones embedding themselves in her palm.

She watched as the girl sprinted past Douglas, Em and Alex who had caught up with her. Em tried to intercept her as she flew past, but missed by a hairs-breadth. Turning to Riva, she looked for direction.

Riva shook her head, breathing hard thanks to the magic that was pooling in her veins. "Let her go." she said.

She hoped that the girl was able to run to a safe place, that she had stopped the attack in time.

She looked across to where the attacker now lay in a heap, groaning in front of the fence. His dark green shirt soaked through with sweat from his exertions.

Riva's mouth went dry.

Another one. How many were there? How many men thought that it was okay to treat women this way? How many had gotten away with it?

He was scrambling to his feet as Riva advanced. The smirk that drifted across his face as he beheld a teenager disappeared quickly as he noticed the traces of her magic. Power was emanating off of her body in waves.

"What are you?" He asked, his voice trembling.

Riva lifted her right palm up in front of her face, her Goddess Mark burning white-hot.

"Justice." She said, releasing a bolt of lightning from her palm.

"Riva no!" Alex's scream rent the air but it was already too late.

It connected with his chest, strong enough to lift him several feet into the air against the metal fence. Blood was rushing in her ears and her nerves were practically singing with her power as she held him there, twitching and writhing as she shocked him.

His cries of pain fed her magic. Each one telling her that she was doing the right thing. He needed to be punished, like she had failed to adequately punish Stuart.

This was what it felt like to be a Goddess. This was what she was meant to do. Protect the weak and avenge the broken. Nature was ruthless and so was she.

She lifted her left hand up in front of her and a second bolt of lightning cracked its way across the junkyard. Her hair was flying around her, eyes aflame as her magic sang its song of revenge.

"Riva, stop!" Alex cried again.

It wasn't her voice, nor the slight pressure on her arm that told her that Alex had tried to pull her away, but the whimper of pain that finally broke her focus.

The lightning disappeared with one last almighty crack and the man fell to the ground in a smoking heap. He didn't move.

Turning, she saw Alex lying on the ground several feet away, Douglas and Em leaning over her.

"Hey, hey Alex. Open your eyes." Douglas was shouting, shaking her shoulders.

Fear pooled in Riva's stomach. Had she done this? What had happened?

Alex's eyes fluttered open and she swatted Douglas away so she could sit up. He gave her enough space, but remained close by her side. "Are you okay?" he asked, concerned.

Alex shook her head from side to side like she was trying to clear water from her ears.

"Yeah I think so." She said, coughing once and then wincing. "I guess I shouldn't have touched her."

All three of them turned to look at Riva, still standing there, the glow from her eyes and Mark fading fast as she realised what had just happened. She had hurt her best friend.

Panting as the magic drained away, she looked over to the body of the man she had practically been barbecuing and felt like she was going to be sick. Looking down at the Mark on her hand that was fading back to an innocent pink, her stomach rolled.

"Oh my god." She gasped, "What have I done?"

Alex, quickly regaining her wits, scrambled over to her, just a little unsteady on her feet.

"Don't panic. I know why you did it Riva, you're ok and I'm ok. You're safe."

Riva shook her head, another wave of nausea shooting through her.

Alex grabbed her head and forced her to look into those chocolate brown eyes. "We are safe. Do you hear me? Safe. He's not going to hurt you."

Breath coming in great gasps, Riva started shaking. She could feel the heat coming off of the body of the man lying behind her. "No it's not, I-I killed h-him."

She wrenched her face out of Alex's grip and dove for the junkheap just in time for her stomach to empty itself up into the hollowed out seat of a car. The retching continued until her eyes were streaming and her stomach was cramping.

"Honey you were just trying to protect that girl." Alex said as she brushed Riva's hair out of her face. "Anyone in your situation would have done the same."

Laughing somewhat hysterically, Riva sat back heavily against the hot metal of the car, avoiding looking at the chain-link fence. "Not everyone would have had the means to kill him though." She thrust her Marked palm up under her friend's nose. "Having this is like walking around with a loaded gun I can't control. The magic makes me *want* to hurt people." She swallowed as another wave of nausea hit. "I was *enjoying* it."

Alex's eyes were filling up with tears, her face full of pity and concern.

"Don't do that." Riva growled. "You aren't allowed to pity me. It was just that g-, that girl sounded so scared. I cou- couldn't just do nothing." She said, her voice cracking as angry tears threatened. "There was no-one there to save me."

"I know. I know." Alex said, putting an arm around her shoulders. "And I don't pity you. I just wish I could have been there to save you like you saved that girl."

Riva was still shaking, despite the swelteringly hot day.

Alex looked her up and down and then over at Douglas who had been watching the two of them, not quite understanding their conversation. "I think she's going into shock. Do you have any blankets in the car?" she asked Douglas.

Looking bewildered, he replied. "No, but I might have a couple of beach towels."

"They'll do. Run there and bring them back as soon as possible." Alex fished around in her oversized backpack for her recently purchased reusable water flask.

"Is she going to be ok?" he asked, hovering uncertainly, looking like he wanted to get closer but the strong smell of vomit now emanating from the shell of the car was making him think twice.

Alex fixed him with a glare. "What part of any of this makes you think that any of us are going to be okay?"

He nodded once and took off back to his car.

"I meant it." Riva whispered once he was gone.

"What?" Alex asked.

"I meant to kill him."

Alex squeezed her tighter. "No you didn't sweetie, you just lost control. But you've been working on it to get-."

Riva was shaking her head. She thought that she would have been sobbing by now but she felt strangely numb. "No you're wrong. I knew exactly what I was doing. I could feel my magic telling me that he needed to pay. I wanted him to suffer. I didn't want to let him go."

Alex went very still. Her arm was gone from around Riva's shoulders and then Alex was in front of her, beautiful face set.

"I can't pretend to know what you went through. But if it had happened to me, I think I would want him to die too." Alex said.

Something about the matter-of-fact way that she said it, reached Riva in a way that her earlier words hadn't.

"Really?" she asked in a small voice.

Alex nodded once, grimly. "Really."

With that small admission, Riva finally felt less alone.

Em suddenly shouted from over by the fence. "He's breathing!"

Riva's heart jolted painfully in her chest and pushed herself up from the ground unsteadily, Alex helping her to her feet.

"What?! Are you sure?"

Em was crouched over the man's head and they watched as she pulled out a small pen-knife.

"What the hell are you doing? Trying to finish the job?" Alex cried, sprinting over to her, bright-white trainers flashing across the concrete.

Em pushed her off, "Of course not." She held the blade of the small knife up to his nose and they both watched as his breath steamed the surface, "See?"

Riva clutched her chest, as if trying to put the recently broken pieces of herself back together. Her breathing was coming in short, shallow gasps and she felt dizzy.

He isn't dead. I didn't kill him.

But looking at the prone figure lying on the ground between Em and Alex, she could only see Stuart. Screwing up her eyes, she tried to ignore the memories but they came to her unbidden. His eyes bugging as she forced the ocean into his lungs, the blood seeping from cuts on his back as she dragged him over the shingle. And most of all, that same feeling of revenge. Of justice.

What hope did she have of ever having a normal relationship, of ever being a normal teenager again when her life was this ludicrous? How could she ever hope to hold Kieran's hand, or to kiss him, never mind anything else, when all she ever saw was Stuart's face? When all she ever felt were his hands pushing her down into the sand?

Her magic hadn't allowed her to feel any remorse, nor a shadow of guilt while she had been using it. It was only after hurting her best friend that she had been able to break its hold on her. Rubbing her Mark, she bit her lip, worried. What was she becoming?

Even now she could see Alex holding her right hand gingerly in her left. There had been so much electricity coursing through Riva in that moment, she was surprised her best friend was still standing.

The panic was coming in waves now and she had no idea how to turn it off. She reached wildly towards the car for some support but the roof was burning hot in the sun. She couldn't calm herself with the Earth like she had gotten used to doing, and she didn't want to risk bringing her magic to the surface again in case she decided to finish the job. She had known that her magic was changing her, Gaia had told her to expect as much, but this wasn't who she wanted to be.

"Alex..." she called out weakly, stars dancing in front of her eyes as she struggled to catch a breath. "Alex, I-."

Then her vision went black and she felt herself hit the hard concrete. The stars in front of her eyes burst, creating a writhing blackness which then slowly grew lighter until it felt like rays of sunlight were dancing on her closed eyelids.

13.

"Awaken, my child."

She would recognize the voice of the Goddess anywhere.

"Gaia?" she asked, fighting to open her eyes, blinking furiously.

The image of the Goddess swam into view, bathed in the golden light of sunset, which was dim enough for Riva to open her eyes without pain.

"How did I get here?" she asked, sitting up delicately as her head span. She definitely didn't want to vomit in front of her.

"Your mind sought refuge in the only place it knew would not cause harm to yourself or others." Gaia said, then after a pause, "Your abilities trouble you."

Biting her lip, she traced the swirl of her Mark with her fingers, thinking about the lightning that had arced from her palms only minutes ago.

"When they get out of control they do."

Gaia smiled, rainbows bursting forth from her fingertips to leap across the meadow like some manic kids cartoon. "I have never seen you lose control of your powers my daughter."

She hugged her knees to her chest and looked up at her, astounded. "Are you serious? I lose control of them all the time! Look at what just happened, I almost killed a man!"

"What you perhaps perceive as a loss of control is actually the appropriate response." The Goddess said wisely. "Perhaps it is just your society's restrictions that deems them otherwise."

Riva shook her head, confused. "Societies restrictions? What does that even mean? I'm pretty sure that murder is frowned upon in any society."

The Goddess stared at her with those amber eyes, eyes that seemed to look down into her very soul.

Riva suppressed a shiver, sometimes she forgot just how powerful Gaia must have been centuries ago. If all Riva possessed was a sliver of her power then she didn't even want to think about it.

"Nature is a very complex mechanism." Gaia explained slowly, glancing around the meadow and its surrounding woods. Following her gaze, Riva swore there was someone looking back. Noticing the same thing she did, Gaia spoke again, bringing Riva's attention back to her. "You know what power lies within you. The earth must make the choice between who lives and who dies almost constantly. Death is a natural part of life."

"I swear if you quote *The Lion King* one more time..." Riva muttered.

Gaia held up her hand. "You must realise that you are more than human now. If you take life it is to ensure the balance, to protect, or to nurture those who have been oppressed."

Riva had a brief flashback to when she had been sitting in Lillian's garden, enjoying a carton of Ribena in the sun.

"If one ae them shrubs isnae growin' right then he willnae get enough sun. Then it's my job tae uproot the plant above and put him in the light."

Feeling cold, despite the warmth of the setting sun, she hugged her knees tighter. "So I'm supposed to choose who lives and who dies based on what they have done?"

The Goddess smiled sympathetically. *"No dear one. The natural world exists for the most part in harmony with itself. Sustainable. However where that delicate balance has been disrupted, you may step in to right it."*

For the first time, Riva thought that the Goddess might just be making sense. But there was still that niggling feeling of guilt in the pit of her stomach. "I don't want to kill anyone." She whispered, a single tear falling down her cheek.

Gaia reached down and wiped away the tear with one finger, leaving a tingling, warm trail behind. *"Some things are inevitable my daughter. Trust in yourself and you will find the answers you seek."*

The Goddess faded from view, leaving her sitting among the wildflowers.

Trailing her fingers across the daisies, she sighed heavily and wished she had a reason to stay longer. Feeling like someone was watching her, she turned towards the tree line.

Where a man in a three-piece suit of all things was lounging against a tree trunk.

Thoroughly confused, she blinked. When she opened her eyes again, he was gone.

This crap ends now.

Grumbling, she got to her feet, marching through the stream and over to the tree line. This mystery figure – man – had been driving her crazy for days.

Looking over her shoulder to make sure that the Goddess wouldn't appear again and chastise her for wandering off unsupervised, she got to her feet and padded over to the trees, keeping her eyes peeled. Excitement building inside of her at the thought of finally unveiling the mystery figure.

The setting sun made the light dim under the broad boughs of the oak trees. She almost jumped out of her skin when a starling burst from the branches, trilling its song. Then again as she clambered over a tree root when a squirrel darted across her path.

I'm being ridiculous. There's no-one here.

"Isn't there?"

She whirled on the spot, the soft light of the sunset through the branches making it difficult for her eyes to adjust. Side-stepping out of the sun's rays she saw him. Standing a few metres away in the middle of the path where she had just walked, was the most beautiful man she had ever seen. He was tall and slender, golden skinned with dark hair that looked so soft she immediately imagined running her fingers through it. Completely out of place in the woods, she hadn't been seeing things, he really was wearing a suit, complete with brogues of all things.

"Going hiking are we?" she asked him, mouth dry, unsure of how to proceed. Unsure of if she was in danger.

He chuckled, his strange amber eyes twinkling. "If I was I think I'm a little better off than you are." He nodded to her own attire, covered in dust from her hike. Still wearing her sweat-soaked t-shirt and shorts, she felt thoroughly underdressed next to him. She tried to subtly move her hair in front of her chest to cover herself up.

She looked around, they were completely alone. She knew that she should have felt scared. The man in front of her was clearly more than a man. His power was so tangible she could almost taste it. The usually chattering forest had grown quiet.

"Who are you?" she asked.

He chuckled again. "So direct, Riva."

She narrowed her eyes. "How do you know my name?"

Hands in his pockets, he casually walked towards her. "This isn't your first visit to Eden."

Crossing her arms over her chest, she replied. "And it isn't yours either. Make a habit of scaring teenage girls do you?"

Smirking, he stopped, inspecting his nails like he had nothing better to do all day. "No. Eden is my home. Although the word betrays the reality let me tell you."

The smile slipped from her face as she realized what he was. "You're a God." She breathed. Gaia had told her that there were others here, those who had survived and lived off of the remnants of their power within Eden's boundaries.

He laughed bitterly. "Why thank you for giving me what I assume was meant to be a compliment." He replied.

She was now thoroughly confused. "So… you're not a God?"

He shook his head, his raven black hair shining in the sunlight. "No. I'm not a God."

"Then what are you?" She hardly wanted to know. For some reason her pulse was racing in her ears and she felt breathless.

He took several slow, deliberate steps towards her until she could smell him. Her breath caught in her throat as she met his amber eyes again. He was utterly intoxicating. His smell, his voice, his face. He was barely three steps away from her now. Why couldn't she move? Why didn't she want to?

His full lips parted, the bottom one slightly too big for the top as he said. "I'm a titan."

"Um, sorry, a w-what?" she stuttered, heart fluttering as his strangely captivating scent washed over her again. The word sparked a faint recognition in her mind but she was so lost in his eyes that she could barely remember her own name.

He smiled lazily, eyes sparkling mischievously as he fiddled with the collar of his shirt. "You have already met my mother. Have become quite well acquainted with her in fact." He looked her up and down slowly, with enough appreciation to make her feel self-conscious. "I see a lot of her in you now. Too much if truth be told."

That comment stung more than she should have allowed it to and she shook her head to clear her thoughts.

"W-why are you wearing a suit in a forest?" she asked, immediately regretting asking such a dumb question.

He laughed again and looked at her like she was something much more interesting than she thought she was. "I tell you I'm a titan and all you ask me is why I choose to wear a suit?"

Riva didn't want to admit that she still had no idea what a titan actually was so she stayed quiet.

"Is there something else you would prefer to see me in?" He asked in a hushed voice, leaning in to her.

The thought crossed her mind before she could stop it and she blushed deeply. He grinned wickedly at her.

"Not today my beauty." He said, his voice deepening until she felt her very core turn molten.

"Why did you summon me here?" she asked, mentally berating herself for acting like a damsel in distress around him. "What do you want with me?"

Again, that glorious laugh. "Oh there are many things I want with you Riva, but none of them appropriate for this conversation."

Her pulse quickened again.

There was a sound to their left, out by the meadow – like the cross between a lightning strike and a wave breaking. They both turned and she saw the barest glimpse of fear cross his face.

Who could possibly make someone with so much obvious power feel scared?

"Our time is up I'm afraid." He said, that cool exterior back in place as he smoothed the jacket of his suit. He reached out to pick up her hand. Hardly daring to breathe, he kissed the back of it, sending jolts of electricity scattering through Riva's body so she could barely think straight. "Until we meet again."

Those eyes, those impossibly beautiful eyes left her face as he turned to leave and Riva could feel Eden slipping away.

"Wait!" she called out after him, not wanting him to leave just yet. "What's your name?"

He turned once again and the look he gave her sent a thrill of both fear and anticipation though her.

"Cronos." He said with a secret smile.

Eden faded away and as much as she wanted to cling on to the image of him, the swirling darkness took her again.

*

"Riva for goodness sake if you don't wake up I swear I'll have Em throw you over her shoulder." Alex was whispering furiously in her ear.

She opened her eyes, blinking in the harsh sunlight that was a far cry from the gold-bathed sunset meadow. Thankfully Alex's long blonde hair was blocking most of it from view like a perfectly styled curtain.

"Sorry, I'm back." She replied sitting up, thoughts completely muddled. "How long have I been out?"

Alex looked nervously over her shoulder towards where Em was still kneeling beside the unconscious would-be rapist. "Just a minute or so. Douglas isn't back from the car with the towels yet."

Time must move differently in Eden. It had felt as if she has been gone for at least half an hour.

Riva swallowed, her throat dry but her hands steady. "It's ok. I don't need them. I will take the water though." Alex handed the giant bottle to her and she drained the whole thing in one, the water's cool sweetness restoring her. "Thanks." She gasped, handing the empty bottle back. "We need to finish our discussion about the titans."

Completely thrown, Alex narrowed her eyes. "That's random."

Riva dumped the water bottle back into Alex's beach bag. "Not when you find out who I was just talking to."

Alex looked intrigued but at that moment, Douglas came careening around the broken cars with two large beach towels and a second bottle of water clutched under his arm.

"Here you go, I hope this is enough." He said as he handed them to Alex, clearly feeling out of his depth.

"Thanks." She said briskly, grabbing it without looking at him and ignoring Riva's protests, fitting one of the towels snugly around her shoulders.

"Really, I don't need it. My issues aren't physical." Riva muttered, glancing quickly at Douglas she braced herself to say the words. "Being beaten to within an inch of my life and almost raped tends to leave a mental scar once the physical ones disappear."

Douglas's eyes widened as he finally understood Riva's reaction.

"I know. But I'll be here every step of the way to help you through it." said Alex, squeezing her shoulder.

Riva fixed her best friend with a stare. "You can't be. Not anymore."

"What?" Alex's brows furrowed, shock palpable on her face.

Riva sighed. "If you stay around this magic you will just get hurt again. I can't risk that."

Ales was already shaking her head. "You just gave me a little jolt. Like playing a game of operation and accidentally touching the sides." Alex huffed.

Riva scoffed. "You never touch the sides."

"Yeah, surgeon in training remember?" Alex muttered sadly, looking down at her hands.

That was when Riva caught a glimpse of the angry red blisters covering Alex's right hand.

"Crap, Alex! Why the hell didn't you tell me sooner?" She grabbed her slender wrist and twisted it up so she could see it properly. The right hand was swollen tightly and yellow pus was oozing from the burst blisters. So much for surgeon's hands, this hand couldn't even hold a pen let alone a scalpel.

"It's fine, we'll go to the hospital in a minute, just don't touch it or put anything on it until we get to the burns unit." Alex said warningly.

Riva's heart broke at how brave her friend was trying to be. "I'm so sorry Alex. I never meant to hurt you." she whispered.

Douglas moved over to her and gently put his arm around Alex's shoulders, "I'll drive."

Alex looked up at him in surprise, waiting for the sarcastic comment, but when none came she let him help her up.

"No." said Riva, quickly pulling the towel off her own shoulders and scrambling to her feet. A quick glance over her shoulder told her that Em was still huddled over the rapist. Whether to make sure that he was alright or that he never got up again she wasn't quite sure.

"What do you mean no?" Douglas asked, arm still across Alex's shoulders protectively.

"I mean no, Alex isn't going to the hospital." She said.

Both of them stared at her, perplexed.

"She needs the hospital Riva. Heck she needed the hospital ten minutes ago." He made to move her towards the hole in the fence but Riva reached out and grabbed her good hand.

"Ow!" Alex gasped in pain as the movement jolted her and Douglas dropped his arm, face thunderous.

"Let me fix this." Riva breathed, looking up into her friend's face.

Understanding dawned on Alex and she nodded in relief, holding out the burned hand.

She needed to stop being afraid of her magic. Gaia was right. She was no longer human, those rules no longer applied to her, whether that was ethical or not. But whatever mistakes she did make, she could also fix.

Tapping in to her magic, she let the palm that held her Mark float above Alex's ruined hand.

As she summoned the Earth, she felt that familiar rush of exhilaration that came with it and she allowed that essence to wrap its way around the three of them. She saw Douglas start in surprise at the breeze and the summery scents of lavender and fresh hay that soon encompassed them.

The glow from her Mark intensified and then drifted, covering Alex's hand in bright white light.

"This feels insane." Alex breathed, a joyous smile on her face. "Like I've got pins and needles all over it."

Removing her hand, Riva let her magic melt away. Feeling stronger in the fact that she had been able to control it. Or if what Gaia had said was true, guide it appropriately to her will. Her friend was now standing, staring at her perfectly healed palm in disbelief.

"It's good as new." Douglas said, grasping Alex's wrist to get a closer look, "The burns are completely gone." He shook his head. "The skin is perfect."

Alex blushed. "You think my skin is perfect?"

They both seemed to realise their closeness at the same time and Douglas took one giant step back and cleared his throat. "You know what I mean, perfectly healed."

Alex rubbed her palms together slowly, as if testing it out. "Don't worry, I won't let it go to my head." She replied breathlessly.

"Hey guys," Em called over, "I hate to interrupt whatever weirdness is going on between you three but this guy isn't looking so good."

Riva steeled herself and walked over.

Ignoring the guilty weight in her stomach, she assessed the damage she had done. She stared at the tattered clothes and burns that seeped all across his body, skin charred and angrily pink in places. Alex's hand had been nothing compared to this guy's body.

She didn't need the doctor in training behind her to tell her that even if they took him to the hospital that he probably wouldn't make it.

She sighed, summoning her magic.

As her eyes began to glow again, her three friends began to protest.

"What are you doing?" Douglas asked.

"Riva, calm down, you don't want to do this." Alex said.

"Should we stop her?" Em asked half-heartedly.

She ignored them and held out her hand towards this stranger she had never met but who now had made the second biggest impact on her life. Two men. Two would-be rapists. One who had taught her to fear, and the other who had taught her that she was the one who should be feared.

Letting the healing powers of the Earth pour from her Mark to cover his body, Em quickly jumped out of the way and grabbed her other hand.

"Riva..." Em stepped towards her, "Are you sure this is what you want?"

As the healing magic left her and set the man's body afire with that same white glow that had coated Alex's palm, she looked into her friend's jade green eyes.

Em's face was serious.

"I've taken life before. Both human and Mer. I know what that costs someone." A shadow passed across her face. "But sometimes it has to be done."

By way of answer, Riva knelt down and rolled up the man's tattered sleeve to reveal a perfectly healthy dermis layer. Lifting her Marked palm in front of her face she waited until it was glowing white-hot and then pressed it forcefully onto the man's forearm.

"Aaargh!" he woke abruptly, screaming in pain and fear.

Looking down at him with nothing but contempt on her face she replied. "He will live. But now any time he thinks of doing what he just did, that is what he will feel."

Releasing him, he now had a shiny brand on his forearm that looked exactly like the Mark on her palm. Em smiled ruthlessly at her as they both listened to the man's whimpers of pain from the still-glowing brand.

She threw his arm back down as if it would contaminate her and turned to Em.

"Now do what you do best." She said in a cold voice, turning away from him for the last time.

Em smirked and looked around for a dull weapon.

"Riva what did you do?" Alex asked, sounding frightened as she turned to her.

"I gave him a second chance to be a better human being. But if he chooses wrongly, there will be consequences." She said, grabbing Alex's hand and pushing Douglas towards the fence. "Come on, let's get out of here."

She marched them out of the depressing junkyard and slipped through the fence with a clatter. Briefly closing her eyes she listened to Em test the weight of her weapon of choice by tossing it from one hand to the other. The metal pipe a dull smack in her strong hands.

Em bent down in front of him, lopsided grin across her face as she tapped the pipe against her palm. His cries of pain and protest ceased as Em smacked him over the head with the rusty exhaust.

Alex and Douglas turned back at the sound, worried looks on their faces.

"I hope he's up to date with his tetanus shots." Was all Riva said.

14.

The mad twittering of sparrows outside her window woke her up. Realising that she had one leg out of the blankets that was now an icicle had her burrowing deeper back under her duvet for some warmth.

Peeking out from under her eyelids, she saw that the day had dawned pewter grey with a heavy chance of rain. Suppressing a groan she rolled over and wished that they were back in sunny California.

Rubbing her eyes, she vaguely remembered the dream she had been having and blushed. She had no idea why she always dreamed of eyes, but the burning amber pits of desire that she had fallen into last night had been nothing like she had ever dreamed of before.

She avoided thinking about who those eyes belonged to. They certainly hadn't been the chocolate-brown hue that fit the boy she was supposed to be dating.

Judging by how light it was outside, they had slept until late afternoon, jet-lag having hit them the minute they got back home. They had barely been able to do more than tell Douglas where the bathroom was before everyone passed out.

Gathering her courage, she flung the covers off, grabbed her dressing-gown and slippers and nudged Em in the back with her toe from where she was snoring violently in her nest of blankets on the floor.

"Come on, get a move on or we'll never sleep tonight." She croaked, opening her door with a creak.

Em just gave out a long moan and rolled back over again.

Oh well, her choice.

Padding down the stairs, the house was quiet so she figured that everyone else was still asleep. Her parent's cosy in their bedroom and Douglas on his air mattress in the living room. Sighing, she was just thinking about how she might make herself a hot chocolate and enjoy the peace and quiet for a minute when someone started hammering loudly at the door.

Jumping out of her skin, she almost skidded down the last two steps.

"Rise and shine! I brought coffee!" Alex said cheerfully, bouncing through the door with a tray of take-away coffee cups from the café. "I knew you would need someone to help you get over the jet lag. Just call me your alarm clock!"

"Jeez, how many have you had already?" Riva asked, wishing not for the first time that her best friend had a volume button.

Without giving an answer, Alex marched herself into the living room and through to the kitchen. By some miracle her pounding at the door hadn't woken Douglas, who was lying sprawled out across the air mattress, shirtless.

Seeing Alex staring, Riva cleared her throat loudly and then gave Douglas a swift kick.

"Time to get up sleeping beauty." She said firmly as he groggily came to.

Rubbing his eyes, he sighed deeply. "Good morning to you too."

She pushed him out of her way. "Budge up, I need to stoke the fire, this place is freezing."

Hoisting himself up on his elbows so Riva could squeeze her way to the grate, avoiding bashing her head on the chair-side table, he finally realized who was in the room with him.

"Oh, morning." He grunted, staring blearily at Alex.

"Morning." Alex replied, with a shy smile, taking a dainty sip out of her cup.

Riva stuck her head into the fireplace to avoid them. The entire journey home they had been studiously avoiding each other.

Scrunching up some newspaper under the fresh logs, she summoned a flame – the scent of bonfires and fireworks conjured with it – and closed the grate.

"Right, that's that done." She straightened up, dusting her hands off on her dressing gown. "Did you only bring coffee Alex?" she asked in trepidation.

Alex plucked a small cup from the tray and extended it to her. "It's a mocha."

Riva wrinkled her nose.

"It's got chocolate in." Alex rolled her eyes, thrusting the cup towards her.

She accepted the warm paper cup and took a tentative first sip. There was definitely a slight bitter taste from the coffee but it was masked enough by the chocolate that she took a second gulp.

While Alex was distracted by pretending not to stare at Douglas as he searched for his shirt, she grabbed the whipped cream from the fridge, popped off the lid of her cup and squeezed in a generous amount. They heard thumps from upstairs which signified that Em had woken up and her parent's bedroom door opened.

"Alex, what a lovely surprise." Riva's mum said, somehow managing to sound genuine despite having just spent the last four days together.

As usual, her mum scanned the room and started calculating how many mouths she would have to feed. Anticipating her needs as usual, Riva's dad was already zipping up his coat, heading for the door.

"Already on it." he said, car keys between his teeth.

Riva's mum beamed at him. "Thanks Dylan darling. Just the two loaves should do it but we might need some more Lorne sausage." She glanced at Douglas as he pulled on a shirt over his six pack. "A dozen eggs as well and some bacon wouldn't go amiss either. And don't try to parallel-park again! Mrs Lowrie still hasn't forgiven you for scratching her Mini!" she called out as he strode out the door – no doubt glad to enjoy the privacy of a solitary car ride.

Riva decided that this definitely wasn't the moment to tell her mum that Douglas was a vegetarian. Squinting at the ceiling, she realized that everything had gone quiet.

"Can you check on Em? I think she's fallen asleep again." she asked Alex who was engrossed in her phone.

"Hmm? Oh yeah sure."

Grabbing her sickly sweet drink, Riva ducked down the small hallway that led to her parent's bedroom and closed the bathroom door. She was about to draw the hottest, deepest bath imaginable and soak in it until she was a prune.

The pipes creaked as she filled up the ancient copper tub and as the room filled with steam she felt herself relax for the first time in days.

Had they really only left for California four days ago? Or was it five? She was completely lost with the time difference. So much had happened that it felt like she had been away for weeks.

Easing herself into the roasting hot water with a blissful sigh, she rubbed her palm absentmindedly. With so many thoughts swirling about her head it was hard to keep track. Gods and titans, Gaia's powers, her destiny, her fledgling relationship with Kieran that she was pretty sure was going to end before it had even begun.

She sighed, grabbing the bar of soap and lathering it between her hands.

Cronos.

Her stomach tightened at the thought of him and she dropped the soap. She made a mental note to get more information out of Alex about him before she went back to Eden. She had a lot of questions for him.

Her phone binged with a text and she reached down from the tub, bubbles pooling on the cracked tiles.

Are you home?

It was from Kieran. Her stomach knotted guiltily, both from the way she had been ignoring him and from the thoughts she had just been having about a certain mysterious titan.

Yeah, do you want to come over? We all just woke up and my mum's making a feast.

She leaned back against the tub and breathed in the chemical strawberry scent of the bubble bath. In just a few days she would be leaving here again, and she genuinely didn't know if she would be coming back. They had Douglas, she had her powers, and Em had been all for charging down to Oceana straight from Venice beach.

Thankfully Riva's father had talked her out of that idea, figuring that it was better they all attacked this plan from a place of familiarity. That and the fact that no-one wanted to spend another night in that dingy motel.

She also wanted to help Douglas get a better handle on his ocean magic before they went charging in all guns blazing. He was completely untested and they were about to go up against an entire army. Alone.

Her phone pinged again.

I'll be there in 20mins?

She found herself smiling in spite of everything. The one normal thing in her life. Even though she was immeasurably more powerful than he was, he made her feel safe. Maybe she was ready to try that kiss again.

I wonder what Cronos's lips would feel like...

She stopped the thought as it was forming. What was wrong with her? She didn't have time to be stressing over one boy let alone two. Not that Cronos could ever be called a boy.

Her phone pinged again.

Should I bring anything?

Not only was Kieran handsome, he was incredibly thoughtful too. She really didn't deserve him.

No, just yourself. I guess this means I should maybe get out of the bath now? ;)

Feeling just a little bit flirty, and not stopping to think about why, she closed her phone and left him with the visual. Maybe Gaia had been right. Maybe she didn't need to be just one thing, maybe it wasn't as simple as being good or bad. Perhaps she could be both.

Listening to the clattering and banging going on through the door as her mum rustled something up in the kitchen and Em and Alex laughed together, she wished that this was her life. That it could be as simple as having a family meal together with no hidden agendas or secrets.

She ran her fingers through the bubbles, and plucked one from the top with her index finger. She watched the rainbows streak across its surface before allowing it to float away from her, its flimsy surface undulating gently. Her magic soon had the room filled with bubbles, all floating around the room like misshapen snowflakes or little foamy planets.

Who am I kidding? I'd take this over normal any day of the week.

Evaporating the bubbles with a flick of her wrist, she pulled the plug in the bath and got out, dripping. After drying off, she pulled on her dressing gown so she could bolt upstairs and find something decent to wear before Kieran arrived.

Ten minutes later, she was coming back down the stairs in her favourite lilac shirt and jeans to find the cottage bursting at the seams with people.

"No sausage for me thanks Helen!" Alex shouted over from where she was sitting cross-legged in front of the fireplace. Douglas was folded into the armchair, legs crossed and studiously ignoring her.

"Who wants wholemeal and who wants white?" Her mum was shouting, taking stock of a show of hands from where she held down the fort in the kitchen.

"Whatever's easiest mum." Riva said, almost tripping over Em's boots as she made her way over to her. "But I'm afraid there will be another mouth to feed, I invited Kieran over."

Her mum beamed at her, halfway through spreading Lurpak on what looked like an entire wholemeal loaf. "That's wonderful darling!"

A little taken aback at her mum's enthusiasm she placed her cup in the sink. "Are you sure you don't mind? It's already a lot of people."

Her mum waved the butter-knife around the room. "Feeding people is what I do best love." She said, giving her a squeeze as Riva's stomach grumbled. "I wonder why?" she chuckled.

"Is dad back already? You did tell him about speed limits right?" Riva asked.

The sound of the ancient boiler straining to heat up after her own bath gave her the answer she needed. He must have barrelled down to the village going at least seventy miles an hour to be back this fast.

Opening the cupboard she wrapped her hand around the pipe. A few seconds later she heard the shout of surprise come from the bathroom.

"Oh good grief!" her dad yelled as the water heated from ice cold to scalding.

Smirking to herself, she plonked down on the sagging couch beside Em who was observing her quietly.

"What?" she asked, fluffing up her damp hair from underneath and glancing at the door.

Em looked shrewdly at her. "You're ready." Was all she said.

"What do you mean?"

Em just stared, those green eyes bottomless. "You know what I mean. You're a far cry from that scared girl struggling to get control of her powers three months ago. Your plan is going to work."

Riva snorted. "Em you know as well as I do that we don't have a plan yet."

"You will. I have every faith that you'll figure it out. You always have before."

Her friends eyes were sparkling like the gemstone she was named for in the light from the roaring fire and Riva squeezed her hand. "Who would ever have thought you would be this comfortable around humans eh?"

Em laughed. "It has pretty much everything to do with your mum's cooking. She won me over."

They both looked over at her mum. She had the whole stove going and was rustling up enough grub to feed a small army but was resolutely refusing help from anyone.

"I still wish you guys would let me come down there with you. I want to help." Alex tore her gaze away from her phone as it became evident that she had been eavesdropping.

"We already talked about this." Riva sighed.

Alex pouted and crossed her arms. "Barely. All you said was that I have no magic to protect myself so I had to stay here. How do you think I'll feel being left behind worrying?"

Riva glanced awkwardly at her mum. She knew all too well the feeling of being left behind. Thankfully with all the banging of pots and pans she hadn't heard.

"Em doesn't have magic so why is she allowed to go?"

Riva looked pointedly at the Mer girl sitting beside her. Mostly her fierce tattoos, wiry muscles and no-bullshit attitude.

"Ignoring the fact that she is a literal mermaid, were you trained from birth as an elite soldier and do you know your way around underwater to guide us?" Riva asked pointedly.

Alex went from pouty to upset, fiddling with a bald spot on the rug. "I just want to help this time."

Riva leaned forward, elbows on her knees. "I know. But I'll be able to concentrate on what we have to do much better if I know you are safe up here." She said.

"I agree. We can't waste time or put ourselves in danger trying to protect you. You need to stay here." Douglas said.

Flushing furiously, Alex stared up at him. "Fine. I know where I'm not wanted."

Sighing, Riva dragged a hand through her hair. "Alex, you know that's not what we meant. My parents aren't coming with us either and look how hard my dad argued his point. Longest plane ride of my life. We just don't want to see you get hurt." She said, reaching over to smack Douglas. "Right?"

"Right." He said with enough sincerity that hope flashed in Alex's eyes.

Riva rolled her eyes. "Look, Alex. You start university next week, you are the only one here who has the opportunity to keep living your life like you wanted to. I highly suggest that you do it."

She couldn't see her friend's face as she looked down at the rug she was still picking, her curtain of golden hair obscuring it from view.

"I want to know that when I'm down there at least one of us is making irresponsible choices at Fresher's week." She was sure she saw the ghost of a smile lift the corners of Alex's mouth. "Think of all the cute boys you'll get to meet."

Riva didn't miss Douglas shifting awkwardly in his chair, or the way his lips thinned. Alex however, perked right up.

"I suppose you're right. Maybe Dundee is a good place to meet someone. California was certainly…" she paused. "…lacking."

The word seemed to hang in the air like both insult and invitation. Alex and Douglas avoided looking at one another.

Em looked inclined to bash their heads together.

"Besides, there is something you can help me with." Riva said, changing the subject before things could get any more awkward.

Alex looked up, intrigued.

"I need you to do some research into the titans. Specifically Cronos. Does the name ring any bells?" Riva asked.

Forever grateful for the fact that academia would always win her curiosity, Alex didn't ask why she needed to know. "It sounds familiar but I can't remember why." She replied, already Googling.

"Why the sudden interest in mythology?" Douglas asked, his dark eyes suspicious.

Riva got up off the couch. "Just want to have all the facts before I make any decisions." She said in what she hoped was a casual voice. "Stop picking at the rug Alex, if you make that bald spot any bigger then it's going to look like the time you tried to give yourself a bikini wax."

Douglas guffawed with laughter as Em asked, "Why would you want to put wax on a bikini?"

Glad that they had been distracted from the topic of titans, Riva searched for somewhere else to be. Thankfully, there came a loud knock at the door.

"Who's that?" Alex asked, deep in a Google search, still looking a tad flustered.

"It's Kieran, I invited him." Riva explained.

Alex squealed, thoughts of titans forgotten as she bounced on her knees like an overexcited puppy. "Meeting the whole family??" she mouthed, gesturing around the circus of a room.

Riva pointed firmly at her and then mimed zipping her lips. She didn't want any drama. Especially not from her now-extended dysfunctional family.

She got up, fiddling with the edge of her shirt and opened the door, careful to close the door to the living room behind her to give them some initial privacy. She wished that she had put on a jumper instead of the shirt. It was one of the prettiest things she owned but she was freezing in it. Opening the door, her stomach twisted in a not-entirely-unpleasant way as she took in all six feet of the handsomely smiling Kieran.

"Hey." She said shyly, hoping that he wasn't mad at her for being such a flake on their calls.

"Hey yourself." He replied, holding out a box of jam doughnuts "I know you told me not to bring anything but I got your favourite."

Riva smiled, closing the door behind him, the draft that blew in making her want to run upstairs for a cardigan. "That's so sweet, thank you." she said with a smile despite the fact that her favourites were chocolate glazed.

Close enough.

"So how was your trip?" he asked as he hung up his jacket. "I guess you don't tan very well. I know you were away less than a week but I thought you would have managed to get some sun."

Riva laughed nervously. "Well, we did spend some time at the beach but we didn't get much sunbathing done." She pulled the edges of her shirt down nervously, just now realizing that she had brought someone into the cottage who didn't know the secret. "We, uh- actually went there to find my cousin. He came back with us, so he's going to be here visiting for a while."

"Your cousin?" Kieran asked, intrigued.

"Mm-hmm." Riva said quietly.

He fidgeted with the toggle on his jacket as he hung it up on the coat peg. "This may sound like a strange question but, your cousin isn't Black is he?"

Slightly taken aback, she replied. "Uh, yeah actually. How did you know that?"

Kieran's neck flushed and he ran his index finger across the collar of his shirt. "I just saw a couple of photos on Alex's Instagram that's all."

Riva groaned inwardly.

"When you didn't call I was wondering if he was the reason why." He laughed awkwardly. "I'm sorry. You two don't exactly look related and in the photo it looked like you were pretty close. I mean, you had your arms around each other and I just put two and two together because he was really good looking and I mean I know we never made anything official before you left but I just-."

Standing on her tiptoes, Riva cut him off with a kiss. It was brief, but his lips were soft and tasted faintly of jam.

Pushing the thought to the back of her mind that while she may not have met someone in California who she had been attracted to, she had certainly met someone in Eden that she couldn't stop thinking about. She banished all thoughts of her dream out of her mind.

When she pulled away, Kieran was wearing an expression of someone who had just been hit over the head with a surfboard. She should know. Surprising herself, she giggled.

"You already snuck one of the doughnuts didn't you?"

He grinned wickedly. "Guilty."

She took his hand, feeling comforted by how small hers felt in comparison. "Well I guess you'd better come meet everyone properly."

As they stepped into the living room, everything was comforting chaos. Her mum was plating up breakfast at four thirty in the afternoon so everyone was huddled around the tiny breakfast bar like hungry orphans in a workhouse where knives and forks were clattering loudly.

"Oh Kieran darling, hello how are you?" her mum asked, spotting them over the numerous heads fighting over her scrambled eggs. She wiped her hands on a dishtowel and walked into the living room.

"Thanks for having me Ms McLaren." He said warmly, giving her a peck on the cheek. "Riva thinks I'm here for her but it's really for the food." He said with a wink.

Her mum, flustered, shooed him away with the tea towel and scurried back into the kitchen.

"You shouldn't have said that. Now she's going to give you double helpings." Riva said.

Kieran nudged her. "Maybe that was my plan all along. I wore my stretchy jeans."

Riva eyed up the light blue shirt collar sticking out from underneath the navy jumper that accentuated his broad shoulders. He'd made an effort again. For her. Her stomach felt pleasantly warm from something that had absolutely nothing to do with the food. She briefly wondered how quickly boys grew. It didn't seem normal.

"Hey man, I'm Douglas. Riva's cousin." Douglas wiped the hand that had been pouring maple syrup onto his pancakes on his jogging pants and shook his hand. "Please don't ask how we're related, I've barely gotten it straight myself." He said with a wink in Riva's direction.

"No problem, nice to meet you." Kieran said with a smile, shaking his hand firmly and squeezing her around the shoulders a little more comfortably. Riva realized that Douglas had effectively saved them all a painfully awkward cover story by being so smooth.

"So which plate is mine Ms McLaren?" he asked, settling himself down at the table beside Riva like he had always been part of the family.

Once the food came she no longer wondered why boys grew so quickly. Both Kieran and Douglas ate like their stomachs were bottomless.

Since the dining table was too small to fit all of them around it they ate across the living room.

"Douglas you haven't touched your bacon dear." Riva's mum scolded from the kitchen as she spied his plate, empty save for three rashers of the butchers' finest smoked back bacon.

Embarrassed, he massaged his stomach. "Sorry Aunt Helen, just trying to stay in shape you know?"

"Of course dear." Her mum said, starting on the washing up. The look on her face told everyone exactly how she felt about people who refused her food to 'stay in shape'.

Riva had never known her mum to give up on force feeding someone so easily. Maybe it had been his easy use of the word 'aunt'.

"I'll have it if you don't want it." Em piped up from the armchair. "I can't believe I've lived my whole life without it."

Kieran's mouth practically dropped open. "You've never had bacon before?"

Em, clearly forgetting that he wasn't in on the secret, almost gave the game away. "No I only tasted it for the first time last week when Helen made it for me. Bacon just isn't available when you're a-."

"Pescatarian." Alex jumped in. "Em was raised by strict pescatarian parents. She's here on a gap year and decided to try something new." She finished with a stern glare that warned Em that she wouldn't have her back next time.

Realizing her mistake she took the plate that Douglas passed her, and then sunk back into the chair. "Yes. Right. All seafood-diet. Thanks for showing me the other side Helen."

"Any time dear." She answered weakly, elbow deep in the sink.

Seeing that Kieran had finished his plate, she decided to get him out of there before someone else accidentally spilled the magic beans.

"I need some fresh air." She said, offering a hand to Kieran.

Stretching his arms above his head, Douglas looked like he was about to join them, until Alex grabbed him by the back of his belt and pulled him back down onto his chair with more force than she looked like she was capable of.

As Riva pushed Kieran past the kitchen and out into the garden she mouthed a thank you at her friend.

"I can't believe she doesn't know how to play monopoly." Kieran said, still shaking his head at one of the other oddities Em had managed to mention as they ate.

Riva faked a laugh along with him, "Yeah, I don't think it's as big a deal in Australia you know."

"Hmm, I thought it was a worldwide thing. Anyway." He took a deep breath and as it puffed out it created a cloud of steam in front of him. "It's cold, even for September." He said, rubbing his hands together.

Riva looked around the damp garden. Thanks to the rain the birds were quiet, the sky heavy with the rain yet to come. "Yeah. I hate this weather." She muttered. "We should have stayed in California."

Noticing Kieran's hurt expression too late, she moved closer, "Crap, I didn't mean it like that."

"It's okay." He said quietly.

"Thanks for coming over." She said.

He looked down at her, molten chocolate eyes warm with affection. How was it possible that she had to look up so far to meet his eyes now?

"Any time you want me, I'll be here." He said, equally as quietly.

Something about his words made Riva inexplicably sad.

They were close now, but she still felt safe locked in his gaze. His eyes really were the same colour as her favourite chocolate.

"You know I really wasn't here just for your mum's cooking right?" he asked, moving even closer.

"I know." she breathed.

He bent towards her and his lips touched hers ever so gently, a questioning flutter. A few moments later she broke away, a smile on her face. Not even the faintest glimmer of panic.

Kieran smiled, baffled. "What?"

"Nothing. And everything." She said, waiting for a flashback that never came.

He reached out and linked their hands together, drawing her into the warmth of his chest.

"I've wanted this for a long time, Riva." He said.

She smiled against him. "Everyone at school has been telling me for long enough. Trust me, I know."

He chucked, "Then why have you made me wait so long?" Only she could detect the genuine hurt in his voice.

"It wasn't anything you did. I just - needed to find a part of myself that was missing first."

Even though he didn't understand how literally she meant it, he bent towards her again. He brushed her lips with another kiss and she was delighted to find that she wanted to kiss him back.

"We should go back inside, it's starting to rain." He murmured into her hair.

She buried her face in his t-shirt, inhaling his aftershave. "In a minute."

He laughed and she felt it vibrate through his sternum.

"Just don't disappear on me again okay?" he said after a pause, sounding vulnerable.

She pulled away but kept their hands linked, "What do you mean?"

"I know you have this new family abroad and all that but the next time you go away, please don't leave without saying goodbye." He said.

Riva sighed, already dreading what she was about to have to say. She had just gotten back, how was she supposed to tell him that she was potentially leaving again tomorrow?

"Um, that's just the thing. You see, I do need to leave again soon." She said, dropping his hands.

The disappointment on his face was crushing. "You're kidding me. You just got home."

She reached for his hands again but he had crossed his arms. The movement hurt her more than she wanted him to know. "I know, I'm sorry. But there are some complicated things going on with my uncle and my cousin's here to help us try to fix it."

Kieran studied her face quizzically as the drizzling rain got heavier. "Is he a criminal too?"

"What?" she replied, utterly confused.

Kieran looked frustrated, "Was he in prison with your dad too?"

Remembering the ridiculous cover story that she and Alex had come up with a week ago, she tried desperately to remember what she had said.

"No, no. of course not." She said. "He's just having some problems that we all want to try and fix so that we can finally be a big happy family. Oh, and my dad isn't a criminal either by the way, he just made a mistake when he got involved with the gang."

"I thought it was drugs?" Kieran asked.

Crap.

"Uh, yeah. That's what I meant." She stuttered. "I mean, same thing really. I prefer not to ask the details."

Kieran still looked suspicious.

"He doesn't like to talk about it much, I think he's ashamed of his past so I don't bring it up."

He went from looking suspicious to more than slightly annoyed, and reached for her hands again. "I was just hoping to spend some more time together before the summer was over." He said quietly.

"I know. This summer hasn't exactly been what I had hoped for either." She replied. If only he knew the half of it.

"When will you come back?" he asked tentatively.

"Soon I hope." She said, trying to be vague. "But we don't exactly have a return date set either."

She left out the fact that the return date wasn't set because she quite literally might not be able to return at all. Not that she had a plan, but whatever she managed to come up with would undoubtedly be dangerous. If something went wrong...

"I'm so sorry." She said, "All I do is mess you around."

"Hey, no don't say that." He reached across and tucked a strand of her hair behind her ear. She'd only ever seen people do that in the movies before. "Your family is important. I get that. I just have to start uni in ten days and I was hoping we could spend those days together."

"Wait, you got in?!" she exclaimed, forgetting everything. "What course did you pick in the end?"

"Nursing. In Inverness." He said, blushing furiously to the roots of his red hair. "I like helping people."

Riva beamed at him and threw her arms around him in a huge hug, "You'll be an amazing nurse."

"Thank you." he said, kissing the top of her head. "So do we have some time to be together before you go?"

Riva bit her lip. "I'm not entirely sure when we're leaving. It could be as early as tomorrow or the day after though."

Kieran groaned, "Can't you delay it a few more days?"

She shook her head. "As much as I want to, this can't wait."

"Okay. Well I need you to at least promise me you won't leave tomorrow." She tried to interrupt him but he put a finger up to her lips, she could smell the sausages on it. "No. I need to take you on a proper date before you go."

"Kieran I-."

"Nuh-uh. One date. That's all I ask. So that if you do end up meeting some ridiculously handsome guy who isn't your cousin this time, you'll know what's waiting for you back here." He said firmly. "Surely you can't deny me that?"

Riva could have kicked herself for picturing Cronos's face.

Despite herself, she smiled. "Alright fine."

"I'll pick you up tomorrow at six then okay?" He said, beaming.

She nodded, incredibly thankful that despite the insane mission she was about to undertake in Oceana, that she could be a teenager going on her first official date for just one night.

She followed him back into the warmth of the house, ignoring Alex's very pointed looks at their entwined hands as they sat down.

In the end it hadn't mattered one bit that Em had never heard of Monopoly before as she cottoned on incredibly quickly. They had all swiftly been bankrupted by her in quick succession in the most cut-throat game that Riva had ever witnessed.

As they were all gathered on the floor around the Monopoly board while Em counted her paper money, Riva wished she could ignore the weight in her stomach that told her that her time was up. They had found Douglas, it was time to go back to Oceana.

15.

"Careful, not so loud!" Riva shushed Em and Douglas, casting glances around the depths of the shadowy bay. Even though this was her home, the murky waters definitely made sneaking around in the shallows much more nerve-wracking than it had been in the sun-dappled waters of California.

"I thought you said it was cloaked?" Douglas asked in a hushed voice as he swam over to her, the dim light making his outline blur.

She shivered as she looked out towards the bay entrance. She couldn't see it but she could feel where it gave way to the open ocean. "My cloaking works for sight, not for hearing. Just keep it down. I'm on edge enough doing this as it is."

Closing her eyes and reaching out with her senses, the only creatures she felt in the wild waters outside of the bay were jellyfish, eels and small fish.

"Just maybe be a little less enthusiastic with the rock throwing okay?" she asked with a tight smile.

Em and Douglas both grinned.

After Kieran had left her house the day before, Riva had had a mini freak-out as everyone started setting up the Cluedo board. Realising what little time they had to plan, she ordered Em and Douglas into the garden for an emergency recon session. Unfortunately the heavens had opened moments later so they had all had to trudge upstairs into Riva's room instead.

Taking offence at being excluded, Alex had shown herself out and as her parents snuggled up in front of the TV, Riva had snuck both of them out of the house to come down to the bay for some real-world ocean practice. As guilty as she felt about leaving Alex out, she had next to no time at all to get Douglas up to speed.

Unfortunately three hours of underwater bootcamp hadn't made much of an improvement. As she floated at the bottom, the undulating seaweed tickling her toes, she watched his attempts at summoning currents with a groan.

"Try it again." she prompted, as he span out of it for the fourth time. "The best thing to do is get the slipstream in front of you properly in place before you summon the current behind you. Otherwise you'll lose your balance."

Douglas nodded, a determined look on his face as he floated horizontally in his swim shorts, equidistant between the surface and the bottom. Riva could just about make out the slipstream as he summoned it and watched as he bent it around the front of his body, the water just slightly smoother than in the rest of the bay.

"Not so much, you need to make it thinner or you'll lose control." She instructed.

Biting his lip, he took her advice and slowly built up the current behind him. Riva and Em watched with baited breath until he released himself like he was shooting out of a cannon. Completely misjudging his propulsion power, he drove himself headfirst down into the ground with a crunch.

She locked eyes with Em and they both had to press their lips firmly together to stop from falling about laughing. They swam down to where he was just about managing to extract his head from the deep furrow he had left in the floor of the bay and Riva grimaced, seeing the deep cuts on his forehead and cheekbones.

"Oh, those look like they sting." She said, reaching out her hand almost automatically.

Looking warily at her eerily glowing palm in the murky water, he replied. "Well I guess that's what you get when you faceplant into rocks."

Her Mark stopped glowing, the cuts sealing themselves shut. "There you go. Good as new." Riva said. "Try again."

Douglas's shoulders slumped. "Seriously? That one doesn't merit a five minute break?"

Both her and Em shook their heads.

"How long did it take you to get the hang of this way of swimming?" he asked dejectedly, prodding his newly healed face with the pads of his fingers.

"Don't worry, Riva was terrible at first too." Em piped up, grey tail flitting back and forth lazily, and she raised her eyebrows at Riva's questioning look, "What? I distinctly remember you catapulting yourself over the rooftops of Oceana like a mad scarecrow."

Riva stuck her tongue out at her as she stretched her fins and turned back to Douglas. "You'll get the hang of it don't worry." She said, "It's easier out in open water, there's less stuff to bump into. And when you're in the travel current you won't have much of a choice about what your body does anyway."

She felt faintly sick at the memory and was already dreading having to go through the equivalent of a spin-cycle tomorrow. Not that their task would get any easier once they arrived.

Em seemed to be able to read her mind and swam back to them in that eerily agile way only the Mer and marine animals could master. "Your plan will work." She said confidently, green eyes sincere.

"Oh yeah? You sound very certain." Replied Riva sceptically. The hurriedly pieced together plan seemed decidedly ramshackle to her.

"Yeah, well failure isn't an option so we can't afford to be pessimistic." Em said, clapping her on the shoulder.

"Lovely." Riva said sarcastically. "Right, breaks over."

Douglas swam back to his position, grumbling about the fact that it had barely been a minute but Riva made her way to the surface. She was supposed to have her date with Kieran tonight. While she had wanted to back out, Alex had told her that if she had to remain behind while the rest of them went to Oceana, then Riva had to go on this date before leaving.

Nervous as she was about returning to Oceana, she was almost more nervous for the date. She still wasn't convinced that she should be breaking her focus, but then she thought about those chocolate eyes filling with disappointment again and made up her mind not to let him down again.

Breaking through the surface, the air returned to her lungs with that not-uncomfortable sharp sting, followed by sweet oxygen as her lungs expanded. Trying to figure out where the sun was in the sky was almost impossible through the blanket of cloud, but trusting her gut, she figured it was probably time for her to head back home if she wanted to look halfway decent.

Diving back down to Em and Douglas, she made the transition back to the ocean almost effortlessly as the oxygen switched from travelling through her lungs to her entire body.

Delighting in the bubbling eddies that she could feel sweeping in from the open sea, she sighed happily. If only she could have discovered that she was part mermaid and then just go travel the ocean instead of having to save it. Her quick dip in the crystal Californian waters had given her a taste and she was itching to see the rest.

"Argh!" Distracted with daydreaming, she hadn't been paying attention to where she was going and Douglas had zoomed straight into her, knocking them both flying. "Watch it!" she cried out, summoning her own flitting current to right herself.

"Sorry!" he apologized, now spinning like a top. "But I think I did it right that time!"

He was still fighting with the current, spinning dizzily around and around vertically, his facial expressions growing more comical with each turn as he tried to stop himself.

She glanced at Em who was trying just as hard as she was not to laugh.

"I'm sure you were." Riva replied, trying to keep a straight face. "Let's just attempt to be able to swim in a straight line for more than five seconds before we leave tomorrow okay?"

Seeing that Douglas was still struggling, she stilled the waters around him and he came to a sudden stop. If he had been a cartoon, his eyes would have been rattling around in their sockets.

"Don't worry, I managed to coach you through it, I can handle him." Em said appraisingly.

Riva looked her up and down. "Yeah because all of your lounging around *observing* did so much to help me understand my powers." She laughed.

Em just shrugged but assumed the gaze of a PE teacher who had just been given a sick note by a very obviously not sick pupil.

"Don't even think about trying to call it a day." she said to Douglas, holding up one finger to his chest as he looked between them, beseechingly.

Douglas brushed Em's finger away and then crossed his arms across his chest, shivering. "Come on, I'm freezing my balls off down here."

Mr California Surfer really hadn't adapted well to the frigid North Sea waters at all.

"Well get used to it, it's just as cold down in Oceana as it is here. And it's not your balls you should be worried about. Although if they fall off before we travel it will just give you one less thing to be embarrassed about." Riva said.

Douglas flushed. When Em had first removed the necklace he hadn't known where to look. Not because of her tail but because of the way she unabashedly bared her rather spectacular breasts.

"Don't you have a spare pair of those leggings?" he whined, eyeing up the seal-skin that encased Riva's legs.

"Nope. Sorry. You're just going to have to make do with those swim shorts and hope that they don't get ripped off in the travel current." She said with a backwards wave.

"Enjoy your date!" Em called out after her. "I'll keep a close watch on this one."

Douglas started protesting but Riva just hissed. "And please keep your voices down if I'm not here to protect you both."

Clearing the surface, she walked barefoot up the cliff path, stopping to grab her rain jacket and boots at the top. She walked back over the fields towards home, steaming as she dried herself off with her magic.

Thanks to both her date and the return to Oceana looming, her stomach was in knots. She was keeping her fingers crossed that her plan would work but there were so many things that could go wrong.

She was relying on Douglas being able to master at least some of his own powers. It had been Em's idea to try and talk to her other uncles, getting them on their side couldn't hurt, especially Murray and Murphy. But the truth was, they had no idea what awaited them at the bottom of the ocean, or what the king would say when he met his son.

Given that there wasn't much of a resemblance, all they had to go on was his age, the bracelet and memories of his mother. There was every chance that the events surrounding Queen Noelani's death had wiped any positive emotions from Duncan's mind completely.
Riva was willing to do whatever it took to free the Mer and save the ocean, but Douglas was their best shot at doing it peacefully.

*

"This was a really great idea." Riva said as they walked out of the cinema, tucking what was left of her giant bag of Minstrels into her handbag. "I can't believe you remembered that I hate popcorn."

Kieran laughed and pulled his jacket tighter around him against the chilly wind, "Yeah you always say it's overrated. I figured you'd be safe with your favourite chocolate."

She took his hand gently, happy that this time he had remembered her actual favourite, as they walked down the main street, its few restaurants closing down as the pubs opened.

"Well, thank you. The great chocolate and good company definitely made up for the terrible movie." She laughed.

Kieran blushed. "I'm sorry, Kirsty told me that she went last week with her boyfriend and loved it. I thought you'd like it."

"Kirsty has a boyfriend now?" she asked, genuinely interested, remembering with a shudder that before the summer Kirsty had been crushing on Stuart.

"Yeah. It's recent though, but they seem happy. Have you not spoken to her in a while?"

Now that she thought about it she hadn't spoken to anyone from their school friendship group since their exams. "I guess when you aren't around as much you learn who cares to keep in touch." She said.

Kieran stopped walking and looked at her, "It takes two you know."

"What's that supposed to mean?" she said indignantly.

He laughed at her scandalized look but she could see that there was hurt behind his eyes. "You do have a tendency to disappear and lose touch. It's not so nice being the one left behind."

Was he ever going to let her stop feeling guilty?

"You know I never meant to hurt anyone. It was just a really stressful time and so many things happened that you don't even know about that made me go away so quickly without telling you and-."

Kieran was holding up his hands in a 'surrender' motion. "Riva, I didn't mean it like that. Just, maybe you should think about texting Laura or Kirsty when you get back from this next trip. I know they would appreciate knowing more about what's going on in your life than what they can get from Alex's Instagram."

She could hear the truth in his words and as he reached across to tuck a flyaway strand of hair behind her ear again, she softened. "You're right. I will. And if you see them before I do then please tell them I care about them and that these last few months have been-." She searched for the right word, "-extraordinary."

"I'll tell them." he said, "What about Stuart?"

She stiffened. "What about him?" she spat out.

"Should I tell him too?"

She had the feeling that he was waiting for an answer but all she could do was clench her jaw.

"I'll take that as a no…" he said awkwardly. "Come on, you can't still be mad at him over the whole boat accident thing surely? It was months ago now and he's definitely been punished enough for it."

A giant gust of wind rushed down the street towards them, banging open doors and knocking over dustbin lids.

"What the hell?" Kieran cried out at the sudden inclement weather, looking up at the sky.

Whatever punishment he got from his father for taking that boat out will never make up for what he did to me.

While Kieran was momentarily distracted she took a deep breath and centred herself, calming her magic before her eyes could start glowing and give the game away. She surprised herself when it actually listened. She was still pissed, but her magic remained under control, buzzing faintly in her blood.

"Wow that wind really came outta nowhere." Kieran said to no-one in particular, apparently trying to get over the awkward lull in their conversation.

"Mmhmm." She replied.

"So why don't you tell me." He said quietly.

"What?" she replied, still looking down at the pavement in case some of the glow still hadn't faded.

"Tell me what it was that made you leave without saying goodbye." He asked. "I know you didn't want to talk about it on your birthday, but I'm here if you've changed your mind."

She looked up at him and wondered if she could tell him. Or which part. Which reality would hurt him the most? The fact that she wasn't quite human or the fact that his best friend had tried to rape her? Looking away she realized that she just couldn't do it. Kieran was so… *normal*. He deserved a normal life, far away from vengeful Mer people and titans and whatever other ridiculousness that swept her away from him.

There was one face that swam into her mind that belonged to someone distinctly *abnormal*. Cronos's flashing amber eyes and dangerous beauty had her stomach clenching in an entirely different way than it did when she was with Kieran.

He met his gaze again and realized that she couldn't tell him. She wouldn't destroy his safe, predictable world like that.

"I'm not ready to talk about a lot of it yet. Some really bad things happened. Scary things." she motioned for him to stay quiet as he looked like he was going to interrupt. "There were amazing things too, I mean I found my dad, but the whole thing was just – messy. If I'm honest I should probably go to therapy about it." she huffed a laugh, trying to brush it off.

Yeah right, if I went to therapy and started telling them anything resembling the truth then I would be locked up in a mental institution before you could say the word 'straightjacket'.

Kieran squeezed her hand, "Well just know that when you are ready to talk about it, I'll be here."

She squeezed his hand right back. "You have no idea how much I appreciate that." Even though she was smiling, she was silently wondering how long he might be waiting for her to come back.

She felt a buzzing coming from her bag, "Hang on someone's trying to call me." She said, fishing around and feeling a few loose chocolates at the bottom, "Crap, I think the Minstrels bag split open."

Finally emerging victorious with her mobile clutched aloft, she answered to hear her mum's panicked voice on the other end of the line and her heart squeezed painfully.

"Wait, slow down mum, you aren't making any sense. What's wrong?" she gabbled into the phone.

The line went quiet and suddenly it was her dad on the other end. "Darling, are Em and Douglas with you?"

Fear shot through her stomach, white-hot. "No. Why? Are they not at the house? They told me they would be home an hour after I left." Quickly looking at the time on the digital display she could see that that should have been three hours ago.

"They aren't here and we just went down to the Maiden's to see if they were still there since that's where you said you were practicing."

Riva already knew what his next words would be.

"They're gone." He said.

She must have looked frightening because Kieran suddenly looked like he wanted to catch her in case she fainted. She clutched the phone tighter.

"I'm coming home. Don't move. Don't call anyone else and for God's sake, do *not* go back down to that bay." She said, hanging up. She was now shaking with the effort of keeping her powers in check. "I'm so sorry, there's a problem at the house. I really have to go."

Despite his confusion he nodded briskly, "We're parked just a couple of streets over, I'll get you back as quick as I can."

They both sped up, Riva's boots cutting into her heels.

"Is everything ok?" Kieran asked

Without looking at him, teeth gritted against her magic, she replied, "No. Everything is absolutely not okay."

Once safely ensconced in the car and speeding up the country lanes, scaring the sheep with their headlights, Riva called Alex.

"Your mum already called me an hour ago to ask if Douglas had come to see me. I have, like, no idea why she would have thought that." Alex said, sounding worried and also faintly like she was sitting in the middle of a washing machine.

"Well obviously he didn't." Riva replied frustratedly. "Where are you? It sounds mental."

Alex sighed, sounding equally as frustrated as she did, "On the bus. Dad refused to drive me because he'd had a glass of red with dinner and mum was bathing the twins. I should be at yours in fifteen."

Riva looked at the time on her screen again, eight thirty. Four hours since she had been down in the bay with them and potentially three hours since they had gone missing. There were so many scenarios running through her mind. Where had they gone? Who had taken them? Had they left willingly? Or had Em betrayed her for a second time…

No. I refuse to believe that.

"Riva?"

She snapped out of her thoughts and back into the speeding Corsa. "It's fine. I'll figure something out. I'm almost home. See you soon."

Ending the call she threw her phone back into her bag and willed Kieran not to ask any questions. Hands balled into fists on her thighs, her fear fuelling her magic, willing her to use it to protect her loved ones.

Miraculously he didn't say anything. Five minutes later he pulled up behind her mum's Kia and killed the engine, leaving the headlights on like searchlights pointed at the cottage. The thought made her uncomfortable. They were too visible. If Em and Douglas had been kidnapped then someone else could have stolen the necklace and be up here looking for her or her father already.

She threw open the car door, letting in a blast of cold air, but Kieran reached out and grabbed her arm. She whirled around and looked down at it.

"Look, I know you don't want to tell me what's going on but I'm worried about you." He said, confusion etched across his features.

Sitting uncomfortably with her handbag across one shoulder and one foot already on the gravel she looked into his eyes.

"Please, Riva. You can trust me." He said again, his expression earnest. Though his grip was loose on her arm, she didn't like the fact that he thought to restrain her at all.

Extracting her arm firmly, she reached back into the car, placing her other hand on his cheek.

"I'm sorry Kieran, I can't afford to trust anyone right now." she said.

He jerked backwards out of her touch, a muscle pulsing in his jaw.

"Alright." He barked out stiffly, face set and staring straight out the windscreen, avoiding looking at her.

Riva couldn't fight the feeling that this had been inevitable. She would always have been the one to break his heart.

She hurriedly backed away from the car. Looking back over her shoulder as she reached the cottage, she could make out nothing behind those bright headlights. Glancing around as if expecting someone to jump out of the shadows, she hurried into her house.

16.

"Right. What do we know?" she asked the minute she was in the door, not even bothering to take off her coat.

Her mum and dad sprang up from where they had been huddled on the couch, deep in conversation.

"Oh darling, I'm so glad you're safe." Her mum said reaching out to her for a hug.

She embraced her mum but was looking at her dad's grave face. He held out his hand, dangling from it was the necklace. "We found this tucked behind some rocks in the cliff."

She reached out and took it from him. It was the first time she had held it. It felt springy but also surprisingly strong. The magic within it tingled against her fingertips. Closing her eyes she could feel exactly how its power worked to change the people who wore it.

Riva sighed, keeping one arm around her mum. "So we can safely assume that they haven't run off somewhere together on land then."

A darker thought was visible on her father's face. "There is the possibility…" he began.

"No." Riva held up a hand to stop him. "I won't believe it. She's done nothing but help us since she came back. She wouldn't betray us again."

Her father took the necklace away from her.

"Riva, think about this logically. Do you really think that she could have gotten this necklace out of the Vault by herself? As logical as her story may have sounded to you, I know the Mer and I know our magic. Smearing my blood across the entrance wouldn't have been enough. Only those of Royal blood or the head Elder can get inside. And there's just no way that she could have escaped Oceana without being noticed, especially not with every Guard known to Mer out searching the ocean for us."

Shaking her head, she tried not to let the doubt creep in. "Then how do you explain her knowing about Douglas? She led us right to him! She practically handed us the key to Duncan's undoing on a silver platter."

Her father laughed hollowly. "Maybe Duncan knew all along and he sent her. Douglas is his one weakness. The one thing that could sow a seed of doubt amongst his people and potentially destroy his plans to eradicate humans from the ocean. Perhaps he told Em where to find him so that she could bring him back to be executed, strengthening his position within the Kingdom."

Her throat had dried up. Why hadn't she thought of that? It was possible of course. Kieran's words haunted her. She had been right to say that she shouldn't trust anyone anymore.

"Then why would she have come to us first?" Riva asked, desperate to believe that Em hadn't betrayed her again. "Why not just go straight to California and take him to Oceana forcefully by herself?"

Her dad shrugged. "I don't know my darling. I don't have all the answers but the facts are clear. Douglas and Em are gone. Voluntarily or not. The question now is what we do about it."

"What we do about it?" she asked. "Well that much is obvious. We go after them." Looking between her parents she felt the need to clarify. "I go after them."

Her mum clutched her tighter and her dad set his jaw.

"You'll be alone." He said gruffly. "That was never the plan."

She looked up into the sharp angles of his face and the faint shadow of stubble across his jaw, "I think I can handle myself now." she said.

He stared straight back at her and she wondered what he was seeing. His daughter standing in front of him, a little windswept from her first, albeit failed, date or the reincarnated spirit of Mother Nature ready to save his people?

Expecting an argument, she was surprised when all he said was, "Alright."

Steeling herself, she broke away from her mum and looped her arms around her dad's neck. She might only have known him for a few months but she had loved him her whole life.

"I won't let you down dad." She whispered.

He squeezed her tighter, "You never could my darling."

All three of them jumped as the front door banged, signalling Alex's arrival. Realising that it was open, she barged in. "I got here as fast as I could." She said, chest heaving. "What's the plan?"

Riva's mum looked like she was about to burst into tears and her dad put a firm, supportive hand on her shoulder.

"I'm going after them." Riva said.

Alex nodded her head. "Okay, I'm coming too." She said, unwinding her scarf.

Riva was already shaking her head. "You know you can't, it's too dangerous."

"Don't you dare start with that again. I went to Nationals with you, I know how to swim." Her eyes went to the necklace now lying innocently on the dining table. "And if you let me wear that I'll have a tail. So I'll probably be faster than you."

Riva rolled her eyes as she thought about how unlikely that was. "It's not about being a good swimmer or having a tail, it's about being a liability." Immediately she could see that she had used the wrong word. Alex looked outraged.

"I don't mean it like that. Just think about it. If you are spotted in Oceana wearing that necklace it's basically like having a giant target on your back. Everyone will know what you really are, tail or not."

"So cloak me then like you did with Em in California." She said, a pleading note entering her voice.

"Even if I cloaked both of us and got us in undetected, I would still be too worried about protecting you instead of focusing on what I really need to do down there." She said.

Alex looked upset and mumbled. "Rescuing Em and Douglas?"

"No. Overthrowing Duncan." Riva said. Both her mum and Alex looked shocked but her dad looked like he had been expecting this all along.

"Look, of course I will try to rescue them, but they both knew what they were getting into. We discussed the possibilities of what might happen if we got separated or captured. Granted, I didn't think it would happen this soon, but it changes nothing. Our end goal remains the same. Forcing Duncan to realise that his way will not work and if he can't see that then removing him from power for the good of both humans and Mer. Goodness-only knows what he has already started putting into motion down there, but if it's anything like we've been seeing at the surface, I can't allow that to continue. Too many people will die if I don't. Too many people have already died."

The images of the sunken cruise liner came back to her suddenly. How many children had died that day? She'd never gotten up the courage to find out.

Alex's brown eyes were furious but her jaw was set. "You better come back to me alive."

"I'll do everything I can to make sure I do." She said, knowing better than to make any promises she wouldn't be able to keep.

"I guess I better go get ready then." Riva said as she turned on her heel and climbed the stairs to her bedroom.

Her attic bedroom was full of a watery light that filtered in from her window. She grabbed the seal-skin leggings and kelp top off her window seat from where she had left them to dry before her date. Had she really been watching that terrible rom-com only an hour ago?

Holding the items of clothing up in front of her she felt a strange mixture of excitement at getting to go back to Oceana and pure fear at what awaited her there.

"Some of your better style choices." Alex said with a large sniff as she stood in her doorway.

Turning to see that her best friend had followed her upstairs, she smiled sadly. "You know I'm making you stay to protect you right?"

Alex nodded and pushed off the door frame with a shrug, "Doesn't mean I have to like it though."

"Are you still good at doing braids?" Riva asked as she pulled off the sweater dress she had been wearing for her date, hoping that having something to do would make Alex feel less dejected.

Alex walked into the room, dodging the piles of clothes on the floor. "Yeah mum makes me do the twins hair before school every day why?"

Riva tossed her tights onto the bed on top of the dress. "Because it will be much easier to see where I'm going down there if I don't have all this floating around my face." She said gesturing to her mass of waves that now tumbled thickly to her lower back.

Rolling up her sleeves as Riva pulled on the skin-tight leggings with some difficulty, Alex asked, "What do you think about a Katniss vibe?"

"Perfect." Riva answered, glad that the tension seemed to have melted away. She knelt down as Alex sat on the bed and started combing her fingers through the thick waves.

"God, I remember when you used to beg me for hair conditioning treatments." Alex sighed, "Do you even use anything on it to make it look this good?"

Riva shook her head smugly, resulting in a sharp tug from Alex's delicate fingers.

"Any chance you could come back with some Mer hair care this time?" Alex asked lightly, "Maybe a seaweed wrap or algae hair mask or something?"

Riva smiled ruefully. "I'll see what I can do."

They were quiet as Alex's deft fingers pulled Riva's hair taught to her scalp.

"I did some research like you asked." Alex finally said as she tied off the braid with a hair bobble.

"On what?" Riva asked, momentarily confused.

Alex threw the long braid over her shoulder with finality and Riva turned to look at her.

"About the titans, Cronos in particular."

Riva's excitement faded to apprehension as she saw the look on Alex's face.

"What's wrong?" she asked.

Alex hugged her knees. "I don't know why you asked, but if you think Duncan is dangerous then he's going to be nothing compared to them. I seriously hope that you're just doing research into your powers because if they are real people…" she swallowed. "They're not good."

Riva thought about her conversations with Gaia. The way the Goddess made her feel simultaneously calm and on edge.

"Please be careful Riva. Because Cronos… he's the worst of the lot." Alex said shuddering.

"You can't be serious." Riva replied, mind drifting back to the image of the handsome man in the oak wood, perfect lips drifting closer to her face, amber eyes aflame to match her soul as his gaze consumed her.

Alex scrutinized her expression worriedly. "Oh I'm sure. He was the first son of the two original titans – Gaia and Uranos. Goddess of the Earth and God of the Sky."

Gaia is Cronos's' mum. Interesting, I wonder why he seems almost afraid of her…

"Apparently there was a prophecy that Cronos would be overthrown by his son so each time his wife Rhea gave birth he swallowed his children to prevent it from coming true. Only one of them survived, they named him Zeus and he supposedly overthrew his father and became King of the Gods."

Riva was immediately reviewing every fantasy she had ever had about Cronos. "Okay, definitely creepy."

Alex was still looking worried. "Please tell me they aren't real."

Looking up into her friends face, Riva realised that she didn't know what to say. Whenever she visited Eden it was only in her mind, but that didn't mean that these Gods, or titans or whatever, weren't real.

"Whatever they are, they aren't important right now." she said, standing up, pushing thoughts of Cronos out of her mind for now. "I've got bigger fish to fry. Literally."

Adjusting the kelp top, she looked at herself in her bedroom mirror.

"Badass." Alex breathed from behind her, echoing her thoughts.

Pale skin glowing in the moonlight pouring in from her bedroom window and the glow from her lamp, she looked Mer. The pronounced cheekbones and thick hair only reinforced that resemblance, but the high colour in her cheeks and the light dusting of freckles across the bridge of her nose betrayed what was left of her humanity.

Calling upon her magic she let it well up inside of her until her eyes and Goddess Marked palm were shining bright gold. The whole effect was quite startling.

"Duncan doesn't stand a chance." Alex said, sounding half-awed, half-terrified.

Turning to her friend she said, "Take care of Kieran for me. It didn't exactly go well tonight but I still care about him. If I don't come back then let him think the worst of me. Keep him out of all this craziness."

"Riva don't say things like that." Alex said.

"Please."

Setting her jaw, Alex nodded.

Letting her magic recede, she turned away from her reflection, "Come on. I can't waste any more time."

The girls hopped down the stairs to meet her parents in the living room. Her mum had one hand over her heart and once again Riva was doubly glad that her dad would be staying with her while she was gone.

"We'd better get going." She said, pulling her coat off the side of the sofa where she had flung it and slipped her bare feet into her boots again, the blister on her heel protesting loudly.

"Let me just grab my car keys." Her mum said breathlessly.

Riva started pulling on her coat and looked at the three people who meant the most to her in the whole world.

"Remember, if Duncan's spies are up here using the ancient magics then they can only come ashore for a very short period of time. So even if they find you, run. Run as far inland as you can get. Go to the mainland even. They won't be able to reach you there." Buttoning her coat she inclined her head, "Actually that wouldn't be such a bad idea."

But her parents were already shaking their heads, "No Riva. We'll be as close as we can be." Her mum said shakily. "You have already given us more than enough protection."

Riva turned to Alex. "You need to go to Dundee."

"But it's literally the other side of the country." Alex started to protest.

"I don't care. The further you are from all of this the better." Riva took in all five foot two of her best friend. "Go start uni and be that amazing doctor you were always meant to be."

Overcome with emotion, Alex looked down at her watch and paled, "It's almost nine thirty."

"Right, let's go." her dad said authoritatively, pulling on his own jacket.

"Hang on." Riva said making her way to the kitchen.

"They could be halfway to Oceana by now." Alex said anxiously. Picking up on her tone, Riva raised her eyebrows at her as she yanked out a Tupperware full of leftover chicken drumsticks from the fridge. "You don't even know how far away Oceana is. Care to tell us exactly why you are so anxious that I rush off in pursuit of Em and my cousin who you have been studiously avoiding?"

Alex blushed furiously as Riva strode past them all out the open front door.

"Don't worry, I'll get there much faster on a full stomach."

They all piled in to the tiny Kia and were soon trundling off across the lanes towards the Maidens once more. She didn't even feel hungry, but there really wasn't much by the way of sustenance in Oceana. At least not any sustenance that she particularly enjoyed. The thought made her savour the crispy chicken skin as she ripped into the drumsticks.

Her mum pulled the car over in a lay-by just one field away from the cliff path. Putting the now-empty Tupperware into the foot-well she looked at the three faces in the car.

"I'm not going to say goodbye if that's what you're all waiting for." She said as they all hurriedly tried to wipe the concerned looks off their faces. "I love you all." She opened the car door. "And I'll see you soon."

Opening the car door she took off across the field, barefoot and dressed in only her Mer garments without looking back.

As she scrambled down the cliff-path, she set her mind to her plan. A modification of the original plan that she, Em and Douglas had hatched together. She was still going to find her uncles and bring them over to her side. The more protection she had from within the palace walls, the safer she was. And the more likely she was to be able to rescue Em and Douglas.

But could she trust them?

Do I really have a choice?

She knew the answer was no. And as her toes hit the frigid waters she knew what she had to do.

Throwing herself forward, she shot under the waves, summoning her currents like old friends immediately, barely noticing the shift as the ocean welcomed her back. Summoning her courage alongside them, she propelled herself into the inky depths.

17.

Oh my god I shouldn't have eaten those drumsticks...

Was her first thought upon exiting the travel current. Her second was to immediately check her cloaking and glance wildly around to make sure there were no Guards in the area.

The travel current back down had been just as violent and stomach-churning as her route back to the surface a month ago. She had thought it safer to once again conjure her own current rather than use one of the main routes into or out of Oceana as she was sure Duncan would have them all heavily guarded – cloaking or not.

The only thing she had managed to control about the current once it was summoned was where it spat her out. She had imagined the large, empty space on the outskirts of the crumbling city where she had once saved a small Mer boy from the jaws of a starving shark.

This area of Oceana was a far cry from the centre of the city where most buildings were still standing. Here the Mer lived mostly in caves, having abandoned their homes as they fell into ruin.

She floated there, the sand beneath her churning in the current's wake, and prayed that no-one would hear the roaring water and come investigate. Given that this area was less populated and in extreme poverty, she was hoping that it would be less heavily guarded.

She had been right, to an extent.

As the current sealed itself shut behind her leaving nothing but opaque water and the kind of silence you hear after the washing machine finally clicks off, she held up her hand in front of her. Sighing in relief she saw that it simply blended in with the water and rocks surrounding her, the faint rays of light that kept Oceana in perpetual twilight passing through it.

But just as she was about to swim off towards the palace, she heard a shout.

"It came from over there!"

"Intruder!"

Heart racing, she ducked behind some rocks just in time. Even though her cloaking rendered her invisible, she was still solid.

Three Guards came barrelling around the corner, spears held aloft and tails pumping furiously. One was dragging a bedraggled young Mer woman by the arm.

"There is nothing here!" one of the Guards yelled, rounding on the woman.

She cowered away from him, her knotted hair and dirty nails telling Riva that she was one of the poorest members of Mer society. Peering out from behind the rocks she could also make out several half-healed welts across her dark grey tail.

What on earth are those?

"Please, I promise you I saw a current open." The Mer woman pointed at the exact spot where Riva had emerged only moments earlier. "It was just there, I swear it!"

The Guards cast glances around and above, spears still held aloft. One of them swam off in the opposite direction to investigate towards the boundary line.

"You have wasted our valuable time with your lies." The largest Guard said, his spotted tail flukes flicking angrily back and forth, "You shall be punished."

Riva had to clap a hand over her mouth to stop from crying out as the Guard slashed at the Mer woman's tail with his spear. Her screams echoed through the barren wasteland but no-one came to help her as a fresh slash of red joined the other marks on her tail.

Riva's hand was aching from where she clutched the rocks in front of her. As much as she wanted to intervene, she couldn't reveal herself or the whole plan would be ruined.

Without stopping to listen to her pleas for mercy, the Mer woman was dragged off between the other two Guards, the three of them heading in the direction of the palace.

She tried to make sense of what she had just witnessed. In spite of their sometimes savage traditions and wild appearances, she had never known the Mer to turn on one another. Yes they had been hostile and sometimes downright violent towards her, but she was demi-Mer. She had never seen this kind of violence and mistrust between the Mer on her last visit.

Granted, she had spent most of her time in the palace, but the way that Mer woman had looked at the Guards, the panic etched on her features, and the way they eagerly sliced open her skin…

This was Duncan's doing. She had been prepared to find out more about the attacks he had been launching on humans, hell she had already heard about a lot of them as they were reported on the news all month, but she hadn't stopped to think about what he might be doing to his own people.

Just stick to the plan Riva. You can't help anyone without finding Em and Douglas. Besides, if Duncan's turning his own people against him all on his own then he's just making it easier for me.

Peeking out from behind the rocks, and feeling her cloaking magic flutter against her skin, she pushed off from the sand and swam towards the palace herself. As she made her way through the lower town and the crumbling remnants of their once glorious city, she couldn't shake the feeling that something was wrong. Swimming further into the underwater kingdom, past the markets and the square, she realised what was different.

It was silent.

Stopping short in the middle of the deserted square, she strained her ears. It was late evening, so the majority of the Mer would be in their homes instead of outdoors trading or socializing, but she hadn't seen a single soul since the Guards had dragged away the young Mer woman.

Even the eerie singing that usually permeated the entirety of Oceana had been muted.

Spinning around and summoning the fastest current she could, she raced towards the palace. If there were no Mer in the lower town and not a soul to be found in the inner city, then they must all be gathered somewhere else. There could be no mass exodus from Oceana's boundary lines as it was the only place left in the ocean where the Mer were hidden. Where they were safe.

No, a gathering was the only option, and there was only one reason Riva could think of that would cause the entire population to gather together.

She thought back to the day she had first arrived in Oceana and headed straight for the amphitheatre.

As she drew closer to the arena, she could hear cheers and shouts coming from what sounded like an enormously large crowd. She had found the Mer, but what else was she about to discover?

Swimming high above the building, cloaked by both her magic and the shadowy waters, she peered through the roof. The arches interlocked but didn't touch, which allowed the water to flow through the space. She peered down into the audience hall and once again had to put her hand over her mouth to muffle her gasp.

Douglas was floating at the floor of the chamber in the same spot where she had been brought upon her arrival in Oceana. Mer flanked three sides of the chamber, seated in rows of benches that snaked high up the walls. On the fourth side was an ornate throne carved from hundreds of different types of coral. Riva half expected to see her grandfather sitting atop it, but unfortunately the face that she gazed down upon was that of her uncle. His sharp cheekbones were accentuated by his vicious sneer and his jaw was tense as he looked down at Douglas who was floating just above the marble floor.

If only he knew that he was looking at his son. Would that even make a difference?

As she took in the lines of hatred on Duncan's face, she felt like they had been stupid to think that he would be swayed by an illegitimate half-human child. She hoped that someone had added stinging fire coral to that throne he was sitting on.

Duncan's voice boomed through the chamber. "How is it that we find you, another half-breed monstrosity, flouting your unnatural magics in the exact same place where we once found the traitor Riva?"

As she gazed down at Douglas, she felt powerless once again. His back was criss-crossed with deep lacerations, the blood spiralling away from his body in the water. The two Guards standing beside him didn't even need to restrain him anymore.

They had only been gone a couple of hours. How could they have done so much damage to him already?

"I already told you, I don't know." Douglas replied, his voice cracking. He sounded so tired.

Duncan raised his chin ever so slightly in the direction of another Mer who sported the same indigo tattoos that marked him as an Elite. Riva quickly scanned the hall for any other Mer with similar markings. There were a couple of them all skulking in the shadows, but none of them with cropped dark hair or brilliant green eyes. Fear hit her painfully in the gut. Either Em had been kidnapped and killed already, or she really had betrayed them and had handed over Douglas in exchange for her freedom.

Her eyes widened in horror as she saw what was clutched in the Elite Mer's hands. He was advancing on Douglas holding what looked like a fish's skull with a saw attached. Dropping herself quietly into the chamber, she slid down the marble arches. When she was halfway down she wished that she had a plan. The Elite was advancing on Douglas with the sawfish skull. Rows and rows of sharp teeth arranged in such a way across the flat rostrum that it looked like it could do unfathomable damage.

They aren't actually going to use it, it's just a threat. His back is already raw from the spears. She told herself, even as she sped up her descent.

As she reached the benches, she came to an abrupt halt as Douglas's screams assaulted her eardrums. She hid her eyes just in time but no matter how hard she pushed her hands over her ears she couldn't block out his screams of agony. What made it worse was the cheering from the Mer that came afterwards.

Please don't be dead, please don't be dead.

She dared a glimpse below her and had to fight with her gag reflex. The flesh on Douglas's back was flapping open in several places, the water around him stained red with his blood. He was bone white but she could see him fighting to stay conscious.

Pressing herself flat against the back of the amphitheatre, just above the highest benches, she looked around the cheering Mer gathered here and felt truly frightened for the first time.

In spite of her powers she felt seriously out of her depth.

So much for her thinking that Duncan was turning the Mer against him, he was turning his people into monsters instead.

"My fellow Mer." Duncan cried out, addressing everyone as the cheering subsided, Douglas on all fours on the cold marble floor. "We have suffered at the hands of humans for too long!"

More cheers.

"Did I not promise you that I would restore our people to their rightful place?"

Unearthly clicks and snaps were now coming from some of the Mer along with the cheers.

"Here we have yet another abomination cowering before us. The last time a half-breed entered our borders she almost destroyed us. Do not forget her trickery, or how she used her magic to hoodwink us into believing that she was anything other than abnormal. Do not forget what crimes this boy's predecessor committed! The murder and mutilation of our glorious King, of my father."

You filthy liar!

Her stomach grew hollow. She knew that he would have spread lies and misinformation to discredit her. She knew that Duncan would want to undo all of the work she had put in to show the Mer that she was an ally. But to say that she had been the reason for the Kings death? Why would the Mer believe that? There had been witnesses to the King's fatal injury outside the borders. Her uncles had been witnesses to his death and to Duncan's treachery.

She glared at her twin uncles, Murray and Murphy, as they stood witness to the brutality inflicted on her cousin as they floated just behind the throne. There was no sign of her other uncle Declan. Maybe he at least was standing up to his older brother. The twins were floating to the far right of the throne, almost in shadow so it was hard to make out their expression, but she could see that they weren't cheering.

Why have they not stood up for me? How could they have allowed this to happen?

Duncan was still speaking and she barely heard him through the blood roaring in her ears.

"How can we forget the half-breed's blatant disregard for the sanctity of Mer life after the abduction of my dear brother who we now believe to be dead, as well as her destruction of the palace hospital resulting in the unnecessary deaths of some of our strongest warriors. Warriors that were seeking refuge and healing from injuries caused by humans."

Hold the phone. What.

He was telling them all that she had *kidnapped* her father? But of course, he would never have made it public knowledge that she was his niece. He would want her to be as far removed from the royal family as possible. But what the hell did he mean about the hospital? Yes, she had destroyed the cave where the King's body had lain in order to escape. She had quite literally blown up the wall to create an exit for her and her father. But she hadn't destroyed the hospital, had she?

Looking around at the Mer who were cheering their new savage King, she wondered if she had accidentally killed some of their family members in the blast. Had she really hurt their loved ones, their children?

"Never again." Duncan continued. "Never again will we allow humans or their kind to pick us off like vermin. We shall rise, glorious in victory and take the ocean back for ourselves!"

The shouts and cheers were now reverberating off the walls while the clicks and whistles vibrated through her chest cavity to the point of pain.

Duncan swung his icy eyes back to Douglas where he seemed to be losing consciousness, his own blood a cloud around him in the water. Although it seemed to be slowing already.

"Now." he said when the cries had once again faded. "Our laws clearly state that any half-breed discovered in our rightful territory should be executed on sight. My father made a grave error in judgement by showing mercy to the girl Riva."

There was a fiery glint inside those ice-cold eyes and Riva shivered involuntarily.

As the bloodlust seemed to overcome most of the Mer gathered and they bared their teeth, she summoned her magic and got ready to use it. She hadn't wanted it to come to violence, in fact she wasn't even sure that she could overpower so many Mer at once, but if the only way to save Douglas's life was to blast her way through the crowd, rescue him and escape the same way she did with her father then so be it.

However as she got ready to release her magic, Duncan did something surprising. He raised his hand to ask for quiet. "While I will show no mercy to this boy, I cannot deny that executing him prematurely would further hurt our cause."

This statement was met with some confused murmurs in the crowd.

"We know that the half-breed girl was found in the same spot. I am making a calculated guess that they know one another. During her confinement to the palace I unwillingly learned much about her personality and I am willing to assume that her love of theatrics will make it impossible for her to resist coming to save him."

The crowd was starting to smile once again. Riva was gritting her teeth. Love of theatrics indeed. Who was the one making the dramatic speech?

"Take him to the cells." Duncan said, and before Riva could even raise her hand, the burly Guard with the midnight black tail had hit Douglas over the head. He slumped forwards, completely unconscious. They dragged him away through the marble doorway, but as much as she wanted to follow him, Riva stayed. She was scanning the rest of the room for the other person she desperately needed to find. Em. What she wouldn't give to see that boyish grin appear over her shoulder now.

Where the hell is she? Riva thought, trying to calm her thoughts. *I know she didn't betray us again. She has to be here somewhere.*

The Mer filed out of the room in a great rush. Again baffling Riva with their rigid attitude of entering through doorways when they could all quite easily swim out through the gaps in the ceiling. Although she was admittedly glad they didn't or they would have all bumped into her.

Once the hall had cleared, she floated down to the bottom of the amphitheatre until her bare feet brushed the cool marble floor. Sinking to her knees she ran a hand across its perfectly smooth surface and raised her eyes to stare at that monstrous throne, in front of which the water was still slightly cloudy with Douglas's blood.

The last time she had stood on this spot she had almost been executed. But she had used her powers to bargain for her life. Why had Douglas not done the same? Had he simply been too weak?

I should have been with him Riva thought, kicking herself for leaving them alone and defenceless back in the bay just so that she could go on a date.

"Murray, Murphy!" Duncan shouted briskly, startling Riva into attention.

Her uncles swam slowly from behind the throne towards their elder brother who floated on the top step of the marble dais.

"Yes?" they asked in unison.

Duncan's features softened slightly, although they remained a far sight from kind, and he grasped each of them by their shoulders. Riva floated closer, careful not to disturb the bloody water too much lest they catch a glimpse of her outline.

"This new regime has been difficult to implement. Despite what you saw here today, many have been resisting my new orders. The palace dungeon grows fuller by the day. Do not forget the role I need you both to play."

"Yes Your Majesty. We are doing our best." Murphy said quietly, stealing a glance at his brother who remained quiet.

Your Majesty?

Riva was puzzled. Her grandfather had never insisted that the family use his title. Being happy instead for his sons to simply call him father. She ground her teeth together at Duncan's arrogance. He had been bad enough as a Crown Prince, a title that had never even been meant for him. He would be insufferable as King.

"I know what you wish us to do Your Majesty, but many feel that you are completely disregarding the policies that father worked years to-."

Duncan held up a hand, cutting Murphy off "Father was too lenient." He said warningly, "Do not forget that it was he who allowed that *girl* into our home, to mix with Mer of the purest blood, of the highest ranks. He let down his guard and she ended up being his downfall."

"Riva wasn't the one who killed father." Murray interrupted, brow furrowed.

Faster than Riva thought possible, Duncan whirled around and delivered a crunching blow to Murray's jaw with his tail. With a sound like eggs cracking, he collapsed to the floor, his own tail – white like his brothers, trembling.

Riva paddled back a few metres, heart pounding.

"She may not have been the one to deliver the killing blow, but she had everything to do with his death." Duncan growled, advancing once again towards Murray but his twin brother darted between them.

"Yes." Murphy said quickly. "You are right. He just needed a reminder, but we will do better in future."

With narrowed eyes the ruthless king looked down at where his youngest brother cowered on the ground and grunted. "Make sure that you do. She will be back to rescue the other half-breed, mark my words. And we better be ready when she does."

Flanked by the last remaining Guards, he exited the chamber. Leaving the twins and Riva alone.

18.

Murphy immediately joined his brother on the floor, tenderly taking the face that was so like his own in his hands, gingerly inspecting the damage. Murray was groaning through clenched teeth, the jutting angle of his jaw telling both Murphy and Riva the same thing. It was badly broken.

"We need to get you to the infirmary." Murphy said, his hands shaking as he pulled Murray's arm across his shoulders.

As she watched him struggle to lift his brother, who clearly wanted to remain a pile of misery on the floor, Riva made her decision. He had said the words out loud - that Riva was innocent. The twins didn't want this. They might be trying to placate their brother for now, whether to save themselves or to buy them time she didn't know, but she knew that they could see the truth behind his lies.

With Em missing and Douglas imprisoned on pain of death, she didn't have any time to waste. Casting outwards with her senses, she made sure there were no prying eyes, noting only a couple of Guards swimming back and forth outside in the square, as well as a few reef sharks circling above the auditorium and she felt safe enough to remove her cloaking.

Letting her magic shimmer its way across the surface of her skin, she revealed herself inch by inch and like a wave tumbling across the sand, she materialized.

Murray was the first to spot her and started frantically screaming in the back of his throat, mangled jaw still too painful for him to move.

"Sssh, you can't try to speak. You will do more damage." Murphy said, attempting to drag him off the dais.

Shaking his head wildly, Murray lifted a finger and pointed directly at Riva.

"What is it?" his brother asked, sounding royally ticked off. "Seriously you can stop your theatrics now, it's entirely your fault we got ourselves into this situation in the fi-." His words choked off at the end as he saw what his brother was pointing at. "Riva?" he breathed, almost dropping his brother.

She summoned a current and closed the distance between them quickly. "Hello uncles." She said. This close she could see the confusion and worry in their hazel eyes.

"I need your help." She said, hoping that Murphy wouldn't start shouting for the Guards.

"How are you here?" Murphy asked, eyes flitting towards the door. "This was incredibly stupid, even for you Riva. Oceana has changed. You won't find it so accommodating this time around."

Riva snorted. "Oh, because you were all so welcoming last time?"

Murphy frowned. "That's not fair. We welcomed you with open arms, even before we knew you were our niece."

"Yeah but the rest of it was no picnic. Look, I need your help." She said, nervous without her cloaking.

"Why would we help you?" Murphy asked, eyes narrowed. Murray was moaning through his teeth, trying to speak.

She crossed her arms across her chest and narrowed her eyes at her uncle. "Because we are family and family help one another. That boy who just got sliced and diced on Duncan's orders five minutes ago? Also family."

Her uncles' confusion redoubled.

"But even if you don't care about that, you know that I am the best chance the Mer have for survival. You saw what I could do with my magic before, imagine what it will grow into."

Moving slowly so as not to alarm either of them, she stretched out her Mark towards where Murray was still sitting. Murphy swam backwards to give her space which she took as a good sign.

Kneeling on the cool, smooth floor, she just barely touched her fingertips to his jaw. It was enough. With a grotesque popping sound as the white light healed him, his jaw moved back into place and he collapsed against his brother in relief, wiggling his chin experimentally.

Murray looked up at her as he continued massaging his jaw, Murphy had one eyebrow raised.

"The glowing's new." He said appraisingly.

Riva rolled her eyes. "Yeah, so I'm even more of a circus freak than the last time you saw me." She felt like sticking her tongue out at him.

"Better?" she asked Murray.

He was still poking at his skin tentatively. "Yes, much. Thank you."

They both got up from the floor and she looked both of them in the eyes.

"I'm sorry that we never got the chance to talk as family before I had to escape. You found out that Dylan is my father about five seconds before Duncan tried to kill me so…"

"We don't actually know much about what really happened." Murray said sheepishly.

Murphy patted his brother on the back, "What happened in the infirmary that day is all a bit of a blur. We aren't sure how much of what Duncan says to believe, as I assume you saw…"

Riva nodded. "Thank you for standing up for me." She smiled at Murray, "I had nothing to do with the death of my grandfather. In fact, quite the opposite. He had been planning to publically accept me as his granddaughter and grant me an ambassador role to attempt to heal the divide between humans and the Mer. But then he went with the Guards to fight when the mine exploded and, well, you know." she finished lamely.

The twins were wide-eyed. "Father, knew?" they asked in unison once again.

"Yeah. Not for long though. We told him at the summer solstice. But I think he had suspected from the beginning. Duncan certainly had."

"How is our b-your father?" Murray asked, sounding desperate for news. "When you both disappeared we couldn't believe it, his shackles were supposed to bind him to Oceana for life. Duncan told us all that there was no way he could have gotten out alive."

Riva was furious that Duncan had let his brothers believe that their own brother was dead. A new low, even for him.

"My father is alive and well." She said firmly.

Both twins shared a relieved glance. "How is that even possible?"

"How is any of this possible?" Riva asked, generating a quick whirlpool around the three of them that was interspersed with flecks of electricity. The dancing light reflected the fear and awe in her uncle's eyes. "I have more power than even I understand." She let the lightning storm die down before it attracted too much attention.

"So did Dylan come back here with you?" Murray asked, craning his neck around Riva as if expecting his brother to pop out from under one of the benches.

"Uh, No. He couldn't. He um, well, he sort of doesn't have his tail anymore." Riva shifted uncomfortably, wondering how they would take this latest news.

"What do you mean he doesn't have his tail anymore?" Murray half-laughed, confused.

She help up her hands in an almost apologetic way and let her Mark glow by way of explanation.

"No." Murphy breathed, flicking his fins to take a step back from her. "No-one has that kind of power."

"Well, for some reason I do." Riva said, glancing around them once again, "Can we go somewhere more private to talk? This is kind of a long story."

The twins shared a look and then nodded. "Follow us."

With them leading the way, and her cloaking firmly back in place, she followed them out of the doors and across the now-bustling market square as Mer of all ages gossiped about the new half-breed arrival. Clearly the news was worth staying up late for. Heads turned in their direction as the twins swam, making way for the two youngest princes of Oceana.

As they drew away from the town, the sprawling coral reef that lay at the foot of the palace greeted them and Riva couldn't keep the smile from her face. Brushing her consciousness against the creatures below, she almost gave away the fact that she was there as they rose up to greet her. Brightly coloured clownfish rubbed gently against the soles of her feet, eagle rays glided over and above her, their velvet-smooth wings caressing her skin. Even the coral itself seemed to grow more vibrant as she passed.

She had missed this giant splash of colour. As they swam over it she felt as if the reef was calling out to her, and in the same way the ocean itself sometimes sang to her, so did the creatures below. Taking a deep breath she allowed the elastic-band feeling her magic sometimes held to expand across the entire reef and let a pulse of it leave her body.

Almost instantly, the entire reef flourished. Corals grew by inches, schools of fish of all colours and shapes spiralled up and across the tips of their rocky coves to spill out across the water above.

"Riva, if you want to stay hidden down here, maybe don't make it so obvious that you're there." Murphy said drolly.

"Sorry." She whispered, waving off a school of parrot fish who had started swimming around her head.

The twins smirked to themselves, but she could see the awe in their faces as they looked out across the thriving reef. This reef had remained largely unaffected by the warming sea temperatures that had caused most of the reefs outside of Oceana's borders to bleach and die already. Hopefully she would be given the chance to heal them too.

The reef faded away behind them as they reached the foot of the palace.

As they passed through the entranceway, there were several Mer milling about. Riva adjusted her currents so as to make their flow more subtle. The last thing she wanted to do was to arouse suspicion.

Unfortunately as she smoothed the water, a pair of feline-like eyes swept across the large atrium to gaze at where she swam. Elder Iolana was swimming sedately through the space with two other Mer.

Panicking, Riva glanced down to confirm that her cloaking was still in place and her heart stopped flapping in a panic when she saw that it was. Looking back up at Iolana, she furrowed her brow in confusion.

Can she see me?

The corners of the Mer Elder's mouth lifted slightly as if to say that she had been waiting for her to arrive. Riva hoped it was a good sign. If Iolana was in her corner then she felt confident that she could win this fight. Perhaps the ancient ocean magic that Iolana possessed, and her rank as Head Elder would tip the scales in Riva's favour. The ancient Mer swam serenely away, the barnacles on her tail lethal-looking in the dancing light of the bioluminescent palace.

Realizing that her uncles had swum around the corner, she bolted off after them, making a mental note to thank Iolana when this was all over for giving Em the key to finding Douglas.

Catching up with the twins, they swam through the entryway and up the sweeping stone steps towards the royal quarters.

Riva had never been this way before. Her modest room that she had been confined to had been on the other side of the palace. As prisons went it had been okay. A decent sized sponge bed, a cracked mirror, some kelp curtains that she had once tried to fashion into a bandeau until Em had taken pity on her and made the one she was currently wearing.

Her chest constricted uncomfortably and she wished that they would hurry up. She needed to explain her plan to them so that she could find Em and rescue Douglas before they got hurt. Well, hurt more than they already had been. The image of Douglas's tattered back flashed through her mind and she fought against another wave of nausea.

"How much longer? We don't have much time." She whispered.

"Not far now." Murray hissed back as a servant carrying a basket of bright black urchins passed them, a puzzled look on her face.

After what seemed a never-ending labyrinth of corridors, they finally stopped in front of an enormous clam-shaped door. Murphy stretched out his hand but instead of knocking, placed his palm flat on the glimmering surface and the door opened, lowering slowly to the floor.

"Colour me impressed." Riva muttered quietly. Murphy smirked.

Upon entering the room she could see that they were inside royal living quarters.

Large archways offered an unparalleled view of the reef below through silken curtains that fluttered pleasingly in the small currents as they darted in and out of the room.

There was a comfortable-looking sponge which was shaped luxuriously into a couch-like shape. There were several other smaller sponges, all of the same peachy-pink colour, that she assumed served as chairs, grouped around an impossibly smooth shell table that Riva was sure she would be able to see her reflection in.

As she peered around the corner she could just about make out the edge of the stone dais upon which sat a large bed, draped in more of those silken curtains.

She hoped that the twins, while they did most things together, did not in fact share a bed.

"Whose room is this?" she asked bluntly, revealing herself instantly, dropping her cloaking.

Unfortunately, as she did so, someone swam around the corner.

"Ah finally, I thought you two were never going to turn up to- ARGH!" her other uncle Declan cried out as he saw Riva floating in the middle of his living room.

She raised one hand in a pathetic wave, "Hi."

Declan was clawing at his throat like he couldn't breathe. Riva wanted to remind him that he was Mer and that wasn't actually a necessity for him.

"Declan, wait. She's here to help us." Murray said, advancing on his elder brother while Murphy swam to the archways and looked out, as if searching for eavesdroppers.

"But she, she's wanted for m-murder." Declan gasped, "We watched her swim away with Dylan. She's the reason he's d-dead." He glanced wildly around the room, "She can't be here. If Duncan finds out we were in contact with her we'll all be dead." He hissed at them, shooting her accusatory looks.

Riva folded her arms. "I hadn't taken you for a coward."

Declan broke free of Murray's arms and swam towards her, thick white tail flukes stirring up eddies within the room, making the curtains swing open.

"Is it cowardly to want to protect my family?" he growled, advancing on her, a furious expression on his face.

Without thinking about it she held her hands up in front of her and a sheet of golden light flashed up between them, stopping her uncle from reaching her.

"Stop." She said threateningly, "If you want to protect your family then you'd better listen to me. Duncan wants a war with humans. I am here to prevent it."

"A war with humans. You speak as if you weren't one." he said, looking her up and down, taking his time on her legs.

"I'm not human." Riva stated simply. That shut them all up. "Well, at least not entirely. Not anymore." She rubbed her Marked palm against her thigh uncomfortably.

"Now. Are you going to listen to me or not?" she asked, looking between all three of them.

The twins nodded immediately, both sitting down on the sponge-couch. Declan remained impassive.

"Come brother. You should have seen what she did to the reef just as we were swimming over it. I haven't seen it that alive since we were children." Murray said. "She also informed us that apparently father thought that she could help us too. There is so much that Duncan kept from us. We want to hear what she has to say."

Murphy remained quiet, looking between where Declan floated rigidly and Riva's still-outstretched palm. Declan moved over to the curtain as if to put his younger brothers' words to the test. Eyebrows lifting slightly, he let the curtain fall back into place.

"You spoke with our father before he passed?" he asked quietly.

Riva nodded. "I did." Her heart twisted as the grief passed over Declan's face. "He was a fair king. And he had been ready to accept me publically as his granddaughter. He understood that I could help the Mer."

Completely surprising her, Declan's face crumpled. Slightly at a loss for what to do, she floated there, mouth opening and closing wordlessly as Murphy helped him sit down gently. So much had happened over the last month that sometimes Riva forgot that they had only just lost their father. Of course the grief was still fresh.

This whole situation was messed up.

"Declan, it's alright. You will get past this." Murphy said, patting his brother on the back. "It was a terrible loss but there will be other chances for you."

Slightly confused, Riva tried to find words to console him. "I'm truly sorry that you all lost him. I can't imagine how confusing this time must be for all of you. It must be so difficult to..." she searched in her brain for a phrase Alex liked to use, "Properly process your grief."

Proud of herself for not rambling for once, she plastered what she hoped was a genuine smile on her face but was met with sad looks.

Declan looked positively miserable.

"What is it?" Riva gulped, "What have I said?"

Declan closed his eyes again and turned away from her so it was Murray that spoke from behind her.

"The baby." He said quietly, glancing over his shoulder towards the bedroom, "He didn't survive."

Riva swung back around and saw Declan's true grief for the first time. Tears sprung to her eyes unbidden. She had spent time with Declan's mate. Declan's heavily pregnant mate.

"When?" she breathed, her eyes burning as the tears escaped and then disappeared into the water.

Declan lifted his head. "Two weeks ago." His voice was strained. "My sweet Maya laboured for days. We were delighted when she birthed a healthy boy and survived, but even as he nursed he grew weaker. We tried everything we could think of. But only a few days after he was born, he slipped away."

Not knowing what to say, Riva averted her eyes from the expression on Declan's face. She couldn't even imagine what it must feel like to lose a child. The Mer had been severely impacted by the pollution levels in the ocean and as a result Mer children were few and far between. Some of their most backward laws, the same laws that forbid Em from loving who she was born to love, were a result of their desire to successfully reproduce.

"Declan, I'm so, so sorry." She said, hugging her arms around herself as her uncle regained his composure. "This should never have happened."

Pinching the bridge of his nose, he sniffed once, "Thank you." He looked over to the open archway that led to the bedroom, "If only my Maya could realise that it wasn't her fault."

Riva turned to watch the silken curtains flutter around the foot of the bed within the room. There was something about their undulating movement that called her to them. Without even realising that she was doing it, she had started swimming towards the bedroom. She could hear voices in her head and it felt like something was propelling her forwards against her will.

As she turned the corner into the room, Maya was lying sleeping on the bed. Her auburn hair a fiery halo spread out across the flat sponge around her head. Her lightly flecked tail twitching slightly as she dreamed, the slight swelling around her middle still visible, mammary glands red and inflamed where her baby was supposed to be nursing. The voices in her head intensified, keening, lilting voices that made her want to weep.

Riva's breath caught as she fully understood the significance of a mother's loss. All of these physical reminders that she should have a baby in her arms.

As she approached the bed, Maya's eyelids fluttered open, but she didn't start at the sight of Riva, in fact she stared straight through her.

"Maya?" she breathed, reaching out to take her cold hand.

The Mer woman looked down at the touch but simply laid her head back down on the sponge like lifting it was too much effort. Riva's chest tightened. She had seen that very same look on her own mother's face one too many times.

The voices grew stronger, and as they reached a peak she realized that they were the voices of all the women Gaia had chosen before her. Singing their own songs of loss, of grief and of suffering.

Allowing her magic to guide her, surrendering herself to whatever force was drawing her to the Mer woman, she gave herself to it and placed her right hand on top of Maya's stomach.

"What are you doing?" she heard someone shout behind her.

Without replying, she closed her eyes and allowed her magic to pour out of her as the song in her head intensified. The stone dais around the bed was cold on her knees as she knelt there, but she focused on the sensations within Maya's body in order to heal her.

Her magic travelled around the grieving mother's body, healing all pockets of infection, taking away the pain of blocked milk ducts and childbirth itself. Restoring her body to how it had been before.

As she rode the wave of euphoria that often came alongside using this much magic, she looked deeper as Maya's body healed. Towards the cause of her baby's death, and found what she had been looking for. Tiny particles of unnatural plastics and pollutants that lived within her very blood.

It was just as Em had explained to her before.

Furrowing her brow she concentrated her magic on those particles, hoping that she could do something, anything to help. The voices in her head urged her on, but no matter what she tried, Ocean magic, Earth magic, any and all elemental powers that she possessed, nothing would get them to disappear.

She wasn't aware that she was crying as the song of the women who had come before her faded, until she felt a hand on her shoulder.

"I'm so sorry. I wish there was something else I could do." She gasped.

Her uncle was shaking his head. "You have already done more than I could ever have imagined."

Maya was now sitting upright and there was life behind her eyes again.

"Declan." The Mer woman gasped, reaching out her arms for her husband.

"Oh sweetheart, you've come back to me." He said, swimming forward to curl himself around her protectively.

Pushing herself up off her knees, Riva started to swim out of the room, not wishing to intrude.

"Wait!" Maya called out, sniffling.

She turned around, "Yes?"

"Can I ask you something?" she said quietly, voice still laden with sadness, but she could detect a trace of hope there too.

"Of course."

"Did you fix this?" Maya asked, her voice catching, as she gestured to her abdomen.

Declan was looking between both women, face full of hope that she didn't want to dash.

Riva struggled to know what to say, "I cannot promise that if you have another child that the same thing will not happen again. But I can promise that there will be another child. And I vow to change things so that in the future this will be the exception and not the rule."

Riva had expected sorrow, but surprisingly it was grim determination that filled Maya's eyes.

She nodded firmly, "Then thank you. For giving us what you could."

Riva smiled sadly back at her and let herself out of the room, closely followed by the twins, leaving the young couple to their grief.

"Can you really fix all of this?" Murray asked when they reached the living room.

Riva sighed and took herself to the edge of one of the archways and looked through the opaque curtains towards the reef below, wondering exactly how many things she was going to be required to fix. The whole damn world apparently.

"I can try."

19.

"Alright, now remember you will only have a few minutes. We can't distract the Guards for long." Murphy said as they walked down towards the palace dungeons.

"That's okay, I only need a few minutes for now." she said, heart racing.

Their plan had been put in place. With three members of the royal family now on her side, she felt confident that they could overthrow Duncan without bloodshed.

She had spent the last hour trying to visit Eden, she had never needed Gaia's advice more than now, but her mind wouldn't shut off enough for her to make the connection. She kept telling herself that it had absolutely nothing to do with wanting to see Cronos again.

Duncan had announced the execution of Douglas at sunset in three days' time. Apparently he assumed that if Riva hadn't appeared by then to save him then he wasn't worth keeping. So with the help of her uncles, she had conspired to break into the dungeons tonight to free both him and Em. None of her uncles had seen Em, nor had they heard her name so much as mentioned since Douglas appeared. As much as that little voice in her head whispered that maybe Em had betrayed them again, she refused to believe it. She would overturn every stone in that dungeon to find her if she had to.

As they wound their way into the bowels of the palace through underwater caves and chambers that were bathed in shadow as the eerie bioluminescence lit their way, Riva sincerely hoped that she could get them out quickly. This place gave her the creeps.

"I'll wait out here." Murray whispered, inclining his head to a shadowy alcove.

Riva rounded the corner with Murphy.

"Good morning." Murphy greeted the Guard on duty warmly in his loudest voice.

"Your Highness." The Guard replied in a musical voice that was a stark contrast with her fierce appearance.

Murray flanked her, turning on his most charming smile. "How are you this morning Fiona?" he asked, trying to lure her away from her position to give Riva enough room to slip past. The tunnel leading to the dungeons was only large enough for one person to swim through at a time. Meaning that even with her cloaking, slipping past undetected was going to be a challenge.

"I am on duty Prince Murphy, as you well know. I don't have time to talk." She replied, studiously avoiding his gaze, clutching her spear in both hands.

Crap. I thought Murphy said that he knew her?

They had waited all night until Fiona had taken up her post at Murphy's insisting. He had seemed so sure that he would be able to lure her away.

Murphy, seemingly unfazed, sauntered towards her and trailed his fingers up her spear, lightly brushing her own. "Come on Fiona, you can take a break for five minutes surely? It's first thing in the morning. No-one is even awake yet."

As much as his shameless flirtation made her lip curl, she breathed a sigh of relief when she realized that it was actually working. A slow smile spread across Fiona's face and she brushed an imaginary hair away from her face, even though her blonde locks were tied back in a severe braided style.

"That's my girl." Murphy breathed, taking her hand and yanking her away from the middle of the tunnel, pressing her up against the stone wall as she let out a giggle.

Almost certain that, despite the severity of the situation, Murphy was enjoying himself very much- if the obscene noises the two of them were making were any indication. They had given Riva just enough space to squeeze past and she shot off down the dark tunnel.

The glowing bioluminescence made the shadows dance and she braced herself for something to jump out at her behind every bend in the tunnel. Her stomach was in knots at the thought of what awaited her. What if Douglas and Em weren't there? What if she wasn't able to break them out and get them back to Declan's rooms in time?

Her uncles had offered to shelter them all, figuring that the best place to hide would be right under Duncan's nose. Riva had to admit she was looking forward to bringing him down from within.

There was a strange whooshing noise in the tunnel, almost like she was swimming through a vacuum, and it eventually widened into a cavernous room that was lined with hundreds of tiny caves that spiralled upwards as far as the eye could see.

Her jaw dropped open. How the hell was she supposed to find Douglas in here? Now out of the claustrophobic tunnel, she could hear the moans coming from the Mer behind bars. Some were weeping, others keening softly to themselves, and yet others were muttering things in a language Riva didn't understand.

The floor below her was strewn with stains and objects she didn't even want to find out the use of. Averting her eyes, she swam towards the first tiny cave. There was an elderly Mer slumped against the back wall. Puzzled by the lack of bars or other obvious barrier, she reached out her hand towards the mouth of the cave.

Her fingers made contact with a viscous substance that seemed to cling to her fingers and pull her forwards. As her hand was trapped inside the invisible door, she almost cried aloud in pain and fear as she was suddenly blind to everything but her worst memories.

She was completely incapacitated as she relived her mum's depressive episodes, Stuart's assault, the King's death, Duncan's witch-hunt and even those lacerations on Douglas's back in quick succession. In the space of a minute she was starved, beaten, assaulted and hunted as her brain was flooded with her worst nightmares and imaginings. Fighting the panic and gritting her teeth to stop from crying aloud she wrenched her hand away, the gelatinous barrier sucking her hand back even as she strained to escape its grip.

Finally the images disappeared and she was once again staring into the cave cell at the sleeping Mer. Clutching her hand to her chest protectively, she tried to get a grip on herself.

What the hell kind of magic was that?!

Looking around she saw that every single one of the cells had the same barrier, it was barely noticeable unless you looked towards the corners of the cave opening where there was a faint shimmer. Cheeks flaming hot from pure fear, she tried to swallow but her mouth was dry. Whoever had spelled these prisons knew that bars were not the only effective method of trapping people. Sometimes the mind did that better than anything else.

Rescuing Douglas and Em was going to be much trickier than she had originally planned. Why had her uncles not told her about this? Was it possible they didn't even know?

Keeping herself firmly cloaked, she swam between each and every cell, peering into their murky depths. As she spiralled higher and higher, the floor now far below her, she marvelled at the fact there were no Guards present inside this chamber. Perhaps the Mer figured that since there was only one way in or out that they didn't need to waste their time.

She was so busy mulling this over that she almost didn't recognise the person in the next cell.

"Douglas!" she breathed, heart leaping as she realised it was him. He was lying on his stomach, those great angry welts criss-crossing his back and Riva had to control a wave of nausea when his skin flapped open as she disturbed the water.

"Oh Douglas what have they done to you?" she breathed, fighting back tears.

He looked up at the sound of her voice but seeing no-one he groaned once and lay his head back down on the cold cave floor.

Glancing once more at the floor of the chamber to make sure there were no Guards, she hesitantly removed her cloaking.

"Douglas, it's me," she whispered. Hesitant to raise her voice more should any of the other Mer realise she was there.

He groaned again, lifting his head by a few inches. Even though his eyes were slightly unfocused, they widened in recognition when they saw her.

"Am I hallucinating?" he asked thickly.

She shook her head. "No, but I need to get my cloaking back up, I can't risk anyone seeing me here."

As she became invisible again, Douglas tried to crawl closer to the mouth of the cave.

"No, don't you'll hurt yourself more." She whispered urgently as he trembled with the effort.

He collapsed once again, his broken body unable to support him for even a few steps.

"What the hell are you doing here?" he asked, voice strained with the effort of speaking.

"What does it look like I'm doing? I'm rescuing you, you idiot." She said.

Douglas grinned, his split lip beading blood against the floor, his right eye was sporting an impressive purple bruise. "Well, as you can see I'm in no fit state for an escape attempt. You were right, my dad's a dick."

She raised her hand, Mark starting to glow. "I can fix that." She breathed, hoping that whatever magic was keeping the prisoners getting *out* wouldn't stop her magic from getting *in*.

Glancing up, panting, he saw what she was about to do. "No Riva you can't. If they see my injuries are healed then they'll know you were here."

Not bothering to listen, she let the magic pour out of her and cover him in her healing light. He groaned and gritted his teeth as his ribs snapped back into place and his back knitted itself together. Hands clenched into fists, his knuckles were white and strained over the bones as he endured the healing pain. Selfishly enjoying her own sudden lift in spirits at the magic use, she fought to rein it in before the healing was complete. Her magic tried to fight against her, like an eager stallion wanting to run while its rider pulled him back.

The light faded and Douglas got to his feet somewhat shakily. She was sure that without the support of the water he would have collapsed. His eye was still purple, although less swollen and the bruises that had bloomed on his torso and arms were now a mottled colour of greens and yellows.

"Turn around." Riva asked.

His back was covered in angry red lines but they all looked weeks old. The skin was still fragile and sore-looking but nothing compared to the raw agony he had been enduring for the last day.

"I'm sorry I couldn't heal you the whole way, I had to let them think that you were healing on your own. The Mer saw my healing powers the last time I was here, so if anyone asks you about it just let them think that you can do the same thing." She sighed.

Douglas approached the mouth of the cave. "I wish I could. It would have come in handy." he grimaced at the memories and swam closer.

"Careful!" Riva warned, immediately regretting raising her voice as it echoed through the chamber but glad that Douglas had stopped before touching the barrier. "It's spelled. Just trust me, don't touch it." She shuddered involuntarily.

Douglas looked up at the corners of his cell, fear plain as day on his face. "Remind me again why I decided to help you with this crazy mission? What the hell kind of place have you brought me to?"

Wishing that she could comfort him properly, she replied. "I'm sorry. This isn't the Oceana I remember either. It's all Duncan. These cells are filling up because of him. But some Mer are rebelling, my uncles have told me there's apparently a secret underground network working against him. They might be able to help us." She whispered.

His onyx eyes widened, the dark circles underneath them betraying his exhaustion. "You spoke to the princes?" he asked.

She nodded, looking over her shoulder and down to the floor to make sure no-one was listening and no Guards had decided to make an appearance. "Yeah. They promised to give shelter to all of us while we bring Duncan down together."

Wiping her hands nervously on her silky leggings she eyed up the invisible barrier, wondering how much magic it would take to break through it. "Alright, come on, we have to get you out of here."

"You can't, not yet." Douglas said, backing away slightly.

"What are you talking about? We have to. They're planning on executing you in a few days." She replied.

He was shaking his head. "Riva, if I escape then he'll hurt Em. I can't let him do that. She fought so hard to protect me when we were kidnapped. I even almost got away at one point…"

A lightning bolt of panic shot down her spine, jarring with the relief that Em hadn't betrayed them after all. "Who captured both of you? What do you mean 'hurt Em', does he have her?"

Douglas's eyes had taken on a hollow look. What kinds of things had he witnessed in the last twelve hours to make him look like that?

Riva's mouth was dry. "Where is she?"

"I don't know, they separated us as soon as we arrived." Douglas asked, his voice cracking, "I haven't seen her since."

Fear bubbling in the pit of her stomach, she replied, "Well then, we need to find her."

"He said he was going to kill her." Douglas said hollowly.

Fighting off a stronger wave of panic she replied, "It's all mind games Douglas. Trust me. It's going to take more than that smarmy, self-centred, self-proclaimed king to finish off Em." she looked around the dungeon, "We need to find her too."

"She's not here." He said miserably.

"How do you know?"

He looked down at the ground, "Because I spent all of last night screaming for her. I didn't hear any drawling Australian telling me to shut up and let her sleep."

Riva balled up her fists in frustration, nails digging in to her palms. "I swear if he hurts her I'll kill him."

Douglas snorted weakly, "Well from what I've seen of my dear old dad so far I wouldn't blame you. But I need to stay in here until you find her. If they discover I'm missing then they'll kill her just to get even with us."

"Crap." Riva pulled at her hair, "You two getting captured wasn't the plan you know."

He smiled wryly, looking down at his torso which now resembled a black and purple tie-dye sweatshirt. "Well this certainly wasn't my plan A either."

"I don't even know what letter of the alphabet my plan has anymore." She sighed, wondering how the hell she was going to find Em now. "Just please stay alive until I come back for you okay?"

Douglas nodded. "You too."

She stepped back from the cave, glad to be away from that nightmarish barrier. "I'll be back as soon as I can."

20.

It hurt her heart to leave Douglas but she knew he was right. She needed everything in place if she wanted to confront Duncan. She couldn't leave anyone that she cared about unprotected. As much as Em was able to handle herself, she was only one Mer against a whole army. She needed to find her friend.

Praying that she was still alive and wasn't enduring some unimaginable torture someplace else, she froze as she heard a noise come from the tunnel. Hesitating at the entrance, she realized that she had already wasted too much time and needed to get through before Fiona lost interest in Murphy.

Cloaking firmly in place, she snuck silently along the tunnel as quickly as she dared. As the mouth of the tunnel opened she stopped dead at the X-rated scene that awaited her and realised that she had seriously underestimated Murphy's charms. Floating silently above the two of them she averted her eyes and went to join Murray where he waited for them in the shadows.

"It's me." She breathed, sidling into the alcove with him as he jumped a mile at her voice.

"Oh my!" he clutched his heart. "I was getting worried." Murray said, trying to brush off his scare, "Were you successful? Where's Murphy?"

"Still busy apparently." She said drolly.

Sighing, Murray swam off in the direction of his brother. All she heard was him clear his throat loudly and a couple of minutes later both twins swam towards her, Murphy grinning roguishly.

"So how did it go?" They both asked, staring at a space two feet to the left of her.

"Not great. We need a new plan. Fast." She replied, still invisible.

Both twins groaned.

"Hey, stop being so negative. You two know the palace a hundred times better than I do, why can't you think of something?" she said grouchily.

Before either of them could reply, eerie singing started up above them in the palace proper.

"What in ocean…" Murphy muttered as the singing reverberated through the walls, making Riva feel like it was vibrating in her very blood.

"What is it?" she asked, "What's happening?" She grabbed onto Murphy's arm and he looked extremely uncomfortable with feeling something he couldn't see.

"Something bad." He replied, eyes wide.

Her blood turning to ice, she summoned the fastest current she could, "Then what are we waiting for?" she growled, thrusting them all down the deserted corridor.

As they finally emerged from the palace and swam out through the giant entranceway, Riva stopped dead, causing Murray to swim into her.

"What are you doing?" he whispered out the corner of his mouth.

She had seen what he hadn't. Far out beyond the reef lay the town square which was now packed with Mer. Mer who were singing what Riva now recognised as a death march.

Wishing that what she was seeing was just one of those horrible prison barrier-induced nightmares, her chest tightened painfully. Em was being led out into the square, restrained by several other Elite, marked as they were by their indigo tattoos.

"No." She breathed.

"Riva, think about this for a second, this isn't part of the plan." Murphy said, finally seeing what she had. "You can't risk exposing yourself. It's too late for her!" He made a wild grab for her that missed by more than a foot as she summoned another current and was gone.

Her blood was racing in her ears, a combination of adrenaline, fear and fury as she flew invisibly over the reef, completely blind to the ocean creatures that rose up to meet her.

As she approached the square, she halted abruptly above the scene. Desperately wracking her brains for some way out of this mess.

Crap! Come on Riva, think dammit!

Her friend was being dragged out on top of several smooth flat rocks that had been piled up in the middle of a platform that had been erected in the middle of the square. The singing became almost too much to bear as the inside of her skull felt like it was buzzing with the vibrations. She couldn't think straight.

"My dearest Merfolk."

Looking down through the gathered crowd, she saw Duncan materialize behind Em, keeping his distance from the Elite. Just his voice was enough to make Riva want to kill him. Right there and then. At the thought, her magic welled up and she wanted nothing more than to release a bolt of lightning or fling one of those rocks to crush him.

Just one flick of my hand and I could end this right now.

But even as she thought it she knew that she couldn't. The Mer would never trust her, or any human, if she killed their King in cold blood. Especially when most of them believed that she had also killed the previous King.

What was it Alex had said when she had almost killed that rapist in California? Something about not stooping to his level no matter how much he deserved it?

As much as she hadn't wanted to admit it at the time, giving him a second chance had been the right decision. That was what Douglas was supposed to have been, Duncan's second chance.

But the new King was making it *really* difficult for her to want to give him one.

Turning her attention back to the raised stones, a bizarre visual came to her mind of the scene from *The Hunchback of Notre Dame*. With Em playing the part of Quasimodo and Duncan perfectly fitting the bill as Frollo. Well, she had always wanted to be Esmeralda when she was a kid.

Remembering her favourite scene from the movie she smiled wickedly. She knew what she had to do. And she was going to enjoy it. Waiting for the right moment, she floated above the square, watching as the Elite dragged Em across the platform. She was even more bloodied and broken than Douglas had been. In fact, she was barely conscious.

They draped her across one of the rocks and she lay there, blood slowly trickling from her fingertips and spiralling up through the water. Her beautiful grey tail was mottled with bruising and sported so many gashes that Riva wondered how she was even still alive.

"My dearest Merfolk." Duncan repeated again once the crowd had quieted, "You are gathered here today to witness the execution of the traitor who lies before us." He pointed one finger down at where Em lay, barely stirring. "This once-Elite Mer has betrayed us not once, not twice, but more times than I can count. Each and every single one of those times she thought that she had found a way out. Well not today!"

He was met by cheers all around. Riva could barely stand it as she watched the crowd grow more bloodthirsty, Duncan's words holding them captivated.

"This Mer used to be sworn to protect us. She was one of our Elite warriors, the guardians and defenders of our race." Duncan said, gesturing over to where the small group of Elite were gathered. At his recognition, they all pulled one hand into a fist over their hearts to salute him.

Duncan smiled shrewdly at the group of soldiers that Riva knew he was using to target humans ocean-wide. She wondered how many of them it had taken to bring down that cruise ship on her birthday.

"Treason in any form will not be tolerated. But this Mer betrayed our race in more ways than one. By breaking one of our most sacred laws." He continued mysteriously, the entire crowd hanging on his next word. "This Mer before you, refused her duty to mate. Refused to continue our noble work in restoring our race to its former glory. No, instead she entered into a relationship with another Mer of the same sex."

Even though she had been expecting it from Duncan, she hadn't been ready for the angry reaction from the Mer gathered around her. As one they surged forwards towards the rock and had to be held back by the Guards surrounding the platform. All of the Mer, especially the women, looked like they now wanted to tear Em limb from limb.

Riva's jaw dropped open. She had underestimated just how desperate the Mer were. She was looking at a people who would do whatever it took to get their lives back, and Duncan was promising it to them while simultaneously satisfying their need for revenge. As she watched the Guards barely able to hold back the angry crowd, she wondered how on earth she would be able to convince them that there was a better way.

Duncan was now shouting over the roar of the crowd, a sick grin on his face. "The other Mer traitor who was involved in this disgusting partnership has already been executed for her treason. However betraying her own race comes so naturally to Emerald here." He swam circles threateningly around where Em lay, struggling to hold her head up.

Duncan's tail was dragging slightly on the smooth stone, his crown gleaming atop his head.

"You see, Emerald offered herself in service to me as payment for her crime, claiming to have seen the error of her ways." Here he stopped to make a self-deprecating bow to the public, "And I, ever merciful. Agreed."

There were appreciative murmurs through the gathered crowd at this news. Riva had to stop herself from screaming. There was nothing merciful about the man floating in front of her.

"However, as I expected all along, Emerald soon broke her word by assisting the half-breed Riva in her murder of my father and the kidnap and subsequent death of my dear brother."

This time, cries of sadness made their way through the crowd as Duncan played them all for fools with his careful web of lies.

How much Riva now wished that she had been able to bring her father down here too, maybe his appearance would have lent some credibility to her cause. As it was, she was now beginning to realise that her uncles' supposedly air-tight plan B was now dissolving around them.

Duncan continued to speak and he stopped directly behind Em. Her eyes were still out of focus but she was trying to lift her head. "We searched for weeks for both the half-breed disgrace and this traitorous witch but failed to find any trace of them. Until yesterday, when we discovered Emerald together with yet another half-breed. Unfortunately not the girl we were seeking, but the boy whom you all saw flaunt his apparent 'power' in a bid to escape our Guards."

Several of the Mer laughed and flashed their unnaturally white teeth. At the sound, Em finally raised her head, her eyes swimming into focus and for the first time, Riva saw her register what was going on.

"While I stayed the execution of the half-breed in an attempt to lure the traitor Riva down here to his rescue, I offer no such leniency to Emerald. A Mer who has defied not only her King, but her people too many times." Duncan extended his arm towards the Elite and a very large Mer swam out from within the group to hand him a sword.

"Emerald, you have been charged with high treason for conspiring against your King, betraying the sacred laws of our race and the murder of two members of the royal family." He gripped the ornate sword in both hands. "I will have your head!" Duncan proclaimed, raising the sword high above his head in a ceremonial fashion.

At that exact moment, Em lifted her gaze to the spot where Riva floated invisibly, as if she could feel her presence.

Riva dropped her cloaking.

"Stop!" she yelled, dropping to the platform so quickly that some of the warped wood underneath her feet cracked.

Em's eyes widened in surprise as pandemonium broke out amongst the Mer gathered in the square.

"Half-breed!"

"She's here!"

"She will kill us all!"

Cries rang out throughout the crowd but before she could lose the element of surprise, Riva summoned her magic and cracked the rock upon which Duncan was resting his tail in two with a blast of water that almost sent her reeling. As one half of it tumbled backwards, it caught his tail flukes, causing him to lose his grip on the sword which fell heavily towards the platform, point first.

He wind-milled his arms, trying to regain his balance but the heavy rock was no match for gravity and he fell from the platform, helpless under the weight. His cries for his Guards were lost amongst the cries from the rest of the crowd as his minions tried to restore order to the Mer.

Summoning all of her power, Mark and eyes glowing madly, she saw the terrified looks of the Mer closest to her and smiled, her magic revelling in their fear. She knew she had to work quickly before the Guards overwhelmed her. The ocean sang to her and the currents rose as she created a whirlpool to surround the platform in a frenzy of whirling water, separating herself and Em from the rest of the crowd.

"Argh!" Em screamed.

Whirling around, the churning water whipping her hair around her, she looked for a Guard she had missed. Thoughts of a sneak attack disappeared from her mind as she saw the sword that had been flung from Duncan's grip now buried deep inside Em's left tail fluke.

Riva watched as the blood started flowing from the entry point and Em's face grew even whiter. She landed right in front of her friend and bent down.

"Stay with me." She whispered, giving Em's shoulders a shake.

The whirlpool was gaining momentum and the unstable water made it difficult for her to keep her balance. But even as the impenetrable barrier kept out the Guards in the square, she finally noticed the six Elite now advancing towards her.

Crap. Forgot about them.

The wall of whirling water was the only thing keeping the rest of the Guards at bay so she dared not let it fall now. She was going to have to take on the six of them alone while holding the whirlpool in place.

Unfortunately these Elite were significantly larger than Em. Five of them were male, all of whom looked like they could easily win a bodybuilding contest, their muscular tails practically writhing with anticipation. The female was baring her teeth and had to be at least nine feet tall, her tail impossibly long and thin. Lethal was the word that sprang to Riva's mind.

Gaia help me.

She sent up a silent plea laced with magic, and even at the bottom of the ocean she could have sworn that the warm touch of the Goddess reached her.

All six of the Elite looked like they could deliver death to her in one blow.

She stood up to face them, fighting the buffeting of the whirlpool, Em at her back. Despite her fear, she reminded herself that she was no longer the scared little girl who had accidentally found herself in Oceana two months ago. With the power of Gaia at her disposal she knew it didn't matter how hard they tried. They wouldn't be able to touch her.

The first Elite to advance on her was cocky. But the grin on his face was wiped cleanly away as she wrenched him off the platform by a furious current. Magic coursing through her veins, Riva didn't even flinch when she heard the bright snap of his spine.

The second and third flew towards her, indigo tattoos writhing with their fury after watching their comrade fall. Riva stopped them both just inches in front of her face with two electrical currents that she conducted through the water. This time when her magic encouraged her to finish the job, she did. If she didn't kill them then they would certainly kill her, there would be no time for second chances today.

Riva gritted her teeth while the female cried in agony as she ripped her lightning through her very bones. That slender, inky tail blistering with the heat.

Her magic was surging, and she felt nothing but blessed relief at finally being allowed to stretch. Her fingers crackled and sparked with electricity even as her currents snaked through the centre of the whirlpool, guided to their next target at Riva's urging. Adrenaline was singing in her veins alongside her magic and she swore that she had never felt more alive.

The two remaining Elite exchanged worried glances.

"You are right to be afraid." She said, her calm voice a perfect contrast to the chaos of their surroundings.

A slender, light current brushed past her upper arm and she caressed it with her fingers, letting it slide through her open palm. She made eye contact with the nearest Elite, and for one second she imagined that he wore Stuart's face.

The lithe current sprang from her grip and wrapped around his neck. He writhed against her and clawed at the water, fingers passing through the current to gouge at his own skin, eyes bulging. Even though the Mer didn't need oxygen to survive, Riva imagined that a crushed oesophagus would hurt.

Delighting in the release of her magic, she almost missed the advance of the last Elite as he came at her from the side. Clearly hoping to attack while she was distracted.

Flinging out her right hand, while her left kept the pressure on the other male's throat, she summoned the sword to her.

Ignoring Em's sharp gasp of pain as the sword slid out of her flukes, the hilt met Riva's outstretched arm and she grasped the ancient metal tightly. As her fingers made contact, she funnelled her magic into it and the blade began to glow white-hot. She pivoted, thrusting the sword with all her strength towards her attacker.

I will never be a victim again.

The words flew through her mind as she drove the sword through the abdomen of the oncoming Elite, stopping him mid-stroke. While the sword was large, she was close enough to see the pain in his eyes, as well as feel the warmth from the cloud of blood that pulsed out from his body as she drew back the sword with a wet sucking sound.

As she watched the life drain away from him, his tattoos fading from a vibrant indigo to a dull blue, she twisted her left wrist and felt the current snap the neck of the last remaining Elite, cutting off his choking sounds.

She dropped the sword and looked around, past the strewn bodies of six of Oceana's best fighters.

They hadn't stood a chance against her.

There was a ringing in her ears as she floated there, alone, with the blood of her attackers swirling through the water that supported her. As her whirlpool continued to roar, she looked around for any Elite she had missed. With a jolt, the only face she saw was that of Elder Iolana. She remained on the other side of the wall of water Riva had conjured, but instead of fighting to get through like the Guards or swimming away in a panic like the rest of the Mer, she was simply staring at Riva, features slightly distorted.

Riva stared back, waiting for Iolana to help her, to show her how to get out of this mess.

Even through the whirlpool those mercury-coloured eyes were piercing.

"Show me what to do." Riva pleaded over the roar of the water.

Iolana raised her eyes skywards and then melted into the crowd.

Riva gritted her teeth in frustration.

Are any of these mystical creatures capable of giving a straight answer?

Taking stock of her surroundings, she realised that some of the Guards had managed to regain control of the crowd and were now staring through the wall of water at her, the violent whirling preventing them from reaching her without injury. As they helped civilians to safety, Riva kept her magic close as she swam over to Em.

The cloud of blood that was flowing from her flukes was worrying. She knelt beside Em and took her head in her hands, her eyes were closed and her face, always a lighter shade of pale, was now ghostly.

"Half-breed!" came a strained shout from below. Carefully placing Em's head down on the smooth stone, she dove across the platform. Looking down, she saw Duncan still trapped by the falling rock and separated from his Guards by the whirlpool. "You will pay for this." He spat at her, a bubble of blood forming at the corner of his mouth.

She clutched the side of the platform as if to keep from launching herself at him. Looking down into his murderous eyes she wanted to finish it. She had him completely incapacitated and at her mercy, without the threat of a Mer army coming to save him. This was her moment.

But even as her magic begged her to finish what she had come here to do, Duncan raised his right hand and she spied the bracelet. The same one that Douglas always wore. She let her magic drain away as the fight went out of her. No matter what he had done, he was still Douglas's father, he was still her father's younger brother.

"Do it." Duncan choked out, pointing up at her.

Looking into his ice-blue eyes she called down, "I might have to in the end. But until I have absolutely no other choice, I'd prefer not to kill my family."

Hands shaking with the effort of restraining her magic, she grasped Em under the armpits and pushed off the rock into the clear water above. She let the whirlpool implode in a cacophony of swirling water that swept the remaining Guards and Mer in the square away in a typhoon of chaos.

21.

Crap, crap, crap she thought, her currents propelling her through the upper city as she dodged buildings and bewildered Merfolk who felt her but couldn't see her. She had slammed her cloaking back into place the minute she had launched herself out of that whirlpool and had extended it to Em.

She needed to stop the bleeding coming from the stab wound in Em's flukes before it became too noticeable.

Adjusting Em's weight in her arms, she had an uncomfortable flashback to the last time she dragged an unconscious Mer through Oceana. Looking behind them she knew they weren't yet being followed but it was only a matter of time before the Guards spotted the pile of bodies that she had left behind. Her mouth filled with saliva and she willed herself not to be sick.

As she wove through the crumbling remains of the lower town, she wracked her brains for somewhere to go. There was no way she would be able to get back to the palace without being detected. She didn't trust Duncan not to place a barrier like that of the prison caves across the whole reef. She should have fled directly towards Declan's rooms, but she had panicked and set off in the wrong direction entirely. Interpreting Iolana's skyward gaze as a sign.

An exit current was also a no-go. If she summoned one now she didn't doubt that they would be able to get out of there, but they would never be able to get back in without being captured, cloaking or not. Not after what she had just done.

She slowed her currents down as they meandered through the outskirts of the city. She just needed somewhere for them to take shelter and give her time to figure out how the hell she was now going to rescue Douglas and save the plan that now lay in tatters. What if Duncan decided to move up his execution as revenge?

Her stomach twisted as she dragged Em towards a small cave. With Em's blood starting to cloud the water she swam them right to the back until they were cloaked both in magic and shadow.

Looking into the corners to make sure it was completely unoccupied, she ran her hand along the ledge at the back. It appeared to lead to a smaller chamber but it was really only wide enough for a small child to fit through. She kept it in mind for a hiding spot if the Guards decided to conduct a thorough search.

She lay Em down on the stone floor and unveiled them both, comfortable enough that the shadows concealed them. There wasn't an inch of her body that hadn't been broken, bruised or beaten. Her skin, always pale, was now dangerously so, and the edges of her lips were free of colour. She didn't have much time left.

Assessing her injuries, Riva knew that this healing wouldn't be quick. She was already drained from all of the magic she had used back in the square but she gritted her teeth.

Double checking the entrance to the cave, she toyed with the idea of cloaking it. But just before she released the magic she realized that would only make it more obvious that this was their hiding place. That was exactly how Em had found her on Skye. No, better to wait and see if the Guards came looking and then hide themselves.

It would be nice to have some sort of warning system though…

Closing her eyes, she extended her consciousness.

She knew that the outskirts of Oceana were home to some of the larger marine animals that found navigating the various buildings of the inner city a struggle. There were often tales of Mer-animal accidents happening at the border. Both purposeful and accidental.

The Mer here were poor and would try to hunt whatever came passing through. But the animals were just as hungry. Shuddering, she remembered how Em had killed a shark while she had still been inside its mind. She had felt every morsel of its hunger, every grain of despair, and then she had lost herself for a split second as she experienced its death.

She looked out towards the mouth of the cave with a small shiver of fear. The animals down here were struggling just as much as the Mer were.

Her consciousness still searching, she finally made contact with what she was looking for. She brushed the whales' mind tentatively, not wanting to alarm her. Where the shark's thoughts had been focused on his sense of smell, this mind was scarily like her own.

Images, both reality and memory flitted through her brain, disorientating her. Then the mind she was connected to seemed to accept her curiously, questioningly.

Conscious of Em's condition she quickly explained her need for a warning and protection. While it didn't exactly feel like she was *talking* to her, there was definitely an exchange of sorts.

Riva pulled away with thanks and brought herself back to the cold cave floor.

Kneeling down on the hard stone, she rolled Em over gently onto her side so that she could assess the damage. Mark glowing, she held it above the stab wound on Em's tail and watched as the skin slowly knitted back together. Working her way up through the deep cuts on her tail she was relieved when it took on its usual silvery colour and the lacerations that marred Em's alabaster skin disappeared.

Halfway through the healing, Em regained consciousness.

"Hey sleepyhead, you missed the show." Riva said drolly, still hovering her Mark over her broken arm.

"Aaah-Argh!" Em cried aloud as the bone snapped back into place with a crack.

Riva quickly shoved a hand over her mouth to stifle the cries, anxiously looking up at the entrance to the cave.

Em bit her.

"Ow, what was that for? I'm the one healing you here!" She hissed, jerking her hand away.

"Oh is that what you call it? Feels a lot like you're doing more damage." Em grumbled, cradling her now not-broken arm to her chest. She looked around the cave groggily. "Where are we?"

Riva gently prodded her forearm with the palm of her hand, trying to sense if there was any infection inside and reducing pockets of swelling as she went. "I'm not really sure. Some random cave in the outskirts of the city." She glanced up at the mouth of the cave again, anxious that someone had heard Em' scream of pain, but the water was still. "I saved your life, you're welcome. Now sit back, I'm not finished."

Even though she was starting to feel dizzy from the magic use, she kept going. Those dark bruises across Em's stomach indicated internal bleeding. At least sitting through endless episodes of *Grey's Anatomy* with Alex hadn't been for nothing.

But Em grabbed her wrist to stop her. "Wait, you mean that Duncan knows you're here?"

Riva tried to get her hand out of Em's surprisingly strong grasp. "Yes, but that's hardly the most pressing problem at the moment."

Em was shaking her head, gripping tightly onto her wrist. "No, Riva we have to go!" she looked frantically over her shoulder as if an entire army were chasing them. Which, Riva had to concede was pretty much true. "You don't understand, he's mobilized the Elite and the Guards together. He's not just targeting humans anymore, he's targeting human sympathizers among the Mer. We have to get out of here before he kills you!"

Riva finally twisted her wrist free and coaxed Em down. "I already know all of this. I spoke to my uncles. Besides, I'm not going anywhere until we rescue Douglas."

Em was still pale. "Riva, he's using people's loved ones as leverage. The dungeons are filled with more Mates than rebels themselves. He'll do the same to anyone who gets in his way."

Riva's gut twisted as she thought of her parents tucked away in the cottage, of Alex probably on a train headed for Dundee, and even Kieran. The thought of Duncan sending someone to hurt them made her seriously regret not finishing him off when she had the chance.

"He doesn't have the necklace, my parents are keeping it safe. No-one can come further inland than a few miles or for more than a few hours with the magic of the Elders. Alex isn't that close to the coast and my dad would be able to protect my mum and get them to safety."

Riva didn't know if she was saying it aloud because she believed it or because she needed to hear it said.

"Besides, Iolana is helping us and she's the one who would have to enchant whoever is sent ashore. I think we're fine." She pointed to the mottled skin on Em's stomach. "Now can you stay still enough long enough for me to heal this mess?"

Em gritted her teeth. "Get on with it then."

As she felt three of Em's ribs snap back into place with a satisfying 'pop', the Mer girl sighed and stretched in relief. Wincing only slightly.

"Thank you." she said quietly.

"Don't mention it." Riva murmured, reaching up to heal the last of the open wounds on Em's face.

"There. Perfect." She finished, leaning back heavily on the cave wall, exhausted.

"I wouldn't call me that." Em said bitterly, sitting up, tail curled protectively around herself.

Riva looked over and saw that Em was looking up at the roof of the cave and biting her lip as if to stop herself from crying.

The cave was silent and cold. The only sounds Em's sniffling and the gentle whoosh of the tide.

"I don't know how much you heard of what Duncan said but it isn't true." Riva said, her voice hollow in the echoing cave.

Em laughed hoarsely, "Of course it was true. Every word he said."

Riva unwrapped her arms from around herself and swam closer to Em.

"Even if you made mistakes in the past you aren't that person anymore. Douglas told me how hard you fought to get away from the Guards that kidnapped you both. You don't need to prove whose side you are on anymore."

Em smiled but it didn't reach her eyes. "You aren't understanding. I don't have to agree with him, but every word he spoke was true. My sexuality, my support of humans, my ability to betray the crown for those I love? Those are all parts of who I am, but it still hurts that my own people were cheering for my execution because of them."

She floated down beside her friend. "You have nothing to be ashamed of." Riva said, putting an arm around her shoulders. She couldn't even imagine the torture that those Elite must have put her through, never mind having hundreds of Mer celebrate her imminent death. Watching that sword descend towards her neck…

She tried summoning her magic to heat the water around them as Em started shivering but all she could manage was the barest hint of a rise in temperature. Sighing, she leaned her head against Em's shoulder. She needed to rest. Without her powers at full strength they were sitting ducks.

"I don't want to live down here anymore." Em whispered, her shaking growing more violent.

"What do you mean?" Riva whispered, not daring to lift her head for fear of what she would see on her friends face.

"If we – *when* we get out of here, I want you to turn me human." Em said.

Stunned, Riva turned to face her. Em was looking at her with glassy eyes, full bottom lip trembling.

"Uh, wow. Okay. I mean, are you sure?"

Em nodded slowly, fringe waving down into her eyes with the movement and she brushed it away impatiently, sniffing.

"Being up there with all of you for the last two weeks has shown me a whole other world that I didn't know existed. I'm not saying that it is perfect, but there is nothing left for me down here, even if we do succeed... the Mer have long memories." Her face took on a haunted expression. "If I keep this tail then I might as well have died today on that rock-."

"Don't say that!" Riva interrupted, but Em cut across her.

"I'm serious. I don't have a future down here but up there... it gives me hope."

"Are you sure?" Riva asked.

Em nodded decidedly. "Yes. I've never been more sure about anything in my life."

Riva narrowed her eyes, "Because you know I probably wouldn't ever be able to turn you back right? And I don't even know if it's something I can do on a whim like that. When I turned my father human I was asking the Earth to save his life. There aren't even any guarantees that it will work on you. I still don't even really know how I did it to my father in the first place." She said.

Em was running her hands down her smooth tail. "You still underestimate yourself. Look at how you just healed me. I was pretty much dead only minutes ago." She raised a hand to stop Riva from interrupting, "I know what the Elite do to deserters and trust me, I felt every calculated blow. The public execution was just to send a message, in a few more hours I would have been dead anyway. You brought me back from that."

Riva was swinging between so many emotions she didn't know how to keep track. Her voice small, she said. "I can promise to try for you. When we get out of here, I will try."

"Thank you." Em replied, reaching out to take her hand.

They both sighed, exhausted, and leaned back against the cave wall, staring towards the entrance.

"So fill me in. What happened while I was – detained?" She stumbled over the last word. As much as she was trying to put on a brave face, Riva could tell that what had happened had left its mark on her. "You said you found your uncles, were they willing to help? I heard that they were fully in support of the King, or maybe it was just for show. What about Douglas? Where is he?" she asked, looking around the cave as if expecting to see him lounging against the far wall.

"My uncles swore to help us, although now that we've been separated I don't know how much help they're going to be if we can't communicate." Riva mused.

"Can't you just get into their heads?" Em asked.

Riva shook her head. "No. They're too far away, besides human minds are more complicated than animal minds. Trust me, you don't want to be in another person's head for too long."

"I can imagine." Em wrinkled her nose in disgust. "But what about Douglas?"

Riva groaned. "He's in the palace dungeons."

"What?!" Em cried.

"Sssh, keep your voice down, every Guard in Oceana is out looking for us." Riva smacked her wrist and looked nervously at the cave entrance.

"I wouldn't be so sure about that." Em said shrewdly.

"What? Why not?" Riva sked.

Em smiled lopsidedly. "You just took out a whole squadron of Elite without blinking while simultaneously incapacitating the royal Guard. If they weren't terrified of you before, they certainly will be now."

Despite her gnawing hunger after the magic use, her stomach turned at the thought of what she had done to those Elite. Em clocked her expression and put a hand on her thigh.

"Hey, it's okay. What you did was self-defence. If you hadn't killed them then they certainly would have killed you, and then me. And then Duncan would have had them go and kill a whole bunch of humans." She paused, judging Riva's face. "You saved more lives than you took."

Riva blinked quickly, her eyes burning. "I know, but that doesn't make it any easier to bear."

"But at least you will *live* to bear it." Em said, squeezing her leg in what Riva thought was supposed to be a comforting way but she was pretty sure Em had just given her a bruise. "I wish I had been in my right mind to see it. I bet you were badass." She grinned lopsidedly.

Riva groaned. "That is a huge problem Em. I'm supposed to be winning the Mer over, not pushing them further away."

Em shrugged. "Depends on the type of Mer you want on your side."

Riva frowned, "What do you mean?"

"Didn't you look around to see which Mer were cheering for my execution? Who was all gathered in that square? Or who Duncan has locked up in the dungeons?" Em asked, leaning back on her elbows, tail stretched out on the rocky floor.

Riva shook her head, "No, I was a little too busy paying attention to the fact that he was about to cut your head off if I'm being honest."

Subconsciously massaging her neck as if to make sure that it remained un-severed, Em continued. "They were all members of the nobility. All of them Duncan's puppets, buying in to his human-hating propaganda. They aren't the Mer you need to win over. You need the support of the masses. The people who live down here." She pointed outside of the cave towards the ruins of the outer city. "These Mer have lived in oppression even before Duncan came to power but now he's filling the dungeons with them, torturing their loved ones, and using them as cannon fodder in his bid to eradicate human presence from the ocean."

"How do you know all of this?" Riva asked, growing worried.

Em shrugged. "Elite are trained to listen. Even under torture." The mask she sometimes put up to protect herself was firmly in place, "I picked up a few things in between my own screams."

Wincing, Riva wished that she could heal her friend's mental wounds as easily as the physical ones. But she knew better than most that the mental damage was significantly longer-lasting.

"Alright. I believe you. But we won't be any good to anyone dog-tired like this." She yawned hugely. "Try to get some rest, I have a feeling we're going to need it." She said, feeling her magic already starting to flood her system despite her exhaustion. She warmed the water around them so they could both stop shivering.

"What if the Guards do come looking?" Em asked nervously, glancing at the mouth of the cave.

Riva's eyelids were already drooping, "Don't worry, I've got an alarm system in place."

22.

One minute she was staring at the back of her eyelids and the next they were fluttering open in the now-familiar meadow of Eden.

Sitting up, she looked around, the dappled sunlight and soft grass immediately easing her anxieties about Oceana. As she got to her knees, there was movement in the tree line.

Standing up, she walked closer to the towering oaks that seemed to protect the meadow.

Padding softly through the buttercups in her bare feet, the sun warm on her back, she could see a figure standing in the tree line, cloaked in shadow.

"Cronos!" she called out, hand outstretched. Stomach leaping in a way that both worried and exhilarated her.

As focused as she was on Cronos, she almost jumped out of her skin when Gaia appeared beside her with the sound of a lightning strike.

"Hello again my daughter." The Goddess said, standing in a beam of bright light.

Riva skidded to a stop, hand over her heart as it raced in her chest. "Crap, you scared me."

Gaia lifted one perfect eyebrow in either amusement or condescension. "Expecting someone else?"

Mouth dry, she shook her head. "Oh, no. Of course not." She looked towards the oak trees that were now completely empty.

Feeling like she probably shouldn't mention Cronos to Gaia, given his reaction the last time she had almost caught them together, she brushed it off. "I just thought I saw something moving in there. Probably just an animal."

Gaia made a noise of suspicious agreement but Riva didn't miss her fathomless eyes darting across the tree line. She really hoped she hadn't just gotten Cronos into some sort of trouble. He had looked like he could handle himself either way.

"I didn't realise I would be able to get here from Oceana." She said, attempting to redirect the conversation.

Gaia's eyes focused on Riva once again. "Well of course you can. It is wherever you are after all."

Riva looked at the Goddess who she thought should be becoming more familiar by now, but for some reason, every time she looked at her she seemed to be changing. Taking a deep breath of the sweet, fresh air, she flexed her fingers, warmth returning to them.

"I guess I forgot how cold Oceana can be." Her stomach rumbled and she rubbed it uncomfortably. "I knew I was right to eat those leftovers before I left home. You don't have any food around here by any chance do you?" she asked, glancing around hopefully.

The Goddess didn't answer.

"Right. Of course not."

Gaia strode towards her, the train of her dress shedding dahlias across the ground as she walked, "How goes your quest to free the Mer? I heard you call for me."

Riva's stomach twisted, anxieties returning in full force. "Not so great actually. I mean I found Em and Douglas which is good and they are both alive, for now. I managed to escape with Em but I have no idea what they are going to do with Douglas. I might be able to rescue him but this was supposed to be so much more than just a rescue mission, you know? I need to get the Mer to listen to me but I don't know how to do that without them trying to kill me."

The Goddess was now inspecting a low-hanging tree branch.

"Sorry. I'm rambling." Riva said.

"Oftentimes speaking our thoughts aloud allows us more clarity." Said Gaia. Riva watched her touch a finger to the branch and crisp white blossoms bloomed from the bark.

"That's what Alex always says." She paused, chewing her bottom lip, wondering if she should utter her next words.

"I killed some people today."

Gaia remained impassive, focused as she was on the branch's blossoms. "You made your choice."

Her words rattled Riva.

"My choice? What the hell is that supposed to mean? You were the one telling me that nature is all about balance." she shouted, "What happened to being *above it all* and there being no right and wrong? How can you stand there and talk about my choices when you forced this on me in the first place?"

Gaia's face suddenly changed into something darker. Before Riva could blink the meadow flashed into fire and blood, the wildflowers crunching under her feet, nothing more than blistered stalks as the trees withered into ghostly skeletons, their fingers reaching out to throttle her. She had to steel herself to avoid cowering to the ground in terror.

The Goddess's eyes were pits of fire. "Nature is ruthless my daughter, yes I told you that. Our magic is woven into the very fabric of the Earth and as such, so are we. We restore balance, we *choose* what is right and what is wrong." Her skin was now red as a winter sunset as she advanced upon Riva, who started backing away nervously, crows calling out overhead across a blood-red sky.

Gaia stopped only inches from her. "No one dares tell a God what choice to make. We made this world, we can just as easily unmake it."

Her voice had gone from a rising crescendo to a cold fury. Riva started looking around to see which way she could flee but couldn't see an escape route that wasn't covered in burning embers. She backed up until her back hit tree bark.

Seeming to realise that she was scaring her, Gaia straightened. "Your own conscience is what you will have to live with. And that is no concern of mine, only that you are continuing down the right path. How you get there matters not."

The terrifying colours faded slowly, the sky lightening gradually to its periwinkle blue as birdsong replaced the crows' death call. The Goddess turned back into the form Riva was most used to seeing her in, with coppery skin, golden eyes and a waterfall of hair the colour of every woman on Earth.

Riva hugged her arms around herself, not quite sure what she had just witnessed. "So you think I made the wrong choice?" she dared to ask.

The Goddess stared at her, "You have yet to understand. Only you can decide whether your choice was right or not. But either way, it has already been made and we cannot wind back the clock."

Wondering if she would ever understand anything the Goddess said, she nodded but couldn't quite bring herself to approach her. The image of the fiery spirit that had stood before her only moments ago was still too fresh in her mind.

Gaia seemed able to sense her fear. "You need not be afraid of fire. It is a part of you. Fire, flood and destruction are as crucial to the balance of this world as are the harvest, fertility and your healing powers."

"There's so much I still don't know." she said quietly staring at the Goddess mark on her palm.

"Remember your path my daughter. Stay on it and you will not easily go astray." Gaia seemed to sense Riva's unease. "Rest here until you are able to return to your task. My faith in you has never wavered."

Riva tried to force a smile onto her face but before she could so much as turn up the corners of her lips, the Goddess had faded into a sunbeam. Alex had been right, these titans were trouble.

Once Gaia was completely out of sight, she finally loosed a breath.

"Beam me up Scotty…" Riva breathed, rolling her eyes.

"Who's Scotty?"

Whirling around, heart racing, she clutched the branch for support as she realised Cronos had been standing directly behind her. His breath had tickled the back of her neck and she ran a hand over it as it tingled.

"What the hell do you think you're doing sneaking up on me like that?" She cried, looking around nervously, still not recovered from Gaia's split personality episode.

He smiled devastatingly, his amber eyes gleaming with mirth. "Your reaction was quite entertaining."

Riva crossed her arms and she wasn't sure if it was to protect herself or stop her from reaching out and touching that perfect chest of his.

"Yeah well, in the future I would like a nice, clear announcement of your arrival." She fought to even out her breathing.

He chuckled low in his throat and the sound made her bones want to melt. "You find me unsettling?" he asked.

She licked her dry lips and looked him up and down. Still wearing that ridiculous suit, one hand in his pocket, the other propping him up against the tree. Roguish grin on his face, dark hair tousled. Unsettling was one word for it.

Clearly reading her expression, he chuckled again. She felt her cheeks flush.

"What do you want?" She asked.

He raised one eyebrow. "So touchy." He took a step closer to her, unbuttoning his suit jacket to reveal the perfectly fitted shirt beneath. "I told you, I find you *intriguing*."

The closer he got to her, her brain was screaming at her to take several large steps back, but for some reason her feet wouldn't obey.

"Alex told me that you're dangerous." She blurted out, saying the first thing that came into her mind to try to break his perilous spell.

He smiled, stopping only a foot away from her. "I suppose I am." He reached out a hand to toy with one strand of her hair again, rubbing it casually between his thumb and index finger. "But what about you?"

He was standing so close to her now, it was all she could do to remember to keep breathing as those fiery eyes searched her face hungrily. "What about me?" she breathed.

He let the strand of her hair fall and the absence of his touch had her suddenly taking a step closer.

"You are dangerous in ways you don't even comprehend." He replied, his face now so close to hers that she could make out the flecks of pure gold in his irises. Standing so close to him for the first time she realised how tall he was, she had to crane her neck to look into his eyes.

He reached down and encircled her wrist with his hand, turning the palm up and running his thumb over her Mark. She had never felt like this. Never. Not even when Kieran kissed her had her stomach being doing loop-the-loops while her blood practically boiled. While the sensation had her practically gasping, the lack of eye contact allowed her to gather her scrambled thoughts.

"I killed some people today." She said, repeating the words she had given Gaia, wanting him to give her a more satisfactory response.

She waited for Cronos to interrupt, but he was now idly tracing the spiral of her Mark with his index finger.

"I did it to save Em. I mean they were coming at me so fast and it was self-defence really. I didn't have a choice." She continued, trying not to think about what those deft fingers might feel like elsewhere.

"We always have a choice." He said gravely.

His repetition of Gaia's words were like a slap in the face and she wrenched her hand out of his grasp. Having expected some resistance, she almost lost her balance as he released her easily.

"You're one to talk." She spat. The spell well and truly broken now.

Adjusting his suit, he stood there, maddeningly calm. "I see." He brushed an imaginary speck of lint off his cuff. "What stories have you heard about me then?"

"That you are Gaia's son. That you have a wife, that you *ate* your children." As the words came tumbling out of her mouth she was disgusted at herself for ever fantasising about this man.

"The Greeks did love a good tragedy." He said, eyes dancing.

Riva shook her head. "What the hell are you talking about?"

Cronos adjusted his shirt collar and she tried her best not to notice how well it fit his broad shoulders. The pale blue of the shirt complimented his golden skin perfectly.

"Aesop, Homer, they did like to exaggerate." He said. He hesitated and then gestured to the path through the trees in front of them.

"Walk with me?"

Worried to say yes and worried to say no, she figured that the best option was to go with him and then end this dream-vision as soon as possible if things got out of hand. Trying not to think about the last time she was alone with a boy in a copse of trees, she stepped onto the dirt path in her bare feet.

Realising that she was wearing the same outfit as she had been in Oceana, she felt thoroughly underdressed in her leggings and kelp top.

"How come you wear a suit?" she asked.

He smiled again. "Are you propositioning me again? I told you I can just as easily take it off…"

Riva blushed furiously and eyed up his shirt buttons worriedly. "No. You can definitely keep it on. I was just wondering why you seem to dress like a human when your mother… doesn't."

"Let's call it an unhealthy obsession that I've had for millennia and just leave it at that shall we?"

Millennia??

He interpreted her facial expression correctly. "If you're about to ask me how old I am don't waste your breath. I'm sure your friend Alex told you that my mother and father created the Earth itself. It doesn't take a genius to figure it out."

Riva's mouth had gone dry. She was making such a fool of herself thinking that Cronos had any interest in her whatsoever. It didn't matter that she had powers, she had only just turned eighteen and he was… a God.

They continued walking in silence, save for the birdsong that had once again returned after Gaia's fiery demonstration. Cronos mistook her ruminating over her attraction to him for fear.

"Since you yourself have just taken life, you must at least allow me an explanation for the sins you think I have committed." He said.

She glared down at her feet, his words cutting into her stomach like a knife. "Fine." She grumbled.

"You have met my mother. Volatile being that she is, she picked a good host in you. My brothers and sisters you have not yet met since she has been keeping you protected in the meadow. And for good reason."

Riva shivered involuntarily. "How come you were able to find me then?"

Cronos smiled, displaying a row of perfectly white teeth. "I have some tricks up my sleeve."

Riva's breath hitched at that devastating smile and focused on her feet again. His face was far too distracting.

"So you didn't kill your father?" She asked.

"Oh no, I definitely did." He said so nonchalantly that she whipped her head up to look at him, stopping them both dead in the middle of the path. He met her eyes and shrugged.

"The bastard had it coming."

Her heart rate accelerated, and this time not out of anticipation.

"Riva, you have nothing to fear from me." He said quietly.

Despite his earnest expression, she looked behind her and became slightly unnerved that she could no longer see the meadow.

"You just admitted that you killed your father and you expect me to be fine with it?" She asked.

"Aren't you plotting to kill your uncle at this very moment? Didn't you just take six lives at the bottom of the ocean less than an hour ago?" he replied, his power surging out from him, making the hairs on Riva's arms stick up.

"That's not fair." She spat. "It's not the same thing at all."

He advanced towards her, grabbing both of her wrists to stop her from fleeing, that energy radiating out from him reverberating in her chest. "But it is Riva. It is exactly the same thing. Do you really believe the very worst of me after these two brief meetings? Do you want me to be the villain everyone paints me to be?"

His lips were a hairsbreadth from her own and she couldn't make sense of her emotions. Did she want to kiss him or kick him?

"I did what I had to do to protect the rest of my family from a monster. Now tell me that you are not planning to do just that." He growled.

Heart stuttering, she gazed into those fathomless amber eyes and realised that she could quite easily get lost in them forever. If what he was saying was the truth, then he was just as damned as she was. He was no hero, but maybe he wasn't the villain after all.

For the first time, she noticed that he was breathing heavily, a muscle in his jaw twitching. She must have really pissed him off.

"What about your wife? And where did the eating your own children rumour come from then?" she dared to ask, trying not to look at those full lips.

The fire in his eyes was momentarily dampened by pain. He released her wrists but remained standing in front of her. "My wife died. As did my children. I played no part in it."

The misery in his voice had her believing him immediately, she felt guilty that she had even asked.

"I'm sorry." She breathed.

Cronos straightened, brushing his fingers through his dark hair.

"The guilt of taking a life fades over time, but you will never forget their faces, even if you know you made the right choice." He reached out to take her hand again and she let him. "You will have more battles to fight before this is all over Riva. You will need to make your peace with the cost of changing the world."

He lifted her palm to his mouth and brushed the hint of a kiss across her Mark. Where those lips touched her skin she thought that she would implode from the sensation.

"Until we meet again." he said.

Her lips parted and she drew in breath to protest, but before she could close the gap between them, the trees faded from view and the last thing she saw were those amber eyes once again dancing with hidden fire.

*

She was awoken by a shrill whistling sound and the sensation of someone trying to fight their way into her head.

"Ouch, what the hell?" she said, groggily coming to.

Em was already up and shaking her shoulders. "Is this the alarm system you were talking about?" she cried over the piercing noise.

Riva placed her hands over her ears but it did nothing to block out the sound. "Yes, although I did think she would be a little more subtle about it."

Trying to focus, she connected with the whales' consciousness and communicated to her that she had received her message loud and clear. Being inside the matriarch's head, Riva caught glimpses of what was going on outside of the cave and she saw that she had brought her entire pod with her. They were circling above the outskirts of the city like black and white angels.

"Thank you." she said, both her voice and her feelings passing through the bridge in their minds.

The whale seemed to want to hang around to see what would happen and Riva caught a glimpse through her eyes of the approaching Guards. Tinted as the world was in more vibrant shades of blue and green, she could still make out the sheer size of the force headed their way.

Panic shot through her as she realised that the only reason they had been afforded any time was so that Duncan could amass a force strong enough to go up against her. While she had wasted time sleeping and dreaming of handsome titans, Duncan had been busy.

Cowering against the back of the cave, eyes blind to everything but what she was seeing through the whales' eyes, she worried that she wouldn't be strong enough to survive this.

She was still weak from her magic in the square and from healing Em and Douglas earlier on in the day. She hadn't had anything to eat since before she had arrived in Oceana the day before.

Crap.

"They're coming for us." She said gruffly to Em, pulling herself away from the whales' consciousness.

Em turned to her, eyes wide in fear. Elite soldier she may be but she knew that the two of them didn't stand a chance against an entire army.

"Cloak us quickly!" she said.

"They already know about my cloaking, they'll probably fill every inch of every cave until they touch one of us or even worse – just throw spears randomly until one of them hits us." Riva said, beginning to panic.

"So what do you want to do?" Em asked, voice gaining strength. "We can't just sit here panicking. They are coming for us either way."

Riva stood up and grabbed at her hair as it floated away from her skull like a mad halo, "I know, I know, give me a second to think."

"Maybe I can help..." piped up a small voice from behind them both.

"Argh!" Riva squealed, her cry muffled by the hand that Em quickly clapped over her mouth.

They stared up at the ledge at the back of the cave and the dimpled face of a small Mer boy stared back at them. He must have been around eight or nine by Riva's guess, although the Mer aged very differently to humans.

"Who are you?" Em whispered incredulously, "How did you get there?"

The little boy was grinning, "I was sent to watch you, but you'd better hurry up, they will be here soon. You need to hide." He piped up excitedly, beckoning them to follow him as he disappeared into the dark recesses of the cave.

The two girls shrugged at each other, deciding they had nothing to lose and swam through the small gap. Riva had been right, there was a sort of shelf but as far as she could see the cave wall ended just a few feet in front of their faces. The Mer boy had disappeared.

"What the hell?" she breathed.

They swam forward horizontally, beginning to feel a more than a little claustrophobic in the tight space as they wiggled forward, sure they were about to hit the wall, when the Mer boy popped his head out in front of them.

"Down here! Come on!" he said grinning.

Em and Riva gawked in disbelief at the natural illusion. Where the shelf met the cave wall there was a natural crack in the rock that was completely obscured unless you were directly over the top of it. It looked like nothing more than a dark tunnel from what Riva could see.

Em gave her a shove from behind in response to the growing noise from the approaching army and she steeled herself.

"Here goes nothing." She said to Em, diving headfirst down the tight squeeze.

Summoning a swift current to get her through the claustrophobic tunnel as quickly as possible, she soon shot out into a sealed cave that was pitch black.

"Hello?" she whispered and almost shrieked again when Em landed on her back.

"Sorry, can't see a thing down here." Em apologized, clinging on to her arm.

"Where's that little boy?" Riva asked, voice echoing strangely.

They swam forwards, arms outstretched, completely blind.

"Alright, that's enough of this." Riva said impatiently, and raised her palm, funnelling magic into her Mark so that its golden light illuminated the passageway in front of them. Riva tried to ignore the memory of a certain someone's lips on her palm.

"Handy trick." Em commented as they advanced together.

The chamber sloped downwards and as they descended, she could see natural light filtering through from another cave just ahead of them. Judging by how far they had swum, they had to be directly beneath the Oceana boundary line. Trying to figure out how that worked magic-wise, she felt a headache coming on.

"Oh my goodness Riva, look!" Em grabbed her arm as they rounded a corner and emerged into a massive underwater cavern.

Holy crap!

There were Mer everywhere. All of whom looked like they had been camping out here for weeks. There were carts and woven algal baskets of what looked like provisions pushed up against the walls. Families were huddled together on top of sponges and wrapped in kelp fronds. And the biggest surprise of all, there were Mer children gazing up at Riva in awe.

She looked to Em for an explanation but her friend was clearly just as bewildered as she was.

"What is this place?" Riva breathed.

"It is our sanctuary." Said a voice behind them.

Turning, they faced a strikingly beautiful Mer woman with a jet black, lethal looking tail that blended perfectly with her midnight black torso.

"At least until you make the ocean our sanctuary once more." She smiled fiercely.

23.

Mer rebellion. Who knew?

She sat in a quiet corner of the cavern, gnawing on a dried piece of seaweed to try and stop the hunger cramps. The past few hours had been surreal to say the least.

Aoife, the leader of the resistance force, had shown both Em and Riva around this intricate network of underground caverns, introducing them to those who were on her side. As she shook hands and watched Mer greet her warmly for the first time (some of them were even smiling) she felt like she was in a dream. How any of this was possible she didn't know, and she had to remind herself to focus on what Aoife was saying half the time as she zoned out. It was too much information to take in at once. She had gone from feeling completely alone in this fight, to having people who actively supported her, who had been *waiting* for her to return.

Aoife had been one of the Kings Personal Guards for two decades. She had been injured in the same explosion that had killed Riva's grandfather. She had lain in the infirmary, on a pallet close to the cave where the royal family had been gathered around the King's body and had heard everything. Riva's revelation, her father's confirmation of their relationship and Duncan's lies.

Knowing that she hadn't much time, Aoife had quickly fled under cover of Riva's destruction of the infirmary. Several more Guards had also overheard, taking any Mer who would listen to them as they went. It turned out that these missing Mer were the ones Duncan had been trying to pass off as the casualties of Riva's destruction.

She pursed her lips at the saltiness of the seaweed and rubbed her forehead against the headache that was forming behind her eyes. There had to be close to two hundred Mer gathered here.

Finding out that the Mer had rebelled against Duncan's merciless attacks on humans from day one had been a revelation to both her and Em. Those who had escaped a jail cell had ended up in these underground caves. As word had gotten out, more and more Mer had left Oceana for the protection of this underground network, preferring to wait for a saviour who may never come than face a tyrant they could never overthrow alone.

She sighed, throwing the seaweed away in disgust. She needed real food. As she looked at the Mer huddled and hiding in the cavern she could see that they wouldn't last much longer without help. Was she even capable of being their saviour?

"You shouldn't waste that, these people are starving." Aoife said, swimming around the corner.

"Sorry. I just can't get used to the taste." Riva said, picking up the strand of seaweed guiltily even though the prospect of eating any more of it made her stomach turn.

Aoife held out her hand for it. "Yes well, it's not exactly part of our regular diet either." She took a bite, wrenching the chewy stalk between surprisingly sharp teeth. "But we don't have much of a choice right now. We're getting by with what we can find."

"How long have you all been here?" Riva asked.

Aoife shrugged, chewing thoughtfully. "Some of us have been here since you escaped, so - around a month. More turn up every day. It's only a matter of time before the usurper figures out where we are." She fixed Riva with an intense stare. "It's a good thing you turned up when you did."

She thought about how she had dawdled back home, going out on dates and for birthday dinners while these people had been risking their lives for her. Her stomach twisted again, but this time it wasn't through hunger.

Aoife noticed the look on her face. "Don't think like that. You came back, that's all that matters now." She finally finished chewing and swallowed the seaweed with difficulty. "I hope that our gatherers come back with something better today. Even we are struggling to stomach this."

Riva laughed hollowly. "This isn't going to be easy you know."

Aoife laughed too, except it sounded more like a snarl. "None of us are very used to easy around here young Goddess. We have fought hard for our liberty. Some of us still bearing the scars from those battles."

She twisted her torso and Riva got a glimpse at a large pink welt that ran from her left shoulder blade all the way down to her left hip, the scarred tissue marring her ebony tail.

"You got that from humans?" Riva asked with trepidation.

Aoife nodded, "A boat propeller from a Naval vessel. They were carrying out drills that created such noise and confusion underwater. I have never seen the animals so disorientated. We were ordered to destroy the ship but we failed." Her dark eyes had gone glassy with memory, "Those of us who were lucky escaped with scars."

Riva looked around the other Mer gathered. Some were trying hard not to look like they were staring at her. Others were shivering under kelp blankets or busying themselves sharpening swords and spears.

"So what makes you all so ready to support me now? Humans have never been kind to your people. The last time I was here the Mer made it very clear that they wanted nothing to do with me." Riva asked, "I am half-human after all."

Aoife smiled shrewdly and pointed at the Mark on Riva's palm, looking innocently like a scar itself when it wasn't glowing.

"You are so much more than simply half-human these days." She looked up at a group of dark-haired Mer who were swimming past exchanging whispers, darting glances at Riva.

"We Mer have been fighting a losing battle for a century. The usurper's new regime is only successful in spreading fear and sowing more misery and loss among our people. He may be successful in snuffing out human life, but he is spilling more Mer blood in the process. In these last few weeks alone more Mer than I can count have either been thrown in those dungeons for breaking his ridiculous new laws or died on his insane missions. I won't let that continue."

"Riva!"

Both her and Aoife looked up at the sound of Em's voice as she came careening through the group of Mer who were still speaking in hushed voices. They started as Em stumbled into two of them.

"Shit, sorry!" she said by way of apology, swimming up to the more secluded corner where Riva sat with the leader of the resistance.

"Riva, you'll never guess what?"

"What?" Riva replied, torn between exhaustion and curiosity.

Em puffed up proudly. "They want me to help train the rebels to fight. Because of my own training and insight into the workings of the palace they think that I'm *uniquely positioned* to help give them, us, the best advantage possible."

Her eyes were alive with hope, and as Riva searched her face she could see just how much Em had been floundering without a purpose. After what she had just narrowly escaped, having something to focus on was probably exactly what she needed.

"That's great Em. I think you'll do amazingly well." She said as Em's tail flitted happily back and forth. She wondered briefly if this would make her change her mind about wanting to be turned human. If she found somewhere that she fit in down here after all would she choose to stay?

Shaking a smile onto her face she pushed the thought to the back of her mind. Better to make sure they all survived the battle that was about to come and worry about the rest later.

"We are honoured to have you on our side as we fight." Aoife said solemnly, twisting her hand over her heart in salute. "We have precious few Elite on our side. Having you stand with us will give us an edge that the usurper is not expecting."

Em blushed at the compliment.

Riva turned back to Aoife. "Why do you call Duncan the usurper? I mean technically he was next in line to the throne so how can he have usurped something that was rightfully his?"

Aoife brushed her long braids behind her neck. "The throne was never meant for Duncan. You should know that better than anyone *princess.*"

Riva cringed. "Yeah, don't call me that. Goddess was bad enough but I'm definitely no princess." Em snorted with laughter that made it obvious that she agreed.

But the way that Aoife had easily called her Goddess... Was that why she felt her connection to Eden growing stronger by the day? Was that why she felt so drawn to Cronos?

She traced her Mark with her left index finger, an echo of the touch she had felt only hours ago.

"Well, it's not like I had a choice in being given these powers or being born into a royal line, but if I had to pick? Then I know which one I would choose." She let her magic rise up, pooling through her veins until her Mark glowed. "Besides, I certainly don't have time to do both."

The corners of Aoife's mouth lifted. "You have only known your father for a short while. We trained to protect him as Crown Prince for centuries. We watched him grow, learn to fight, learn to love his people and want to protect them himself. He was the rightful King."

Riva was seriously surprised. "You stand by that now? Even after he ran off with a human and my grandfather shackled him?"

Aoife smiled again, like she was in on a secret Riva wasn't. Even Em was leaning in to hear more. "Your grandfather never wanted to shackle your father in the first place."

Riva's jaw dropped, Em looked like someone had slapped her across the face with a limp fish.

"What do you mean? He told me that his father wouldn't speak to him for years after his return." Riva asked.

"Because he was bitterly disappointed, and scared for the future of the family. He knew as well as anyone that Duncan was never going to be the right person to rule. He was too quick to anger, too irrational, and far too selfish to be a fair king. Your other uncle, Declan is much too wet behind the ears to ever rule. Look how he continues to do Duncan's bidding even now when he has shown his true colours. Your grandfather *wanted* your father to succeed him." Aoife looked around to make sure no-one was listening.

"He came to his rooms after he found out the truth about who you were and started putting plans into place to remove Prince Dylan's shackles. He felt that once the Mer were given a chance to fall in love with you, to learn that you weren't a threat, then he could give your father his title back." She sighed sadly, her onyx eyes clouding over. "He thought that he had time."

Riva stared at the uneven rocky floor, her mind far away in a cottage on the Isle of Skye where her father probably sat with an arm around her mum. The picture of a simple, happy life. That was the life he had wanted, that he had sacrificed everything for.

"Things would be very different if my grandfather hadn't died that day." Riva said sadly. "But it's too late for that future now. Duncan is the King, whether we like it or not, and now we have to do whatever it takes to stop him."

Looking around the cavern at the rebel Mer, she wondered if it was even possible for them to overthrow what was left of the Elite and Duncan's army of Guards. They were just a bunch of rag-tag Mer who had probably never held a spear before in their lives. The majority of them were gatherers, precious few were hunters and the rest were children.

"I've never seen so many Mer children before." Em said, echoing her thoughts as a small group swam past, playing keep-it-up with a spiny purple urchin.

Aoife smiled warmly at them, the skin around the corners of her eyes crinkling. "Yes. They are our greatest gift."

Em squirmed uncomfortably and Riva threw her an understanding glance. After almost being publically executed for her choice to never mate, she was undoubtedly still feeling a little on-edge.

Aoife continued. "The majority of the Mer that you see before you have lived the poorest of lives. Even the hunters take only the smallest scraps of meat before they sell the rest to the nobility." She inclined her head towards Riva. "You spent most of your time here in Oceana in the palace so you must believe that fish and other luxuries are in ready supply."

Riva thought back to the large and opulent banquets that were thrown for the Mer nobility in the royal ballroom. Most of the dishes she had been presented with she had been unable to stomach, but now looking at the jutting bones and hollow faces of the Mer around her she felt terribly guilty for being so wasteful.

Aoife covered Riva's hand with her own, "It is both a blessing and a curse. You see, eating lower on the food chain means that their blood holds less toxicity. They are hungrier of course, but their reproductive systems are healthier. For most of them a diet of sea grass and kelp is a small sacrifice when they are rewarded with their children."

As the children swam circles around each other, pealing, bell-like laughter cascading from the group, Riva could imagine a better future for the Mer.

Em coughed loudly, interrupting. "So what is your plan?"

Aoife peered around Riva, studying Em closely. "I respect your background and all you have sacrificed in the service of our young Goddess. However, you still made the choice to betray your rightful King, and pass critical information to Duncan."

Em bristled beside her and Riva threw her a warning glance.

"Please, Aoife. Em has proved herself trustworthy to me several times over. Her lapse in judgement from siding with Duncan is all but forgotten. Besides, don't you think she has already been punished enough?" Riva asked, jumping in before Em could say something she would later regret.

Aoife's other hand clenched and unclenched around her spear as she looked Em up and down. "I trust your judgement young Goddess. That will be enough for me." Aoife finally said.

"Thank you." Riva replied, looking worriedly at Em who seemed dangerously close to falling into a dark pit of thoughts. She reached out and took her hand. Those jade eyes met sapphire and she gave her a small smile.

"Come." Aoife said, grabbing her spear and rising majestically from the sea floor. "There is something you both need to see before we can discuss our plan of action."

Pushing off the rock she was sitting on to follow, Em went automatically to drop Riva's hand but she held on tightly.

"No. From now on you don't pretend to be something that you're not." Riva said warningly to her. "I am your friend and you need me right now. Let me be here for you."

Only Riva could see the red outline around Em's eyes as she hid behind her floppy fringe, but she felt the grateful squeeze in her fingers nonetheless.

Both Riva and Em scrambled after Aoife, through a small tunnel and out into a dimly-lit cavern that they hadn't been shown earlier.

The only light that permeated the darkness here came from a small hole in the top of the cave. Bizarrely it reminded Riva of Ariel's grotto in the Disney movie. She half expected to find Sebastien swimming out from one of the shelves or a collection of dingle hoppers.

Letting her advanced eyesight adjust to the low light, she looked around at the shapes huddled around the edges of the cave, some moaning quietly.

"Who are these Mer?" Em whispered.

Aoife tapped the butt of her spear against the floor of the cave, the noise reverberating across the chamber. "My finest warriors!" she called out, her melodic voice joining the clatter echoing off the walls, "The young Goddess has returned to us."

Riva really wished that she would stop referring to her as 'the young Goddess'. But her announcement was met with feral sounding clicks and whistles from all around her until soon the cavern was filled with a cacophony of sound. Some of the figures on the floor rose up and swam closer to the spotlight.

As they advanced slowly, Riva could see that the vast majority of the Guards who had followed Aoife here were wincing as they moved. Some unable to swim properly, so they dragged themselves across the ground to get a better look at her. Even more stayed where they were, leaning against walls or atop rocks, either unwilling or unable to move closer.

"They're all still wounded." Riva breathed.

Aoife smiled proudly around the room. "We will heal in time. We are stronger than we look."

Hand to her mouth, Riva looked around at all of these Mer who believed in her cause so much that they were willing to suffer for it. How many of them were still healing from the explosion a month ago? She could see some Mer with severe burns huddled in the shadows. How many more of them had been injured while escaping Duncan? And who in their right mind had chosen her for this role?

"We will fight for you." Aoife said proudly.

Looking around her, she decided that she didn't want these people to fight for her. They were barely able to swim. She could never ask anyone in this condition to pick up a sword and hurt themselves further. Her palm began to glow automatically and even as her stomach cramped from hunger, she knew what she had to do.

Before she could swim towards the Mer closest to her, she heard Em shout out beside her.

"Finn?"

Turning, stemming her magic, she watched Em hurl herself into the arms of a hulking Mer. Their matching tattoos made it hard for Riva to tell where one of them ended and the other began.

"How the hell did you end up here?" Em exclaimed when she pulled back.

The humungous Mer -Finn - smiled brilliantly down at her and ruffled her cropped hair affectionately. "I deserted the other day when they brought you in. You didn't think that I would help them torture my best student did you?"

Em floated back a few feet as if to get a better look at him, her face crumpling at his words as she tried not to let the emotion show on her face. She turned to Riva to introduce them.

"This is Finn. He was my mentor." She paused, glancing up at him almost shyly. "And friend." She said in a quieter voice.

Riva extended her hand. "Nice to meet you." she said, her fingers swiftly crushed in his strong grip.

"Likewise." He said gruffly as Riva winced. "So you managed to rescue her from the clutches of our brothers and sisters on the dark side eh?" he asked.

Riva frowned, not sure if he was joking or not. "Um, yes?"

He nodded once as if satisfied. "Good. Any Elite working for Duncan deserves what is coming to them. We swore allegiance to the ocean. Not to any King." He stood up straighter and then hissed through his teeth, face contorting in pain.

"Are you hurt?" Em asked, her voice sounding strangled.

Finn started to shrug but Riva saw him wince and she swam forward. "You are."

Turning to Riva, Finn bowed stiffly. "It is nothing, Goddess. Please there are many others here who are suffering more greatly than I."

"Okay, everyone seriously needs to stop calling me that." Riva said.

"What have I told you about trying to play the hero?" Em scolded, grabbing his muscled shoulders and turning him around.

Both of them gasped as they saw his back. From his neck down to the base of his spine, he was peppered with arrowheads.

"We didn't want to pull them out all at once in case I bled out." he explained as Em's face took on a furious expression.

"They did this to you on Duncan's orders." Em spat out, eyes ablaze. "Since when did we start turning on our own?"

"Since Duncan started pitting us against one another." Aoife said ominously from behind both of them.

Em looked distraught and there was only one thing Riva knew that she could do to make this situation better. She reached up and pulled out the first arrowhead, muscles straining as she grasped the sharp metal. She tried not to grimace as it came away with some tendons and muscle.

"Argh!" Finn cried out, reaching around with his arm to try and put pressure on the wound which had started puffing out clouds of blood. "What are you doing?"

"Saving your life." Riva scolded, swatting his hand away, letting the arrowhead drop to the floor of the cave. "Now hold still."

Calling on her magic, she basked in the surge of joy that came with it. Welcoming the flood of power into her veins she funnelled it into her Mark once more. It had only been a few hours since she had healed Em's extensive injuries, but she had to do something.

Palm aglow with healing light, she worked her way down his back methodically, pulling out one arrow, healing the wound and then moving on to the next. Minutes later she was staring at Finn's broad back, now marked only by his swirling tattoos.

"Incredible." He breathed, running the back of his hand over the base of his spine, rolling his shoulders.

Em cleared her throat, "Um. Riva? You've got an audience." She lifted her chin in the direction of the walls.

Looking away from Finn's back, she saw that even the more severely wounded Mer had inched closer to watch the healing. Hope and hunger in their eyes.

Aoife studied the crowd closely and made her way over to her, leaning across to whisper in her ear. "Are you strong enough for this young Goddess? I can order the less severely wounded to wait until you have recovered your strength?"

Riva gritted her teeth against the exhaustion that was already threatening and pushed Aoife gently away. "No. Bring them to me."

Cronos's words floated across her mind as she took up her position. Perhaps if she healed enough of the Mer, and saved the rest, then she could make peace with what the upcoming battle would cost.

And so she sat in the spotlight in the middle of the cavern as each Mer came to her for healing. Some needed broken bones put back together, others were simple lacerations. But the ones that took all of her strength to face both mentally and magically were the Mer sporting burns so extensive that she could never even have dreamed them up. It went against everything she understood of biology for someone underwater to be burned. Perhaps that was why they were taking so long to heal.

As she wove their wounds together with magic, they told her stories of how they had been injured escaping the dungeons, or fleeing their ranks. Each and every one of them glad to be in her presence and happy that they risked their lives for her.

Riva knew if she hadn't been there to heal them then they would have succumbed to infection in a matter of days. As she watched their oozing, pus-filled pockets of flesh fold back into smooth pinkness, her vision started to swim.

"That's enough." Em said firmly, and she felt two strong hands on her shoulders pulling her away.

"I'm almost finished." Riva protested, reaching towards Mer with more minor injuries, barely noticing that she was slurring her words, "I can do this."

"You have finished young Goddess." Aoife's voice now joined Em's as she was led away to a quiet corner, "Now sleep."

24.

It was bitterly cold when she woke.

She had been having such a peaceful dream. She had been lying in the meadow, gazing at Cronos as he stroked her cheek. The fire dancing in those amber eyes had matched the burning sensation his fingers left on her delicate skin.

The best part was that it had been warm.

Shivering, she turned from the bed of kelp she assumed Em had placed her on and looked at the sleeping forms of Mer huddled together throughout the cavern. Without any of the sun's rays to warm the water, it felt like the inside of a refrigerator. Wishing she was back in that sun-drenched meadow she wrapped her arms around herself. It had definitely been a dream right? She hadn't actually gone to Eden this time? Surely if she had then Cronos would have at least said something instead of just lying silently with her.

Whatever. You've got bigger problems.

Pushing herself off the stone floor, she tried to heat the water around her. But, as she expected, having been in Oceana for days, all she could manage was a small current of heat to take the gooseflesh off her chilled arms.

Trying her best not to think about that chiselled face, she rubbed her tired eyes. She could see no sign of Em or Aoife so she swam silently in search of them, trying not to disturb the sleeping Mer as she went and passed through the underground chambers like a ghost. She didn't bother to cloak herself as she went, she highly doubted that these Mer would stop her from doing anything she wanted to.

Slipping quietly through to the largest chamber, the sentry Guards nodded respectfully at her as she passed.

When she reached the hidden entrance to the tunnel on the outskirts of Oceana, she saw Aoife slumped, half asleep, still clutching her spear.

"Hey, Aoife." Riva whispered, prodding her shoulder.

She jumped out of the way just in time as the Mer Guard woke up, brandishing her spear lethally.

"Wow there." She laughed nervously.

Aoife put a hand to her head, her eyes still drowsy with sleep. "My apologies young Goddess, I must have drifted off."

Riva extended a hand to help her up off the floor. "Don't worry about it. But please just call me Riva."

"As you wish." Aoife said.

"Why do you call me Goddess?"

Aoife looked puzzled at the question and leaned on her spear. "Because that is what you are." She said simply.

"But how do you know what a Goddess is? What God's do the Mer worship?" Riva asked, curiosity getting the better of her.

"We do not worship any God's or Goddesses specifically. Instead we celebrate the solstices and celebrate the natural magic of the world. As you have inherited the spirit of the Goddess you call Gaia, you are a part of that." Aoife explained.

Riva's eyes widened. "You know about Gaia?" She still hadn't told anyone but Alex about Eden.

Aoife smiled. "You'd be surprised what one hears at the bottom of the ocean after a few centuries."

Riva looked the woman up and down in surprise, she didn't look a day over fifty. How old was she? Perhaps she had heard enough to be able to answer her next question.

"Do you know what a titan is?" she asked, crossing her fingers.

Aoife's blank expression told her enough. "No, I'm afraid not. Is it something to do with God's and Goddesses, or magic?" she asked.

Riva sighed. "Unfortunately I think it has everything to do with all of that."

She wished that she could pick up a phone and call Alex. She was starting to realise that this was probably all part of some 'bigger picture', or even worse – fate.

She jerked herself out of her daydream again as she remembered just how good Cronos had looked lying beside her. For once he hadn't been in the suit, instead his golden torso and rippling muscles had been bared to the world, but all she had been able to focus on had been that perfect face. Now wide awake, she felt slightly worried about how much he was popping in to her thoughts. Was he manipulating her? She needed to be more careful.

Briefly another face swam into her mind and she thought of how badly she had hurt Kieran by telling him that she couldn't trust anyone. Then why was she so willing to trust Cronos?

I'm in trouble…

She needed to get a grip of her hormones before she messed everything up further.

Needing something to distract her from her thoughts before she drove herself crazy she turned to Aoife. "Have you seen Em?" she asked.

Aoife's eyes darted into the dark tunnel and she looked back at Riva nervously. "She was supposed to have returned by now."

"Returned? Returned from where? Where did she go?" Riva hissed, trying to keep her voice down so as not to wake everyone up.

Aoife sighed, "She went to find you something to eat. We both know you are no good to us if you can't use your magic and she told me that you need sustenance for your powers to work properly."

As much as Riva resented being told that she was useless without her magic, she knew that was it true. She also knew that there was a serious shortage of pepperoni pizza underwater, so the fact that Em was risking her life for some meal that Riva would most likely have to plug her nose to swallow made her furious.

"What an idiot." She hissed, "It's not like I didn't almost get myself killed rescuing her. Wait until I get my hands on her."

She summoned a current and made to shoot through the tunnel when Aoife grabbed her arm.

"Riva, don't go out there. We need you alive, Em is an Elite. She knows how to avoid trouble."

Narrowing her eyes, Riva looked at the leader of the revolution. "I don't care if she's the freaking Queen of Sheba. If you want me to lead this revolution then the next time my friend makes a stupid suggestion you stop her. Elite or not, okay? I know you said you still don't trust her and I don't know if this was some test of yours, but Em is one of my best friends. You offer her the same amount of protection you would offer me."

She cloaked herself, causing Aoife to let go of her arm in surprise and sped off up the tunnel like a worm in a hole.

Crap, I forgot how claustrophobic this is.

Trying not to let the dark, confined space freak her out, she finally popped her head out of the concealed cave entrance and looked around. Everything was still. Planting her hands on the ledge she hauled the rest of her body out of the tunnel and into the cave.

Gliding through the space, invisible, she poked her head outside. It was eerily quiet and she couldn't sense anyone close by, but even with her cloaking she was nervous to leave the cave. The force that Duncan had deployed to find her had been substantial. She dreaded to think what the consequences had been when they had returned to the palace empty-handed. She just prayed that Douglas was still alive.

Em what the hell were you thinking?

Getting a grip on herself, she swam free of the cave and drifted higher, hoping that she would be able to have some sort of advantage in spotting Em or any patrolling Guards. As she circled the city outskirts from this high up she could just about make out the gleaming palace in the distance. All she would have to do was stay cloaked, swim up to Duncan's bedroom window and finish the job. They would all be free and she could go home.

But then Douglas's father would be dead, your own father would never forgive you and you would have killed your uncle.

She squashed the thought as soon as it occurred to her. Her stomach still churned at the memory of what she had done to those Elite yesterday and that had been self-defence. Slaughtering Duncan as he slept was something entirely different, no matter what he had done to possibly deserve it.

Scanning the ruins of the old city, she tried to spot Em between the crumbling buildings and rocks. As her stomach grew hollower and she started to wonder if she might actually just join Em in her hunt for food, she spotted her. She was swimming slowly under an overhang of rock, clutching something to her chest, tail undulating slowly. Riva's relief at having found her alive and in one piece was short-lived as she spied two Guards swimming side by side, headed for the exact place Em was sheltering.

Judging by Em's crouched stance, she was planning on making a break for it, but if she revealed herself now, she would be spotted by the Guards immediately.

Riva shot straight down, the water rushing in her ears, praying that she would reach her in time. The voice in the back of her mind was already preparing her to have to silence the two Guards if they saw either of them. Quite probably in a permanent way.

The overhang of rock rushed up to meet her and she swooped around it, slamming into Em just as she flicked her tail to swim out.

"Ah---." Em cried.

Riva clamped her hand down over Em's mouth as she let out a surprised shriek and managed to cloak her just as the Guards rounded the corner. She pushed both of them as far under the overhang as possible, not willing to risk the Guards feeling so much as an out-of-place current.

She could feel Em's heart pounding through her chest. Her own heart seemed to want to give them away it was so loud. But the Guards swam sedately through the pass, spears aloft and eyes darting around.

Once they had passed, Riva grabbed Em by the forearm and summoned a swift current that carried them immediately back to the cave. Shoving Em, still cloaked and protesting down the secret tunnel before her, she didn't speak until they were once again in the relative safety of the underground cavern.

"What the hell do you think you are playing at?" Riva cried as she stripped them of their cloaking.

"Ocean's above! What's going on?!" cried out Aoife as their surprise materialization woke her from sleep again. Riva couldn't help but be glad that she wasn't the only Mer on guard duty.

Em looked flabbergasted. "I went to get you some food. You looked so exhausted when I put you down, I thought you'd be grateful." She held out three very dead lobsters in front of her and Riva's heart twisted. Em knew that lobster was one of the only things that she could stomach down here. Giving up on her anger, Riva smacked away her outstretched arm and instead pulled her in for a fierce hug.

"Don't you ever scare me like that again okay? I can live without lobster but I can't live without my best friend." She said.

Pulling away she was slightly embarrassed to realize that she was crying.

Em was sporting a sheepish grin, "I thought Alex was your best friend?" she asked.

Riva grabbed one of the lobsters off of her. "You know what I mean." She said, wrapping both hands around its body and increasing the water temperature around its shell until it was boiling. As the lobster grew red, Riva sighed with exhaustion and started ripping off the shell.

"You should've just eaten it raw." Said Em, concerned.

Riva closed her eyes as she chewed, happy just to have a mouthful of something that didn't make her want to vomit. "Well you went to all that trouble of getting them for me, I thought it was worth the effort."

"Here." She stretched out the third lobster to Em and Aoife. "Eat. You two need your strength as much as I do."

"I couldn't possibly." Protested Aoife.

"It's for you, Riva." Em protested.

She gave them a glare that soon had them accepting and halving the lobster up between them. Needless to say, they ate it raw.

After she had finished the first, she started on the second. This time the heating took no time at all and she could already feel her strength returning.

"I thought you were on my side now about the human vs. Mer food debate." She asked Em as the Mer girl eagerly sucked the meat out of a claw.

"Well, yes. But there are still some things I grew up eating here that I love. Lobster being one of them." she said.

Ripping open the second crustacean eagerly, she had just hooked a hunk of meat on her index finger when a small voice came from behind her.

"I like lobster too."

The three women turned slowly to see a small Mer boy, aged around five or six, swim shyly up to them. There was something vaguely familiar about him.

The three women shared a look.

"Well it just so happens that we've got some to spare." Aoife said gently, offering him a claw from her half of the lobster.

The little boy approached the women carefully, eyes darting to and fro, before taking the claw ever so gently from Aoife's hand.

"Thank you." he said quietly, nimbly picking the meat out of the shell. When he had finished, he sat staring hungrily at Riva's meal so she broke off another claw for him too. Only slightly begrudgingly.

"Are you going to save us?" he asked so matter-of-factly that it took Riva off guard.

She hesitated. Trying not to accidentally make a promise she couldn't keep. "I'm going to try." She said.

The little boy seemed to be speaking absent-mindedly now as he focused on his food. "My mama says that you are. She says that even though a lot of folk say you're a bad person, you use your magic for good things."

Riva frowned slightly, "Oh really? And how does your mum know things about my magic?"

The little boy was busy with his teeth and needed a second to reply. "She saw you use it once." He paused and then looked up at her, "Can I see some now?"

Riva laughed at his enthusiasm and threw him what was left of her lobster. While she was far from full, she could count every single one of his ribs. Just one more thing on her list of reasons to overthrow Duncan.

"You'd better get back to your mama before she worries where you are." Riva said gently.

The little boy nodded and as he stood up, she got a good look at his tail. Strongly resembling the bottlenose, not far off the same shade as Em's, his tail was marked by large half-moon scars. The kind of scars that might be left by shark teeth. She looked over and locked eyes with Em who had just realized the exact same thing. This was the same little boy that she had saved a few months ago.

Riva felt a lump appear in her throat. The fact that he was here alive, albeit starving, dirty and on the run, reminded her that she did know how to keep the balance. There was a time when she could justify taking life, but there were many more times when she would save it.

The little boy was still staring at her, his eyes two moons in his face.

"Don't worry, my mama will know I'm safe if you're here." He said.

Before he swam off he seemed to hesitate and then wrapped his arms around Riva's neck, still clutching his lobster claws. The warmth of his little body hanging there made her feel so indescribably lonely all of a sudden.

"I think my mama's right. I think you will save us with your magic." He whispered into her ear and then swam off happily back to wherever his mum was.

The three women looked at each other. Em with one eyebrow raised, Riva unsure of how to feel and Aoife with a steely glint in her eye.

"Well, I'm with the boy." Aoife said crossing her arms.

Em threw away the shell she had been fidgeting with. "You saved him, now it's time we help you save the rest of us." She said.

Riva looked between them both and knew that the time had come. "Then what are we waiting for?"

25.

"Everyone form a line, time is of the essence!" Aoife barked out, chivvying stray Merfolk into the queue.

Riva was standing before the members of the resistance in the largest underground chamber, hoping that their plan would work.

They had spent the entirety of the previous day in meetings with one another. Em and Finn had flitted in and out in between sessions of the crashiest of crash-courses in combat Riva had ever seen.

Granted most of the harvesters still looked more comfortable with a scythe than a sword but beggars couldn't be choosers. She had spoken with Aoife, and her circle of senior Guards who had spent hours arguing, going back and forth with one another, and changing their minds until they all finally agreed on a plan of action.

After seeing Riva's handy cloaking trick the day before, Aoife was eager to get her to use it. Making the obvious argument that it would give them an unparalleled advantage. The only problem was that even if Riva could cloak everyone individually, she might not be able to sustain it for very long.

That was when Em had ever so helpfully piped up that her only limitations were the ones in her mind. After that, she had lost all arguments and had been bullied into cloaking each Mer individually so that the whole army of rebels could move into position undetected at the time of Douglas's execution.

There wasn't going to be a rescue, there was going to be a battle.

She rubbed her chilled hands together and tried to calm her churning stomach. She really didn't need a raging case of IBS right now. Every member of the rebel force willing to fight was gathered before her. Almost a hundred and fifty people that she needed to make invisible.

The first Mer approached her. A young woman with creamy skin and auburn hair that was braided in a similar fashion to Riva's own. She grasped the wrist she had extended with her Marked palm and centred herself around her magic. She felt it pooling in her bloodstream and come cascading out through her Mark into the Mer woman.

Invisibility flowed through the Mer's body until she was nothing more than an insubstantial wraith.

A murmur of both apprehension and appreciation rippled through the rest of the Mer gathered. Riva scrutinized her work, if you swam past her without knowing she was there then you wouldn't look twice, but as she examined the edges of the Mer's body, she could just about make out a slight edge to the cloaking. Either way it would have to do.

Gesturing for the Mer woman to swim to her left where Aoife and Finn were splitting the groups up, she beckoned the next Mer forward to be cloaked.

Their surprised exclamations did bring a smile to her face as they watched their bodies disappear.

Once the entire group was successfully cloaked, including Aoife, Finn, Em and herself, she turned to the faces she could no longer see, holding her Mark aloft.

"Riva what are you doing?" asked Em's disembodied voice.

Without answering, she connected to her magic again, somehow able to feel every single person she had cloaked individually – as if they were still connected to her. Her magic pulsing in her chest and in her Mark, she let it expand from her.

She was working on a theory. A theory that, if proved right, would be her ticket to giving the Mer their lives back.

Her magic spiralled through the people gathered, connecting them like golden threads on a tapestry of the sun. Eyes closed, she felt rather than saw what she was doing. One by one, she snipped the cords that bound them to her, like the clean cut of an umbilical cord. After the first cut, she smiled. It was working.

"Riva?" Em asked again and she felt her move closer.

"Just. Wait." Riva replied, eyes still closed, feeling her way through the people with her magic.

Carefully releasing each Mer from her, she made their cloaking permanent, channelling the magic from the Earth instead of from herself. She wanted to kick herself for not thinking of it before. To save herself from exhaustion all she had needed to do was find another source, and her connection to Eden had shown her that Earth magic existed even at the bottom of the ocean.

Once each individual had their own self-sustaining cloaking in place, she flexed her magic out from her like a giant bubble until it covered them all.

And now for the piece de resistance…

Crossing her fingers and praying that it worked, she turned the cloaking magic inside out. Like a two-way mirror, they would be able to see out, but no-one else would be able to see in.

Cries of dismay went up through the crowd as almost two hundred Mer suddenly re-materialized.

"Riva what happened?" Em asked, rushing up to her finally. "What went wrong?"

None of them were expecting her to smile.

"Oh it worked alright. And even better than I had hoped." She grinned. "Duncan isn't going to know what hit him. Literally."

Aoife now approached, shaking her head as Finn and the other Guards attempted to hush the now-panicked Mer. "Explain yourself."

She pointed to the rabble. "Find a way to shut them up and get them focused on me. I'll be right back." She said, summoning a current to carry her off to the chamber where the families were hunkering down to wait out the battle.

She re-appeared moments later, swimming hand in hand with the little boy she had saved from the shark. He was sucking his thumb and seemed utterly confused as to why she had brought him to an empty chamber.

She had linked each cloaked Mer together permanently. Meaning that they could see each other, but any Mer left uncloaked would be blind to their presence.

The rebels were silent as they watched them approach and she halted just in front of them.

"Alright Sammy." She said, floating below him so that they were eye-level. "Tell me what you see?"

The little boy gazed around the cave with wide eyes. "I dunno, rocks?"

Riva smirked and nodded encouragingly. "Yes, rocks. Anything else?"

"Um. Kelp?"

The rebels began to whisper and the noise seemed to unsettle him as he tried to find the source of the noise. Riva grasped him by the shoulders. "Can you see any Mer people in this cavern Sammy? Look really closely." She asked.

Too nervous now to speak, he shook his head dramatically and went back to sucking his thumb.

Beaming, Riva straightened up. "You see? If you have been cloaked you will be able to see one another. However you will remain invisible to all others out-with the cloaking magic." Realization dawned on the features of the Mer that she could see but that Sammy was still blind to.

"Who are you talking to?" he asked in a small voice.

She looked through the ranks, at the women and the men, all of them too skinny, all of them dirty and unkempt. But all of them willing to fight for their freedom.

"To our people." She replied quietly. Finally, she felt like she was one of them. Her Mer blood sang in her veins.

She realised they were all waiting for her to say something else so she raised her voice, hoping that she wouldn't ramble too much. Sammy clutched her hand tightly, his little grip somehow giving her strength.

"You fight for me today in the hopes that I can give you your freedom. Not only from a tyrant king but from Oceana itself. For too long you have had to seek shelter in a crumbling city. For too long you have been away from your true homes."

The Mer began to bare their teeth and lash their tails back and forth, her words stirring their blood.

"Duncan believes the answer to your problems lies in eradicating humans, but he has used you and banished you and tortured you to get his way." As she spoke she made eye contact with each individual. "And for what? This city is still the only safe haven in all of the oceans. While our people cower here, the ocean itself falls to ruin without us there to protect her. So I show you now, there is a better way. With this cloaking you will be free to roam the oceans as you please, your sacred duty to guard and nurture her will be returned to you. Together we can reverse this damage and save her before it is too late. So I ask you now. Will you fight?!"

The roar was more than she had anticipated. Clicks and whistles punched through her chest and she staggered backwards. Poor Sammy was now terrified of the invisible people in front of him.

"Pretty speech but I thought we were supposed to remain inconspicuous?" Em asked through the corner of her mouth as Aoife rushed to regain control on the rebels again.

"Oops. I didn't think about that." Riva bit her lip as the few people in charge attempted to silence the crowd.

By the time she had taken Sammy back to his bewildered mum and returned to the chamber, the mood was serious once again.

Heeding Em's reminder she called out, "Remember, this cloaking won't stop Duncan's Guards from being able to feel or hear you so you must remain quiet and aware at all times until we are in position."

The rebels began to file silently out of the underground caves through the tunnel one at a time.

Em reached across to pat her on the shoulder, "Don't worry, this will work." She said confidently.

Her stomach was in knots again. "I hope so. Douglas's life depends on it." She said anxiously as she watched a young Mer girl with a black and white stripe on her tail enter the tunnel.

"As long as everyone plays their part, our plan is faultless." Said Finn, his deep voice inherently calming.

Even as she watched them leave, she knew that the element of surprise was all they had. If they were somehow discovered before they were in position then they might still lose. Even though all of the Mer here seemed convinced that Riva could defeat Duncan's entire army by herself, she wasn't so sure. She certainly didn't want to put it to the test. As strong as she had become over the past few months, her powers were still tied to her body's limits, even if she drew power from the Earth. If she got too tired or weak to fight then her magic would be useless.

"Are you ready?" Aoife asked quietly.

She slipped through the tunnel, following the leader of the rebels, with Em bringing up the rear. Popping her head out of the cave she had sought sanctuary in, she saw their army already split up into their units, waiting for their next command. She had to hand it to Finn. He ran a tight ship.

Aoife swam up and down, inspecting the ranks one last time. Riva cast her consciousness out for any Guards but found nothing. She nodded her head towards Aoife. Who addressed their people one last time.

"My dear friends, today we rise as one to help our young Goddess and to welcome the beginning of a new future. Freedom, not only for ourselves, but for the generations to come." She pointed her spear in the direction of the palace. "Now, we follow her. To whatever end."

Goosebumps prickled on her skin as they all swam silently away from the cave. This was really happening.

"Alright." Riva whispered to Em who was on her right. "The prison break team go in first remember."

They both looked over at the group Finn was leading. Around twenty Mer, almost none of them fighters, but all armed with small explosives of Riva's making.

She had stunned everyone the night before, including herself, when she had sat over a small underwater hot spring and heated it until it was an underwater volcano. As the magma poured up from under the sea floor, it turned brown and released steam. This had delighted the shivering Mer who, albeit used to the cool temperatures, had been struggling in the cavern after weeks without any access to the sun-warmed waters.

She had formed as many magma-mud-pies as she could, infusing them with her lightning so that when they hit any barrier they would explode. Hopefully. She hadn't been able to think of another way to get past those nightmare-inducing jail cells in the palace dungeons. All she could hope for was that her own magic would negate the magic in the barrier long enough for whoever was in the cell to escape.

Finn soon disappeared over the ridge with his group and the rest of the rebels waited for Riva's signal. She cast out her consciousness again and found only a whale shark, meandering slowly between two travel currents high above.

"Okay. Let's move." She said, nodding once again to Aoife on her left.

Rising from the cave as one, the rebel Mer formed a tight group behind the three women.

As they swam through the ruins, Riva noticed the water draw more shadows as they approached nightfall. Even though Oceana pretty much existed in perpetual twilight thanks to the depth, there was still a noticeable difference between day and night.

Trying to calm her nerves, she reminded herself that Duncan had said sunset on purpose. He wanted her to turn up, and she was sure he would be ready for her.

"Why have we not encountered any patrols yet?" Em whispered anxiously.

Riva shrugged and kept swimming. Aoife was looking like she didn't want to think about the answer. Already dreading the kinds of nasty surprises her uncle had concocted in the past two days, she swallowed her nerves.

More than a hundred Mer fanned out as a group behind her, most clutching spears recently whittled, the few Guards that were dotted between them as assigned group leaders clutched their own lethal-looking weapons. She reminded herself that she wasn't alone anymore.

She looked through the group and marvelled at the sight. Mer of all shapes, sizes and colours united with a common purpose. Flashes of blonde, red and black hair mingled with the pumping tails of darkest ebony to the lightest grey. The sight really was quite breath-taking. Thankfully she was the only one who could see it. As long as they remained quiet, Duncan shouldn't suspect a thing.

They swam high over the tops of the buildings as they entered the lower town, avoiding the crush of the streets below. As they crested the rise to enter the city proper where the buildings resembled actual pieces of architecture instead of just crumbled ruins, Aoife held up her hand to call their group to a halt.

Riva almost groaned aloud but knew she couldn't let any of the Mer behind her see how worried she was.

Duncan had called in reinforcements.

The entire square was full of residential Mer belonging to the upper classes or nobility. All of them decked out in their finest for this special day. Cloaks of woven algae draped the shoulders of some, while others sported headpieces made of shells or bracelets of coral for the occasion. Encircling all of the Mer in the square, both in the inner circle around the platform and on the outskirts of the square, were Guards. Floating rigid and alert, ready to take on any foe.

"There are Elite here as well." Em breathed softly in her ear, surprise clear in her voice. Her face not betraying her feelings about seeing the execution platform again.

Riva swallowed uncomfortably.

The Elite were dotted through the crowd itself which would make their plan difficult. Riva had wanted to separate the general public from the Guards, giving their group a clear idea of which Mer to protect and which to fight if it came down to it. This way they were going to have to fight on all fronts.

Aoife nudged her with an elbow and then pointed skywards.

"Crap." Riva breathed, clenching her hands.

More Elite and Guards were posted every ten feet in a spiral rising upwards from the town square. There was no way their group would pass through unnoticed even with their cloaking.

"What do we do?" Em breathed quietly and Aoife turned to remind the Mer behind them to remain silent, as some nervous whispers had started.

Riva took her time observing the layout of Duncan's security. "I need a minute." She said.

The path to the palace across the reef was clear, but Riva was worried about whether or not Finn's group had managed to get to the dungeons unimpeded or if there were more surprises waiting for them too.

Clearly Duncan was expecting her to keep her fight outdoors. Possibly anticipating a repeat of how she had rescued Em. By placing the majority of his forces around the public, he could also claim that he was protecting his citizens. Did he know that she had an army with her? Had someone tipped him off? Or was he really this afraid of her?

"There isn't much space down on the ground for us to infiltrate." Aoife muttered, studying the packed square. Mer were floating shoulder to shoulder from the buildings bordering the square almost to the platform itself.

"I know." Riva whispered, making up her mind. "Okay, here's what we are going to do. Aoife, make sure each group splits up, half will make their way into the streets that feed into the square in small groups. There is enough space there for them to wait for my signal and to hide inside buildings in case any Guards pass by." She looked down at where they were tightly wedged in by the public and upwards at their spiral formation. "But I highly doubt they will be moving around much."

"Of course." Aoife answered.

"The other half of the group will squeeze themselves in beside the platform, forming a circle around it, facing the line of Guards. I know there isn't much space to manoeuvre but it's our only choice right now. Try to divide our own Guards up equally so that each group has at least one with them."

Aoife nodded and made to swim away to give the directions to her troops, but Riva shot her arm out and grabbed her.

"Make sure that no-one so much as brushes one of the Mer down there by accident." She said. "This plan is hanging by a thread. We can't afford to give ourselves away."

Riva and Em floated, observing as Aoife directed the Mer into their positions quickly but quietly.

Every time another one of the rebels swam undetected past one of the sentries, Riva felt the weight on her shoulders grow simultaneously heavier and lighter. They might have succeeded in getting into position, but nothing was over yet.

"So now we wait for them to bring Douglas out." Em said quietly from where they still floated just outside the town square.

Riva lifted her gaze past the large buildings towards the reef and the glistening palace that lay beyond.

"No. Now I call in reinforcements." Riva replied.

"What?" she whirled to face her "You can't deviate from the plan now!" Em hissed, her Australian accent getting more pronounced with her worry. "What if you don't make it back in time? You know that we can never win this fight without you."

Riva was already backing away in the direction of the palace. "Em. Don't worry. Douglas is still being held in the dungeons. If I see them bringing him out I will be back here in a flash. But there's something I have to do first. Just wait here and stick to the plan." She said, summoning a swift current and bolting out of there.

26.

Circumnavigating the town square that was quickly resembling a battlefield, at least to the Mer who were able to see through her cloaking, she sped off over the reef.

Guiding her currents, she felt like she was flying as she whizzed off through towering corals that were now spiralling towards the sky and dodging rays who came to play in her slipstream. Clearly the magic she had imbibed on the reef just the other day had already taken root. The reef had never seemed so vibrant.

As she reached the base of the palace she followed her gut instinct and shot vertically up the side, nose almost touching the pearlescent walls. Easing off on her currents as she reached the familiar silken curtains, she hovered just outside, listening.

At the first archway she could hear nothing and peeking in she realised quickly that it was the wrong room. Skirting the side of the towers she cautiously glanced inside each archway hoping to find her uncles. Just as she was beginning to think that she was too late and began to worry that Douglas would be meeting his death any second, she heard the twins' voices.

"She's disappeared. What are we supposed to do? If she doesn't come back to save her…"

"I don't blame her though, do you? This isn't her home, why should she fight for it?"

"No. You're wrong. She'll be somewhere, she thinks that boy is related to her. I just don't know what's taking her so long."

Riva brushed the curtain aside and let down her cloaking as she swam into the room where her uncles were gathered together, talking in hushed voices.

"I hope you all know that this is treason." She said, standing right behind them, arms crossed.

All three of them jumped at the sound of her voice. Their expressions ranging from happiness to fear, to panic.

"Are you mad to come into the palace today?" Declan said, making a grab for her wrist, eyes darting all around. "Duncan has spies everywhere."

Riva brushed him away. "He isn't the only one. I have a plan."

"As air-tight as your last one?" Murphy said scathingly.

Riva chose to ignore that comment.

Murray closed the gap between them and put his arms around her gently. "I'm so glad you're safe, niece."

"Thanks." She said. "At least one of you cares." She looked pointedly at her uncles but let her mouth betray her smile. "There's no time to waste. I need your help."

Her three uncles looked between themselves.

"Tell me what you know." she asked.

The three of them looked worryingly guilty.

"We didn't want to help him you know." Murphy said.

"Believe us, we wanted no part in it, but he is our brother." Declan added.

Murphy said nothing but was looking shiftily at the floor, hands clasped behind his back.

What the hell are they talking about?

She raised her hands up to get them to stop. "Look, at this point it really doesn't matter. I just need to know exactly what he is planning so I can stop him." she said.

Murphy raised his eyes slowly from the ground. "He's expecting you to be here. He knows that some of his army has deserted so he isn't expecting you to be alone."

Riva nodded, her spine was tingling, conscious of time. "So that's why he's spread out his Guards, he doesn't want me to be able to incapacitate them all at once again."

"Exactly." Murphy continued. "He thinks that you will attack at the moment he brings Douglas out. He wants a spectacle, for you to paint yourself as the villain. You should see the things he was saying about the way you killed half of his Elite force in minutes."

Riva fought down the nausea. "I'm not sure I want to know."

Declan's voice was soft. "It was self-defence Riva, no-one can blame you for that."

She was subconsciously rubbing her Mark against her sealskin leggings as it throbbed uncomfortably, her magic eager to be let loose again.

"Well I have a few surprises up my sleeve that he won't be expecting." She said quietly. "And I need your help with that." She addressed the twins.

"Whatever you need." They said in unison.

She quickly explained her plan regarding the dungeons and how Finn was already down there with a small group of Mer.

"So I need you two to make sure they have clear access to the dungeons when the time comes. Distract the remaining Guards, do whatever you have to, but make sure that they are in there when I give the signal."

"Which is what exactly?" Murray asked.

Riva smiled shrewdly, "Oh you'll know."

"What do you ask of me? We're supposed to be at the King's side during the execution. Our dear brother keeps going on about 'unwavering royal support'. He will be furious that the twins have disappeared but he won't have time to look for them by the time he realizes that they are missing." Declan asked, wringing his hands.

Riva thought about it. "No. Stay with him. When the time comes, I might need you close by to convince him about Douglas if things go south." She looked at them all, her heart heavy but happy that her family was on her side.

"Convince him what about Douglas?" Declan asked slowly.

Riva looked blankly between the three of them. Had she forgotten to tell them? Or had they really not worked it out for themselves yet?

"Douglas is Duncan's son." She said.

Jaws dropped and Declan turned white as a sheet. "Impossible." He breathed.

Riva pursed her lips. "Well that's what I said at first but it really had more to do with a woman actually wanting to have sex with Duncan and not with-. Never mind." They were still staring at her with stunned expressions.

"The aim is to solve this without violence. Hopefully by revealing who Douglas is to Duncan he will hesitate long enough for us to convince him. No-one else needs to die because of this."

Murphy went to move towards her. "Riva, we didn't expect something like this." He said, looking to his brothers as if for support. "We had no idea."

She looked over her shoulder through the archway, she didn't really have any more time to waste. "It's fine, it's my own stupid fault for not telling you sooner, but we thought that I would be bringing him back here after getting him out of the dungeons. We all know how that plan worked out." she laughed hollowly, the miserable looks on her uncles faces making her anxiety grow.

"What is it?" she asked.

They all shared a shifty glance.

"What aren't you telling me?" she asked again, louder this time.

Drums started outside and her blood ran cold. She looked towards the archway, her long braid swinging across her shoulder.

"It's time. You must go." Declan said, chivvying her quickly back towards the curtains.

"But wait, I want to know-."

Before she could ask them any more questions, the door to the suite had drifted closed behind the three white tails.

Cursing her secretive family, she rushed out of the archway on the back of another current.

The drums grew louder and more ominous as she swam towards the ground. The Mer beat their drums in formation and with every resonating boom her heart pounded harder. She hoped that Douglas had enough faith in her to know that she wouldn't let him die. Floating invisibly just outside the pathway from the palace, she watched as two Guards led Douglas out of the dungeons.

He was limp in their arms, but more alert than Em had been the day Riva had thwarted her execution. His eyes were darting all over the place looking for something. Looking for her. She wished that she could give him a sign so that he wouldn't lose hope but she couldn't risk it.

Just behind the Guards swam the council of Elders, led by the ancient Iolana, sporting her usual macabre cape. Remembering the way the velvet-soft rays had danced with her on the reef made her sad to see such a giant being made into a garment like that.

Regardless, Riva was glad she was there. She might need the woman's help if it came to a fight.

After the Elders came Duncan, with Declan just a little ways behind him. He looked composed enough but his rapid blinking gave away his nervousness. Riva studied Duncan's face. He looked furious but determined. She supposed that he was angry at the twin's apparent desertion. At least they had listened to her. For a second she hadn't been sure if they would.

The small procession was now swimming over the reef, so Riva sped off in a wide arc towards where Em was still waiting for her.

Em visibly relaxed when she spotted her. "Cutting it a little close aren't you?" she hissed, looking at the approaching executional party.

"Don't worry. I found help." She whispered.

Ignoring Em's questioning glance, she turned her attention back to the square where the gathered Mer had grown silent at the approach of their King.

Douglas was thrown forwards to his knees on the platform, overbalancing slightly in the water and he fought to right himself, his hands bound by rough-looking rope behind his back.

The Elders spread out behind him, their barnacle-covered tails scraping against the rough wood of the platform. Duncan took his place in the centre and Declan melted away into the background, eyes on the floor.

What the hell is he so nervous about? I didn't ask him to do anything that difficult.

"My dear Merfolk, here we are gathered to witness a traitor brought to justice once again." He paused and looked around at his adoring public. "However be assured that this time the sentence will be carried out in full."

Cheers from the crowd set Riva's teeth on edge and Douglas glared out at them all. She briefly wondered if he would ever forgive his father for this. Or if Duncan would ever be willing to believe that Douglas was his son.

"Before me kneels the half-breed companion of the traitor Riva who still awaits punishment for her own crimes."

Seemingly unable to hold back any longer, Douglas yelled out to the crowd; "What crimes? What crime is it to be born? Riva and I didn't choose this, you Mer chose it for us when you willingly mated with a human. Why should we be punished for your choice?"

Before he could finish, one of the Guards hit him between the shoulder blades with the butt of his spear, winding him. She could see that he was missing a tooth and had several new cuts and bruises that marred his dark skin. They must have taken him from the dungeons to get information out of him since her healing.

More cheers rose from the crowd as Douglas spat blood and Riva started counting down on her fingers. It was almost time.

"You hear the lies he spouts from his own inferior mouth. Today we shall take one more step towards eliminating his kind and preserving the purity of our blood!"

He extended his right arm to grasp the same sword that Riva had pulled from Em's flukes just a couple of days before.

Now! She shouted in her head.

The water directly above the square ripped open and they poured through the entrance current she had created in a great rush. All of the Mer gathered shrieked at their sudden appearance. Ten glorious black and white whales swam through the current, all of them vocalizing at such a frequency that every Mer gathered clapped their hands over their ears and shrunk away from the sound. The King included. Sword forgotten, he was on the ground, white tail curled up around him in pain.

Riva and Em smiled, she had plugged the ears of the rebels with a cushioning of air to stop them from being affected. As the killer whales swooped down and through the regimented ranks of Elite and Guards, they knocked Mer sentries flying with their tails as others became swept away by the strong slipstreams, breaking their spiral formation.

In the confusion, the Mer gathered in the square crouched low to the ground, figuring it was safer than being buffeted around in the currents created above by the pod of whales.

As the piercing vocalizations faded away, the matriarch swam up towards where Riva floated, still invisible. She slowed to a stop directly in front of her and Riva gazed into her eye. Completely black, ringed in the palest blue, Riva reached out a hand to rest on her ebony skin.

Thank you.

The whale thrummed out her own version of thanks before gliding smoothly away, Riva's hand slipping off her silken side. Avoiding her powerful tail flukes, she watched as the pod swam away from the square and she opened an exit current for them as they headed for the surface once again.

The Mer down on the sea floor were murmuring nervously as the Guards and Elite dotted through the crowd attempted to restore calm. Duncan looked shaken but he was regaining his composure, waiting until he had the full attention of his audience before picking up his sword again.

Bloody drama queen.

Just as the sentries scurried into formation once more, a resounding boom came from the palace. This time screams and cries erupted from the crowd as everyone dove for cover. The sea floor beneath them shook and every Guard turned towards the noise, panicked. Riva saw Duncan give the order to investigate and at least fifty Guards shot off towards the palace.

Right on time, one of the rebels called out in a clear voice. "It's the dungeons! The rebels have released the prisoners!"

From his position in the square, anyone could have said it. But the nobility quickly repeated the rumour, fuelling the panic down below.

Confusion reigned as the Guards posted on the outer edges of the square attempted to keep the Mer inside. Creating even more fear and panic than if they had been allowed to leave.

Hearing the shout, Duncan swam up above the rooftops to get a better look, and sure enough, there was a cloud of dark smoke, something that looked so out of place underwater, rising from the direction of the dungeons.

Giving the signal to the rest of the Guards who remained floating above the square, he sent them off to investigate.

"Just like we planned. " Em said delightedly as they watched the majority of Duncan's force swim off into the path of the rebels.

Down on the ground, Duncan was attempting to gain control over the public. The Elders were shifting uncomfortably behind their King, eyes darting around the open water above them. Iolana remained unflinching.

"My dear people, stay here where you are safe. We will provide you protection from this latest attempt by the traitor Riva to destroy us. She has turned her attention towards freeing criminals and traitors, turning her back on her own friends." The public were slowly calming down, realising that they didn't really have a choice.

Riva turned to Em and grinned. He was playing right into their hands. "Showtime."

She was met with a grin as Em swam down to join Aoife, grey tail flashing and Riva slowly sunk down through the water.

She descended slowly, weaving her way through the few Guards that were left floating above the platform and avoided the heads of the Mer still floating in the square. She steadied herself so that when her bare feet finally touched the wooden platform, they didn't make a sound.

Still cloaked, she inched towards Douglas as Duncan continued to make his rambling speech. She no longer cared what he was saying.

Halting in front of her cousin, she could see a nasty new wound on his head, just visible amongst the tight curls. Brushing her hand against Douglas's cheek, she whispered in his ear. "Get to a sword when you can."

He flinched visibly and his onyx eyes widened in surprise but she held his head tightly between her hands, stopping him from looking up at her.

"It's going to be ok." She whispered again, letting her hands slide from his cheeks. Relief was palpable on his features.

Positioning herself between Douglas and the King, she now had to live up to all of her promises. Closing her eyes, she connected to her magic and sent up a silent prayer to whatever God was listening that she was ready for this.

"My people. As our ever-faithful Guards explore what has occurred in the palace dungeons, do not be afraid. If there was a loss of Mer life then it will have been Mer who were convicted of crimes against the crown. We stand here today, about to witness one of the final acts necessary in protecting our race. Once we have weeded out these traitors, we can begin to rebuild our people."

Duncan reached for the sword again and Riva planted her feet firmly on the platform directly in front of him, the warped wood felt strange under her bare feet and she wondered briefly if she was about to get a splinter.

He raised the sword, and she watched it glint in the eerie half-light. Summoning her magic, her Mark and eyes began to glow. She watched as Duncan paused, eyes narrowing in the direction of the three golden lights that had now appeared in the water before him.

She dropped her cloaking just as the sword swooped down towards her.

"Hello uncle." She said with a smirk as the sword fell.

"Half-breed!"

Duncan's roar was deafening as he slashed wildly with the sword which would have easily clove her in two if she hadn't deflected it with a stray current.

"I prefer demi-Mer if you don't mind." She said lazily.

At her sudden appearance, screams and cries rang out across the square as the public fought to get away but found themselves trapped between Guards.

Her uncle lunged for her again, ancient sword gleaming and white tail slashing madly as she dodged him. Weaving her way around him with the help of her currents, while simultaneously using them to hinder Duncan's own movements.

Every time he lunged, he met a wall of solid water. Each time he parried, she deflected with a current. He couldn't get within two feet of her.

"You murdering *witch!*" He growled, redoubling his attack.

Riva set jet after jet of water to meet his sword. "Funny that you call me the murderer when you're the one swinging a sword at someone's head."

She sent out a wall of solid water to stop his advances and he was left floating there, two hands clutching the hilt, unable to move it.

Raising her hand, enjoying the fury and fear that was evident in his ice-blue eyes, she warped the water around the sword, twisting his wrist painfully until he cried out and dropped it. It fell to the floor between them with a thump.

"Kill her!" Duncan cried wildly, making a wild grab for the sword.

As the few Elite and Guards left among the crowd advanced towards her, she raised her glowing Mark, spreading her arms out from her body and asked the Earth to stop cloaking the resistance.

The sudden appearance of over a hundred armed rebels surrounding the platform and the square sent a wave of panic among the crowd and the fighting began in earnest. Guards hurled spears and rebels brandished scythes and the rest of the Mer fought to escape the melee.

Duncan made another desperate swipe for the sword and Riva stretched out her hand, asking the ocean to bring it to her. The sword came rushing into her open palm and she grasped the cool hilt as Duncan's hands closed around empty water.

Riva, seeing the moment she had planned for present itself and knowing that it would last only moments, threw the sword point down into the platform with a dull thud.

Before her uncle could lunge towards her, she threw out her right hand, immobilising Duncan in a whirlpool that encased his tail, and turned to address the crowd. Turning her back on the council of Elders made her more than a little uncomfortable, but Iolana's narrowed eyes were laser-focused on her.

"Listen to me!" she cried in the strongest, steadiest voice she possessed.

Her voice struggled to permeate the riot going on all around her. With a groan of exasperation she centred herself, drawing up her magic which she then pushed down into the sea floor. The ground began to rumble and as both Duncan's army and the rebels paused to observe the greater threat, she cried out again.

"Listen!"

The shrieking cries and clash of weapons slowly subsided. She knew that she had one chance at this. She needed them to know who she really was in case Duncan didn't survive. Her plan for the future would never work if less than half of all Mer trusted her. The rebels were on her side, but they wouldn't be enough.

"You have come here today to witness an act of unthinkable violence, I am here to stop it. You have been told that I am a traitor, a monster, an *abomination*" she thought back to her arrival in Oceana months ago and the words that Duncan himself had used to describe her.

She looked her uncle in the eye as she said it and hatred was etched into every line on his face. His jaw was set and his ice blue eyes unforgiving.

"But that is a lie. I know you all have reason to hate humans and what they have done to your home. I possess the power necessary to give you back your lives. King Malcolm could see that and asked me to help before he died."

Duncan was struggling against his bonds, "Lies!" he hissed, but Riva held her audience captivated with her words.

"I am the daughter of Prince Dylan. I am the granddaughter of King Malcolm and Queen Noelani and I am here to restore peace to Oceana." She turned to look at her uncle Declan and reached out her hand.

"Your King has been conspiring to murder his own niece and he did so in full possession of the truth. While my father was still resident in Oceana he revealed who I really am and Duncan wanted to murder him for it too. I fled Oceana under pain of death little more than a month ago, taking my father with me to save our lives. I am here to inform you that my father, your once-rightful King is alive and well today."

The crowd buzzed with murmurs and shocked whispers, which grew only louder when her uncle Declan swam past the still-immobilized King and stood shoulder to shoulder with Riva, adding his voice to hers.

"Every word that my niece speaks is the truth." Declan said, his hands shaking.

As she looked out into the crowd, she could see Guards who had been ready to kill her five minutes ago, holding their spears loosely by their sides. Confusion was etched on their faces as they tried to make sense of her words and of their brothers in arms amongst the rebel force who were holding raised weapons against them.

Riva gestured to the rebels circling the platform and the outside of the square. "You see how many of your brothers and sisters have already joined my cause. They can see the bright future that I can give you all. So I ask you now. Will you turn your back on this tyrant king and try for peace? Or will you hold on to your hatred until it destroys you?"

Finishing her very much on-the-spot speech, she wrenched the sword out of the platform and cut Douglas's bindings in one motion. Genuinely surprising herself that she didn't chop off his hand in the process, she helped him to his feet. The three of them stood there, a Mer Prince and two Demi-Mer royals, waiting to see what the crowd's reaction would be.

Then, a cry came from the middle of the square.

"We will never be ruled by a half-breed!"

The shout was followed by a faint whistling sound and she spotted the dagger a fraction of a second too late. As she dodged just in time, she felt the hot bite of metal as it sliced her cheek. Shocked, she ran her fingers over the stinging wound and was surprised when they came away red with blood.

Pandemonium ensued.

Her momentary distraction thanks to the pain had been enough for her to waver in her magic, letting Duncan release himself as her whirlpool faltered. The act of defiance from one of the crowd sparked others to follow suit and soon the rebels were fighting a mob as the Guards remained unsure of which side to protect and which to fight. Some Mer appeared to be trying to get to the platform to finish Riva and Douglas off themselves, others seemed to want only to escape the confines of the square.

Once freed, Duncan launched himself at Riva, white tail beating furiously, but just before he made impact, Declan intercepted him. The two brothers collided with a bone-shuddering crunch and they turned over each other, fists and tails flying until it was difficult to make out who was who with their almost identical blonde heads and blindingly white tails.

Unable to look away and unable to get involved, she stood there and watched as the two brothers laid their fists and flukes into each other.

"What was that?" Douglas asked weakly, pointing over Riva's shoulder in the direction of the palace to where the smoke had been replaced with a large cloud of steam.

"Oh, you know. Just a little volcanic eruption." She said, flinching at some of the sounds coming from the square around them.

"A what?!" Douglas exclaimed.

No sooner was the word out of his mouth than Finn's group of rebels crested the reef and spilled into the higher water above the square. His rebel group and freed 'criminals' were fighting furiously with the bulk of Duncan's Guards that had been sent to investigate the explosion. The rebels were outnumbered two to one, even with the addition of the prisoners.

Seeing that the majority of them were wounded, Riva threw out both of her hands and sent a current up to separate the two groups. Snaking the water around the rebels like a giant bubbling serpent to give them time to regroup.

"Give me a hand would you?" She asked Douglas. If she hadn't been underwater the sweat would have been pouring off of her with the effort.

Weak as he was, he helped her guide the currents until Duncan's soldiers were fully separated from the rebels. Finn looked down at Riva and gave her a wink, a large gash on his bicep weeping blood. He quickly turned his attention to his forces, regrouping them and sending the severely wounded to the back of the square.

Diverting her attention from above for a second she took in the battle surrounding them.

Duncan and Declan were still fighting each other with tails and fists and most of the Mer were simply trying to find their way out of the mess of writhing bodies but the rebel forces either side of them made it difficult. Most of the rebels were fighting Duncan's Guards furiously.

She made the mistake of looking below the platform where several bodies lay strewn on the sea floor, eyes open and unseeing.

"This wasn't supposed to happen." She breathed, staring down at the body of a Mer who was lying broken on the compacted sand.

Douglas followed her gaze and grabbed her wrist. "Well there's nothing you can do about it now. What's the plan?"

Fighting down the nausea and dizziness, unsure if it was from what she had just seen or the magic use, she gritted her teeth.

"I need their attention." She said desperately, an idea coming to her. "Keep an eye on them up there would you?" Jerking her head in Finn's direction.

Diving off the platform and onto the sand below, she swam past the bodies towards an open square of sea floor. Trying not to shudder as she got to her knees, she buried her fingers in the ground, connecting herself to the Earth. The Mer around her shrank back, rebels and soldiers alike as her eyes started to glow.

Feeling every slight fissure and crack beneath her, where each grain of sand connected to another, she anchored that familiar pulsing ball of energy in her chest and let it expand.

Instead of keeping it constrained like she usually did, letting only a small amount seep out at a time, she unleashed it.

Her magic blasted through the ground, breaking it apart.

The ground beneath them began to shake violently enough that the water became unstable. The buildings around the square cracked and as if in slow motion, they began to crumble. The falling stones threatened to squash the fighters at the edges of the square and screams filled Riva's ears as both armies scrambled for safety. Herding even more Mer into the square until there was barely a square inch of space left to draw a sword, as the last remaining structures in Oceana came crashing down around them in a great cloud of sand that engulfed the entire square. The clash of metal on metal faded slightly as the earthquake disorientated everyone on both sides.

It's working. She thought delightedly.

She revelled in this magic, the feeling of joyful adrenaline that it brought with it. When she was connected to it like this, she really did feel like a Goddess. She would use it to save them all. No one else needed to die. Reaching down into herself again, prepared to clear the turbid water and halt the fighting, she revelled in her power.

Then, without warning, it stopped.

She jerked her hands out of the sand like she had been electrocuted. Panicking, she tried to connect to that now-familiar swirling ball of energy in her chest and felt nothing. Her magic had turned off, like someone turning the knob on a tap. One minute it had been flowing freely and the next it was just, gone.

Freaking out, she looked up at the open water above the square, squinting to see through the sand. The current she had been using to give Finn's forces a respite had disappeared and soldiers were now resuming their massacre of the rebels. Some of them descending on the crowd too.

"Riva, what happened?" Douglas called down to her over the deafening whirling of the water.

She was gazing at her Mark, after using so much magic it should have been glowing brightly, but instead it was sitting dully on her palm.

"I don't know." she replied, her voice shaking.

She pushed off the sand and swam, infuriatingly slowly without her currents, to land on the platform beside Douglas. As her feet touched the raised platform she felt dangerously exposed. Without her magic she felt treacherously out of her depth and glanced around them in case anyone brought the fighting to her. "My magic. It's gone."

Douglas's eyes widened. "How?"

"I have no idea, one minute it was fine and then the next it was just gone. I don't know how."

Douglas shot his hands out in front of him and Riva's hope disappeared as she saw no current shoot from his fingertips. Douglas looked down at his own hands, terrified.

Riva lifted her gaze to where the Elders floated in a line, holding hands and chanting under their breath.

Iolana was the only one with her eyes open, and they were fixed on Riva.

As Douglas connected the dots, his own eyes filled with fear, "We're in big trouble."

"I couldn't agree more." Said an arrogant voice behind them.

Duncan was floating on the other side of the platform, and she followed his gaze to the ground where the body of his brother lay.

"Seems like he grew a conscience all of a sudden, I guess his little mate doesn't mean so much to him after all." Duncan sneered, his usually sleek blond hair messed up from the fighting.

Riva swam over to her uncle and desperately felt his neck for a pulse. As she knelt beside him, she let out a sigh of relief when she felt it. It was weak, but it was there.

"What are you talking about?" Riva spat, peering up at the King through the gritty water and glaring daggers behind her at Iolana, who was still chanting, binding Riva's powers.

Duncan smirked and she longed to wrap her hands around his throat. But she didn't dare advance on him without access to her magic.

Maybe she could distract Duncan long enough to connect to Eden, get the help of Gaia, or even Cronos if he had enough power.

"You see, after your little stunt the other day, I saw that I needed more leverage." He glanced behind him. "And my poor unfortunate brother here was only too willing to help me get it once I locked up his precious Mate."

Duncan kidnapped Maya? Crap, we need help.

Riva had been about to try and find Em in the fray and ask for her help, or start pummelling Iolana in the face until she stopped chanting, when she followed Duncan's gaze and saw an Elite soldier moving towards the platform with a Mer woman in his arms.

Her tail was strange. Slightly misshapen and a weird shade of pink. But as soon as Riva's eyes left the tail and found the necklace that sat around her neck she felt like her heart had left her body.

It was her mum.

27.

"You bastard!" she screamed, so loudly that her throat cracked and she launched herself at him. It was only thanks to Douglas throwing his arms around her at the last minute that stopped her.

The tears came unbidden and she felt a fury like she had never felt before in her life. Her mum who had lived in fear of the ocean since her dad had disappeared. Her fragile mum who she had taken care of her entire life. Dragged to an underwater kingdom in the middle of a bloody battle to be used as leverage.

I should have forced her to go to the mainland.

Her mum's brown eyes were wide in her face. There was fear there yes, but also a plea. Riva raked her eyes over her mum's body. If he had touched even one hair on her head he was dead. She no longer cared that he was Douglas's father. She would kill him in an instant, completely safe in the knowledge that her own father would agree. God, she hoped that he wasn't hurt.

"Give me my magic back!" She screamed at the Elders, and she felt blood vessels pop in her eyes as she strained both against Douglas's grip and to summon her magic. The hulking arms of the Elite soldier pressed harder and her mum gasped in pain. If she had been able to access her magic they would all have been obliterated.

With the two opposing Mer groups busy fighting all around and above them, it felt like the three of them were in their own little bubble. Still restrained by Douglas, she searched wildly around, squinting against the sand storm to try and signal to Em, or anyone who could fight with their hands, that she needed help.

"Neat little trick isn't it?" Duncan sneered, glancing behind him at Iolana, who was still staring at Riva like she was the villain.

Riva wrenched her gaze over to Elder Iolana. The very same Mer that she had been convinced was on her side. "Why would you do this?" Riva cried. "Can't you see that I'm trying to help your people?"

Iolana looked down on her pleas disdainfully. "I warned you when you first visited our city that your powers, when wielded by one singular individual, especially an individual as young as yourself could be dangerous."

Those mercury eyes were swirling clouds of venom.

"I allowed Emerald to leave with the necklace, and gave her the information you needed to find your cousin." Her voice rasped across the platform and Riva found herself instinctively cringing away from it.

"I placed my own spells around the borders of your home island, enchantments that would inform me when you had found one another and used magic together."

Rive thought back to that evening in the bay when she had corrected his currents. Her stomach dropped.

"So you helped me get to this point only to kill me?"

Iolana's wrinkled face was nothing but a cold mask as she said, "I brought you both down here to assess whether or not all half-breeds possess the same control over our ocean home as you do. Evidently, they do not."

Those swirling silver eyes passed over Douglas derisively.

"You were dangerous to us before while you possessed only the magic of your Mer blood, but we see now that your power has been amplified to a level beyond all comprehension. A level that you yourself do not yet fully understand."

Riva looked down at her Mark, praying for so much of a sliver of that supposedly limitless power to make an appearance now.

"We cannot allow you to roam the oceans unchecked." Iolana said with finality and resumed her chanting.

She couldn't believe this, Iolana hadn't been helping her at all, it had all been a test.

"Your discrimination against demi-Mer makes you incapable of seeing what my powers can do for all of you." Riva shouted to be heard over the growing chanting of the Elders. "You cloak Oceana on each solstice to protect what is left of your people. I can make sure that they are able to return to their homes again. Together we can rebuild this city and the entire ocean!"

As she stared up pleadingly into the face of the withered Elder, she knew nothing she could say would change Iolana's mind. She would never be able to trust a half-human who had the power to make or destroy the ocean.

She looked around frantically for Em, or Aoife, or even Finn. Anyone who would recognise what was happening and come to their rescue. Anyone who knew how to use a weapon.

"Mum." She called out to her in despair, Douglas's arms slackening as she swam slowly forwards. "Mum, it's going to be ok. He won't hurt you."

Her mum didn't even look able to speak and Riva's hands curled into fists. Just because she couldn't see any physical damage on her mum's body didn't mean that the lasting mental effects of her capture wouldn't destroy her.

"Why did you take her?" she turned to her uncle, voice cracking in despair. Hands balled into fists by her sides.

Duncan smirked again, hands clasped behind his back, looking like he had all the time in the world. "Because I could. And because I know the importance of leverage. If this boy wasn't going to be enough to make you co-operate then I found someone who would be."

"How did you find her?" she growled, taking up a defensive stance even though she knew she couldn't hope to fight her way out of this.

Duncan glanced over at his brother's unconscious body. "It's unfathomable the lengths that some people will go to for love."

How could he do that to his own brother?

If Duncan had really taken Maya hostage… Then yes, she believed that Declan would do anything to protect his mate. And she couldn't hold that against him, she would do the same for her mum. Duncan's conniving little brain had worked it all out. Declan would do anything for Maya, even betray his niece and brother in order to go ashore in the same place he had eighteen years before. This time to capture her mother instead of her father.

Dad must be going out of his mind with worry…

Her heart gave a painful lurch as she thought about how he would have tried to save her. How he probably tried to follow her into the waves. But she had taken his tail away.

Taking advantage of her momentary distraction, Duncan shot forward, grabbing Riva by the throat.

His hands locked around her windpipe, pressing down so forcefully that she thought her neck might snap. It didn't matter that she didn't need to breathe down here, one twist of his wrist and she was gone. She thought back to the face of the Elite as she had crushed his throat the exact same way only the day before.

Shocked and terrified that she didn't have her powers, she clawed desperately at his hands, her nails leaving deep gouges in his skin.

"My people don't need help from humans." He continued, his face pressed close to hers so she could see the hate in his eyes, hear the venom lacing his every word. "Humans are what got us into this mess in the first place. You are nothing. Look how pathetic you are without your magic. How could you ever hope to know anything about how to save the Mer when you aren't even one of us?"

His grip tightened again and she struggled to find purchase on the platform with her toes, anything to get him off balance. Even though she knew that she was absorbing oxygen from the water, she still felt like she couldn't breathe. As she struggled against his death-grip, Duncan's features twisted and morphed into Stuarts, before flickering back again. She clawed uselessly at his wrist, the feeling of suffocation overwhelming her.

I'm nothing without my magic. She thought despairingly. *I was so stupid to think that I could do this.*

Stars burst in front of her eyes as he squeezed, she felt something give in her throat and she gagged.

"Now you will watch as I destroy everything you have, just like your kind did to me." Duncan said.

He released his grip on her neck without warning and she would have sagged to the platform if he hadn't moved behind her. He placed his hands either side of her head, forcing her to watch what happened next.

The Elite holding her mum raised a small dagger that glinted menacingly in a stray sunbeam that had penetrated the sand storm and drove it in between her mum's ribs.

"NO!" Riva's strangled cry tore up her damaged throat as she began writhing in Duncan's grip. She watched as Douglas shot forward and grabbed the Elite that was at least a foot taller than him by the wrist with both hands, desperately fighting to disarm him as Riva's mum slumped to the ground in a cloud of blood.

No, this can't be happening.

Still unable to escape Duncan's grip as he clawed at her face, she sent out a plea with her mind, a desperate attempt to survive this.

Please, help me...

Her vision flickered and she saw a blurry image of a tree branch, a swift flash of golden light and then there they were, the most beautiful eyes she had ever seen.

I need your help.

The vision faded and she slammed back into reality, heart stopping as she gazed at her mum's limp body.

Suddenly, the hands holding her head were gone and she hit the platform. Whirling around she could see that Douglas had somehow managed to stab the Elite Mer and had now tackled Duncan and was pummelling him in the face. Unfortunately Duncan was both larger and stronger than him on account of his tail and he soon had Douglas pinned to the ground.

The Elite soldier was clutching his side but still looking as solid as an ox. She dared not touch him without her magic and looked around in desperation as he advanced towards her mum's body. The pain in her throat was almost unbearable. Without her magic she wasn't healing.

With the Mer fighting on all fronts, she couldn't see a way out. She started to hyperventilate.

Where the hell is Em??

She looked all around her, desperate for help. She had been so sure that Cronos had heard her but maybe she had just hallucinated those eyes. The Elders were still chanting, binding her powers with their own ancient magic. She didn't have a hope of overpowering that Elite soldier and freeing her mum, who now looked like she was retreating further inside herself as she bled out.

She turned on Elder Iolana.

"Why are you doing this?" each word sent lances of pain up her throat. "I thought that you were on my side? You sent Em to me. You told me that I was the answer." She looked up into the withered face and felt like crying in frustration. "You told me that I had great power. You wanted this!" she gestured at the carnage that surrounded her.

The Elder Mer finally opened her eyes. But before she said anything there was a great flash of light that blinded her.

Throwing her arm up in front of her face, she was blasted to the side as the light split the platform in two. She hit the sea floor with a thump, some of the wood hitting her in the back. She whirled around.

Cronos?

Lifting her head, she saw that the battle was suspended, frozen in time.

Douglas and Duncan locked in what could be mistaken for a father-son embrace if it weren't for the twin expressions of utter loathing on both of their faces.

She pushed some of the wood off her, sending it floating upwards and peered through the dust.

He was standing on the sea floor, just a few feet away from her. He was still in that clean-cut suit but there were shadows all around him, little remnants of his power that flashed and gleamed brilliantly.

"How did you get here?" she croaked out, completely weirded out by the utter silence that now surrounded them.

He walked towards her. Walked. Not swam. "A thank you would be nice." He replied rolling up his shirt sleeves to reveal muscular forearms.

"What did you do?" she breathed, swimming towards him, stopping before they touched when what she really wanted was to throw her arms around him and sob.

He glanced around them. "I gave you time." Focusing on her face, he traced the line of red where the dagger had cut her, his expression unreadable. His hands were warm, and dry.

"How is this possible?" she asked. "Are you even real?"

He smiled, that impossibly beautiful face wrenching her heart. "Always so many questions." But she didn't miss his furious expression when he glanced at the bruises now blooming across her neck.

He gazed above them to where she could see Em frozen mid-dive, clearly on her way to try and help.

"Well maybe I'll stop asking so many questions when you start answering some." She retorted, grimacing at the pain in her throat.

Cronos continued to smile, but his expression grew strained. "I gave you time, now you must use it. My powers aren't what they once were." He looked seriously at her, almost as if he was worried about the outcome of this battle. "Use it well."

Leaning forward, he kissed her forehead, his smooth lips sending shivers all the way down her spine that had nothing to do with the cold. Then he disappeared.

Not waiting around any longer, she jumped into action.

The Elite Mer was once again clutching the dagger and before he could finish what he started, she hoisted herself up onto the broken platform. Not stopping to think about an alternative, Riva grabbed it out of his frozen hand and slit his throat. The dagger was so sharp that it felt like she was slicing through the breast of her mum's roast chicken. Frozen as time was, no blood flowed, but she knew that when time started up again he would be very dead. She surprised herself by feeling glad about it.

Looking down at her mum, she knew that she had to get her magic back in order to heal her. Pushing herself back across the platform, so painfully slowly without her currents, she swam frantically back towards where Iolana was still linked to the other Elders.

As time began to unfreeze, she watched as the Mer around her began to move like they were in super slow-motion and she finally reached the only part of the platform that remained intact.

Grasping the wrists of two Elders, she wrenched with all her might as the sounds of the battle came back to life and she could see things speeding up. Her time was running out.

Finally severing the connection between the Elders, she moved on to the next pair on the other side of Iolana.

Just as time returned to normal and Em ploughed into the destroyed platform with an almighty crash, she succeeded in breaking the spell.

Her magic came back to her in a great rush and she felt suddenly drunk with power.

Eyes and Mark once again glowing like golden beacons, she moved her neck from side to side as she felt it heal.

"That. Was a mistake." She said, rising up in front of Iolana.

Her electricity danced across her skin as she rose to float above them. No longer contained to her hands, it flickered across her entire body. Three of the Elders scattered, terrified, but the others remained standing by their leader.

Thrusting her hands out in front of her, she loosed several bolts of lightning that arced through the water, illuminating the battle beyond the now-murky square. The first bolt connected with Iolana's chest and the others hit the other Elders. They crumpled instantly but Iolana fought her. As the skin on her tail began to flake off, she looked up at Riva from behind fathomless eyes and croaked out;

"Your power will be your undoing."

Sick of whatever her twisted agenda was, she loosed another bolt of lightning with a roar and the Elder splintered into ash.

"And yours." Riva spat bitterly, reining in her power, ridiculously grateful that it was a part of her once again.

It was utter madness. The clashes and bangs sounded even more threatening now that she could barely see the two armies thanks to the sand that had been churned up by the earthquake and the dagger wound on her cheek was stinging as it sealed shut, making her eyes water.

Em was still trying to extract herself from the broken platform, having been thrown off by Cronos's jet of light and misjudged her speed.

"Was that you?" she cried out as Riva helped yank her tail out of the rubble.

"Part of it." She groaned, heaving her friend upright. "I'll explain later. Protect my mum, I'll deal with Duncan."

Em's eyes widened. "Your *mum*?"

She followed Riva's gaze and they both saw a Guard crawling across the ground, his tail badly damaged from the blast, in pursuit of her mum. Riva tried not to look at the body of the Elite she had killed, his blood now staining the water a red so dark it was almost black. Her mum was scrambling to get away, clearly unused to the cumbersome tail.

Without asking for an explanation, Em launched herself at the Guard, and Riva, abandoning Duncan for the moment, dove for her mum.

Unfortunately, while she had been distracted by Em, Duncan had gotten free of Douglas and reached her mum first. At the same time a sharp crack sounded behind her, telling her that Em had successfully disposed of her mum's pursuer, Duncan grabbed her mum by the wrist and held her up like a human shield.

"No!" Riva cried out, arm outstretched, Mark aglow.

Duncan grinned maniacally, blood on his teeth. "Not so fast there. You might have your magic back but you wouldn't dare hurt dear old mummy in the process would you?"

She gritted her teeth and felt Em come to stand behind her.

"Let her go." she growled threateningly, summoning her lightning again. It crackled and bounced off the sand in front of her in great arcs, illuminating the fear in her mum's eyes.

Good. Her mum was still conscious, the dagger must have missed anything vital. She was trembling and her eyes were glassy but she was alive.

Duncan tutted. "Uh, Uh. Careful now. Wouldn't want any accidents to happen." He taunted, pulling another small knife out from behind his back and held the tip of it up to her mum's neck. She tensed, ready to pounce.

"Riva..." Em breathed as both warning and question.

She didn't know what to do. If she surrendered to Duncan then all of this would have been for nothing. All of the Mer who had died or were dying, all of the rebels who had pinned their hopes on her would have been for nothing. They weren't going to win this battle without her. Finn was holding the line above them but just barely. She hadn't seen Aoife since the battle began but she didn't think it was going well for the rebels in the square.

But she couldn't lose her mum. She wouldn't.

"What do you want?" she asked through gritted teeth, frustrated tears pricking at the corner of her eyes.

Duncan twirled the knife lazily, blood beading on her mum's neck as he did so. "You know, I like to think myself a pretty good judge of character. But you… You took a while to figure out. But everyone can be bought for the right price. Not with jewellery or empty promises – but with *love*." He scoffed at Em. "Look at all of your allies Riva. All of them. Every single one brought to my feet because of love. Just like you have been in the end."

Fists clenched, magic barely constrained, she asked him again through gritted teeth. "What do you want?"

He smirked. "I want you out of the way."

And he ripped the necklace off her mum's neck.

"NOOO!!" she screamed, launching herself at her mum even as Duncan threw her body away from him.

He swam away cackling madly. "You can only choose one of us Riva." The knife glinting in his hand, he headed straight for Douglas who was slowly regaining consciousness.

Riva leaped forward to catch her mum as her tail disappeared. Two slender, very human legs appeared and Riva knew that human lungs would follow. All she could hear was the blood pounding in her ears as she watched her mum's eyes widen in panic as she felt the intense pressure encroach on her skull and her lungs began to convulse.

"Em!" she screamed, summoning her friend to her side.

Thanking whatever God existed that she had moved on to *The Goblet of Fire* on the plane ride back from California, she summoned her magic.

Working quickly, she waved her hand and formed a giant bubble around her mum's mouth that was filled with oxygen before her lungs could betray her and suck in water. She clung on to Riva tightly, fingers fluttering weakly for her daughter.

"Try not to breathe too much. That oxygen is limited." She said quickly, making her decision.

She shoved her mum into Em's arms, though she was fighting to stay with her. "Get her out of here now!"

"I don't unders-." Em began, scooping Riva's mum to her chest.

"NOW!" Riva screamed, pushing them both skywards as she raised her Mark to point above the square and opened the swiftest travel current she could summon.

The current rent the water open above them, scattering rebels and Guards alike. Even though the last thing Em wanted to do was leave her alone to deal with Duncan, she nodded firmly and swam straight up into the current as fast as she could, Riva's mum clutched safely in her arms, reaching behind her towards her daughter.

"I love you." she whispered as her mum disappeared.

The current sealed behind them with a wet sucking sound.

She turned around, her last sob dying in her throat, feeling like her chest was hollow and zoned in on Duncan.

"Riva!"

Douglas's shout came from just a few metres to her left where the dust was beginning to settle. Duncan had abandoned the knife in favour of the sword that Riva had discarded and was stooping to pick it up. Not even bothering to check that Riva was still there, simply assuming that she would have chosen her mum, he was inches away from it.

Pushing off of the platform, she dove with the help of her currents and reached the sword before him. Sliding between his outstretched arm and the platform, she grasped the hilt and rose to her feet.

She was swift enough to see the surprise in his eyes just before she twirled the hilt and drove the sword down through Duncan's thick tail flukes and into the ground. The king screamed in pain and fury.

"You half-breed monster!" he cried, tail trembling. "You will pay for this!"

Pinned as he was by the sword, Douglas dove behind him and quickly grabbed his arms to restrain him.

"Do it Riva." Said Douglas gruffly, lip swollen. "Do it before it's too late."

Her magic was screaming the same thing and she had to take a beat to steady herself. This wasn't a decision she could be influenced into. Her anger at what he had done to her mother, her father, her cousin, Em, hell pretty much everyone she knew, was telling her to end him.

But she had put so much effort into sparing his life. Every plan she had come up with, every decision she had made had been to resolve this peacefully. What had it all been for if she was just going to drive a sword through his heart now?

She looked between them both, for the first time together, and she could see the slight resemblance.

"Are you sure? He's still your father." She said quietly, shaking with rage. The fact that she was even asking this instead of ripping his heart out was a miracle.

Douglas fought to keep Duncan in place. "I don't care anymore. He had me beaten and tortured without a second thought. He's not my father. He's a monster."

Finally their words seemed to reach Duncan's ears and he stopped fighting against Douglas's restraints.

Riva advanced, magic bubbling within her, wondering how she was going to do it. The battle was still going on around them, although she could hear things slowing down. The clashes of metal and hearty shouts had now been replaced with dull thuds and groans.

"Did you hear that *uncle*?" she sneered at him this time. "You almost executed your own son."

Instead of listening, he gnashed his teeth at Riva. "What is this foolish trick? Do you think that I would believe anything that comes out of your mouth, half-breed?"

Riva smiled. She was going to enjoy this.

"I know you won't believe my words. But maybe you will recognise that." She said, pointing to Douglas's wrist. She nodded at him in encouragement, if she was going to kill him, then she wanted him to know the truth before he died.

Douglas released his father's arms and stepped in front of him, extending the wrist that held the woven bracelet. Duncan remained kneeling on the platform, white tail tucked under him.

"My mother made this for me." Douglas said stiffly, refusing to make eye contact with his father.

Duncan, still pinned in place by the sword, made no move to remove it even though his hands were now free, but instead looked between his sons bracelet and his own. Both identical.

"My mother's name was Isabelle Ryan. She lived in Monterey, California. My birthday is October 12th 1991."

Riva gazed between them both, and watched as Duncan slowly fiddled with his own bracelet while scanning the face of the half-human he had been so desperate to kill only moments before. She contained her magic, waiting for the right moment.

"Impossible." The king breathed.

Douglas looked like he either wanted to cry or hit something. "My mom used to make bracelets like these for sailors. St Christopher medallions. To keep them safe on their travels."

Duncan's mouth was opening and closing like a fish. "A son?" he asked softly, almost to himself, finally lifting his eyes from the bracelet to look into his son's face.

Then before Riva could do anything, Duncan had twisted around to wrench the sword out of his tail and launched himself at Douglas.

"No!" she cried out, arcing lightning through the water a split second too late and it hit the bare sand.

She watched in horror as Duncan flew through the water and Douglas scrambled to get away. A flash of silver distracted Riva and she watched as the sword sunk heavily towards the sand. When she finally looked up, the two of them had switched places and it seemed as if they were embracing.

Or they could have been, if it wasn't for the large spear protruding from in between the king's shoulder blades.

"STOP!" Riva screamed. Her shout releasing a wave so powerful that it blasted away the sand in the water, rendering the town square-turned battlefield completely visible.

Knocked off balance by the wave blast and distracted by her shout, the fighting stopped as hundreds of pairs of eyes turned to look at what was happening atop the ruined platform.

Douglas held his father, supporting him as the colour drained from his face.

"My son." The king repeated with difficulty, gazing up into his boy's face. "Forgive me." Was all he managed to choke out before the life left his eyes.

"No." Riva whispered in shock, her magic evaporating.

Douglas, as furious and betrayed as he had felt by his father, was crying. The Mer all around them had dropped their weapons and a heavy silence hung over the square.

"No." Riva repeated. Duncan hadn't grabbed the sword and launched himself at Douglas to kill him. He had been freeing himself to protect his son from the spear that had been headed directly for him.

She closed the short distance between herself and where Douglas knelt, still clutching his father's body and she put her arm around him.

Unexpected tears burned at the corners of her eyes and after a few moments she stood up and faced the two armies who were now floating together as one people.

"The King." The lump in her throat blocked the next words. Swallowing, she tried again.

"Is dead."

28.

Riva looked down at the reef from her perch on one of the palace turrets. Given that the Mer tended to obey social etiquette much better than she did, it was one of the only places she could find that she could get some peace.

The last week had been one huge stressful nightmare and it was taking its toll. She longed for the surface again. She wanted to see her mum, to check on her properly. Em had returned a few hours after the battle had ended on one of the main travel currents to tell her that her mum had survived. That she had been taken to the hospital in Inverness to get her wound stitched up but that it wasn't life-threatening.

As much as she had wanted to return home immediately after the battle was finished, she simply couldn't. There was too much to organize. Duncan's death had left the Mer without a ruler and the battle had caused a rift within its people. Not to mention the absolute state of the city thanks to her mini-earthquake.

She knew that Alex was probably going out of her mind with worry. She wondered if Kieran was waiting for her to come home or if he hated her now. She thought of her father going out of his mind with worry about both his daughter and the love of his life. But the one face that had been swimming across her mind all week hadn't been human.

She had been used to eyes haunting her nightmares for months, but now a different pair stalked her dreams. It was utterly ridiculous that in the aftermath of everything that had happened that she should be thinking about romance, but she couldn't get his face out of her mind.

The way he had come to her rescue with those glittering shadows, the way he had somehow been able to stop *time*... she bit her lip to keep the smile off her face.

Riva knew that he was dangerous, that he was in possession of some crazy powers but she couldn't stop thinking about the fact that he had come to rescue her.

As much as she had wanted to see him again, she hadn't dared to visit Eden again. For some reason, she had a feeling that Gaia wouldn't be happy with them knowing one another.

He had been able to get outside of its boundaries, something that Gaia told her was supposed to be impossible for all the ancient Gods, or titans, or whatever they all were.

Her stomach growled loudly, jerking her out of her thoughts. She wouldn't mind heading up to the surface for a piece and Lorne sausage either. Massaging her hollow stomach, putting all thoughts of Cronos and Eden from her mind, she gazed down at the reef that had grown more vibrant by the day since Riva had touched it. She wished all the ocean's problems could be resolved so easily.

After Duncan's death there had been a lot to figure out, and most of that responsibility had fallen to Riva. From healing the wounded on the battlefield to organizing the funeral. Many of them had been expecting her to pronounce herself Queen after the battle, with many of the rebels even being surprised when she hadn't.

"Hey!" a voice called from below her, "You up there hiding again?" Douglas's face appeared from an open archway just below her.

"You finally found me. Well get up here then." She said, amused.

He swam out of the palace on an impressively smooth current and landed lightly beside her.

"You're getting better at that you know." She said.

"Practice makes perfect right?" he scratched his nose, trying to appear uninterested. "Speaking of, have you rehearsed your speech yet?"

Riva resisted the urge to roll her eyes. "You know very well that I haven't." she sighed. "If only Alex was down here with us. She'd have a speech drawn up for me in no time. In fact, she would have had that treaty signed on the dotted line in half the time it took us to get it straight."

Douglas leaned back on his elbows, "In a quarter of the time probably."

Observing how soft his voice was when he spoke about her, Riva said. "Oh does this mean that you've finally seen the light?"

Douglas punched her on the arm. "Shut up." But he blushed.

"You two are idiots. It really took a near-death experience for you to admit you like her?" she asked.

"Yeah well, call me emotionally unavailable." He scoffed, rubbing his leg absentmindedly.

Riva nodded at his new leggings. "I see you finally retired the swim-shorts…" she stifled a laugh.

"Yeah, I wasn't sure how I would feel about wearing tights but those things were definitely no longer suitable in public." After the battle the pale blue shorts had been in tatters and showing off those family jewels was not the way she wanted to announce his royalty publically.

He traced the dark rings on the silken fur of his leggings. Em had practically wrestled him out of his shorts and stuffed him into this new pair of leggings less than a day after the battle. She had apologised for not being able to find any leopard seal on such short notice so harbour seal would have to do instead.

Riva tried not to think about the cute doe-eyed animal that had died to keep Douglas's legs warm, but she was happy that if the hunters had managed to catch a few seals then at least more of the Mer would sleep with full bellies tonight.

She fidgeted with her white corset-type top that Em had insisted that she wear to the ceremony. She had worn it once before on solstice, but preferred the easy movement that her kelp top provided her.

"Do you think you'll go back to the surface soon?" Douglas asked.

Riva shrugged. "I mean technically after today we're free to come and go as we please." She hesitated. "Do you want to leave?"

He gazed out at the reef and then looked directly above them, the strange half-light making it impossible to tell if there was a surface miles above them or not. The reason why Riva had always imagined Oceana as a giant bubble.

"I do and I don't, you know?" he eventually replied. "I mean, my life was great and I was happy before all of this. But I just feel like I've got more to learn from this place. I don't think I'm done yet."

Riva rubbed her hands up and down her arms, trying to get some feeling back into them. "Suit yourself. I'm heading in the direction of a warm bath and a steak pie as soon as I finish that damn speech." She laughed.

"Don't you like it at all down here?" Douglas asked.

Leaning back to join him, the pearl-smooth surface of the palace roof was cold on her elbows. "I don't know. Sometimes when I'm back on land I yearn for it like you can't even imagine."

Douglas looked at her wryly.

"Alright fine, maybe you can. But then when I'm down here I long for the surface. It was less so the last time I was here but I didn't have my Mark back then. Or my other powers. I think that keeps me tied to more than just the ocean now. Reminding me that I can't spend eternity down here. Besides, I think the ocean has more to offer than just this city. If we can even call it a city anymore." She muttered guiltily.

Douglas hissed through his teeth "Nah, I think this place was due an upgrade."

She looked down at the colourful reef. The one part of Oceana besides the palace that was still standing.

"You know I used to sit at my bedroom window and stare out at the ocean. I used to be so afraid of it."

"Really?" Douglas exclaimed. "I thought you were like some champion swimmer or something?"

"I was." Riva nodded, hair billowing out behind her. "But only in a swimming pool. No, the ocean was one of my biggest fears. And my mum's. I'll never forgive Duncan for bringing her down here." She couldn't help her fists clenching in anger. Douglas fidgeted uncomfortably.

"But do you know the only other thing I was more afraid of?" she asked.

Douglas hit her playfully on the arm, "Seafood?"

"Shut up." She said, smacking him back. "No. Being stuck on that island forever. Our trip to find you in California was the first time I had ever been away from Scotland. Not counting my first trip here of course. Other than that I've lived my whole life in one place." She leaned up to wrap her arms around her knees. "I think I'd like to change that."

After a moment Douglas sat up too. "I don't think you're going to have much of a choice about that anyway." He reached over and took her hand, turning it so her palm faced upwards to display her Mark, innocently pink without its magic. She wondered if Eden counted as international travel or something even further afield.

"Don't remind me." She sighed heavily, noticing how quiet the palace had grown. "We'd better go. Duty calls."

Pulling her hand away she dove gracefully down and through the archway to her chambers.

After the battle had ended, she and many of the other rebel leaders, including Em, had been given rooms in the palace. The past week had been filled with meetings where they had only one topic of discussion. The future of Oceana and the Mer.

Her stomach roiled at the thought of the speech she was about to have to give.

It had been decided that instead of being ruled by a single King or Queen, their power should fall to a council instead. One where every Mer voice had representation.

Declan was chosen to have a seat thanks to his royal blood. Her uncle had been extremely grateful for Riva's forgiveness in the part he played to kidnap her mum, but as he clutched Maya to his side like he was never going to let her go, she had found that she understood.

The twins were both offered seats on the council as well but politely declined, seeing this as a way to finally win their freedom from Royal duties. She pitied the Mer women of the wider ocean as she had looked at the grins on their faces.

Aoife had been chosen by popular vote to lead the council and represent the interests of the people and Finn had been given a seat as the representative from the Elite. The most shocking turn of events had been when Riva had turned her own seat over to Douglas.

It had taken over ten minutes of shouting for order for everyone to stop arguing and listen to her reasoning. But she had known that she had made the right decision. There was definitely such a thing as too much power and she already had more than she could handle.

Douglas had seemed both pleased and humbled by the gesture and she could tell that he was looking forward to this new responsibility. Riva only worried that it would break her best friends' heart if he decided to stay in Oceana permanently.

She would instead fill the role that her grandfather had envisioned for her. An ambassador to Oceana, who would travel between the surface and the underwater city periodically, providing insight and helping in the fight to restore the oceans to what they once were.

As she swam through the shining palace by Douglas's side, they greeted the Mer they passed warmly. She still couldn't get used to how accepting they were of her now. Being able to move around Oceana without having to endure narrowed eyes and hushed whispers really made the place much more welcoming.

The audience hall was the only building still standing, aside from the palace, that could hold all of the Mer who resided in Oceana. As they swooped down from the reef and she beheld once again the destruction she had caused, she felt slightly worried that they might ask her to help them clean it up.

As they entered through the open double doors, a hushed silence descended upon the hall. The Mer gathered were solemn as Douglas and Riva swam through the bottom of the bowl-shaped room. Even though the rebels had been victorious, it hadn't felt like a victory. There had been no celebrations and there had been more than a few Mer who had opposed the change – primarily the nobility who had stood to gain the most from Duncan's regime.

As they made their way towards the coral throne, the eyes of all the Mer in Oceana upon them, they both paused at the side of the large marble table upon which the King's body lay.

His face looked softer in death than she had ever seen it in life. Those cold, calculating eyes had closed forever and his lips were left in a relaxed smile instead of his usual sneer. Despite all that he had done, she had found herself feeling sorry for his death and fiercely glad that it hadn't been by her hand. He had died honourably, to save his son from a spear that had meant to end his life. It was that final act that had allowed him a state funeral.

Douglas squeezed her hand tightly and she looked at him out of the corner of her eye. His face was crumpled in on itself and her heart ached. He had been robbed of any time they could have had to heal what had passed between them.

"His last act was to save your life." she said softly, resting her head on his shoulder. "He would have been glad to know you, in the end."

Douglas nodded and sniffed. "I know. But that doesn't change what he did to me before he knew who I was." He said thickly. "I still hate him for that."

"You're allowed to feel both." She said in hushed tones. "There's a fine line between love and hate." Riva said quietly, covering his hand in both of hers, "You can hate him for hurting you, hate him for leaving you and even hate him for dying before you got to know him. But you can still love him for saving your life amidst all of that."

Douglas sniffed loudly. "When did you get so wise?"

"I think it has something to do with sharing the powers of an ancient Goddess…" she laughed miserably. "Come on, it's about to start."

She took his hand and they swam to float on the dais in front of the throne beside their uncles. Many of the Mer had been surprised at their abolishing of the monarchy. Many more had protested against it. But from the inside, Riva could see how broken the royal family really were.

Declan was barely surviving his grief, the twins had absolutely no desire to rule anything except the party lifestyle, and that left two Demi-Mer royals who didn't know enough about Mer politics to get anything done properly. No, it was better this way.

A hush fell over the crowd as they gathered on the dais. Then they began to sing.

One by one, Mer children swam though the giant doorway and laid gifts atop Duncan's body. Brightly coloured starfish, prickly urchins, intricately woven kelp and blankets of sea grass until all that remained visible was his head. Atop which sat his crown of intricately woven corals. The last King of the Mer.

Once the children had swam back to their parents and the singing faded, Declan stepped forward to speak. His face pale and his voice more than a little unsteady. Riva wished that she could give him a whiskey, he looked like he needed it.

"Today we gather to lay our King to rest. My brother was far from perfect, but he loved his people fiercely and only ever wanted what was best for the Mer." He said shakily. Riva hoped that he had something better coming because she could see some of the expressions in the crowd darkening. Probably those of the rebels.

"Today we say our goodbyes and we welcome a new dawn. Let today be the day we choose to walk away from hatred, and from grief. Let today be the day where Mer support Mer, where we can flourish in peace and unity once more. Let us honour my brother, and my father with that legacy."

His voice rang out across the chamber as he stepped back. Riva had to admit, he had finished strong. Realising that there was a significant pause, she freaked for a minute, thinking that she had forgotten that it was her turn to speak, but then she remembered that Aoife was supposed to go first. She peeked out across the line, but the warrior woman was looking stoically ahead.

Then the Mer began to sing again. Riva had only heard this type of singing once before.

Usually the endless yodelling down the long corridors and open waters set her teeth on edge, like someone was dragging their nails across a chalkboard, but this music was something different.

The voices of every Mer gathered, from those sitting at floor level, to those rising high on the benches that swooped above their heads on either side, were joined as one. The music wove its way through the room until Riva felt like it was thrumming inside of her. It was a melody made to heal and what grief there was in her heart at the passing of her uncle, it was now partnered by hope.

It took her a moment to realise that the singing had stopped, and a moment more to realise that they were all looking at her.

"Oh, crap. Right." She muttered under her breath, stepping forwards. She had forgotten the task she had to carry out before her speech.

And they had wanted me to rule the Mer. I can't even remember the Order of Ceremony.

Focusing on the marble plinth in the middle of the room, she extended her hand towards it.

Aoife's voice rang out through the hall as Riva's mark began to glow.

"As we are born from the sea, so shall we be returned to it."

Riva barely heard the murmurs coming from the gathered mourners who had let to see her magic. A whirling circle of water opened up behind the plinth in the middle of the room, blocking her view of the doors on the other side. She had tried to make the current as gentle as possible and so instead of writhing and swirling violently like her travel currents usually did, this one simply swished invitingly.

Raising Duncan's body off the plinth, she funnelled her magic into the offerings that surrounded him so that they flourished with her guidance, sprouting colourful sea flowers that wrapped around every inch of the King.

"Goodbye uncle." She said sadly, summoning a second current to push him slowly through the wall of water. As all of the Mer gathered bowed their heads, she turned to look at her family floating beside her. Their faces glowing in the ethereal light that emanated from the current. Eyes ringed in red.

She pushed her hand forward gently and the King's body vanished peacefully into the abyss. She allowed her hand to fall to her side and stepped back into line beside her family.

After a respectable amount of time, Aoife took up her position in front of the throne and hushed whispers spread throughout the crowd. This seemed to be the real reason that most of them had come.

Aoife observed her people. Her long braids tied back with a leather tie, and her biceps and tail flukes decorated with one strand of gold paint. If anyone here looked like a Goddess it was her.

"Merfolk. We have just said goodbye to the last King of the Mer. We have discovered to our downfall how dangerous it can be to give one man so much power. Therefore from now on we will rely upon our own people to decide what is best for them. With the guidance of a new council-."

Riva craned her neck to see where some of the remaining Elders were gathered at the side of the door. After how they had stripped her of her magic to give Duncan an advantage, they were lucky she was letting them live.

"- who will take into consideration the demands of the people and strive to always foster peace."

Aoife gestured for the other members of the council to swim forward and Riva stood back to allow Declan, Douglas, Aoife and Finn their moment. The Mer children swam forward again, this time each with a woven circlet of gold that they placed upon their brows.

Riva didn't miss the surprised murmur that went through the crowd, or the confused glances as hundreds of pairs of eyes flicked to Riva's forehead that remained empty.

"We stand before you as your elected leaders and representatives." She said, gesturing along the line to Finn, Declan, and Douglas. "We will strive to rule our people with a fair hand and a just mind." She finished.

As they all stepped back, the murmurs of surprise were still echoing from the benches. So Riva stepped forward. She was standing in almost exactly the same place that she had been when she had first been brought to Oceana. Floating at the bottom of the amphitheatre had always felt like being at the bottom of a goldfish bowl. At least the Mer no longer looked like they wanted to kill her.

Wishing that she had some flashcards she cleared her throat.

"I know not many of you wanted to listen to me when I first arrived here two months ago, and I understand why. Humans have not been kind to you, I have been able to see that since the moment I took my first breath underwater. I am neither fully human, nor fully Mer, which leaves me uniquely qualified to serve in an ambassador role between our peoples. We cannot achieve peace without understanding and as my time here with all of you has passed, I have seen so many more of you come to understand me."

Looking through the crowd, she found Em's smiling face just to the right of the dais.

"Whether you trust me because you believe in what I say or whether you simply think that I am your best shot at survival, I don't care. My goal is to restore balance to the world as we know it. I have a great responsibility to this world we all share and I cannot accept the responsibility of ruling your people alongside that."

She looked behind her towards her family. "I have complete faith in the council to guide you towards a better future. But before I go, I wish to give you all a gift."

She turned to her uncle, who swam in front of her, thin golden circlet glinting in the half-light. Causing more than a few shocked gasps from the crowd, the former prince bent his gleaming white tail and knelt before her.

Extending her right hand towards him, her Mark shining, she cloaked him in the same way she had done the rebels. Cloaking, anchoring the magic to the Earth, severing the connection and then flipping him under the umbrella of magic. Declan effectively disappeared and then immediately reappeared in the space of a few seconds.

Holding up her glowing palm to ask for quiet as the Mer who had not been part of the rebel force began yammering away, she addressed them again.

"You all sought shelter in Oceana for its protection, but now you shall carry that protection with you wherever you go within your own skin." Riva took her uncle's hand and helped him up. "Once you are cloaked, you will be able to return to your homes. Oceana can once again become a place where you come to reunite with family, trade across the seas and to celebrate solstice instead of simply seeking refuge. This cloaking will make you invisible to all human eyes and allow you to return to your sacred duties."

She had expected a reaction but all of the Mer were staring at her, dumbfounded. The rebels she had already cloaked were grinning from ear to ear, and even the nobility who had originally opposed her were looking at her in awe. Seeing Em's familiar lopsided grin, she gave her a wink.

As the Mer slowly realised that this wasn't a joke, Aoife started barking orders and chivvying the eager Mer into lines in front of Riva.

As the new Mer council directed their people and answered questions, Riva could see the peaceful future that she had fought so hard for. The way the Mer were looking at Douglas with respect and accepting him as a leader gave her hope for any other demi-Mer out there.

They had actually done it. Duncan may have died, but peace had been achieved.

As she cloaked Merperson after Merperson, feeling only the touch of one wrist after the other she let her mind drift, the repetitive magic becoming meditative. Oceana faded away until she found herself dreaming of a sun kissed meadow filled with wildflowers.

"Not exactly what I was expecting but I'm not complaining." Drawled a deep voice.

Turning to her right she saw him. The man who had haunted her dreams, both sleeping and waking. And he was shirtless.

"Would it have killed you to put on a shirt?" she asked, crossing her arms even as she raked her eyes across his toned torso, unable to avert her eyes.

"Why? You don't look like you want me to." He grinned devilishly, "Besides, you kept making fun of my outfit choices. I thought you might prefer this."

She certainly did, but she wasn't about to admit that to him.

He was lounging in the grass, propped up on one elbow so she sat down cross-legged beside him.

"I'm sorry I've been avoiding coming here. I want to thank you for what you did." She said quietly.

He gazed into her face, the expression in his amber eyes unreadable.

She plucked a daisy and fiddled with its petals. "If you hadn't come when you did I don't know what would have happened."

He smiled wryly. "You're going to be a lot harder to kill than you think." He said, smirking.

Riva tried to ignore the twist of anxiety in her gut and started plucking petals. "Without my magic I'm useless. When it got stripped away and there was nothing that I could do to save the people I love…" she willed herself not to cry and sniffed. "I felt weak. I swore to myself that I would never feel that way again."

Cronos hooked a finger under her chin and tilted her face up to his. "So change that." He whispered.

Riva twirled the tiny white petal, its skin so soft and fragile between her fingers. "How?"

He grinned wickedly. "You train."

"What you want me to enrol in kickboxing or self-defence classes or something?" she laughed, trying not to look down at the incredibly muscled torso that made her want to know what kind of training *he* did.

"No. Not kickboxing." He let his hand fall away from her chin. "But you do need to learn how to protect yourself without your magic." He paused for a second, as if weighing his next words very carefully. "I can teach you how."

Riva's mouth dropped open. "What?"

Even as he said it, Cronos looked like he was regretting offering her anything. "I can help you learn how to defend yourself so that you never feel weak again."

She thought about it. There had to be worse ways to learn than being taught by a titan who resembled a Calvin Klein model.

Although if they were going to be getting sweaty together and in close contact then she would have to learn how to keep control of her feelings. Even just sitting on the grass with him was enough to make her feel intoxicated.

Cronos seemed to be thinking along the same lines.

"Of course if you think that you can't handle it then I will rescind my offer." He said.

She glared at him. His words rubbing her up the wrong way.

"No. I accept your offer. I want to learn how to protect myself." She replied. Realising that she never should have relied so heavily on her powers in the first place. Stuarts face flashed into her mind and as it did she realised that the pain that usually came with it had lessened. Not in a way that could make her forget, but it was easier for her to separate herself from it.

"I want to be strong." She said with finality.

For some reason this amused Cronos and he plucked the half-dead daisy from her hand and tucked it into her hair.

"You are already stronger than you know." he breathed, eyes raking her face, making her feel like his gaze was consuming her entirely.

When he looked again at the limp daisy nestled behind her ear, his brow furrowed like something displeased him. He waved his hand around it and she felt its weight become heavier, lusher.

"Much better." he said smiling.

She reached up to pluck the flower from her hair but his hand stretched out to stop her.

"Leave it." he said, his voice husky and he let their hands fall back down to rest on the grass, still touching. His face was close to hers now, much too close. She needed a distraction before she did something she would regret later.

"How did you do it?" She asked.

"Change the flower? I think you could do it better than I could." He laughed.

She tried not to move her hand too much lest he realise that they were still touching and move it. "Not the flower. Coming to Oceana I mean. I thought you titans weren't able to leave Eden?"

Cronos looked uncomfortable. "My brother gave me a little help with saving you, but as you saw I was not afforded the luxury of time. Otherwise I would have done much, much more."

The way he said it had Riva wondering exactly how much more he could do, and why he would do it for her. She briefly pondered what was in it for him.

"Why did you bother?" she dared to ask.

He remained so still he resembled an ancient sculpture. Now she thought about it, there probably were ancient sculptures dedicated to him, although she had a sneaking suspicion that none of them would do him justice.

"Cronos?" she breathed.

The way he looked at her when she said his name, that burning fire in his eyes made her want to rip herself away from Oceana and materialize in Eden properly. But that fire quickly dampened and his expression became conflicted and she abandoned all thoughts of-

"I told you. You intrigue me." he said quietly.

She knew he was lying. There had to be more to it than that. Why else would an immortal titan have any interest in anything she did? She couldn't shield the disappointment from her face and he chuckled. She tried to pull her hand away, even though she didn't really want to and he let her go. She crossed her arms.

"I've been lied to, abused, betrayed and attacked more times than I can count in the last few months. If you're going to train me to help me survive all of that, then you better teach me how to survive you as well."

She almost regretted letting so much of her feelings show as he seemed to measure his next words carefully.

"You would do better not to get involved. There are things happening. Things that have been put in motion since before your birth that even you cannot stop. I wish to protect you from that."

He doesn't want you, he doesn't want you, he doesn't want you.

She was furious to realise that she was about to start crying. She pressed her lips together and looked down at the ground. This was ridiculous. Just because he had come to her rescue, why did she think that meant that he cared?

She stopped blinking and refused to let the tears fall. She wanted to be strong. Well, she wouldn't let him see her cry for him. This would be the first lesson he would teach her.

He got to his feet, rising from the position he had been lounging in with otherworldly grace. He towered above her, face in shadow with the sun at his back.

"When you are ready, we will start your training." He said, his expression unreadable as he faded into nothingness.

She was left sitting cross-legged in the meadow alone, cheeks ablaze, wondering what the hell she was getting herself into.

Checking back in to Oceana, she saw the never-ending line of Mer waiting to be cloaked and decided to stay awhile. Even if it was only a dream-state, she felt a hell of a lot warmer here than she did at the bottom of the ocean.

Wandering lazily towards the creek and a large patch of uninterrupted sunlight, a loud noise sounded behind her. It was the same noise she had heard the first time she had met Cronos. Like a thunderous wave combined with the whip-crack of lightning. Remembering how worried he had looked about his mother catching them together, she figured she'd better make herself scarce before Gaia started grilling her on why she was meeting up with Cronos behind her back. She dove for the bank of the creek and hid herself just underneath the lip.

The noise ended with a great swoosh and then there was silence. Riva lay on the sandy rocks, feet submerged in the creek and dared a glance out from behind the ledge.

Nothing could have prepared her for what she saw.

Lillian, her elderly neighbour who had passed Gaia's powers to her was standing beside the Goddess, fighting weakly against her grip.

Heart pounding, she didn't know whether or not to reveal herself or stay hidden. Going by the look on Gaia's face and the fear in Lillian's eyes, she decided on the latter.

"I know what you have been doing." Gaia said warningly, throwing Lillian down hard to the ground.

The old woman looked up at her, softly wrinkled face unreadable. "I dinnae ken what ye mean."

"Do not toy with me Lillian, you made a bold decision in choosing her. One that might very well work against you in the end."

Lillian smiled, eyes crinkling at the corners. "Aye, it might. But then again I've always been a bit o' a gambler myself. And I rather like ma odds."

"You thwarted me for too long Lilly." Gaia drew herself up to her full height, flowing robes of fire casting maniacal shadows across Lillian's face. "You did me a favour when you gave your powers to such a naïve, young host and decided to pass on. Although I'm sure you never imagined to trap yourself here with me."

Lillian crawled up to her knees and smiled ruefully. "Maybe I just wanted tae watch that *naïve, young girl* take ye down myself."

The Goddess growled softly and looked like she was about to raise her hand to the woman when she instead lifted her head and glanced over in Riva's direction.

Ducking quickly back under the lip of the creek bank, she held her breath and tried to lull her brain back into the dream-state that would get her out of Eden before she was caught snooping on something she clearly was not supposed to see. Her brain couldn't make sense of any of it.

Why was Lillian here? Did that mean she wasn't dead? And what did Gaia mean when she said that Lillian chose her, it had been Gaia who had chosen her, hadn't it?

Staring into the crystal-clear creek water, thankfully she felt herself being lulled back towards reality. But as the audience chamber swam back into view, a reflection of the Goddess's face appeared in the stream's surface.

With a sickening jolt, Riva took in the expression on Gaia's face and felt pure terror for the first time in her life. She watched as the Goddess spat fire and lunged for her. Riva screwed her eyes shut in anticipation of being dragged back into the meadow by a seriously pissed-off titan. But the lithe fingers never made contact.

Opening her eyes, Riva found herself shaking in front of the dwindling line of Mer, firmly back in Oceana.

A strong pair of arms reached out to steady her and she looked at Em's face.

"Hey, you doing okay? Do you need us to ask them to stop?" she asked, confused by the worried look on Riva's face.

Heart pounding, she looked out at the twenty or so Mer she still had to cloak and shook her head. "No, I'll keep going." She looked back towards the line, realizing as she did so that her hand was shaking.

Gaia had caught her spying on her and Lillian *(Lillian?)* in Eden. And she had been mad as hell about it.

"What's that in your hair?" Em asked, wrinkling her nose.

Lifting her hand up, she felt the impossibly smooth petals and tugged the flower from above her ear.

She looked down at the blood red rose that now sat innocently in her palm, both a warning and a promise, completely out of place at the bottom of the ocean. Cronos's gift had travelled between Eden and Oceana with her.

Not only was she was planning on returning to train with him behind Gaia's back, but the Goddess who she thought had gifted her powers to her was clearly keeping some very dark secrets.

As she stroked each delicate petal, the warm glow in the pit of her stomach should have warned her not to get in over her head.

What the hell have I gotten myself into now?

Acknowledgements

First of all I have to thank every single one of my readers and followers on social media. Without you these books would not be out here in the world and without your support I wouldn't have a career as an author. So when I say thank you from the bottom of my heart – I mean it.
The first book in this series (Ocean's Daughter) took seven years to go from plan to draft to published. Earth's Mother took seven months.
I have to thank Paul for his never ending support when I chose to become a full-time author and creator this year which is what gave me the time to dedicate myself completely to this manuscript.
As always a huge thank you to the talented designer of my covers Justine Berthet, you have out-done yourself with this one!
Dee, like with each new book, you give up your time to play the part of editor and sounding board. I couldn't do it without you.

Riva will return in 2022…

Other Titles by Hazel McBride:

- I Still Believe

- Ocean's Daughter

- Earth's Mother

About the Author:

Having been inspired in her early life by her mum to care for marine life, she grew up to become a killer whale behaviourist and carer, working at two prestigious facilities in Europe. This love of marine mammals and her passion to help safeguard the future of the natural world was a massive inspiration for writing Oceans Daughter. Originally from Scotland, she has lived in the Dominican Republic, Tenerife, France and now lives with her Fiancé in the Netherlands working as a part-time author and coach as well as training to become a veterinary technician.

Printed in Great Britain
by Amazon